LAST OF THE FREE

GORDON ANTHONY

Copyright © 2018 Gordon Anthony
All rights reserved.
ISBN-13: 978-1984126146
ISBN-10: 1984126148

The Calgacus Series:

World's End
The Centurions
Queen of Victory
Druids' Gold
Blood Ties
The High King
The Ghost War
Last of The Free

Note on Place Names

The following list provides details of the places mentioned in this story, along with other principal places in First Century Britain. Most of these are marked on the accompanying map.

Bodotria
The River Forth.

Camulodunon / Camulodunum
The Celtic / Roman forms respectively of a settlement which occupied the site of modern Colchester. The name means, "The fort of Camulos". Camulos was the war god of the Catuvellauni. The original, Iron Age settlement was reputedly founded by King Cunobelinos (Shakespeare's "Cymbeline") when he conquered, subdued or assimilated the neighbouring tribe of the Trinovantes. The Romans regarded it as the "Capital" of the Catuvellauni and established their own colony there soon after the invasion. The settlement was sacked by Boudica during her great revolt.

Clota
The River Clyde.

Eriu
The Celtic name for Ireland.

Giudi
One of the ancient Celtic names for the modern town of Stirling, more properly linked to the fortress rock which is now the site of Stirling Castle.

Hibernia
The Roman name for Ireland.

Ister
The Roman name for the River Danube.

Isuria
The Romans established a town they called "Isurium Brigantum" which was built on the site of the modern village of Aldborough in North Yorkshire. The settlement of Isuria in the Calgacus stories is a fictional Iron Age town set in roughly the same location and is where Cartimandua had her home.

Iova
The island of Iona, off the west coast of modern Scotland. There is some evidence that suggests the island was home to a druidical sect long before the arrival of Columba and Christianity.

Londinium
A Roman port and trading settlement built on the site of modern London.

Mons Graupius
The name given by the Romans to the site of the battle they fought against the alliance of tribes reputedly led by a man named Calgacus. The name means, "The Swordsman". The actual site of the battle has never been properly identified and is the subject of much debate among historians. I have selected a northerly location for reasons which are expanded in the Author's Note at the end of the story.

Tava
The River Tay.

Trimontium
A Roman fort and supply base built near the site of modern Melrose.

Chapter I

The amphitheatre was only half full, but that did not really matter because it was only half constructed, much of the audience space comprising nothing more than piled mud and turf which surrounded the oval arena of hard-packed earth.
Serpicius frowned as he looked at the partially constructed venue, his expression remaining clouded as his gaze swept over the sections which had been completed. Around the edge of one half of the oval, rows of stone seating rose in a single tier, the seats filling up with off-duty soldiers who were noisily laughing and joking with one another as they settled down in anticipation of a good show.
"They'll be lucky," he thought sourly.
His cold, unsympathetic eyes scanned the crowd, noting the almost festive air, even though a good number of the soldiers seemed to be suffering from a variety of injuries. He saw arms in splints, men using crutches, many wearing bandages or with silver staples holding their skin together where they had been slashed or gouged by sharp blades. Yet, despite these injuries, they had come to watch more bloodletting.
Such was the way of the Empire, Serpicius reflected grimly.
To one side sat a few dozen civilians, dressed in long trousers and woollen cloaks despite the warmth of the late summer sun. Their long hair marked them out as barbarians, no doubt local villagers who had come to see what all the fuss was about. They sat stiff and self-conscious, looking around with perplexed expressions as if they were not sure why the soldiers seemed so keen to witness the spectacle of formal combat.

They will soon learn, Serpicius thought to himself. They will enjoy it and they will want more. They will demand Roman entertainment and, before too long, they will become Romans without realising what has been done to them. He had seen it before and had no doubt that it would happen here, just as it had happened elsewhere in the Empire.

Turning his back on the arena, he walked away, descending to the outer sections, then going beneath the raised tier of the spectators' area to the preparation rooms. Nobody stopped him. The burly, hard-faced men posted to keep curious visitors out merely stepped aside and allowed him to pass.

That was as it should be. Once or twice, he heard someone whisper, "Serpens", the name of his alter ego. "The Snake", they called him in hushed, almost reverential tones.

Serpicius did not mind the unflattering soubriquet. In fact, he enjoyed the response his reputation engendered. It was right that men should fear and respect him.

It was a name that had stuck with him for as long as he could remember. He liked to tell people it came from the speed and deadly venom with which he struck down his opponents, but he knew it had initially stemmed from his childhood; a nickname given to him partly because of its similarity to his real name, but mostly because everyone who met him remarked on how aloof he was and how cold and dark his eyes were.

Serpicius did not care about that. In fact, he cared about very little, least of all what other people thought of him, as long as they respected him. His pleasures in life were few and his needs simple. The truth, he acknowledged to himself, was that he enjoyed killing. The sense of power that act gave him was what sustained him, what made him keep coming back to the arena.

Even a pox-ridden, half-built arena like this one in the far north of Britannia. It was hardly the same as the great Flavian amphitheatre in Rome, he mused sourly as he moved along the dimly lit corridor.

In the coolness of the lower rooms, he found the place he was seeking.

"There you are!" gasped Italus. "You need to get ready."

"There's plenty of time," Serpicius told him.

The gruff lanista scowled at him as he gestured towards a young slave boy who was standing beside a long, wooden table which was covered by a large towel.

"Have your massage and get ready. You're up last."

Serpicius merely nodded and began stripping off his clothes. Once he was down to his loincloth, he heaved his bulky frame onto the table and lay on his back. While the slave began massaging his body with oil, Italus prowled up and down the tiny chamber.

"Don't you want to know who you are fighting?" the lanista asked.

Serpicius, his eyes closed, grunted, "It doesn't matter. I've watched all your men in training. I can beat any of them."

"You are an arrogant so-and-so, Serpens," Italus snorted. "Just because you used to fight in Rome doesn't mean you are better than provincial gladiators. I know you were one of the best in your day, but you are not as young as you used to be."

"Your concern for my safety is touching," Serpicius responded with undisguised sarcasm.

"I don't give a shit about you," Italus shot back. "Your name has added a few hundred to the audience, but you're not one of my fighters, so I won't shed any tears if you end up leaving the arena through Charon's gate."

"That's not going to happen," Serpicius stated flatly. "Why don't you admit you are more concerned with losing one of your own men?"

Italus stopped pacing and stood close to the table, looking down at the recumbent form of the famous gladiator. Serpicius, like most fighters, ate a diet designed to add bulk, to pad out muscles with flesh so that wounds had less chance of penetrating vital organs. Serpicius' body gleamed under the coating of oil, but the traces of old scars were clearly visible on his arms, his legs and torso.

Gruffly, Italus admitted, "You're right. It costs a lot of money to train a slave up to a decent standard. I'd prefer it if you don't kill one of my best men."

"Then put me up against a *tyro*," Serpicius suggested indifferently.

"We need to put on a decent show," Italus told him. "I can't have you defeating a youngster too quickly. There's a crowd of soldiers out there waiting to see some proper swordplay."

"From the looks of them, a lot of them have already seen plenty of swordplay," Serpicius observed mockingly. "Have you seen how many of them are missing limbs?"

"There was a battle a couple of months ago," Italus informed him. "They say the barbarians stormed the camp of the Ninth Legion during the night. From the sounds of it, the wounded are the lucky ones. They say the Legion lost several hundred men."

Serpicius blew a soft snort of derision.

"That sounds like someone's been pulling your leg," he grunted. "Nobody can storm a Roman fort. I expect the soldiers have been telling tall tales."

"No," Italus insisted. "Everyone is telling the same story. It makes you wonder what those savages up there are like."

"It makes me wonder why the soldiers didn't guard their camp properly," Serpicius snorted.

Seeing the gladiator's lack of interest, Italus sighed, "Yes, well, the Governor is still chasing the barbarians northwards, but the base commander wants a decent spot of entertainment for the soldiers who were shipped back here, so do your best to make it look good."

"I always look good," Serpicius told him.

He rolled onto his belly, allowing the slave to rub oil onto his back and shoulders, letting the young man knead his muscles with expert hands.

"I don't understand you," Italus confessed. "Why don't you give up this life? You're a free man, not a slave. What age are you now? Forty? That's too old for this sort of life."

"I tried retirement," Serpicius replied, his eyes still closed, his body relaxing under the probing fingers of the slave. "It was boring."

With a resigned sigh, Italus gave up.

"Just be ready for your fight. I need to go and check on the others now."

Serpicius did not respond, so Italus stomped out of the cubicle and stalked down the corridor to where the slave gladiators were going through their own preparations.

Serpicius lay perfectly still, enjoying the massage. He did not care what Italus thought. What could the man know of his life or his needs? The elderly lanista might be correct that forty was too old to be a gladiator, but Serpicius knew no other life that could reward him with the adulation of the crowd, the respect of other men and the satisfaction of seeing an opponent die under his blade.

With his eyes closed and the slave kneading his muscles, Serpicius allowed himself to reflect on his past. As a free, but poor, child growing up in the slums of Rome, he had become a member of his local gang at an early age. By the time he had reached fourteen, he had become an accomplished thief and assassin; a brawler, a killer. That was what he was good at; what he enjoyed.

His mistake, he knew, was that he had made no friends. Even his fellow gang members disliked him. Not that he was concerned, for he disliked them in equal measure, but the life of a gang member was a dangerous one and he had made too many enemies. By the time he was nineteen, he had known that his fate would be to end up in the gutter with a knife in his back.

So he had changed his life. The arena offered a chance to fight, to kill, and to be paid for it. Instead of sneaking through the shadows to slit throats, he would fight in formal bouts in front of an adoring crowd of thousands. It had been a decision he had never regretted. The training had been brutally hard and delivered with savage efficiency but, as a free man, he had not been whipped. He could handle the beatings, could cope with the constant exercises that were designed to enhance his speed and strength. The pain, the bruises and the occasional broken bone were small prices to pay.

Out of that forge had emerged The Snake. Serpens had once been the most famous gladiator of them all, a tough, remorseless, killing machine who never lost a bout.

The crowd had loved him. Men had wanted to be like him, and women had been happy to make themselves available to him. He had taken full advantage, naturally, although it had often been difficult for him to conceal just how much he despised these people, these ordinary citizens who were content to remain living in the gutter.

But, after fifteen years, he had known that he could not survive in the arena much longer. He was still fast and strong, but neither as fast nor as strong as he had once been and, sooner or later, he knew, he would have died. After he lost a fight, suffering a serious wound to his shoulder, he had decided to retire.

That had not lasted long, he reflected. As he had told Italus, it had been boring. The crowd had soon forgotten him as their fickle attentions moved to other heroes. Faced with living a life of unending boredom or returning to the savage street gangs, he had decided to travel, to see the provinces and to return to the only life that mattered to him.

Which is why he was here in Britannia, at the furthest edge of the Empire. Here, he could still reap the rewards that the arena offered, and he could do so with less risk than he had faced in Rome. The gladiators Italus had trained were good enough for the provinces, but they were second-rate as far as Serpicius was concerned. He had not been boasting when he had told the lanista that he could beat any of the slave fighters Italus had at his disposal.

It was nearly time to prove that.

The massage was done, the slave boy moving to help Serpicius dress and don his armour; belly guard, leg greave, helmet and shield. All of them were gleaming and polished or painted. That was part of the show, of course. His shield bore the image of a green snake, coiled with head raised and fangs wide. The crowd would recognise it and so would his opponent. That was worth a lot in a bout. Fear of his reputation had defeated several men before now and would no doubt do so again.

He could hear the shouts from above, the cheering, the jeering, the cries of delight or complaint as men's chosen fighter either won or lost. None of the fights would be very good, he knew, which explained most of the jeering and mocking laughter, but there would be heavy gambling among the spectators, and that always added some spice to the show.

The door burst open and Italus barged into the room, nodding when he saw that Serpicius was ready.

"You're on!" he barked.

Wordlessly, Serpicius followed the lanista to the tunnel that led to the arena itself. Another gladiator stood there, a young man wearing identical equipment to Serpicius. The younger man shot him a look before hurriedly turning away and Serpicius knew that he had already won. This boy was one of Italus' better fighters, but he was clearly nervous at the prospect of facing The Snake.

Slaves pulled the doors open, admitting bright sunlight that forced them to blink against the dazzling outdoors. Then the two of them strode into the arena.

The late summer sun was hot, unusually so for Britannia, bringing beads of sweat to his face. The padded lining of his helmet kept his eyes free of perspiration, but the sensation of clammy warmth was unpleasant and he wanted to take his helmet off. First, though, he must dispose of his opponent, and he could not do that too quickly because the soldiers wanted a good show.

The noise from the crowd faded as the two fighters raised their swords in salute to the Master of the Games. This official was some bigwig, Serpicius had been told, an important man who was visiting the camp and had been asked to preside over the show. Serpicius neither knew nor cared who he was. This was a formality and he wanted to get it over with as quickly as possible. He raised his sword, chanted the traditional greeting and had turned away almost before the man in the purple-striped tunic had signalled that the fight should begin.

The two gladiators turned to face one another.

Italus was in the arena, standing behind the slave fighter, sword and whip in his hands, ready to inflict punishment if the gladiator did not perform properly. Serpicius, a free man, had no such deadly prompting. He did not need it, for this was what he lived for.

Dismissing everything else from his mind, he concentrated on his opponent. The young man's helmet had a face guard, identical to the one Serpicius wore, an iron plate peppered with holes to allow some restricted vision and enough air to breathe. He could just make out the man's eyes behind the mask; wild, frightened eyes.

The younger man launched into an attack, clearly hoping to strike an early blow which would weaken Serpicius. He turned it aside easily, vaguely aware of the appreciative cheer from the watching crowd as he did so. Soldiers who trained every day with the sword would recognise skill when they saw it, and Serpicius had more than enough skill to dazzle them.

The two gladiators locked shields briefly, slashed at each other, neither sword finding a target, then they separated and began circling one another.

The fight became a series of feints and jabs, of jumps and barges. Serpicius blocked every attack and made sure that his own were slow enough to be parried while dangerous enough to keep his opponent afraid of him.

The crowd loved it, of course. That was good. It meant that Serpicius would be able to earn some free drinks from the off duty soldiers that evening.

He kept moving his feet, never standing still, always ensuring his sandals kept a firm grip. In some parts of the empire, where the arena floor was made of sand, gladiators fought barefoot to ensure they did not slip or fall but here, where the surface was hard packed earth, hobnailed sandals were ideal.

The younger man was tiring now, Serpicius could tell. He was hot and feeling some strain himself, but he had always had excellent stamina and, despite his age, he could outlast most of the young bucks who thought they could tire him out.

This one was no exception.

It was time, Serpicius realised, to end it. If the fight went on too long, the crowd would become restless and bored.

He allowed the next lunge to draw his opponent in. Blocking with his shield, he stepped in, swinging right to smash his iron-rimmed shield against the other man's right shoulder. As his opponent stumbled backwards, struggling to maintain his balance, Serpicius stabbed forwards, feeling the sharp tip of his short sword smash into the man's belly armour before sliding upwards and burying itself into his lower chest.

Serpicius jumped back, avoiding his adversary's flailing shield which could have broken his right arm if it had connected. His move had been so fast that some in the audience had missed it. Only when the younger man staggered and let his arms fall did they notice the dark, bubbling blood oozing from the gash in his torso.

The man's head slumped but he remained standing, if virtually helpless. The wound was probably fatal, Serpicius knew, but he wanted to make sure. One step, one thrust, and it was done. The gladiator fell to the ground, a soft groan his last sound.

And Serpicius felt sated. Life was good. Life was sweet. And he had killed another opponent.

He dropped his sword and shield, reached up to remove his helmet at last, felt the cool breeze on his sweat-damp face and forced a false smile to his lips as he turned to face the crowd, one arm held aloft to signal his victory.

Let them see him, let them recognise him.

His skin tingled when he heard the roar of approval. This was what victory meant. Later, when he left the amphitheatre, these same men would ply him with food and drink, would even pay for a woman for him if there was one available in this northern wilderness. They would flock around him, asking questions, wanting to be noticed by him.

It was part of the show. He would give them what they wanted in return for the things he desired. Respect, fear and admiration. Food, drink, and women. What else was there in life?

He gave a final salute, then picked up his sword and shield and strode out of the amphitheatre, his job done.

Serpens had struck again. It was a pity the Governor had not been there to witness his victory, but Agricola was in the far north, hunting down the rebel barbarians. Soon, he would have a victory of his own, Serpicius knew, and then there would be further opportunity for a famous gladiator to display his prowess. The Governor would want more shows, more triumphal celebrations to reward his soldiers. And Serpens, The Snake, would be there.

"It won't be long," he told himself. "Rome always wins."

Chapter II

The early morning sounds were more urgent than usual, the shouts of the Centurions edged with a hint of danger; the tramp of feet and the murmur of voices suggesting a mixture of excitement and alarm.

For a long moment, Gnaeus Julius Agricola wanted the noise to simply wash over him like a dream. He had no desire to rouse himself from the small cot and venture beyond the cocoon of his command tent. His sleep had been troubled by memories, by thoughts of what might have been, and those remembrances lingered in his mind, holding him immobile and listless.

His son was dead.

Barely a year old, the child had succumbed to one of the innumerable fevers that were so deadly to the very young.

The news had taken some weeks to reach Agricola. As his army pressed ever further northwards, venturing into lands no Roman had ever seen, pursuing the elusive barbarians step by weary step, mile after endless mile, the messenger had taken a long time to catch up with him and deliver the devastating message.

His son was dead. The son he had barely known, whom he had last seen when he was still a squalling babe, would never grow into a man.

Agricola knew enough of the world to understand that such deaths were not uncommon. In fact, most children were fortunate to survive beyond the first five years of life. But that knowledge did not lessen the hurt.

It was a private grief, though. He could not afford to display weakness in front of his soldiers, the men who looked to him for leadership. For them, he would need to cover his pain and act the part of a Roman Governor.

But for now, while the sounds from beyond the thick, heavy canvas of his large tent told him that something out of the ordinary was happening, he lay in his cot and allowed the grief to consume him.

It was a brief moment of personal and private grieving. All too soon, he heard movement at the entrance to his tiny inner chamber as the curtain was slowly pulled aside and Donnatus, his personal assistant and secretary, cautiously poked his head into the sleeping chamber.

"Sir?"

Reluctantly, Agricola opened his eyes, banishing the dark memories. Already, the morning sun was heating the tent and painting the canvas with a bright backdrop of warmth.

He peered at Donnatus' worried face.

"What is it?"

"The barbarians, Sir. We've found them."

Agricola's befuddled mind struggled to comprehend.

"Which tribe?" he asked.

"All of them, Sir. The whole barbarian alliance is here. Thousands of them."

Half an hour later, Agricola was sitting on horseback, surrounded by his senior officers, all of them staring across the gently undulating plain towards the massed ranks of the barbarians. The worst of Agricola's earlier mood had been banished by the need for action and by the knowledge that, after days of endless marching, he had found the enemy at last. A nagging hurt still gnawed at him, but his professional instincts took over as he surveyed the scene confronting him.

The barbarians were, as usual, occupying high ground, spread across the slopes of one of the foothills of a great range of mountains that stretched far off to the south and west. They were arranged in tribal groups, some on the very summit of the hill, some half way down the forward slope, and others on the edge of the plain at the foot of the hill where their horsemen and chariots raced to and fro, cheering and gesticulating at the Roman fort where Agricola's army was preparing for battle.

"How many would you say?" Agricola asked.

"Thirty thousand?" suggested Silvanus, Legate of the Second Legion, one of the two Legions Agricola had led to the far north of Britannia.

Nobody argued. If anything, the estimate seemed rather low, but numbers mattered little to the Romans. If they employed their usual tactics properly, they could overcome worse odds than two to one.

There was, though, one dissenting voice.

"Thirty thousand that we can see," said Julius Macrinus.

Agricola turned in his saddle to look at the German Tribune. Macrinus, a commander of Auxiliaries, was a veteran of the British campaign. The Governor had been impressed by the man's ability and had recently promoted him into his inner circle of advisers. That decision had been a good one, Agricola thought. Alone of the officers around him, Macrinus was not afraid to voice an opinion, even if it meant disagreeing with more senior men.

"The nearer hill, you mean?" Agricola asked.

Macrinus nodded gravely.

"There's an old hill fort over there," he explained, pointing out a small group of irregularly shaped hills off to their right. "We need to pass it on our right flank to approach their main force. They probably have some men in there, waiting for a chance to attack us in the rear once we have passed."

"Take that hill first, then," suggested Aulus Atticus, one of the younger and more impulsive Tribunes.

"I doubt very much that the rest of them will stand by and watch while we do that," grunted Macrinus sarcastically.

Agricola knew there was no love lost between the aristocratic Atticus and the gruff Auxiliary commander. He prevented an argument from developing by making a quick decision.

"We can deal with that hill without storming the place," he told them. "It is the main enemy army we need to defeat. The Auxiliaries will lead the attack. They will need to extend their line, so I want the ranks to be thinned to half the usual depth."

Macrinus, never one to be overawed by authority, challenged, "Isn't that rather risky, Sir?"

"All life is a risk," Agricola smiled confidently. "But you know the Britons rarely have the power to break through our armoured lines. The greater danger is being outflanked. We need a long line to face so many opponents."

Macrinus pursed his lips but did not argue. Then he asked, "The archers? How do you want them deployed?"

Agricola's response was to shrug, "At your discretion, Macrinus."

The big German gave a grim nod of acknowledgement. Like most Romans, Agricola despised the use of bow and arrow. The Roman way was to close with the enemy and stand toe to toe, using the power of their heavy infantry to overwhelm their opponents. Archers, who killed from a distance, were generally disdained, but Macrinus knew the skill required to use a bow, and he appreciated how their weapons could be used to greatest effect. The Governor had brought a small contingent of archers, barely half a Cohort, but that would be enough for Macrinus' purposes.

"And what of the Legions?" Silvanus enquired. "What do we do?"

Indicating the clump of hills that worried Macrinus, Agricola replied, "Stay to the right. Form up in front of those smaller hills and be ready to intercept any barbarian force that tries to attack the Auxiliaries."

"Are you sure you don't want us to attack the hill fort before the main assault goes in?"

"No need," Agricola assured the Legate. "If we defeat the main force, the fort will surrender. I see no value in wasting Roman lives taking the place."

"And the cavalry?" Atticus asked expectantly.

"In reserve on either flank," Agricola replied. Giving the young Tribune a smile of encouragement, he added, "You may lead the left wing of the cavalry, Atticus."

Atticus' face beamed back at him.

"Thank you, Sir. I will not let you down."

"Nobody will let me down," Agricola nodded. "This is the chance we have been waiting for, gentlemen. The barbarians have nowhere left to run. This time, we will finish them off."

A chorus of agreement met his words, but he noticed that the grizzled, greying Macrinus was frowning as he looked across to the waiting barbarians.

"Is something troubling you, Macrinus?" the Governor asked.

"I'm just wondering what surprises he has in store for us this time," Macrinus answered softly.

The Governor dismissed his concerns, but not before a momentary pause had gripped the others. They were used to facing barbarian armies and winning but, this time, their enemy was one who had repeatedly shown that he knew how to defeat Roman armies.

This time, they faced Calgacus.

Standing high on the windy summit of the hill, Calgacus looked down at the advancing Roman army. Tall, broad-shouldered and immensely strong, he was the very image of a barbarian warlord. He wore a breastplate of bronze on his chest, a scarred and battered piece of armour which still reflected the sun and gave him a martial appearance. On his back hung a huge sword in a scabbard which also gleamed in the bright, morning light. Made from bronze with a line of tin running down its entire length, the scabbard was widely believed to be of gold and silver. Yet its worth was in what it represented rather than the value of the metals from which it was made. Everyone knew about that famous sword. It was the subject of several songs, as was Calgacus himself.

He disliked the songs, scorning them as mere fantasy, yet he had relied on his fame to bring this gathering of tribes together.

"Sometimes, fame has its uses," he murmured to himself as he looked down at the forces arrayed on the hillside and the edge of the plain.

"It looks like he's fallen for it," Runt observed, jerking his chin to indicate the smaller hills that lay to the right of the advancing Roman lines. "Both Legions are forming up to tackle the fort."

Calgacus gave a grim nod of satisfaction. The ancient fort which crowned the low huddle of irregularly-shaped high ground was manned by a mere fifty men who had been ordered to keep moving around so that the Romans would see them and fear that a strong force held the dilapidated stone walls. That ploy seemed to have worked because half of the Roman strength had been neutralised as the Legions had been held back from the main assault on the bulk of the British war host.

"He's going to try to beat us with the Auxiliaries," Adelligus, Runt's son, commented hopefully.

The warriors surrounding them laughed scornfully, but Calgacus frowned as he ran a hand back through his long, dark hair. The confidence of the younger men made him feel older than his fifty-three years. His hair was greying at the temples, he knew, his strength, still prodigious, was not what it had once been, and his speed of movement was less than it had been in his own youth. For the first time, he was beginning to wonder whether he really was an old man.

He did not feel old. His body was inured to hardship, accustomed to long marches and short rations. He could still trek and fight with the best of the younger men, but it took him longer to recover his breath nowadays, and his muscles ached for longer than they had once done.

He shook his head in irritation. It was not his age that was truly bothering him, he knew. What concerned him was that they were about to engage in a pitched battle against the might of the Roman Army.

It was partly his own fault. He had managed to engineer an alliance of tribes and had led them in a daring night attack against the Roman Ninth Legion, storming into their camp and killing hundreds of legionaries. The victory had been so stunning that the Governor had been forced to leave the demoralised remnants of the Ninth Legion behind to garrison forts and occupy conquered territory. It had also meant that, in the few short weeks since that incredible achievement, more and more tribesmen had flocked to join his war host.

Alliances among the volatile Britons were notoriously fragile, and this one had been no exception. Only Calgacus' force of will and his proven record of victories had held the deep-seated animosity between the tribes under some sort of control.

But he had been forced to abandon his preferred method of waging war. There was not enough food to keep so many men together in one place for very long. Their very presence demanded action. He had launched raid after raid on the Roman marching columns, picking away at stragglers, destroying supply columns when they could catch them, but it was not enough. The Romans had remained near the coast so that they could be supplied by their fleet, and they had marched on, ravaging the land, looting and destroying homes and farmsteads on the way.

Frustrated by their inability to halt the Roman advance, the warriors had demanded a battle, and Calgacus had been unable to persuade them not to risk everything on a major confrontation.

"What use is a large army if you are not going to use it?" Broichan, the elderly druid, had demanded. "We have worked for years to bring about a true alliance and now we have it, we cannot afford to throw it away."

Broichan was down near the foot of the hill, exhorting the warriors, calling out curses on the hated enemy. For a man who was normally so cold and calculating, he had been caught up in the excitement of the impending battle and was ranting his fury at the enemy while, all around him, drums beat and carnyx horns wailed their eerily mournful calls of defiance.

Other chieftains were little different, most of them clamouring for a fight and boasting of the Roman heads they would take and the glory they would find in combat.

"You can't tell them not to fight," Bridei had warned Calgacus. "They'll just go ahead and do it anyway. You might as well devise a battle plan and give us a chance of winning."

Bridei, self-proclaimed King of the Boresti, was one of Calgacus' oldest friends, as well as being his closest ally. He was short, stocky, crude and bellicose, but he knew how his rival Kings thought.

"Easier to tell the sun not to rise than tell the tribes not to fight their enemies," he had growled. Grasping the hilt of his sword, he had added darkly, "And I can't say I blame them."

Calgacus understood Bridei's fierce anger. The Romans had pillaged and ravaged the land as they pushed northwards, leaving many of the tribes, including the Boresti, homeless. The Venicones and the Taexali had also seen their lands claimed by the Romans and they, too, were desperate for revenge. Bridei was itching for a chance to reclaim his home, and Calgacus understood that he could not avoid a battle. He had delayed long enough. Too long, some of the Kings were murmuring.

So now he stood on the hilltop, watching the advancing Romans and hoping that his plan might actually work.

"Are our lads in place?" he asked Adelligus.

The young warrior nodded, not quite managing to conceal his frustration.

"They're not happy," he informed Calgacus.

"I know. But they won't miss out on the fighting, no matter what happens."

"They would prefer to be in the battle line," Adelligus persisted, making no secret of the fact that he shared the sentiment.

Calgacus smiled. Adelligus was a fine warrior who had proved himself in combat several times, as the white line of a long scar on his cheek confirmed, but he was relatively inexperienced when it came to fighting major battles.

Calgacus asked him, "Do you remember when Bridei killed that bear last year?"

Adelligus frowned as he nodded, "Yes."

"He didn't stand up and face it," Calgacus reminded him. "He lured it into a trap. We must do the same, because the Roman Army is like that bear; too strong and powerful for us to beat in a stand-up fight unless we are very lucky."

Adelligus looked puzzled as he pointed out, "You didn't tell the other chieftains what you were planning."

Calgacus gave him a regretful smile.

"Sometimes," he admitted, "a War Leader must make difficult decisions. Like Bridei said, those tribes want a fight. If I told them what we were planning, do you think they would put up a decent show?"

Bridei snorted, "The daft buggers would turn and run as soon as the Romans got near them. That would give the game away."

Adelligus was clearly concerned at the thought that thousands of men's lives were at risk because they had not been told the full details of Calgacus' strategy.

Runt put a hand on his son's arm and said, "Cal knows what he is doing. Besides, you never know, those lads might get lucky and beat the Romans without any help from us."

"Broichan certainly thinks they can win," Bridei observed, nodding down the slope to where the grey-bearded druid was still exhorting the warriors to slaughter their enemies.

"We'll find out soon," said Calgacus.

Because, down at the foot of the hill, battle was about to be joined.

Julius Macrinus gripped his short sword firmly in his right fist, wanting to be ready even though he was in the fourth rank and would be unlikely to use the blade in the initial clash. The sword was a comfort, but his main weapons were his eyes, ears and tongue.

He watched the enemy as the Auxiliary troops advanced towards them. Chariots and horses still raced to and fro, with the horde of men on foot continuing to fill the air with their shouts of defiance. As yet, they made no move to stop the Roman advance.

"Archers!" Macrinus yelled.

Some twenty paces ahead of the main line of infantry, a loose cordon of bowmen led the way. They stopped, drew arrows and hastily loosed a volley, aiming at the chariots. Some horses were hit by the deadly shafts, tumbling in their harnesses and creating confusion. A few of the barbarian warriors were also struck, and then another volley of shafts hit home.

As Macrinus had guessed, the provocation was too much for the enemy. They broke ranks and rush at the archers who turned and fled, slipping between the ranks of the Auxiliaries to take up position behind the line from where they would send their arrows arcing over the heads of the infantry. These volleys would be less accurate, but there were so many barbarians, they were bound to find some targets.

Macrinus grinned. The enemy line had been disrupted, and now they were in range of the Auxiliaries' javelins.

"Throw!" he bellowed, his shout being echoed all along the line as the Centurions took up the cry.

The soldiers hurled their javelins, the volley bringing down dozens of tribesmen who, as usual, had no protection except hide-covered, wicker shields.

In response, the Britons released a torrent of their own missiles; spears, slingstones and darts which the Roman troops caught on their large shields. The sound rattled all along the line, temporarily drowning out the shouts and screams of the barbarian army.

"Throw!"

A second volley of javelins flew across the gap between the opposing forces, killing or wounding many more men, but making little impact on the huge numbers facing the Romans.

Macrinus glanced right and left. Far off to the right, the Governor was driving the Cohorts forwards. Agricola had decided to march on foot in the midst of his troops, showing them that he was not afraid to fight alongside them. It was a clever ploy, Macrinus thought, and typical of the Governor's leadership. Some among the Auxiliaries might feel aggrieved at being sent in to face the enemy alone while the citizen legionaries stood further back, safe from immediate harm. Roman blood was being preserved, they might claim, while the Auxiliaries, predominantly Germans, Batavians and Tungrians, were being sacrificed to Mars, the war God. But with the Governor marching in their midst, their potential grievance had been turned into a feeling of immense pride; they had been chosen because their commander trusted them, and he was marching with them, displaying his confidence in them.

Less certain of the outcome of the battle, Macrinus glanced further back over his right shoulder, looking towards the hill fort which now lay behind the right flank of the Roman line. To his surprise, no danger threatened from that fort. He had expected Calgacus to spring a trap, but perhaps the Britons inside the fort had realised that the two Legions, around eight thousand heavily armed and armoured veterans, would pounce on them as soon as they left the shelter of the walls.

The Governor's plan had worked so far, Macrinus acknowledged, but it meant that the Auxiliaries forming the main battle line would be hard pressed.

Away to his left, he saw Aulus Atticus and the cavalry edging forwards.

He cursed. Atticus was too eager to spill barbarian blood. He was headstrong and inexperienced, traits that could lead to disaster. Which was why Macrinus was stationed near him. Agricola understood the potential for Atticus to get himself into trouble and was relying on Macrinus to act as a rock of stability.

But now that rock was about to be engulfed by a tide of barbarians.

Chariots rushed at them, the warriors hurling heavy spears at the Roman lines from close range as they raced past, wheeling around to return time and again. They were, though, largely ineffective. The Romans used their shields to protect themselves and continued their slow, methodical advance while their own archers continued to send arrows flashing overhead.

With a deafening scream of outrage, the barbarian footmen charged.

"Keep moving!" Macrinus bellowed at the top of his voice. "Don't stand still or they'll run right over you! Keep moving! Remember your drills."

The two sides met with a tremendous clash which resounded all along the line like a rolling boom of thunder.

"Stab them!" Macrinus yelled unnecessarily.

His men knew the drill, had rehearsed it time and time again in both practice and in battle. The barbarians used long, heavy swords with rounded tips which needed room to wield properly as they hacked and slashed at the armoured men facing them. But each Briton took up as much space as two Romans, which meant every warrior in the front rank faced two opponents. Not only that, the Romans were armed with short, thrusting swords which they used to jab at their unprotected enemies while fending off any attack with their large shields.

Macrinus had seen it many times before and it had always worked. It worked again now.

The ferocity of the British charge had brought down a few Romans but men from the second and third ranks had stepped forwards to fill the gaps, urged on by their Centurions. The barbarian swords and spears struck shields, glanced off armoured helmets or were deflected by the heavy mail coats of the Auxiliaries, while the short, jabbing swords of the Romans struck home against unprotected flesh.

"Keep moving!" Macrinus called.

And the advance ploughed on.

"'Ware horses!" called a voice from the left.

The chariots were back, flashing in to deliver their mounted men to the battle. There were men mounted on horseback as well, leaning down from their high saddles to hack brutal swings down on the heads of the Romans.

But Aulus Atticus had seen the attack and led his own horsemen in a furious charge to take the barbarians in the flank.

For what seemed an age, the battle degenerated into a frantic melee as men and horses became entangled in vicious brawling. Horses screamed and reared, lashing out with their hooves, while men stabbed and cut, yelled and struggled to kill the men facing them.

Macrinus was stepping over bodies now, using his sword to ensure that any fallen Briton was truly dead. Walking over a fallen enemy was one sure way to end up with a sword in your groin, he knew.

Macrinus continued to urge his men on, but the advance was stalled by the sheer press of bodies and the mounting piles of dead and injured men and horses.

"Keep moving!"

The Romans clambered over dead bodies, struggling to maintain their organised line as they attempted to continue their advance.

The Britons fought desperately, hurling themselves at their enemy with no regard for personal safety, screaming in rage as they took advantage of the gaps created in the Roman formation. Men on foot, men on horseback, men in chariots all battled to breach the Roman line.

"Keep going!" Macrinus yelled as he sensed the vital moment was approaching.

The Roman army operated best when it was attacking, but their lines had been thinned and there was no weight to their advance. As men fell, the Britons surged into the spaces, hacking left and right. Most of them were swiftly dealt with, but Macrinus knew that his ordered ranks could be turned into a disorganised rabble at any moment.

Atticus and his cavalry were still mixed in among the chaos, swinging their swords, the horses virtually immobile amid the bloody carnage.

Atticus!" Macrinus shouted. "Fall back to the wing! Clear the way!"

Atticus could not hear him. Surrounded by his mounted troops, he was swinging his long, cavalry sword as if in a dream, consumed by the thrill of battle and oblivious to the fact that his troopers were impeding the advance of the infantry.

"Atticus!" Macrinus yelled in vain.

The line wavered and buckled, and Macrinus felt his anger rising as the chances of victory seemed about to be thwarted by the sheer mass of men and animals in front of him.

Then Calgacus made his move.

"Now!" Calgacus yelled, raising his arm and slashing it down in an unmistakable signal to release the second line of his war host.

He had formed his army in three ranks on the hill, the middle tier waiting half way up the slope. Now they charged down at the battle raging at the foot of the hill, but they did not run into the mass of death and chaos. Instead, they sped towards the flanks, hoping to surround the Roman lines and trap them.

"We've got them!" Bridei crowed exultantly. "We should join in."

Calgacus shook his head. The men on the summit, forming the third part of the war host, were desperate to join in, but he had long ago learned the lesson of maintaining a reserve.

"Not yet," he said. "The Legions haven't joined the battle yet."

Runt, diminutive in size but as experienced as any man in the alliance, spat, "They've got more cavalry!"

It was true. From beyond the hill fort where they had been concealed from view, came more Roman horsemen. Charging to left and right, they sprung their own trap on the Britons.

Calgacus swore as he angrily slapped his hand against his thigh. He had hoped to destroy the Auxiliaries by surrounding them with his second line of attack. Men who find themselves with enemies in front and behind are prone to panic. If he had been able to break the Roman advance, the Legions would have been forced to fight a defensive withdrawal to prevent a rout. Instead, Agricola had countered his move with a surprise of his own, and now it was the Britons who were caught between two forces.

The battle changed in an instant. Where the two sides had been engaged in virtual stalemate, the tide turned as soon as the British warriors found themselves under attack from the fresh Roman cavalry. Their own plan had been ruined, and they lost heart as soon as the first charge of horsemen struck home.

Even on the hilltop, Calgacus could hear the wail of despair as the war host broke and ran, scrambling for the safety of the hillside with the Roman foot soldiers in pursuit.

"Bastards" hissed Runt, although it was not clear who he meant.

Calgacus turned to Adelligus and Bridei.

Calmly, he told them, "You'd better go and join your lads. Be ready when the moment comes. Don't move too soon, though. We need to make it count."

The two men, one grizzled and bare-chested, his torso decorated by tattoos, the other young and fresh-faced, turned and headed back over the summit of the hill, signalling to the nearby warriors to follow them.

"We should go too," Runt advised.

"Soon," Calgacus nodded.

He watched as the war host he had assembled disintegrated under the threat from the advancing Romans. Men of many tribes, Taexali, Caledones, Venicones, Creones, Smertae and half a dozen others, threw down their weapons and struggled up the slope as quickly as they could, while the Roman Auxiliaries, freed at last from the crushing press that had blocked them, climbed in pursuit.

"Bastards!" Runt repeated. "They've beaten us again."

"We're not beaten yet," Calgacus told him.

Macrinus felt the joy of victory. Calgacus had done his worst, but Roman discipline had triumphed once again. Macrinus' men might be Germans but they were Roman-trained and Roman-equipped. If they lived long enough, they would become citizens of the greatest Empire the world had ever seen, and that Empire had gained yet another victory. The last opposition had been beaten. All that remained was to crush the survivors.

"After them!"

All along the line, the Auxiliary troops were scrambling up the slope, eager to catch their fleeing enemy. Any Briton who stumbled or fell was quickly despatched, any who stood to fight were mercilessly cut down. Red with blood and gore, the Roman advance swept up the slope.

Aulus Atticus was in the forefront of the pursuit. Some of his men had dismounted, either because their horses were dead or injured, or because it was easier to claw their way up the hill on foot. Others, including Atticus himself, remained mounted, kicking at their steeds to scramble after the fleeing Britons.

The regular formation had vanished as the fastest men left the others behind in their eagerness. Relief at having survived and seen the enemy turn tail had ignited a desire to kill and kill again, to utterly destroy the men who had dared to face them.

Macrinus, feeling the weight of his years, followed as quickly as he could, still encouraging his men to continue the pursuit. The enemy was beaten and could not be allowed time to reform.

Ahead of him, he could see Atticus, still on horseback, still holding his sword aloft, still desperate for glory. He watched as Atticus swept his sword down to smash the skull of a grey-haired old man who was dressed in long, dark robes and who had been frantically attempting to rally the panicking warriors. As the aged druid collapsed, Atticus yanked the long blade free from the dead man's shattered skull, kicked at his mount's flanks, and surged up the slope in pursuit of more victims. Beside him, hundreds of Romans, their units mixed up as individuals simply raced as fast as they could, were eagerly following Atticus' lead.

Macrinus paused to catch his breath, taking a moment to look around. He was thirsty, his mouth so dry he could hardly raise a spit. His legs were tired from the climb, and his chainmail armour weighed heavily on his shoulders.

But the battle was won. The Legions had not even drawn their swords and had been mere spectators as the Auxiliaries, supported by the cavalry, had gained the victory. Down on the plain, the Legions were now advancing on the ancient hillfort as its occupants, barely more than fifty of them, Macrinus could see now, fled in near panic.

Then his gaze swept upwards again, towards the crest of the hill and his heart almost stopped.

Calgacus!

He was there, standing on the summit, his long sword still on his back, acting as if nothing were wrong. Beside him, the smaller figure of Liscus, universally known as Runt, was waving at the fleeing Britons, urging them to escape over the crest of the hill. Then, as if he had noticed that Macrinus had seen him, Calgacus turned and hurried away, vanishing over the lip of the hilltop.

Macrinus stood still for a shocked moment as realisation struck him. He had believed the Romans were on the verge of complete victory, but he knew now that Calgacus still had one more trick he intended to play.

Up ahead, Macrinus could see Atticus frantically kicking at his horse to encourage the exhausted beast to chase the famous British war Leader.

"Stop!" Macrinus yelled. "Atticus! Come back! It's a trap!"

There was no chance of Atticus hearing him. A few of the nearest soldiers halted their climb, looking at him with perplexed expressions.

"Form up here!" he shouted, waving his sword and shoving at the nearest men to bully them into some sort of line.

"Standard Bearers!" he called. "Rally here!"

Few of the men carrying the various flags were able to hear him, but one or two halted their headlong advance and obeyed his summons. The soldiers around them, dutifully following the standards, scrambled after them.

"What's going on?" one of the men asked.

"It's a trap," Macrinus declared loudly. "Form up or we'll be dead men."

He heard the thudding of hoofs and turned to see Agricola, now mounted on a horse and accompanied by half a dozen aides, hurrying over to him.

"Why have you stopped?" the Governor asked as he reined in behind the embryonic line of soldiers, his horse struggling to maintain balance on the steep hillside.

"It's a trap, Sir," Macrinus repeated. "We need to bring the men back."

"Are you sure?" Agricola demanded, frowning as he scanned the hilltop.

"Positive, sir. If we go over that hill there will be an ambush waiting for us. I've seen Calgacus use that trick before. In Hibernia."

Agricola's frown deepened at the mention of his abortive attempt to conquer the island of Hibernia, but he knew well enough what had happened to the troops he had sent there.

"Gather as many men as you can and form a proper line," he told Macrinus. "I'll bring the rest back."

Then, with his staff officers trailing in his wake, he was off, pushing his horse up the slope, bellowing at the soldiers to halt their advance and re-join Macrinus.

It was almost too late. As Agricola drove his tired horse to the crest of the hill and an endless vista of mountains revealed itself, he saw Atticus leading several hundred men in a wild, ragged charge into a wooded landscape of hummocks and gullies as they dashed in pursuit of a horde of fleeing Britons.

"Stop!" Agricola yelled in vain.

He rode on, more cautiously now as the ground was uneven and littered with corpses and the debris of war, the detritus marking Atticus' path through the British rout. Swords, spears, shields and helmets lay scattered among the dead and wounded, forcing Agricola to pick a way through the obstacles.

He and his officers caught a few men, ordering them back to the hilltop, then he hurried on, shouting at the top of his voice, attempting to recall the mad, disorganised charge.

He heard the screams and the clash of arms as he neared the woodland. From the depths of the trees came the unmistakable sound of an ambush. He could not see anything of the fighting but he could imagine the scene as hundreds of British warriors leaped out from their places of concealment to attack the disorganised Roman troops, falling on them from all sides, hacking and killing. It was a favourite tactic of the Britons, catching the Romans in terrain where they could not deploy properly and use their disciplined system of fighting. Caught singly or in small groups, the Roman soldiers would be mercilessly slaughtered.

Agricola stopped, staring helplessly at the trees, listening to the awful sounds of his men dying, knowing he could do nothing to save them.

To his relief, Roman soldiers emerged from the tree-filled gullies, running for their lives, the hunters having become the hunted. Even as Agricola watched, he saw one man being pounced on by three wild, screaming barbarians who hacked their helpless victim to death.

"Back to the hilltop!" he yelled. "Form up there!"

Dozens of men were streaming past him, some of them having discarded their weapons in their desperation to escape. Riderless, panicked horses appeared, galloping wildly as they dodged between trees and running men.

"You should go back, Sir," one of his Tribunes advised anxiously.

Agricola turned in his saddle, looking back at the hilltop. He breathed a sigh of relief when he saw Macrinus bringing the bulk of the Auxiliaries into view. They were mixed up, men of different units standing alongside one another in a ragged formation that was driving many of the Centurions into a rage, but they were there, and they were under proper discipline.

"Back to the hilltop!" the Governor shouted again, gesturing wildly to the running men who were streaming past him.

He could have saved his breath because they knew that their only chance of escape lay in reaching the Cohorts who were assembled on the hilltop. Gasping and stumbling, they weaved and staggered their way to safety.

Casting one final, despairing look into the dark shadows of the woodland, Agricola turned his horse and rode slowly back up the debris-strewn slope, feeling tired and depressed. He knew he had won a great victory and, although several hundred men had been caught in the trap Calgacus had laid for them, a greater disaster had been averted thanks to Macrinus' warning.

In military terms, Agricola had won the battle, yet, somehow, he felt as if he had suffered a defeat.

Chapter III

Oil lamps guttered in the tiny inner cubicle of the Governor's tent, casting large, wavering shadows on the canvas walls. Agricola sat at his small desk, his mood still sour. Macrinus stood opposite him, while his chief Secretary, Donnatus, sat to one side, a small, wax tablet held in one hand, a metal-tipped stylus poised in the other, ready to jot down notes.

"It has been a long day," Agricola murmured softly, knowing that the walls of the tent were not capable of muffling his voice from anyone who might be passing nearby.

Macrinus nodded, his expression grim and accusatory.

"Yes, Sir."

"The enemy have fled?" the Governor asked, ignoring the Tribune's unspoken criticism.

"Yes, Sir. We have searched the woods where they ambushed Atticus and they have definitely gone. We've recovered most of the bodies."

"And Atticus himself?"

"Among the dead," Macrinus replied flatly. "Although we identified him from his armour since his head had been removed."

Agricola's mouth twisted in distaste as he gave a slight nod. He could not find any sympathy for Atticus who had allowed his thirst for glory to lead him recklessly into a trap.

"Do we have the final count of casualties?" he asked.

Donnatus glanced down at his beeswax tablet but Macrinus needed no such prompting.

"Seven hundred and twenty one dead," the Tribune reported. "A further twelve hundred and eighteen wounded, perhaps half of them seriously."

Agricola's lips formed a thin line on his face. Around a quarter of his Auxiliary troops had been killed or wounded. When added to the losses they had incurred over the previous weeks' advance, it left them seriously depleted. He could understand Macrinus' dark mood, especially when the Legions had suffered no losses at all.

"Your men fought well," Agricola said to Macrinus. "Tell them that."

Macrinus gave a curt nod.

"Arrange for the seriously wounded to be sent to the coast so that the fleet can transport them back to Trimontium," the Governor went on.

"Very good, Sir."

"And have the dead cremated and the bones buried."

Macrinus gave another nod. He already knew what to do and needed no telling. What he wanted from the Governor was something more than unnecessary instructions.

"And your orders for the rest of the men?" he asked bluntly. "Do we pursue the enemy?"

Agricola could detect the pride in Macrinus' voice. The Auxiliaries may have suffered dreadful casualties, but they would fight again if he commanded it.

"Do we have a rough count of how many men the enemy lost?" he asked.

"We estimate around five thousand dead," Macrinus reported.

"Which means the bulk of their army has escaped," Agricola frowned. "Into those mountains."

Macrinus said nothing, so the Governor raised an eyebrow and asked, "What are our chances of finding them?"

"Virtually non-existent," Macrinus replied instantly. There was no suggestion of defeat in his tone, merely an acceptance of the reality. "Those hills go on for as far as we can see. There are a thousand places they could hide and plenty of scope for more ambushes."

"We have fought in such terrain before," Agricola reminded him.

"Not over such a wide area," Macrinus argued. "But yes, we can do it if necessary. The problem is that it takes time to conquer people who live in such a land. We need to locate every village, destroy every farm, burn their crops, capture their livestock and force them to face us in battle again. I doubt very much that Calgacus will make that mistake a second time."

Agricola sighed, acknowledging the truth of Macrinus' statement. They had conquered the fierce Brigantes who had occupied similar landscape but here in the north, the mountains were higher, the range much larger. And it had taken three years to defeat the Brigantes. Agricola could not afford to take a similar time to destroy the Caledonians and Picts. He had already been Governor of Britannia for more than six years, beyond any Governor's usual tenure. He had wanted to complete the conquest of Britannia before being recalled to Rome and now, it seemed, that chance had been lost. He had won a victory, but the price had been high and the ultimate strategic result inconclusive.

A sense of failure gripped his heart, its power made stronger by the still fresh knowledge of his young son's untimely death. Yet he could not afford to give in to feelings of despair, so he fixed Macrinus with an uncompromising stare.

"We will withdraw to the south," he told the Tribune. "We can cage these rebels in their mountains."

"South?" Macrinus queried, his dark eyebrows arching in surprise.

"It is the most sensible thing to do," Agricola explained calmly. "If we remain here, we risk being cut off from the overland supply routes and being penned in at the coast. It makes more sense for us to base ourselves near a navigable river and establish a secure land frontier zone."

Macrinus nodded his approval.

"I understand, Sir."

"Good. We will find a location from where we can ensure our land and sea communication routes are secure, preferably with a friendly tribe nearby."

The Governor glanced at his Secretary, Donnatus, as he observed, "We could go to the territory of the Boresti. Not all of that tribe followed Calgacus, and those who remain are friendly towards us. Or, at least, their new chieftain is. What is his name again?"

Donnatus replied, "Togodumnus. He is Calgacus' son."

"Yes, a coup for us there," Agricola said with a grim smile. "Although having Calgacus' son on our side does not appear to have persuaded many of the other barbarians to come over to us. So, we require a new strategy. We will create a new base for ourselves where we can watch the passes into the mountains and where we will have access to more fertile lands to the south of us, and a friendly tribe around us. If the rebels see the benefits of cooperation, perhaps a few more of them might surrender to us."

Macrinus made no reply, although his stance suggested he did not share the Governor's confidence in this strategy.

"Very good, Sir," he acknowledged.

"I shall issue formal orders later," Agricola told him. "Now I must compose a report for the Emperor."

Macrinus saluted and strode out, but the memory of his brooding presence left an air of gloom over the tiny cubicle.

Agricola sighed again, taking a deep breath to brace himself for what he needed to do next. The new Emperor, Domitian, would need to be informed of the latest development, but such reports needed to be worded carefully. Fortunately, Donnatus was experienced at presenting matters in a favourable light.

"We must report this as a triumph," the Governor told him.

"Indeed, Sir. Perhaps a slight adjustment to the casualty figures might be in order?"

Agricola gave a soft smile. They were hundreds of miles from Rome and it was unlikely anyone would ever challenge his report. Lying did not sit easily with him, but he appreciated the need for some propaganda. It would, after all, be for the consumption of the Roman people as much as for the Emperor, and the people wanted to hear of Roman victories, not Roman deaths.

Donnatus suggested, "Perhaps reporting three hundred and sixty casualties?"

"Half the actual number of dead?" Agricola frowned.

"The others could be reported later," Donnatus replied. "Perhaps as the victims of plague."

Agricola smiled at that. It was true that, despite the skill of the Army's medical orderlies, deaths from disease were usually more common than fatalities in battle.

"Very well," he decided. "Let us halve the number in our initial report. As for the barbarian losses, these are notoriously difficult to estimate, are they not?"

"Indeed, Sir," smiled Donnatus. "Ten thousand barbarian dead would seem a neat number."

Agricola nodded, "We must report the conquest of Britannia. The enemy have been routed. Only a few rebels remain and they will be confined to worthless, rugged mountain terrain where they can do no harm."

"I am sure nobody could find fault with that assessment, Sir," said Donnatus.

"Draft something for me, would you? In the meantime, I will write orders for the army to withdraw to friendly territory."

"Very well, Sir. I shall see to it."

The Secretary left, having jotted a few notes on his tablet.

Alone for the first time since dawn, Agricola closed his eyes and wished things had turned out differently. He wished his son had not died; he wished Atticus had not led hundreds of men into a trap; he wished he had caught or killed Calgacus.

But he could not change the past. All he could do was deal with the present. He would report a victory for Roman arms, he would report the conquest of Britannia, with all meaningful resistance crushed. The few remaining rebels would be penned into their highland fastness by a series of forts, and he would civilise the tribes who were now under firm control.

As he considered his plan of action, his mood lightened. He had never been one to give in to setbacks. No matter what fate presented, he had always overcome difficulties with energy and purpose. He would do the same now, he vowed to himself.

But he must be careful how he presented his decisions to the Legates. The men who commanded the Legions were appointed by the Emperor and owed loyalty to him. Not that the current Legates had been appointed by Domitian, for the young man had only recently gained the imperial throne, but still the Legates would undoubtedly send their own reports back to Rome. Agricola would need to ensure that their accounts did not contradict his own. Fortunately, these men had fought alongside him for the past few years and he believed he could rely on them to support him. Besides, claiming that Britannia had been finally conquered would do their own reputations no harm.

Agricola's greatest concern was that he would be recalled before he could complete what he saw as his destiny. He had a vision of a Romanised Britannia, of towns laid out in the Roman style, of local people wearing tunics and togas, of roads and aqueducts, theatres and bath houses. He had already begun such projects in the south, and he needed time to introduce them in the north. It would be the work of several years, he knew, time he was unlikely to be granted, but he wanted to lay the groundwork and see the beginnings of a new province.

Time was against him, but Emperors were fickle things and Domitian was reputed to be more volatile than most. Perhaps he could be persuaded that Agricola was the only man who could complete the great work of civilising this distant, barbarian land. The Emperor certainly had many other matters to worry about, and he might not be too concerned about Britannia.

Agricola mentally shook himself. Worrying about what might happen would not help him. His own reputation was secure, he knew. He had accomplished more than any of his predecessors in Britannia. A temporary withdrawal to a secure line of fortifications would not diminish his achievements. Even if he were to be recalled tomorrow, he could hold his head high in the Senate.

And yet there was one other thing that rankled. For all that he had achieved, Agricola felt the nagging irritation of a task left unfinished. There was one thing that left him open to criticism, one thing he had repeatedly failed to do.

He had not been able to kill or capture Calgacus.

Chapter IV

An eagle soared high on a rising thermal, its wings outstretched as it lazily circled, taking advantage of the fine, clear weather of a late summer's day. Not that the great bird had any appreciation of the fine weather except that it offered a chance to locate some fat, succulent prey. Its keen eyes surveyed the mountainous terrain far below, searching out signs of movement. Briefly, it banked its wings and turned towards a woodland where a fast running stream tumbled down a hillside, normally an ideal location to find a hare or young deer. Then the eagle lost interest as it saw that the beasts moving among the trees were men and horses.

The eagle did not concern itself with what these men might be doing. It instinctively knew that the presence of these large beasts sometimes flushed smaller animals out into the open, but it quickly realised that any potential prey had already moved on or was lying hidden. It would find no food here. With a slight adjustment of its long wings, it turned away and moved off, soaring high over the mountaintops.

Far below the great raptor, down among the trees, the sun sparkled on the noisy stream and made dancing patterns of light and shade across a narrow clearing where several dozen men had gathered. Like the eagle, none of them showed any appreciation for their surroundings. All they knew was that this was, for the moment, a place of relative safety.

Calgacus sat on a boulder that was illuminated in a patch of bright sunlight. He was unshaven and his eyes narrowed under the bright glare, but his expression was grim and determined despite the air of defeat which lay heavily on the men around him. He had removed his bronze breastplate, but his great sword lay across his knees as if he were ready to use it.

Warriors stood in a circle around the edges of the clearing, spears in hand, their clothes and skin marred by signs of battle and travel. Some nursed minor injuries, gashes or bruises. All of them had the tired, desperate look of beaten men.

In the centre of the small clearing, two chieftains faced Calgacus.

"It seems you were right, after all," said Bran, the newly-appointed King of the Caledones.

Bran was a small, wiry man with brown hair and a keen intelligence. Some considered him too sly and cunning but, as far as Calgacus was concerned, he had, so far, shown himself to be a trustworthy ally.

"Yet we might have won," Calgacus replied. "Unfortunately, not enough of them fell into our trap."

Gabrain, King of the Venicones, a young, burly, red-haired giant of a man, glowered as he spat, "So, what do we do now?"

"We continue the fight," Calgacus replied calmly. "We have no other choice except to surrender, and I will never do that. There is nowhere else we can go. We are the last of the free people, and only the mountains and the sea lie behind us."

"We cannot defeat their army," Bran pointed out. "You were correct about that."

"We cannot defeat them in a battle like that," Calgacus agreed. "But that does not mean we give up the fight. There are other ways to defeat them."

"Perhaps, but we have lost a lot of good men," Bran went on. "Broichan is dead. Muradach of the Taexali is dead. Most of the northern tribes have scattered and returned to their homes."

"The fighting season is almost over anyway," Calgacus shrugged. "We will rest over the autumn and winter, then gather another war host in the spring."

"How?" challenged Bran. "Without Broichan the druid, it will be difficult to persuade anyone to follow your lead, especially after this defeat."

Bridei of the Boresti, who had been standing to one side, growled, "The defeat was not Calgacus' fault. He advised against fighting a pitched battle, as you know only too well."

Bran returned an innocent smile as he spread his hands in a conciliatory gesture.

"I know that, my fierce friend. I am merely pointing out the realities of your situation."

Calgacus' ears pricked up.

"Don't you mean it is our shared situation?" he asked sharply.

Bran treated him to another smile.

"The season is almost over," he said, returning Calgacus' own words. "My people will return to their homes. We will defend ourselves against the Romans if they should attack us, but I cannot offer our aid in taking the war to them."

"You will make peace with them?" Gabrain challenged angrily, his fists clenching.

"I did not say that," Bran answered smoothly. "But I cannot pledge my warriors to a fight they cannot win when they need to defend their own homes. Our scouts report the Romans are pulling back. I doubt that they will leave us entirely, but one does not provoke a sleeping bear. If we leave the Romans in peace, they may decide not to pursue us."

"They will not leave you in peace," Calgacus assured him. "One day, they will come for you. I have been saying this for years. The only way to oppose them is for all the tribes to unite."

"We have tried that," Bran countered. "You led us to one victory, but it did not stop them."

"Ignoring them will not stop them either," Calgacus argued, managing to keep his voice calm and reasonable.

Bran gave a casual shrug.

"Then let us meet again in the spring. By then, the situation may have changed."

"You are leaving us, then?" Gabrain demanded, his words dripping with scorn.

Bran paid no attention to the younger man's unspoken accusation of cowardice. He merely smiled and nodded.

"We cannot all stay together," he remarked. "How would we feed a large war host over the winter? Better that we return to our homes, gather the harvest, and lay in stores. Next year ..."

He finished with another shrug.

"Next year we may all be dead," rasped Bridei.

"I pray the Gods will not allow that," Bran replied equably.

Bridei grunted, showing what he thought of the Gods' ability to protect them.

Addressing Calgacus, Bran offered, "I must do what I think best for my people. We are far from our homes here, and we need to return to our farms. If you wish to continue the fight, that is your business, but the Caledones will not take part. All I can promise is that we will meet with you again in the spring to discuss what might be done."

"Go, then, coward!" barked Gabrain, his freckled face flushing red.

Bran's warriors tensed, gripping their spears tightly, ready to avenge the insult if their King gave the word, but Bran himself treated the young warrior to a contemptuous look.

He said, "I am no coward, as you know. But neither am I a fool. We have done all we can for the moment. Let us regroup and consider our options. That is what I am going to do."

With that, he inclined his head in a curt bow to Calgacus, then turned on his heel and walked out of the clearing, heading down the slope to where the stocky, sturdy ponies were cropping the thick grass. Within moments, he and his warriors were riding away down the valley.

"Bastard!" spat Bridei. "I knew we couldn't trust him."

"He lost a lot of men in the battle," Calgacus pointed out. "They fought as well as any. I can't say I blame him."

He looked around at the few chieftains who remained. Gabrain, seething with rage, Bridei, gnarled and fiercely proud, Runt, his oldest friend and companion, and young Adelligus whose face could not conceal the hurt he felt at their defeat.

"What do you want to do?" he asked them. "Will you make peace with Rome?"

Gabrain snorted angrily, kicking out at a long strand of grass. Bridei hawked and spat his answer. Calgacus did not need to ask Runt or Adelligus for a response.

"Then we continue the fight," he told them.

"How?" Runt asked sceptically. "I hate to point this out, but without Bran and the Caledones, and with all the other tribes having deserted us, we probably have fewer than four thousand men left."

"Don't worry about that just now," Calgacus told him. "I'll think of something."

Five days later, Calgacus was still in search of some inspiration. They were, though, days during which he was kept busy organising the remnants of his scattered army.

As Runt had pointed out, the loss of the Caledones had reduced the size of their war host to less than four thousand fit warriors. But all of them needed to be sheltered and fed, and many of them had families who had fled to the mountains when the invaders had marched north. They were tired and despondent, grumbling at every minor setback, and it took all of Calgacus' forceful encouragement to keep their spirits up. He accomplished this by ensuring the men were kept busy.

"Autumn is nearly on us," he told them. "We need to split up and establish small camps where the Romans will not find us easily. Your families must be hidden away in the high glens, every approach must be watched, and we need to arrange relays of messages so that we can keep in touch and be ready to deal with any Roman patrols. These are our mountains, and we must keep the enemy out of them. Above all, we need to work together."

That last statement, he knew, was the most difficult to achieve. The bulk of his small war host comprised Gabrain and the Venicones and Bridei's Boresti. Both tribes had been evicted from their homeland and had lost everything except what they had been able to carry away. In addition, there were smaller bands of men from other tribes like the Taexali, the Damnonii, the Vacomagi and the Creones. There were even a few Caledones who had decided to remain with the rebel force rather than return home with Bran and their other comrades.

In all, it was as disparate a force as Calgacus had ever led, but he was grateful that so many had placed their faith in him. These men were the toughest, the hardiest, the ones who hated Rome and would not give in, no matter the consequences.

The problem was that there were far too few of them. However much encouragement Calgacus gave them, he knew he would need a much larger army if he were to have any hope of defeating the Legions.

The thought weighed heavily on him as he and his own small war band made their slow way southwards while their army dispersed into the hills. By the time he and his companions reached the high corrie where they had left their families, he still had no definite idea what to do next.

Wearily, he embraced his wife, Beatha, who knew from his expression that the battle had not gone well. There were many such reunions in the newly created village which clustered around the shore of a high loch that filled an ancient crater near the summit of a forbidding mountain. The evening was spent in recounting what had happened, in naming the fallen, and in singing songs of lament.

The villagers were full of questions and concerns, their eyes betraying their fear that the Romans might yet find them. Calgacus understood their anxiety and did his best to reassure them.

"We nearly beat them," he recounted. "If more of them had fallen into our ambush, we would have destroyed their Auxiliaries, and then the Legions would have been forced to retreat or be surrounded. As it is, their entire army has pulled back, so we must have hurt them. I think we are safe for a while yet."

He attempted to sound positive, but there was no way of concealing the fact that the great alliance of tribes which he had worked so hard to bring together had more or less evaporated.

There could be no celebration as they had hoped. There was relief that most of their men had returned safely, and there was resolve to continue the fight, but as the sun set over the mountains and the stars blazed down their cold light, most people left the communal fire and returned to the shelter of their newly-built homes.

Calgacus hauled himself to his feet but made no effort to go indoors. Instead, he held out his hand to Beatha.

"Walk with me," he said to her.

She stood, tall and elegant, wrapping a woollen shawl around her shoulders to ward off the gathering chill of the night. Then she took his hand and they walked around the edge of the small loch, stopping to sit on a heather-decked tussock from where they could look back at the collection of homes their people had created.

The night was virtually still, only a soft, chill breeze ruffling the dark waters of the loch. If it had not been for the orange glow of the village fire and the faint sounds of voices from the assorted roundhouses, they could have been alone on the wide earth. As it was, this was a spot where they could speak without fear of being overheard.

"So we must spend the winter up here," Beatha commented softly. "That will be hard. The snow covers these hills in winter."

"I know."

"Food will be short."

"Yes."

"And the houses are even more crowded than usual," Beatha added.

That, Calgacus knew, was true. The new village was hemmed in by the bowl of the crater. Each house was filled to capacity. He and Beatha shared their new, makeshift roundhouse with Runt and his small family, as well as Adelligus and Fallar, Calgacus' heavily pregnant daughter who would soon bring a new child into the world. In addition, they shared the house with a collection of sheep, goats, pigs and cattle, with the humans sleeping on an upper alcove which ran around the walls of the house like a shelf, while the animals were brought inside each night. It was a noisy, smelly way of life, but it would protect the animals during the winter and their body heat served to keep the people warm at nights.

The one thing the arrangement did not provide was privacy, which was why Calgacus and Beatha had strolled some distance away from the village to talk. As always, Beatha had recognised his need to unburden himself of his concerns.

Frowning as she pushed one hand through the strands of her long, blonde hair, she told him, "You need a plan."

"I know."

"Do you have any ideas?"

"Only one," he admitted. "We cannot beat them in a straight fight, so we need to lure them into a trap. It has worked before, and it almost worked this time. But they are growing wary of my tricks."

"Then you will need to be even more subtle."

"I know."

"And you will need a larger war host."

He nodded, "More men will join us when they see we have not given up. A few small successes will be enough to bring them back."

"So you will raid the Roman forts, attack their patrols and hope to goad them into marching into the mountains to find us?"

"That's right."

Beatha placed her fingers on his arm as she said, "Don't you think Agricola knows that will be your intention? How can you be sure he will come after you? You admitted that he is growing wise to your ambushes."

Calgacus scowled, "Then I will need to provoke him into doing something rash."

Beatha nodded thoughtfully as she said, "He is not a fool, Cal. You have outwitted him a couple of times, but you can't count on doing it again. You know the entire Roman strategy is based on terror. You know what they will do to us if they come here."

"They won't find us up here," he insisted. "They could march along the valley down below and never know we are here. Even if they did find us, we can move a lot faster than they can, and we'll just find somewhere else to stay."

"That might keep us alive," she commented, "but it won't defeat the Legions. They can bring thousands of soldiers against us."

"True. But, in the mountains, they need to split up. We can isolate smaller groups and cut them off. Besides, the Caledones will re-join us in the spring."

"Are you sure about that?" Beatha enquired gently.

"I must believe it," he told her.

"I know. But it's not much of a plan, is it? Not that I am complaining. I know you have done everything you can, and I know you will keep us safe, but I am so angry at being forced out of my home and needing to scrape a living up here in the wilds just because the Romans want to rule the whole world. I know you never promised me a palace to live in, but

I'd hoped our new grandchild would be born somewhere better than this."

Calgacus frowned and nodded glumly.

"I want that too, Bea. You know that. But wishing won't change the facts. I only know one way to fight the Romans, so that's what I'm going to do until someone else comes up with a better idea. If you have any suggestions, I'd like to hear them."

"There is one thing we could do," she ventured.

"What's that?"

"We could cross the sea. Go to Eriu. Tuathal, the new High King, owes you a great deal. He would let us make a new home there."

Calgacus took a deep breath, staring out over the gently rippling, dark waters of the loch. After a long, reflective pause, he said, "I cannot do that. Not yet. Too many people are looking to me for leadership. I will not run away after one setback."

"We have been forced further and further north all our lives," Beatha pointed out. "What difference would it make if we moved across to the west instead of hiding out in these hills?"

"Because the Romans will pursue us wherever we go. I am tired of running from them."

"I know," Beatha smiled sadly. "I just thought I'd better point out what is at stake for all of us. Apart from Liscus, nobody else will dare to tell you if they think you are wrong."

"You think I am wrong?" he asked sharply.

"No, Cal. I think you are right. I just thought you should know that you have choices."

"There are always choices," he nodded. "Sometimes, though, there are no good choices. But I will not force anyone to stay. If anybody wants to sail to Eriu, or go and live among the Romans, they are welcome to leave."

"Some might consider that," she informed him. "Especially when they hear the news."

"What news is that?" he asked, shooting her a narrow-eyed look.

"I sent a couple of the younger boys down to our old village to find out what is happening," she explained. "They say Togodumnus is back. The Romans have installed him as chieftain."

Calgacus hesitated before responding. The one thing in their relationship that had caused more arguments than anything else was his attitude towards their son.

After some time, he asked, "And what is he doing as chieftain?"

"I don't know," she admitted with a mischievous smile. "But I thought you might like to go and find out."

Chapter V

Togodumnus forced himself to ride with his head held high. In truth, he was tired and feeling low in spirits, but he refused to allow his Roman escort to see that he was troubled in any way. Dressed in his finest clothes of blue and green, his heavy, hooded cloak fastened by an ornate brooch of gold, he made an effort to at least look like a chieftain even if he did not feel like one.

"It is easy to be second in command," he told himself, recalling some advice old Runt had once given him. "It's not so easy to be the one with all the responsibility."

Togodumnus had been too young and inexperienced to fully appreciate the truth of those words. Even now, in his early twenties, he felt too young for the responsibility that had been placed on him. He was supposedly the new ruler of what remained of the Boresti, a chieftain with jurisdiction over a wide stretch of land all along the north bank of the mighty Tava, fertile farmland which stretched from the coast to the distant hills. When he considered how his father had so easily assumed the mantle of leadership, how even gruff, drunken old Bridei had ruled without any apparent doubt, he felt inadequate for the task he had been burdened with.

No, he told himself. Inadequate was not the correct word. He felt trapped. He had not become a leader of the people because of his own merits but because the Roman Governor, Agricola, had installed him as chieftain and backed him up with Rome's military might. It was what he had always wanted when he was younger but now that it had been handed to him, he found the office distasteful. Whatever decisions he might want to make, whatever plans he had to better the lot of his tribe, the knowledge lurked in his mind that he needed Roman permission and Roman power to put his plans into practice.

The simple facts surrounding his new role were that the people despised him and the Romans treated him with disdain. They might call him a King, but he knew that they regarded him as a barbarian first and foremost.

It was not a comfortable situation to find himself in. Nominally, he was free, the Roman horsemen accompanying him for his own safety, but he felt almost as much a prisoner as he had during the difficult days when he had been constantly under guard in the midst of a Legionary fort. That time had given him an insight into how the Roman Army operated, into what the Governor's true objectives were, and it was then that he had realised that he did not feel a part of the Roman world. He had been a prisoner, an outsider, and when his father's war host had stormed into the camp that fateful night, Togodumnus had truly felt proud of his people.

And yet he had stayed when so many others had fled to the hills to escape the Roman invasion. Even now, he found that he needed to justify that decision to himself. It had been the right thing to do, he was fairly sure, although whether he had made the choice for the right reasons was still a question in his own mind. He liked to convince himself that he had elected to remain as a Roman pawn because he was well equipped to represent his fellow Pritani, but sometimes he was forced to concede that he may have made an impulsive decision simply because his father had asked him to return to the wilds with the warriors.

Whatever had motivated him, the truth was that he was no warrior, no swordsman like his famous father. He understood learning, and books, and the growing of crops. He had felt he could do more to help if he remained with the Romans, acting as an intermediary between them and the Britons who chose to remain on their land.

It could still work, he told himself. He should be proud of what he had achieved so far. He was no longer a captive but a chieftain who could demand an audience with the Governor himself. Somehow, though, he felt like an imposter masquerading as a King.

"Nearly there," grunted one of the escorting riders. "We'll head up to the watch tower."

Togodumnus gave a half-hearted wave of acknowledgement. The Roman had not asked whether they should accompany him all the way to his home, but had merely announced that they were leaving him to find his own way over the last few hundred paces. Not that it mattered in terms of his safety, for he was within sight of the village, but the man's attitude rankled. He had simply told Togodumnus what was going to happen. A mere soldier had given instructions to a British chieftain.

The four Romans wheeled away, climbing the slope to where a newly constructed watch tower stood in the centre of what had once been Calgacus' homestead. The tall, wooden perimeter stockade still stood but the buildings, the homes, stores and barns, had been burned to the ground. Now a tall, wooden tower looked out from the crest of the ridge from where the Roman garrison could look out over the wide estuary to the south and across the broad plain of the Boresti to the north.

Togodumnus' village lay on that plain, only a few hundred paces from the tower. There was no defensive stockade, no ditch and rampart, merely a collection of around thirty roundhouses, widely spaced, each with an area of land for growing vegetables and rearing livestock. There had never been any need for a stockade when Calgacus ruled here. From his hilltop fortress, his reputation had been sufficient to protect his people.

Until the Romans came.

Now the village was half empty, many of the homes abandoned. Only a few families had stayed, and they were mostly the elderly or young. They were so few in number that they had more fields than they could cope with. Gathering the harvest had been difficult, a succession of long, exhausting days in the fields and when they were done, the Romans had taken most of what they had gathered.

Which was why Togodumnus had gone to see the Governor. He had travelled alone because his tiny village had few enough men to spare to escort him, and the people of the other villages did not yet trust him enough to go with him. His return journey had been safer thanks to the escort of soldiers the Governor had insisted accompany him, but it had felt significantly less pleasant.

It was over now, though. With the sun easing towards the western horizon, its warmth bathing his back, he trotted past the first roundhouses and headed towards the place he now called home.

At least Thenu would be there. He felt his heart surge at the thought. One achievement he could be proud of was that he had freed her from Roman captivity as a condition of agreeing to become chieftain of the Boresti. The Governor had wanted the son of the famous rebel, Calgacus, to be seen to be an ally of Rome, so he had been prepared to accede to Togodumnus' demand that Thenu be released. It had been a small enough victory, Togodumnus thought. Agricola had no need of the girl once her grandfather had died. She had only been of value while her imprisonment had forced the old man to betray Calgacus' plans. Once Calgacus had discovered the treachery, she was of no use to the Romans.

She would be waiting for him now, he knew. Timid and shy, alone in the world apart from him, she was struggling to fit into the strange environment in which she now found herself.

Togodumnus was not entirely sure that she genuinely loved him. He kept her safe and had offered her a chance of a new life, but he often wondered whether she had agreed to stay with him out of gratitude or loneliness rather than affection. Which was, he knew, simply another worry he had to contend with.

A few people saw him riding in. Some waved, others nodded greetings, while some merely stared or even ignored him. None of them came to speak to him.

I am chieftain of a people who hate me, he thought miserably.

Still he acted unconcerned. Straight-backed and with his chin high, he eased his horse towards the large house near the northern edge of the scattered settlement.

And almost felt his heart plummet to the soles of his boots.

There were extra horses tethered behind his house, he could see. Four of them, with two men lurking nearby, not quite out of sight. And a third man, short in stature, his head balding, two short Roman swords hanging loosely at his sides, the weapons incongruous against the faded and shabby tunic and trousers he wore.

"Hello, Togodumnus," said Runt.

"Hello, Liscus."

"Your father is inside. He wants to talk to you."

"That will be a first," Togodumnus muttered as he reined in and swung down from the high-pommelled saddle.

One of the other men, also armed with a sword, took the reins and wordlessly led the horse away. He was a young man, one of the villagers Togodumnus had grown up with, but the obvious contempt with which he regarded Togodumnus was like a physical blow.

Togodumnus clenched his jaw and vowed not to give these men the satisfaction of seeing that their attitude hurt him. He should not really blame them, he told himself. After all, they believed he was a collaborator with their enemy. The truth was more complex than that, but it was a truth which needed to remain secret.

Runt, who knew what Togodumnus had done to aid the rebels, gave him a sympathetic look as he gestured towards the door of the house.

Togodumnus stood his ground. He glanced up at the ridge, towards the square-sided watch tower silhouetted against the evening sky, where he could make out the figure of a Roman soldier standing high on the rampart.

"They will see you," he warned in as casual a tone as he could muster.

"We've stayed round the back of the house," Runt shrugged. "And we're watching out for any sign of them coming down here."

He cocked his head to one side and gave a boyish grin as he added, "It's just as well your escort didn't come all the way here with you. It would have been inconvenient to have to kill them all."

Togodumnus shook his head, smiling in spite of his irritation.

"You and Father were never short of confidence," he remarked softly. "But why are you here?"

"Let's go inside," Runt suggested.

Togodumnus pushed the door open and stepped into the gloom of the roundhouse, the interior lit and warmed by the central hearth fire. Just above head height, a layer of smoke filled the circular room, adding a measure of insulation as well as serving to keep the thatch free of vermin and insects. On a late summer's afternoon, though, it made the house oppressively hot and stuffy.

His father, though, appeared perfectly comfortable in spite of the heat. Dressed in a loose fitting tunic and checked trousers which were tucked into calf-length, leather boots, he sat beside the fire with his long legs stretched out in front of him while he clasped a mug of steaming tisane in his huge hands. His great sword in its shining scabbard lay on the earth floor beside his chair.

Togodumnus stopped. Even here, apparently relaxed and at ease, Calgacus dominated the room. Sitting opposite him, now half-risen from her chair, Thenu looked tiny and frail in comparison, her expression a mixture of relief and concern when she saw Togodumnus.

"Well, lad, you'd better give her a proper greeting," Calgacus told him.

It sounded like an order, which made Togodumnus dig his heels in and remain where he stood.

Eventually, Thenu came to him, gave him a peck on the cheek and led him to a chair beside the fire.

She took his cloak as she said, "I've got some broth nearly ready. Sit down and I'll serve it up."

She sounded as if she was doing her best to appear calm in the face of an ordeal. Togodumnus could sympathise. He had always found dealing with his father to be an ordeal. Even when he was outwardly calm, there was a steely look in Calgacus' blue eyes, a determination to have his own way and to succeed in whatever he chose to do. It was the sort of look which defied argument, the look of a man used to command and to being obeyed.

But Togodumnus was done with obedience. He might have been wrong about some things in life, but he was determined not to simply submit to his father's whims.

He took his seat and stared across the small hearth fire, holding his father's inquisitive gaze and refusing to be cowed.

An iron pot stood on the hearth stones, its contents bubbling away and filling the air with an appetising aroma of vegetable broth. Thenu busied herself with serving up four bowls and handing them round while the three men sat in stony silence around the smoky fire.

"I hope it's all right," Thenu said in a soft, nervous voice.

"It's excellent," Runt assured her as he ate the first mouthful.

"I'll take some to your men outside," Thenu declared in a rather timid voice as if she expected Calgacus to overrule her. Instead, he nodded his approval. She spooned broth into two bowls, carried them outside, and returned a few moments later, her expression still anxious.

For his part, Togodumnus could barely taste the broth. He was hungry because he had not eaten all afternoon, but he was too worried by his visitors to be able to enjoy any food.

"Why are you here?" he asked bluntly.

"I came to thank you," Calgacus replied evenly. "Your warning about the traitor in our camp helped us defeat that Legion."

Togodumnus dared not look at Thenu. The traitor in question had been her grandfather, compelled to aid the Romans because she had been held as a hostage.

"You certainly caught them by surprise," he observed noncommittally. "But that was months ago. I hear things did not go so well for you in your most recent battle."

Calgacus gave a slight shrug, taking time to eat another mouthful before admitting, "It could have gone better."

"And now you want something from me," Togodumnus guessed. "That is your real reason for coming here, isn't it?"

"You helped us once before," Calgacus pointed out.

"Yes, because I came to see the Romans for what they are, and I did not want our people to be destroyed."

"So, if you understand what the Romans are like, you will continue to help us?"

"That depends," Togodumnus replied evasively.

"On what?" his father demanded.

"On what it is you want me to do."

"I thought you were on our side," Calgacus replied bluntly.

Togodumnus felt a shiver of anger course through his limbs. For a moment, he concentrated on appearing calm, on spooning a mouthful of broth into his mouth and taking his time to eat it, but he felt the old, familiar antagonism that always arose when he spoke to his father.

Eventually, he said, "I am on the side of the Boresti. They are my people and I want to do what is best for them."

"What is best for them is to live freely, without Roman rule," Calgacus stated firmly.

"I agree," Togodumnus nodded. "But we live in a world where things are not as we would always wish them to be. The Romans are here. You cannot prevent that. Each of us must deal with them in our own way."

"And your way is to grovel at their feet?"

"If that is what it takes to keep our people safe," Togodumnus retorted sharply.

Calgacus gave a brief smile as he nodded, "You are your own man, at least. Good for you."

"What is that supposed to mean?" Togodumnus challenged.

Calgacus, his broth forgotten, sat straight in his chair and leaned forwards, his eyes fixing on Togodumnus.

"It means we can help each other," he told the surprised young man. "Your mother suggested that we should perhaps work together."

"How is she?" Togodumnus asked quickly. "And Fallar? And everyone else?"

"They are well. They are safe for the time being."

"But I suspect you are going to do your best to upset that safety?" Togodumnus asked. "You are going to continue fighting."

"It is what I do," Calgacus admitted. "But I need your help."

"My help?" Togodumnus frowned suspiciously.

"There are two things we need," Calgacus told him, ignoring his son's obvious reluctance.

"Let me guess," sighed Togodumnus. "You need food and you need information."

Runt smiled broadly and even Calgacus gave an approving nod.

"Very good. I always said you had brains."

"No you didn't," Togodumnus shot back. "All you ever did was complain that I had no aptitude with a sword."

Calgacus sat back, obviously chastened by the vehemence in his son's voice. With a slow shake of his head, he admitted, "I am sorry for our disagreements. I have made a lot of mistakes in my time. One of them was how I treated you. But being a parent is not easy. You do what you think is right at the time."

He shot a quick glance at Thenu as he added, "Maybe one day you will realise that."

Togodumnus shifted uneasily. He was not accustomed to his father acting in a manner that was almost conciliatory.

He stated, "What is past, is past. We cannot change it. As for the future, I will do my best to make it a good one for our people."

Calgacus nodded thoughtfully.

"Which brings us back to what we need."

"Food is a problem," Togodumnus informed him immediately. "We have little enough ourselves. Most of the harvest was confiscated by the Romans."

Calgacus gave a knowing nod.

"That does not surprise me," he murmured.

Togodumnus was grateful that his father did not give him a lecture on the perfidies of the Empire, especially since his predictions of Roman behaviour had been proved correct.

Togodumnus went on, "I can probably spare a little grain, and perhaps there will be salted meat later in the year, but I can't see the people here starve just to feed you."

"I know. Whatever you can spare will be appreciated. I was thinking of maybe sending a few of our younger boys down every few weeks. The Romans won't suspect kids of doing anything serious, so they could act as messengers and couriers."

"It might be better to meet somewhere away from the village," Togodumnus suggested. "That would be safer for everyone."

Calgacus nodded, "We can work something out, but whatever we do will be dangerous. If the Romans find out that you are helping us, it won't go easy with you. That means we need to let as few people as possible into the secret."

"I understand," Togodumnus sighed. "As for the danger, I am growing accustomed to that."

"As long as you understand the risks," Calgacus said. "Providing us with food will be dangerous enough, but passing information puts your life at risk."

"I am hardly in a position to tell you very much," Togodumnus shrugged.

"You saw the Governor today, though."

"I went to complain about the harvest being seized."

"Did it do any good?"

Togodumnus shrugged, "We shall see. But, whatever else he does, Agricola is not going to tell me his plans."

"But you will still hear things. There is a Roman garrison up in that tower on the ridge. You could befriend them. They will know some things."

"Nothing of importance," Togodumnus argued.

"All information could be important," Calgacus assured him.

Togodumnus gave a small, hesitant nod.

"Very well. I can do that."

"And you can tell me what you saw and heard when you visited the Governor."

Togodumnus sagged back in his chair. He had been beaten again, he knew. He was going to do what his father wanted. He had decided his future months earlier, when he had passed a message to the rebels warning about a traitor in their midst. Now he knew he had no choice but to continue to play the part of a spy.

"He is building a large fort further along the river," he reported dully. "They are quarrying stone and digging ditches. He is also planning to build a line of forts across the country, especially at the mouths of the glens."

"He's trying to block us in," Calgacus mused.

Togodumnus nodded his agreement.

"Containment seems to be his plan."

"What about the Legions? Where are they based?"

"The Ninth, or what is left of it after you raided its camp, has gone south. The Second has also left. The Twentieth are building the fort, and he's kept all the Auxiliary troops nearby. They will man the forts and watch towers, of course."

"And those forts and watch towers will need to be supplied on a regular basis," Calgacus grinned. "Which gives us plenty of opportunity to disrupt things."

"You won't defeat the Romans that way," Togodumnus said, echoing Beatha's advice.

"I know. But it's the best way of keeping the fight going. They have food and weapons. We need food and weapons."

Runt put in, "If two of the Legions have headed south, that evens the odds against us."

"Perhaps," Calgacus shrugged. "But they can always march back again. And even One Legion is still a tough nut to crack."

"Virtually impossible," Togodumnus affirmed.

"Which doesn't mean we are going to give up and accept things. I want the Romans gone from our lands, and the only way to do that is to fight them. They aren't going to sit down and negotiate about it."

"You need something more than continued raids," Togodumnus observed.

"I'm willing to listen to ideas," Calgacus told him, his tone amused at the thought that his unwarlike son might know how to combat the most powerful army in the world.

Togodumnus stood up, running one hand over his face while he thought. Pursing his lips, he began to slowly pace the floor.

"The best way to defeat your enemy is to demoralise them," he remarked, speaking as if thinking aloud.

"Killing enough of them will do that," Calgacus joked.

"Rome has more men than even you can kill," his son shot back. "If you somehow wipe out the Twentieth Legion, they'll simply bring more Legions to stamp on you."

He waved a hand at Calgacus as he went on, "Many of the legionaries already regard you as a demon. They believe you cannot be killed because you have been brought back from the dead."

"That was nothing more than a trick," Calgacus snorted, recalling how he had taken part in what had appeared to be a sacrifice where a witch woman had cut his belly open, spilled his innards on the ground, then resurrected him.

"Trick or not, it worked very well," Togodumnus assured him. "But even that won't drive the Romans back. Individually, they are in awe of you, but their discipline is such that they will not simply run away at the mention of your name. Their recent victory over your war host has given them more confidence."

"So, what are you thinking?" Runt enquired, his expression one of encouragement.

"I'm thinking I need to split a log," Togodumnus replied enigmatically, heading for the door. "Wait here a moment."

They heard the sound of an axe chopping wood, then Togodumnus returned with a short, freshly split log which would normally have gone on the fire. Instead, he clutched it in his left hand as he resumed his seat and drew out his dagger.

The others watched in perplexed silence as he began to carve letters into the flat face of the small half-log. He worked with studied concentration, taking his time to ensure that the writing was neatly laid out. When he was finished, he proudly passed the piece of wood to his father.

"You know I can't read," Calgacus frowned as he stared at the strange characters carved on the wood.

Togodumnus was enjoying the sense of impressing his father for once.

He said, "One thing you taught me was that people are impressed by symbols."

Calgacus nodded uncertainly as Togodumnus went on, "The Romans are no exception. They have their standards, their flags and their badges of rank. Symbols to inspire loyalty and respect. But symbols can work against them, too."

"And this is a symbol?" Calgacus asked, holding up the short section of carved wood. "What does it say?"

"The Latin says, 'Calgacus Hic Erat', which means simply, 'Calgacus was here'."

Calgacus' frown deepened as he stared at the carved letters. In the angular, straight lines of Roman lettering, the words still meant nothing to him.

Togodumnus explained, "You cannot be everywhere, Father. The fact is that the Romans are afraid of you. Even senior men like your old adversary, Julius Macrinus, respect you. But they know you cannot match them if they spread their forces across the country."

"We can move around, though," Calgacus objected, still confused as to what his son was trying to tell him.

"With that, you won't need to," Togodumnus told him, gesturing at the split log. "All you need to do is have lots and lots of pieces of wood carved like that. Every time you make a raid, every time you kill a Roman, leave that message behind. Have them left in different places on the same day."

Realisation dawned on Runt, who grinned, "They'll think we're everywhere at once."

"And they won't know which raids were genuinely made by you," Togodumnus agreed. "With any luck, the more superstitious among them will believe you truly are more than mortal."

Calgacus sat back, his expression one of admiration.

"We can play with their minds while we fight them," he smiled.

"It won't defeat them," Togodumnus warned. "But it will help break down their morale. Then, when they do march against you, they'll be wondering where you are and how many men you have."

"I always said you had brains," Calgacus insisted.

"No you didn't," Togodumnus reminded him.

Calgacus stood up, clutching the carved totem in his left hand. He gave his son a slow, thoughtful nod.

"I did, you know. I just never said it to you. But I'll say it now. I am proud of you."

Togodumnus felt a lump begin to rise in his throat. As a boy, acceptance and pride were what he had always craved from his famous father. Now, though, he was no longer a boy. He was a man, with pride of his own.

He coughed to clear the emotion in his voice.

"You should go now," he managed to say. "You cannot stay here. You are supposed to be my enemy."

To his surprise, Calgacus extended his right hand, waiting for Togodumnus to clasp it. After a moment's hesitation, he did so, feeling the strength and power in his father's grip.

"Whatever happens," Calgacus told him, "I am proud of you. You will make a good chieftain."

"Perhaps you could tell that to the people here," Togodumnus murmured in what was only half a jest.

"I will," Calgacus assured him. "Not because you are my son, but because you are the best man to see them through these troubled times."

Then, to Togodumnus' astonishment, Calgacus stepped around the hearth fire to embrace Thenu. The young woman looked petrified, enfolded in his massive arms.

"Look after him for me," he told her. Then, turning to Togodumnus, he added, "And you take care of her. One thing you will always need is the love and support of a good woman."

Then he was leaving, picking up his huge sword and striding purposefully to the door. Runt gave Togodumnus a quick handshake, then pecked Thenu on the cheek, his face alive with a broad grin.

"He did use to say you had brains," he told Togodumnus as he made to follow Calgacus. "It's just as well you have. Perhaps, with your help, we might actually win this war."

Togodumnus stood, unmoving, listening to the sounds of horses galloping away from the house. Only when they had faded into silence did Thenu put her arms around him.

"I was so frightened when they first arrived," she whispered. "All I could think of was how fierce your father is. He scares me."

"He scares a lot of people," Togodumnus told her, placing a reassuring hand on her cheek. "Including me."

"Is that why you are going to help him," she asked, her brow furrowing uncertainly.

He knew what she wanted to hear. She had been a captive of Rome, held against her will, a hostage whose life had been forfeit if her grandfather had not aided the Romans. Her family were all dead, her tribe enslaved or exiled. She had as much hatred for Rome as Calgacus himself.

It was the way she had been treated that had finally dispelled Togodumnus' own admiration for Rome and everything it stood for. That had not been an easy decision to make. All his life he had wanted to be a Roman but, when the Empire had finally arrived it had not acted as a friend but as a conqueror. He had learned that quickly enough.

He sighed, "I am going to help him because it is the right thing to do. I am standing between the Romans on the one hand and our own people on the other. I would be useless in a fight, but I can do my part."

Thenu relaxed, reaching up to kiss him.

"I will help, too," she told him. "But do you really think your father can beat the Romans?"

Togodumnus pursed his lips and frowned. Then he shook his head.

"It will need a lot more than bravery and a few carved words," he admitted. "An awful lot more. No matter how often he wins a battle, there is no ultimate victory against Rome, I'm afraid. The Emperor demands conquest, plunder and tribute, and what the Emperor demands, the Emperor gets. We cannot change that. Whatever any of us do, our fate will be decided in Rome."

Chapter VI

Flavia reclined on her couch, nibbling at some of the sweetened delicacies set out before her and her guests. It was a small dinner party, with only nine diners including Flavia herself. There were four men, each of whom had brought along his wife or latest mistress, and they lay on couches which were set on three sides of the low table in the traditional Roman fashion, three people occupying each couch.

Flavia had laid on her usual extravagant meal, several courses following in quick succession, with slaves on hand to ensure that guests' wine cups were never empty. Flavia, a rich widow, had a reputation as a generous host, and she worked hard to maintain that distinction.

Other than offering polite compliments, Flavia paid little attention to the other women, because her main interest was in the men who were her principal guests. They were middle-aged, all of them ranked as knights, the second tier in the formally hierarchical Roman society. They were wealthy, with business interests and landholdings scattered throughout the Empire. They were the sort of men Flavia knew she needed to cultivate, so she smiled and talked knowledgeably about their lives and interests, encouraging them to speak freely, ensuring that the wine loosened their tongues while she sipped at a fruit juice.

Her relationship with these men was rather complicated. As a woman, she could not formally be recognised as a patron, but she was wealthy and each of them owed her favours because of the financial support she had given them. She was their patron in all but name but, for the sake of propriety, they all pretended that she was no more than an acquaintance with whom they had occasional dealings. Flavia never insisted on them following her around the city as some patrons did to their clients. She never openly called on them to support her in any political venture because, as a woman, she had no direct involvement in politics. What she did do was have the occasional quiet word with them to apply a little influence here, or lend a little money there, or act as a go-between in some confidential business arrangement. And, of course, she sometimes held small, private dinners where they could discuss their latest ventures.

The evening was a great success. Agreement was reached on some potential business transactions, and promises were made to make discreet enquiries about third parties who might be persuaded to become involved in new ventures.

It was all very civilised, although Flavia found much of the conversation rather dull. Some of the information she gleaned would probably prove useful to her in the future, but she found it difficult to maintain her concentration as she mentally noted who said what, who knew which other influential people, and which of her guests would soon owe her another favour for services rendered through her extensive network of contacts.

At the end of the meal, Flavia gave each guest a small trinket as a gift, assured them that she had their best interests at heart and, late in the evening, bade them farewell with more assurances of her goodwill.

When the last of them had left, she breathed a sigh of relief. After twelve years in Rome, she was finding it more and more difficult to enjoy such encounters. Once, she had revelled in such things, in keeping herself informed of gossip and rumour, in gently guiding people's thoughts in the direction she wished, but, somehow, the joy had gone out of political intrigues, and Flavia recognised that she was becoming bored by it all.

She retired to her private bedchamber where her slave, Iusta, began removing the intricate web of pins that held Flavia's dark, lustrous hair in place.

"I must be getting old," Flavia mused as she gazed into the polished metal disc of her mirror.

"Not at all, Domina," Iusta assured her. "You look better than most women half your age."

Flavia's full lips curved in a faint smile at the flattery. She worked hard to retain her looks but, now nearing her fiftieth year, she knew that time was beginning to catch up with her. Everyone agreed that she did not look a year older than forty, but her feeling of advancing age was not so much physical as mental.

A knock at the door interrupted her introspection as one of her slaves cautiously entered the room.

It was Vericus, her elderly major domo. He gave a stiff nod of apology as he informed her, "Domina, there is a man at the front door. I was going to send him packing because he is on his own, but he insists that he must see you."

"At this hour?" Flavia responded, her curiosity piqued.

She could understand Vericus' suspicion of their visitor. Few people dared to tread the streets of Rome at night unless they had an extensive retinue of slaves to protect them from the street gangs and assorted thieves and cut-throats who plagued the city no matter how many watchmen were employed by the Emperor.

"Who is he?" she asked.

"He claims to bear a message from Annius Persus, the senator, but he insists he must see you personally."

Flavia's eyebrows arched as she turned on her stool to regard Vericus.

"What does this messenger look like?"

"He is elderly, Domina. But tall and well built. He looks strong despite his years. And his accent is atrocious."

Flavia could not conceal a faint smile. Like many slaves, Vericus was an inveterate snob. But his description had confirmed her suspicions.

"Show him to one of the reception rooms," she told the major domo. Then, signalling to Iusta, she added, "You had better put my hair back up. And I think a fresh gown and a little more perfume would be appropriate."

It took her over a quarter of an hour to prepare herself. She was tempted to keep the messenger waiting even longer, but she found that her heart was beating just a touch faster than it had before. Her sense of boredom had been replaced by one of anticipation which she hoped would not evaporate when she met this unexpected caller.

He was waiting in a small, comfortable room off the wide atrium, one of the public rooms where she normally met her clients each morning. Disdaining the padded chairs, he was standing in the centre of the room, drinking from a wine cup which Vericus had provided for him.

As the major domo had described, he was a tall man, with short, grey hair and a weathered, suntanned face that was covered in lines and wrinkles, betraying that he would not see his sixtieth year again. Yet his plain tunic revealed arms and legs that were still strong and powerfully muscled, toned by years of hard, physical labour. Even so, he was not like any labourer Flavia had ever seen. His air of calm self-confidence was almost palpable, an aura demanding attention and respect.

"Not bad," he commented approvingly as Flavia entered the room.

"The wine or me?" she challenged archly.

"Both," he said, casting an appraising look over her. "The years have been very kind to you."

"Thank you for the compliment. You are looking well yourself."

He put down his cup and gave a slight shrug as if her polite words were of no consequence.

"Sit down," Flavia invited as she took a seat facing him.

He did as she said and sat, upright and alert, his clear, blue eyes regarding her gravely.

"You have a message from Annius Persus?" she prompted.

After a moment's hesitation, he shook his head.

"I have come on my own account, but I thought that using a senator's name would make it easier to convince your door slaves to admit me."

"I see. Does the senator know you are here?"

"Not unless my daughter has told him."

"You are a devious man ... oh, forgive me, what name are you going by nowadays?"

"Caradog," he replied. "But you can use my real name."

Cocking her head to one side, Flavia gave him an amused smile as she asked, "You are not concerned that the Emperor might learn that you are still alive?"

"I am past caring now," he shrugged.

"Very well, Caratacus. Since we are in private, I shall use your true name."

"And I shall use yours, Cartimandua."

"I have not used that name for more than twelve years," Flavia responded in a matter of fact tone.

"Nevertheless, it is Cartimandua I need to talk to. You accuse me of being devious, but the woman I knew in Britannia was as slippery as a snake."

"Snakes are not slippery," Flavia informed him. "If you picked one up, you would know that."

"I try not to deal with snakes," he shot back.

"Yet you have come to me in the middle of the night, with your son-in-law, the senator, kept ignorant of the fact. Perhaps you should tell me why."

He gave a slow, thoughtful nod.

"I need your help," he told her bluntly.

Flavia, who had once been Cartimandua, Queen of the Brigantes, one of the most powerful rulers in Britannia, and an ally of the Empire, sat back in her chair and smiled.

"It must have cost you a lot to utter those words," she observed wryly.

"Needs must," he grunted ungraciously.

"Very well," she smiled. "I will listen to you, But Cartimandua is long gone. I am Flavia now, and have been ever since I arrived here."

"The Romans have a saying that a leopard does not change its spots," Caratacus said. "Whatever name you go by, you will be able to help me because I know how you operate."

"Operate?" she challenged innocently.

"You have contacts. You are wealthy and you know lots of people, including the Emperor."

"I have not spoken to the Emperor for years," she replied dismissively.

"You were a guest at the palace only last year."

"One of dozens. I exchanged no more than a formal greeting with the Emperor. My invitation was purely because I knew his father. He has ignored me ever since."

"But you can get close to him if you wish. He would grant you an audience."

She gave a concessionary nod.

"Perhaps. But why would I wish to bring myself to his attention? That is something I would prefer not to do."

"I can understand that," Caratacus grunted. "Domitian truly is a snake. As treacherous and deadly as they come."

"That is not the opinion of the people," Flavia pointed out. "His reign has begun well. He is popular."

"He is another leopard," Caratacus snorted. "He cannot change his nature any more than you can. His reign may have begun well, but how did he become Emperor in the first place? His brother, Titus, wore the purple for only a few years before he died in mysterious circumstances. There are disturbing rumours about the cause of his death."

"They say it was fever," Flavia interjected.

"It could just as easily have been poison," Caratacus retorted. "Domitian hated his brother and has always been hungry for power."

"It does not matter," Flavia insisted. "He is Emperor now, and doing his best to rule wisely."

"Yet, by your own admission, you do not wish to draw yourself to his attention. Does that not prove that you know his true nature?"

"All Emperors are dangerous," Flavia replied evenly. "But why do you care about Domitian? You clearly want me to go to him. Perhaps you should explain why."

"Because I want you to save what is left of our people."

"Our people are under Roman rule," she asserted.

"Some Britons remain free," he argued, sitting upright and leaning intently towards her. "But the Empire still threatens them."

"My people were the Brigantes," she persisted. "Yours were the Catuvellauni. Both are now Roman subjects. I know nothing of these northern tribes who still resist the Empire. They are not my people."

"We have had this argument before," he spat. "Everyone who lived on our island was a fellow Briton. They are all our people."

Flavia held up a hand to calm his simmering anger.

"I know what is happening in Britannia," she assured him. "But let us be frank about this. It is not so much the people you wish to save; it is your brother."

Caratacus relaxed slightly as he gave a curt nod of admission.

"Yes. I want you to save Calgacus."

There was a long silence during which they held one another's gaze, neither of them backing down.

Flavia eventually said, "You are making an emotional appeal? To me?"

"You were close to him once," Caratacus stated. "Very close."

"We were lovers for a few days," she returned. "Until he betrayed me. At your behest, as I recall."

Caratacus ignored the barbed comment. He countered, "But he has saved your life several times. You would not be here if it were not for him. He rescued you when your tribe rebelled against you. You owe him."

Flavia remained calm and almost emotionless as she replied, "Ah, a debt of honour. Is that what you mean?"

Caratacus threw up his hands in frustration.

"I should have known better than to come here!" he exclaimed angrily.

"Calm down, Caratacus. I did not say I would not help. It is just that I find your arguments amusing. You should know me better than to appeal to my good nature. I don't have one."

"That is not true," he insisted, fixing her with a defiant stare. "You hide it well, but I know you have helped several people from Britannia. You have bought British slaves and freed them. You have set them up with businesses so that they can earn a decent living as free men and women."

Flavia regarded him with renewed respect.

"You have been checking up on me," she accused with mock indignation. "What you say is true, but you may have misinterpreted my motives. These people are now in my debt and they can be useful to me."

Caratacus sighed, "Arguing with you is like trying to catch the smoke from a fire. But forget all that. Will you help me?"

"I might consider it," she conceded. "Although I don't see what I can do."

"You can persuade the Emperor to call back his troops, to stop the conquest of what is left of our island."

"Are you serious?" Flavia asked in surprise. "How do you think I can achieve something as important as that?"

"If anyone can think of a way, it is you," he stated flatly.

"So you have no plan," she smiled. "You think all I need to do is ask Domitian to please stop attacking Calgacus and he will do it?"

"You know how to persuade men to do what you want," he asserted. "It is what you have always been good at."

"Twenty years ago, perhaps," she said in self deprecation. Waving a hand to indicate her body, she added, "I cannot compete with young women these days."

"You have a brain as well as a body," he persisted emphatically. "That is why I know you can do this. The only thing I need to know is whether you intend to help me."

Flavia regarded him coolly, not allowing his forceful manner to affect her composure.

"It must have been a difficult decision for you to come to ask for my help," she observed equably. "I presume that means you have no alternative plans?"

"I have one," he told her. "And I will use it if I must."

She gave a soft, knowing smile as she remarked, "Ah, an act of desperation, I expect. They were always your stock in trade. Let me guess. You will attempt to get close to Domitian so that you can assassinate him. A dagger in the back, or something similar. Am I correct?"

Caratacus stared at her, his eyes hard and unyielding. Then he gave a curt nod.

She laughed, "You would not succeed. You would never be able to reach him."

"No man can be safe all the time," he growled. "I will find a way if I must. But you should know that, if I am forced to do this thing, I will confess that it was you who paid me to do it."

Flavia's serene expression did not falter. In fact, her eyes sparked with delight.

She said, "Do not be foolish, Caratacus. You were a fine warrior and a great King, but you were never good at politics. You must know that it would be a simple matter for me to denounce you as a traitor before you could make your attempt. I could easily identify you as a member of Annius Persus' household. The senator and his wife, your daughter, would be executed without trial, as would your grandsons. You would not risk their lives for this, would you?"

The old warrior sat very still, holding her gaze as if attempting to demonstrate that she was wrong.

She continued, "The entire thing would be pointless in any case. Domitian's death would not result in the recall of troops from Britannia."

"It might," he argued. "Domitian has no heir. The Empire would collapse into civil war again, so the Legions in Britannia might be recalled."

Flavia raised a mocking eyebrow as she retorted, "Might? Perhaps? As I say, it is not much of a plan, is it?"

"There are risks to all plans," he grudgingly conceded. "That is why I have come to you. I know you can succeed without the need for anyone to die. What I need to know is whether you will help me."

Flavia sat very still for a long moment then gave him a slow, pensive nod.

"I will help you," she told him. "But not for any of the reasons you think."

"I don't give a damn about your reasons," he told her. "As long as you try, I will be in your debt."

Flavia smiled, "The great Caratacus in my debt? That has to be worth something."

"Enjoy it while you can," he growled ungraciously.

"Oh, I am already enjoying it," she assured him.

The old man sat stiffly in his chair, his expression hard and grim.

He rasped, "I was right about you. You have not changed."

Flavia waved a languid hand at him.

"Neither have you. Your memory is long and far too resentful. But what happened between us was long ago. We live in the present and must look to the future. So, let us turn our minds to how to accomplish this task you have set me."

Caratacus said, "I will leave it to you. But you must hurry. Time is against us. All the reports suggest the Empire is pressing ever further northwards."

Flavia shrugged, "You must know I cannot be sure of success. Emperors are stubborn men. Military triumph is what they live for. I cannot simply walk up to Domitian and ask him if he would be so kind as to call off the conquest of Britannia."

"I trust in your abilities to persuade," he stated with a hint of sarcasm.

Ignoring the jibe, Flavia responded, "You must give me some time. But I give you my word that I will try. In the meantime, I think it would be best if you did not come back here. There are too many eyes and ears."

"You do not trust your own slaves?"

"I have learned that trust is often misplaced," she shrugged. "It would be better to be cautious. We should not meet face to face if at all possible. If you must communicate with me, go through one of my clients. There is a man named Belinus who runs a small cookshop near the new amphitheatre, on the north side. He is from Britannia. I will send word to him to warn him. He will carry messages if necessary."

"So, there is somebody you trust?"

"I trust in his debt to me to ensure his loyalty," Flavia smiled. "I told you my generosity had a price."

She could see the scorn in his eyes, but he made no comment. Instead, he stood up and reached for his cloak which he had draped over one of the chairs.

Flavia stood as well. She held out her hand and, after a slight hesitation, Caratacus gripped it firmly.

"You know I can never truly forgive you for handing me over to the Romans when I came to you for help," he told her.

"Are you not afraid I might do the same thing again?" she asked, smiling to soften her words.

"Of course I am," he growled. "But I am hoping that your affection for Calgacus will keep me safe. Besides, if you do this thing, I will do anything you ask of me."

"That is a dangerous promise to make," she told him.

"I know. Perhaps not quite anything, then. But, as I said, I will be in your debt and I am a man who pays his debts. The chance to have that hold over me is an opportunity the Cartimandua I knew would not be able to refuse."

"I think perhaps we know each other too well," she remarked. "But I have given you my word, for what it is worth. You need not fear betrayal from me."

She thought he was about to make some retort, but he changed his mind and kept his mouth firmly shut. They held one another's gaze for a moment, then he turned and strode to the door without a backward glance.

Once she was alone, Flavia walked to the table and poured a measure of wine, treating herself to a long drink while she allowed memories to fill her mind. As usual, she found that she could not help smiling when she recalled Calgacus but, although her memories of him and her recollections of how much she owed him formed part of her reasons for agreeing to help Caratacus, her principal motive was, as she had told the old warrior, very different. It was a fundamental, almost instinctive response to his appeal which had persuaded her. Already, plans were forming in her mind as she considered the task she had set herself, but those schemes would need a little time to develop. The best thing to do, she knew, would be to sleep on it. In the morning, she would have a clearer idea of how to proceed.

Draining the goblet, she placed it on the table, then left the room. In the atrium, Vericus was waiting, his features clouded by a disapproving frown.

"You may clear the room," she told him.

"Yes, Domina."

"Oh, and one more thing."

"Domina?"

"You saw no visitor this evening. I went straight to bed after the dinner guests left. Is that not so?"

"Certainly, Domina. That is my recollection."

Flavia wished him a pleasant good night and left him to clear away the evidence of her meeting. Still smiling, she returned to her bedchamber where Iusta was waiting for her.

"You seem very pleased, Domina," the young woman observed as she began unpinning Flavia's hair once more.

"Yes," Flavia agreed. "Life has just become interesting again."

Chapter VII

The Roman cavalry patrol halted to take a short rest and allow their horses to drink from a broad stream which flowed along the narrow valley. The commander, a young man named Decimus Claudius Jacundus, surveyed the surrounding countryside, doing his best not to appear nervous in front of the seasoned men of his troop. Satisfied that everything seemed quiet and peaceful, he posted sentries and gave orders that the men should take the chance to stretch their muscles and eat some of the salted meat and hard bread from their rations.

He made a cursory tour of his thirty-strong troop, speaking to the men and trying to appear relaxed, although he harboured the suspicion that their hard expressions masked their contempt for his youth and inexperience. They were never openly hostile, but he found it almost impossible to meet their eyes when they stared back at him. He had been warned against attempting to become too familiar with the men under his command, and he was beginning to understand why. The troopers were citizens of the Empire, but they were mostly from the lower classes of society, men who had joined up because they had no better options in life. Hard-bitten and tough, they were almost like foreigners to Jacundus who had been brought up in a genteel, civilised household.

Unable to oppose the men's indifference to him, he sought refuge in solitude, walking a few paces away from the stream to stand on a small tuft of heather-covered earth, a low vantage point from where he could study their surroundings.

Nothing had changed since the last time he had looked only a few moments earlier. The hills still crowded in on either side, trees still clumped together in forbidding, shadow-filled patches of woodland, birds still soared high above, and the sultry air of late summer still buzzed with insects. Nothing else moved.

Jacundus removed his helmet and ran his fingers through his sweat-dampened hair. He took a deep breath, savouring the fresh cleanliness of the air, sensing the tang of the nearby woodlands which constantly drew his attention.

"The barbarians love to hide among the trees," he had been warned. "Stay clear of woodland if you can."

He had nodded and thanked his more experienced fellows for their advice, but he was not stupid. It would be foolish to take his men into woodland because cavalry could not operate among trees. Everyone knew that.

He could detect no signs of danger, and yet the apparently idyllic country scene in front of him seemed somehow threatening, as if unseen eyes were watching him. Looking back at his men, he noticed that most of them seemed to share his sense of unease because, even while eating their rations or leading their horses to the stream to drink, they cast frequent glances at the trees.

A movement caught the edge of his vision and he whirled to concentrate on it before relaxing and cursing himself for a nervous fool. A large, plump, brown bird had appeared off to his left, noisily flapping its wings as it rose into the air before flying off down the valley. His eyes followed it enviously. He wished he could ride in that direction. Down there, several miles distant, was one of the new forts, a small garrison designed to block the entrance to this valley so that the savages who inhabited the mountains could not approach the larger legionary fortress which the Governor was building on the upper reaches of the river Tava. There were several such smaller forts, each one intended to guard one of the many valleys that led into the mountain fastness. But the Governor was not content to simply sit behind the walls of his forts and leave the barbarians unmolested. Patrols were sent out regularly with instructions to seek out villages and camps and to destroy any crops or stores they might find.

Which was why Jacundus was here, beyond the edge of the Empire's territory, looking for enemies and jumping at shadows.

He was just about to step down from his perch when he glanced at the tree line once again and felt his heart miss a beat.

There were men emerging from the woods, men wearing dull clothing, carrying spears and swords, men with long hair and savage, blue-painted faces. They were crouching low, moving silently but rapidly towards him and his resting troop, dozens of them scurrying across the open ground like a horde of swarming ants.

One of the sentries spotted them at the same time, calling out an alarm. Instantly, the Britons broke into a run, charging towards the Romans and letting out fierce, barbaric yells which echoed around the narrow valley, the sound bouncing from the hillsides as if the land itself had suddenly declared war on Rome.

"Mount up!" Jacundus screamed as he rammed his helmet onto his head and ran for his horse.

One of his troopers was holding the snorting animal for him, tugging it away from the stream so that Jacundus could mount. They still had time, he told himself as he leaped up into the saddle. The woods were two hundred paces away and the barbarians would take time to reach them. If his men could form a fighting wedge, they could destroy the attack thanks to the superior speed and power of their horses.

His men were well trained. Roman cavalry troopers practised vaulting onto their horses' backs so that they could respond quickly to any threat. They put that practice into good use now, dropping their half-eaten food and springing into the saddle, tugging on reins to wheel their horses away from the water and into some sort of formation in order to face the threat.

For a moment, Jacundus struggled to keep his horse under control as it skipped nervously because of the uproar around him. He clamped his thighs against the beast's sides and yanked hard on the reins, bringing a whinny of protest from the horse. Clumsily, he drew his sword and held it high.

"Form up!" he yelled, hoping his voice did not sound as frightened as he thought it did. "Wedge formation!"

They would do it, he realised with considerable relief. Instead of pressing home their attack, the barbarians had stopped their charge, recognising that their trap had failed thanks to the troopers' rapid response. The Romans would soon be ready and the savages were clearly unwilling to face mounted men on open ground.

Jacundus shouted encouragement to his men and prepared to issue the order to charge. This was what cavalry trained for, a chance to ride down a ragged formation of men on foot. It would not be a battle, it would be a massacre. He could feel the excitement rising in his chest and he could already visualise the congratulations of his fellow officers when he told them of his victory. Desperate for a chance to prove himself, he yelled at his men to hurry.

They were not quite ready. Men and horses jostled for position, lances pointed in all directions as the men hauled on reins and jabbed their heels into their mounts' flanks as they battled to form up in the confined space of the riverside clearing

Jacundus frowned impatiently, knowing he had no choice but to wait. In truth, his men had reacted quickly, but he was anxious to strike a blow for the Empire, and the excited, heaving mass of closely packed horses seemed to him to be taking far too long to sort themselves out.

It was then that his impatience turned to stunned disbelief when he saw the real attack.

Naked men had emerged from the river just a short way downstream. There were around forty of them, dripping wet, each one holding a spear or sword as they ran barefoot towards the rear of his newly formed formation.

His eyes gaped in bewilderment as he heard a loud roar from the front and saw the first batch of barbarians resume their attack. Then another shout from behind and to the right revealed a third group of men, also wet and naked, who had climbed out from the depths of the river just upstream from where he had made camp.

Some of his troopers were looking anxiously towards him, oblivious to the danger behind them and wondering why he had not given the order to charge.

He hesitated, frozen by indecision, and then it was too late because the naked men had reached them and spears were jabbing at men's backs, plunging into horses, making the terrified animals scream and writhe, throwing riders to the ground and creating havoc. In the tightly packed wedge, the riders at the centre had no room to move and, as they battled to turn and face the attack, they created even more confusion as they became tangled with one another.

The Romans at the outer edge of the snorting, heaving mass of horses tried to wheel round to face the new threat, but horses take time to turn, and the barbarians swarmed around them, hauling men from the saddle and hacking brutally at their helpless victims.

Jacundus' voice betrayed him. He could not utter a word, could only gape in horror as his troop was surrounded. The naked men were everywhere, stabbing, yelling, screaming and bringing death, while the barbarians from the woods were almost upon them.

Horses reared, lashing out with their hooves, but this only rendered the riders impotent as they clung on to prevent being thrown, and the Britons used their long spears to stab at the horses' exposed chests and bellies, bringing them down in a flurry of screaming, flailing crashes.

Jacundus could sense the rising panic among his men. They were trapped, and faced annihilation unless he could think of some way of turning the tables on the barbarians. But his mind refused to work, and he gaped in helpless horror at the chaos surrounding him, unable to summon the strength to act.

It was one of the senior troopers who made the decision. Mounted men only have an advantage over men on foot if they are able to keep moving. Standing still, surrounded by enemies, they were virtually helpless.

"Run!" the soldier yelled, pointing his lance down the valley, towards the distant fort and safety.

Startled from his impotent immobility, Jacundus took up the cry.

"Run!"

Freed from inaction by the decision, he kicked his heels into his horse's sides and yanked fiercely on the reins, turning its head and urging it into a gallop.

A Briton reached for him, but Jacundus swerved aside, the move saving his life as a spear hurtled past him, then there was open ground ahead of him and he was leaning low over his mount's neck, urging it onwards.

As he fled from the battle, he caught a glimpse of a giant, naked warrior who wielded a massive longsword. The man was issuing commands, while swinging his sword at one of the troopers who was vainly attempting to ward off attacks from all directions. The Roman fell from his horse, which reared in panic, its hooves vainly lashing at the men who surrounded it.

Jacundus knew he should turn, that he should not flee like a coward, but he could not overcome the terror the Britons inspired, and he kept moving because he knew that he would die if he remained here.

He still held his sword in his right hand, its weight and clean, unbloodied blade mocking him. Crouching low over his horse's neck, he twisted round to see how many of his men had managed to break free. Less than half, he guessed, and his heart quailed at the loss of the others.

He briefly considered rallying the survivors and turning to make a counterattack, but the ground to his right suddenly erupted as more barbarians rose from hiding places among the heather to hurl spears and slingstones at the fleeing riders. Jacundus heard a horse scream and go down in a crashing tumble of fear, but he dared not look back. To stop was to die, and he wanted to live, so he kept going, his eyes filled with tears of shame and impotent rage.

The fight was over quickly. Calgacus, still wet and cold from his long concealment in the water, shivered as he surveyed the scene. His men were finishing off the wounded men and horses, some of them already butchering the animals and stuffing great chunks of steaming meat into the nets the Romans used to carry forage for their mounts.

"Gather up the weapons!" he ordered. "And take whatever food you can find!"

He turned, his blue eyes peering down the valley after the fleeing horsemen.

"They won't come back," Adelligus assured him.

The young warrior was grinning cheerfully at the success of their ambush. He had led the men who had been concealed among the trees and who had distracted the Romans long enough for Calgacus and his main force to emerge unseen from the water where they had lain hidden for what had seemed an age.

"Get everyone ready to leave," Calgacus told him. "I want to find my clothes and get dressed. That water was bloody freezing."

"I did offer to take your place," Adelligus smiled.

Calgacus shrugged. Young men were always able to bear the physical hardships of war easily, but it had been his idea to hide in the stream and he knew his warriors would appreciate the fact that he had been prepared to immerse himself in the cold river alongside them.

"I wasn't convinced they would stop there," Adelligus observed.

"It was an obvious spot for them to rest," Calgacus told him. "Either on their way up the valley or on the way back." He grinned as he added, "I'm bloody glad it was on the way up because I think I would have frozen to death if I'd had to wait for them to come back."

"So we go now?" Adelligus asked.

"In a moment."

Calgacus turned to look at the devastation around him. A dozen horses lay dead, the bodies of at least fifteen Romans scattered among them. He noticed two of his own men sprawled amid the chaos and pursed his lips. Casualties were inevitable, but he still felt a pang of guilt at having brought these men to their deaths.

"I wanted one of the Romans alive," he said aloud. "Have we got one?"

"Over here!" a voice responded.

A wounded trooper, ragged and bleeding from a nasty gash to his left arm, was being dragged through the carnage towards him. The Roman had already been relieved of his armour and weapons and looked terrified, his eyes bulging in his face, his right hand clamped to the wound in his left arm, vainly trying to staunch the flow of blood that oozed out between his fingers and ran down to his elbow.

"Fetch a horse for him," Calgacus ordered.

"You are letting him go?" Adelligus asked in surprise.

"Yes. I want him to take a message. Have you got that piece of carved wood?"

Adelligus handed over the small piece of tree bark he had been keeping safe. It bore the scratched markings of Roman lettering.

"Calgacus Hic Erat," Calgacus told him. "Give it to him."

The bewildered Roman was handed the chunk of wood with its short message.

"Take that to your governor," Calgacus told the man in Latin. "Make sure you tell him who gave it to you."

The Roman stood still, confused and barely understanding what was going on, his breath coming in ragged gasps of pain and fear.

"I am Calgacus," the Briton informed him. "Tell your Governor these are our hills. We will kill any Roman who comes here. Do you understand?"

The trooper managed a bewildered nod.

"Put him on a horse," Calgacus instructed his men. "Then let's get out of here before the other Romans regain their courage and come back."

The wounded trooper was heaved into the saddle of one of the surviving horses, a snorting, terrified mare which rolled its eyes and bared its teeth as men clustered round it, shoving the bleeding messenger onto its back. One of the Britons slapped the horse's rump and it broke into a startled gallop, running away down the valley.

"That ought to stir things up a bit," Calgacus grinned.

He glanced at Adelligus as he added, "Let's hope Bridei, Gabrain and your father have had similar success."

Someone had fetched a cloak for him, which he gratefully wrapped around his shoulders. Then, moving quickly, carrying away as much plunder as they could, and leaving the dead for the crows, he and his war band melted away into the hills.

Chapter VIII

The camp was like a construction yard. The sounds of nails being hammered filled the air, accompanied by the rumble of wagons transporting raw materials, and the constant background noise of men shouting and straining to lift heavy pieces of timber or stone. A great perimeter ditch had been dug, an earth rampart raised and covered with turf, but stone facings were now being put in place. Barracks were being constructed, several long buildings, placed regularly in the prescribed manner and position. Stores, granaries, workshops, administration centres, an infirmary, all were needed and even with more than four thousand men available, the work would take several weeks to complete.

Galleys brought supplies up the river, unloading at a hastily constructed dock just to the south of the huge fort, while a constant stream of ox-drawn carts brought great blocks of stone from a nearby quarry, and work parties felled dozens of trees from the area around the fort. The work never ceased during daylight hours as the legionaries fashioned a home for themselves in this northern outpost.

In the centre of the camp would be the Principia, the headquarters from where the Governor and the Legate of the legion would direct the campaign. Nearby would be the private quarters of the commanding officers but, for the moment, both the Principia and the Praetorium were large tents, temporary accommodation until the more essential buildings could be completed.

Gnaeus Julius Agricola sat behind his small desk, studying reports and rosters. With him were Hordonius Piso, Legate of the twentieth Legion, Julius Macrinus, commander of the Auxiliaries, and Agricola's secretary, Donnatus.

Their mood was sombre, the junior men remaining silent while they waited for the Governor to respond to the latest news.

"Another attack?" he grumbled as he threw down a writing tablet. "Eighteen men dead?"

"They were ambushed," Macrinus replied evenly. "It is a risk our patrols take."

"But this ..."Agricola frowned as he picked up a small piece of carved wood. "Calgacus Hic Erat. Calgacus was here."

"He gets around," Piso offered with an ironic smile. "That's the fourth one we've come across in two days, and all from different parts of the frontier."

Agricola gave a sour nod. The other reports contained details of an attack on a signal tower, the ambush of a supply column taking food to one of the minor forts, and a work party being slaughtered while felling trees. All had resulted in casualties, but this latest attack was by far the worst.

"What of the officer in charge?" he demanded gruffly.

"Claudius Jacundus," Piso offered. "He is a young man, newly joined us. I don't blame him, though. He did nothing wrong. It was an ambush, and he was seriously outnumbered."

"Are you leaving him in command of his *turma*?" the Governor enquired.

Piso nodded, "I do not think anything would be served by punishing him any further. He is taking it quite badly as it is."

"He's not the only one," Macrinus put in. "The men are beginning to worry about Calgacus."

He gestured towards the carved wooden message as he added, "They say he is everywhere."

Agricola snorted, "Tell them it's nonsense. These placards are simply being left whenever a bunch of barbarians carries out a raid."

Piso offered, "But it does suggest the attacks are coordinated. We face more than a band of renegades, and our men know it."

"It's worse than that," Macrinus persisted. "One of those messages was hurled over the ramparts last night. The sentries didn't see who threw it, but it landed near the barrack tents."

"I shall address the men," Agricola decided. "They must surely know that Calgacus is merely directing these raids. He cannot possibly be involved in every one of them."

"No," Macrinus agreed. "But it does not help that many of the men still believe he is more than mortal."

Agricola's face darkened as he glowered at the Tribune.

"Is that rumour still going round? I forbade all talk of that."

Macrinus shrugged, "The lads will talk among themselves whatever we say. Besides, some of my men saw him being killed and then being brought back to life."

"It is your job to make sure they do not discuss it!" Agricola barked angrily as he jabbed a finger at the Tribune.

Macrinus stood his ground in the face of the Governor's wrath.

"I know, Sir. But it's difficult to tell them it didn't happen when I witnessed it myself. I still can't explain it."

"You saw him die?" Piso asked.

Macrinus nodded, "It was in Hibernia. He stood outside the gates of our marching camp, and allowed a witch woman to cut his throat, then to slice open his belly. I saw his guts fall out. Then she sacrificed a goat, let its blood fall on him, cast a spell, and he stood up again."

Piso looked horrified, but Agricola snapped, "It must have been a trick of some sort."

"I hope so," Macrinus grunted. "But, if it was, I have no idea how it was accomplished. But my point is that, whether we believe it or not, it helps add fuel to the myth that he is able to be in more than one place at a time."

"He was certainly involved in ambushing Jacundus' troop," Piso remarked. "Several of the survivors saw him, and the man he let go was very clear about it."

"He is playing with our minds," Agricola asserted. "We will not let this affect us. We are Romans, after all."

As usual, the Governor's anger had abated quickly, but there was a short, tense silence while he looked at the faces of the other men.

"Is there something else I should know?" he growled.

Macrinus, never one to hold his tongue when given the opportunity to speak, said, "There is a feeling that, although we won the last battle, we have been forced to retreat. The barbarians may have lost the fight, but they are not beaten. That knowledge does not help morale."

"Morale will improve if we keep the men busy," the Governor insisted. "But, from now on, I want all work parties to be protected by an equal number of armed men."

Piso and Macrinus nodded their understanding and Agricola quickly moved on.

"Is there anything else other than routine sick parades or punishment tribunals?" he asked.

The two officers shook their heads, but Donnatus made a soft clearing of his throat.

"There is one important thing, Sir. A message arrived just before this meeting began."

The secretary held out a small scroll, rolled tightly and bound with a scarlet ribbon.

Agricola frowned as he took it and casually tore off the ribbon.

"Who brought it?" he asked.

"A freedman," Donnatus replied. "In the service of Gaius Popidius Flaccus."

Agricola hesitated for a moment, his frown deepening as he unrolled the scroll and began to read.

"Popidius Flaccus?" Macrinus asked. "Who in Jupiter's name is he?"

Piso ventured, "The name is vaguely familiar, but I can't place him."

Agricola took a deep breath before announcing, "Gaius Popidius Flaccus is our new Assistant Procurator. And it seems he is about to pay us a visit."

"Ah, that Popidius Flaccus," Piso nodded. "Son of a freedman himself, if I recall correctly."

He paused slightly before giving the Governor a meaningful look and adding, "From what I have heard, he is an ambitious man. Not only that, I believe he is a personal friend of the Emperor."

Agricola's face betrayed no emotion, but they all knew this unexpected visit could spell the end of his time as Governor. There was every chance that Popidius Flaccus might be coming north to deliver a message recalling Agricola to Rome.

"Well," he said after a lengthy pause, "we must wait to see what our guest has to say for himself."

"I hope he doesn't mind sleeping in a tent," Piso smiled weakly.

"He will not need to," Agricola said with a satisfied grin. "One of the barrack blocks is almost complete. Let us give it over to him and what I expect will be a sizeable retinue."

"What about the men who were supposed to move in to the new rooms?" Piso asked.

"They will need to stay in their tents for a while longer," the Governor stated.

Macrinus could not help smiling broadly as he observed, "I dare say that will make him popular with the troops."

"Nevertheless," Agricola continued, "we cannot have a friend of the Emperor sleeping in a tent while there is adequate accommodation available."

"Barely adequate," Piso pointed out. "The roof is only half finished. He might find it leaks."

Agricola gave a sly shrug.

"That would be unfortunate," he said evenly. "But we are at war and this is a frontier fort. He cannot expect luxury."

Popidius Flaccus, it turned out, did not expect to find luxury at the frontier, which was why he had brought it with him. His large retinue of freedmen and slaves, along with several dozen trunks of luggage, assorted chairs, tables, beds and other apparently essential furniture, were unloaded from two galleys which had sailed up the coast before venturing into the interior to the upper reaches of the Tava.

Flaccus himself was an unprepossessing man in his thirties, of average build, with dark hair and features which could best be described as unremarkable. His attitude, though, was clearly that of a man who had become accustomed to being obeyed.

Leaving the unloading of his belongings to his senior freedman, he demanded to be taken to see the Governor. Dressed in a purple-striped tunic and a hooded travelling cloak, he entered the fort with the demeanour of a man determined not to be impressed by anything he might see.

When he was admitted to Agricola's tent, he established his authority by greeting the Governor with the words, "His Excellency, the Emperor Domitian, sends his greetings."

Agricola was too seasoned a politician to display anything other than a polite reaction, but Macrinus could feel the tension in the air. Flaccus was clearly in the Emperor's favour, and that made him a dangerous man to cross.

Macrinus had expected Flaccus to ask for a private meeting, but the Assistant Procurator did not seem at all concerned with privacy. He was, Macrinus supposed, the sort of man who preferred an audience for his haughty displays of his own importance.

After the introductions had been made and wine had been served, they took their seats around the small desk.

Agricola said, "We are honoured by your presence, Popidius Flaccus, but I am intrigued to learn what has brought you all the way to this northern outpost. His Imperial Majesty normally sends his letters by less exalted messengers."

"I am here to do my duty," Flaccus stated firmly. "I hear reports that you have conquered the natives and subdued the entire island. It is therefore necessary to assess the locals for the purposes of taxation."

It was not the answer Agricola had expected. He was momentarily caught off guard, both by Flaccus' message and by the slightly sarcastic tone in which it had been delivered, the Assistant Procurator clearly implying that he did not believe Agricola's claim to have conquered the entire island.

Managing to mask any irritation he might be feeling, Agricola calmly explained, "We have defeated the rebel army, but that does not mean it is safe to wander the country. There are bands of brigands still active in the hills, and this area remains under military control."

Flaccus gave a mocking smile as he answered, "Still, my duty is plain. The barbarians must be assessed for tax. The Emperor has sent me here to ensure that Britannia is civilised as quickly as possible and that the Treasury sees some benefit from your success."

Watching the Governor closely, Macrinus was amazed at Agricola's composure. It was no real surprise that a new Emperor wanted tax revenues to fill his coffers, but Flaccus' explanation was misleading at best. To have arrived here so soon, he must have set out from Rome before Agricola's message of victory had reached the city. It was obvious to Macrinus that Flaccus was playing some sort of political game, but whether he was doing so at Domitian's bidding or whether he had some hidden objective of his own was not clear.

To a soldier like Macrinus, such things were unsettling. If he had been in Agricola's position, he would have been tempted to grab the Assistant Procurator by the throat and demand answers. The Governor, though, remained perfectly calm.

"Civilising this country will take time," Agricola told Flaccus patiently. "These people are savages, unused to our ways and customs. You will have seen from your travels further south that we are slowly bringing them round by building bath houses, forums and theatres. These things cannot be done overnight. I'm afraid this is still very much frontier territory."

Flaccus sat back in his chair, crossing his legs and sipping at his wine with feigned casualness.

"I understood that it was normal in such circumstances to persuade the local leaders of the benefits of Roman rule."

He gave a condescending smile as he went on, "You know how it works. You hand out a few payments of gold or silver, and bestow fancy titles on the leading inhabitants. Then the upper classes persuade the ordinary people to accept us."

Agricola's returning smile held its own measure of scornful reproof as he said, "I know perfectly well how Rome brings new people under its control. Those are the policies I have adopted in the south, and they are beginning to bear fruit. The problem with these northern tribes, however, is that every man sees himself as a leader and each of them squabbles with his neighbours over who is in charge. There are few major settlements, and no real upper class for us to persuade."

"And yet they have kings," Flaccus pointed out coolly. "And a War Leader."

Agricola gave a slow nod of agreement, as if understanding where Flaccus was leading the conversation.

"Every man who builds a home on a hilltop calls himself a king," the Governor tried to argue.

"I see," Flaccus sighed theatrically. "That must be why I have heard so much about your problems keeping the barbarians under control."

"The enemy have been defeated and their army scattered," Agricola stated firmly.

"And yet there are some people who have suggested that your claim to have subdued the entire island was perhaps a little premature."

For the first time, Agricola's face grew stern.

"Organised resistance has been crushed," he insisted sharply. "The alliance of tribes has been broken. That is why I can say the island has been conquered. There are no armies left for us to fight. However, small groups of rebels will continue to be a problem for some time. That is inevitable."

Flaccus was not at all perturbed by Agricola's growing impatience. He had the ear of the Emperor, after all, and was impervious to the Governor's obvious antipathy towards him.

"It seems to me," the Assistant Procurator went on, "that you have a rather more serious problem than that. I have heard reports that the rebels, as you call them, are very organised and are led by a man who is notorious for his opposition to the Empire."

He paused for effect before adding, "I refer, of course, to this fellow named Calgacus."

Agricola's mouth twitched in obvious irritation, and his face grew slightly flushed as he replied, "He is certainly notorious, but he has lost most of his followers. All he has is a few groups of bandits. He cannot prevent us pacifying this land, no matter how troublesome he proves to be. And you know perfectly well that many parts of the Empire are troubled by gangs of brigands, even in the civilised territories."

Flaccus gave a supercilious nod as he persisted, "But it would surely aid our cause if you could dispose of him."

"Naturally."

"Especially if you could accomplish that before your term as Governor expires."

A tense, expectant hush fell over the small gathering. All eyes were on Agricola, waiting to see how he would respond to the implied threat.

"I have done more than anyone to extend Rome's rule over this island," he said with calm authority, his words deliberate and careful. "What is important is the betterment of the Empire, not my personal reputation. I believe that is secure enough already."

"A very noble sentiment," Flaccus nodded. "Precisely what the Emperor knew you would say. But he desires this conquest to be completed properly."

Agricola's eyes were hard as he stared at the pompous young man opposite him.

"Are you telling me that I have been recalled to Rome?" he demanded. "If so, please show me the Emperor's written command and I will follow his orders without hesitation."

Flaccus gently waved his goblet of wine in a smug gesture of dismissal.

"Not at all. The Emperor has far too many other problems on his mind at the moment. There is trouble brewing in Dacia, and some of the German tribes beyond the Ister are showing signs of unrest. The Emperor appreciates what you have done so far, and wishes you to continue."

"So I am not being replaced?" Agricola asked, his tone barely civil.

"Not at this moment in time," Flaccus conceded. "Although we all know an Emperor can change his mind."

With a hard edge to his tone, Agricola stated, "Then, until I hear that he has indeed changed his mind, I would be grateful if you would permit me to get on with my job. I and my men will provide you with whatever you need to ensure your safety, but you must remember that we are still in the process of pacifying this territory. I recommend that you return to the southern part of the province until we have completed our task."

Flaccus gave a cold smile as he replied, "I think I will stay here a while longer. I would be very interested to see how you go about subduing the remaining rebels. I am sure the experience of witnessing your success will be educational."

Everyone understood the implied threat. Flaccus was the Emperor's man. Whatever he saw or heard would no doubt be reported to Rome. His rank might be only that of an assistant Procurator, but the Governor's future lay in his hands.

Agricola merely nodded, his expression impassive.

"You are welcome," he said flatly. "I hope our meagre hospitality does not offend you."

"I am sure I will manage," said Flaccus. "I really am very keen to see how you intend to deal with this man, Calgacus. I hear he is terrorising your troops."

"My men are Romans," Agricola replied testily. "It takes more than a few barbarians to terrorise them."

"Of course. But everyone I have spoken to since I arrived in Britannia seems to know of Calgacus and his exploits. Some even suggest he is like a modern Achilles; invulnerable to injury. I do hope you have some sort of plan for dealing with him."

Agricola hesitated, taking a deep breath.

"We are concentrating on establishing this fortress," he said eventually. "Once that task is complete, we will deal with the rebels."

"So you have no plan?" Flaccus pressed.

"We continue to send cavalry patrols into the northern areas," Agricola stated firmly. "In addition, our fleet is harrying the coastal regions. We send envoys to some of the less hostile tribes in order to persuade them towards an attitude of peace."

Flaccus gave a sly, mocking nod.

"All standard procedure, I am sure," he smirked. "But it is not a policy designed to bring matters to a speedy resolution. You have withdrawn from the northern part of the island, have you not?"

"Only in order to preserve shorter lines of communication and supply over the winter," Agricola said testily.

"I see," drawled Flaccus. "And in the meantime, this Calgacus controls the land north of here, is that not so?"

"Some of it. Temporarily," the Governor conceded ungraciously.

Flaccus grinned like a man who had just made a winning throw at dice.

"Ah. Temporarily. How temporary would that be?"

Agricola sat very still, his face hard and unblinking. For all his authority and power, there was nothing he could say to this officious interloper. To argue against the obvious truth would only result in Flaccus reporting his words to the Emperor.

Macrinus decided it was time for him to intervene.

"If I may speak, Sir?" he asked Agricola.

The Governor gave a stiff nod of assent and Macrinus, knowing he was putting his own reputation on the line for the Governor's sake, explained, "I believe I have an idea which may help us."

Chapter IX

The fine weather that had persisted for so many days had changed at last. The land had turned grey, shrouded by low-hanging clouds from which came a slow, unremitting drizzle that soaked its way through all but the thickest and warmest of cloaks. Even remaining under shelter offered little respite from the gloom. Tents hissed under the relentless patter of rain, while brick and wattle buildings seemed to have any warmth drained from them by the gloom of the dreary dampness. The temperature had fallen as well, the dank air having a chill that was borne on a steady breeze which, while biting at exposed faces and hands, did nothing to disperse the endless blanket of clouds.

For one man, even the spurious comforts of shelter were denied. Riding slowly along a valley floor, heading ever deeper into the hills, he shivered despite the layers of clothing and the hooded cloak of fat-smeared wool which kept the rain from penetrating to his skin but did little to warm his blood.

He glanced up again, trying to judge whether the clouds were lifting. He decided they were not. The tops of the hills on either side were still invisible, lost somewhere far above him. To his right, a shallow river flowed swiftly along its bed of pebbles, occasionally pooling into wider, darker patches of water or cascading around and over larger boulders. He was not far from its course but could hardly hear the fast-flowing water because of the incessant sound of the rain on his hood.

His horse plodded on, its legs swishing through the sodden grass, its head lowered as if it, too, shared the misery of its rider.

There was scarcely another sign of life. Birds were too sensible to fly in such drab weather, and any livestock which might once have grazed here had long since been taken away, either by marauding Roman patrols or by the natives who had fled to the wilder, less accessible parts of the mountains. Now, only the occasional abandoned roundhouse showed where people had once lived in the days before this area had become part of the new frontier zone.

And yet the rider sensed that he might not be alone. He knew that what he was doing was dangerous and that a man's senses could mislead him into believing there were hidden eyes watching him, but still he felt a nervousness at being so exposed.

He mentally chided himself for his anxiety. There was only one way to achieve what he had set out to do, and that required him to travel alone. That, in itself, was what was unsettling him, he told himself.

When he looked back over his life, it was difficult to recall a time when other people had not been nearby. In fact, there had often been times when he had sought a little solitude, but he had rarely experienced anything quite like this lonely ride into hostile territory.

"It's your own stupid fault," Julius Macrinus muttered under his breath as he tugged the hood of his cloak tighter in an effort to keep as much of his flesh covered as possible. "You talked yourself into it."

That, he reflected, was true. He had known that, whatever the Governor might have told Popidius Flaccus, there was no prospect of pacifying the northern tribes for several months, if not years. Building the fortress would take a few weeks, laying in stores would take even longer because Roman rules of campaign decreed that each fort must hold at least one year's worth of grain supply in case it was cut off by enemy action or bad weather. It would take dozens of galleys to bring the required amount of grain from the southern supply bases, and the granary was not yet complete anyway. Macrinus was experienced enough to understand that it would be some time before Agricola could devote his attention to resuming the military campaign. That was one of the things Macrinus admired about the Governor. He was thorough and methodical, never beginning a campaign until he was certain that his men were as well provisioned as possible.

There were other factors to be considered, too. Establishing control over the recently conquered areas to the south would require both time and manpower.

Taking everything into account, Macrinus had known that Agricola could not possibly bring matters to a quick conclusion because the year's campaigning season was almost over. Autumn was already bringing shorter days and colder, wetter weather. Winter would be on them in a matter of weeks, and Agricola would not risk marching into the wilderness during winter.

Which meant that the crushing of the last rebels would need to wait until the springtime, which might be too late for Agricola. He may not have been recalled to Rome yet, but he could not expect to be left in place much longer. A year at most, Macrinus guessed, probably a lot less if Flaccus was peering over his shoulder and writing critical reports to the Emperor.

Macrinus had been in Britannia for many years and he knew that, if any commander could complete the conquest of the entire island, it was Agricola. But even Agricola would need more time. It had taken several years of tough fighting to subdue the Brigantes, and the tribes of the north, while less numerous than their southern neighbours, had a far larger wilderness in which they could conceal themselves.

Privately, Macrinus believed it would take at least three years, using two Legions, to crush the resistance.

There might, though, be another way of achieving victory, or at least a semblance of victory.

"Popidius Flaccus is correct," he had told the Governor, framing his opinion as a compliment to the Assistant Procurator. "We need to bring the ruling elite under our influence. And the most important leader the rebels have is Calgacus."

"He will never make peace with us," Agricola had pointed out. "He has fought against us for his entire life."

"And what has it brought him?" Macrinus had asked. "He must know he cannot defeat our Legions. What do we have to lose by asking him to at least discuss terms? You never know, we may be able to come to some arrangement. He might be willing to act as a client King."

Agricola had looked doubtful and, privately, Macrinus shared his scepticism, but he knew that they needed to be seen to be doing something if they wished to prevent Flaccus reporting back to Domitian that the rebels were being allowed to go virtually unmolested.

"I know Calgacus," Macrinus had reminded the Governor. "Perhaps I could persuade him to meet with you to at least begin negotiations."

What Macrinus had forgotten was that Flaccus was a politician who had come to prominence in the convoluted world of intrigue surrounding the Imperial Palace. No sooner had he voiced his half-conceived plan than the Assistant Procurator had pounced on the idea and added an embellishment of his own, proposing a scheme which had appalled Macrinus.

He had tried to protest at the course of action Flaccus had suggested, but he had not been able to argue against it. Even his assertion that it was dishonourable had been brushed aside by the Assistant Procurator.

"It is precisely the same as a stratagem of war," Flaccus had insisted as if he were some sort of military expert.

Macrinus had looked to the Governor for assistance, but Agricola had realised it was futile to argue against the Assistant Procurator.

"Go and see if you can find him," the Governor had told Macrinus. "Talk to him and tell him I would like to meet him."

So Macrinus was out here in the damp, miserable autumn rain, his horse trudging between mist-shrouded hills in the hope that, sooner or later, he would encounter someone who would take him to Calgacus.

He was angry at the way Flaccus had appropriated his plan, and he had been tempted to lie low for a few days before returning to the Governor full of regrets at being unable to track down the elusive rebel leader, but that idea had quickly dissipated. It would solve nothing, merely putting them back to the position he had been attempting to avoid, of Popidius Flaccus complaining about their lack of effort. Besides, everyone knew that this was rebel territory he was riding into, and nobody would believe he could wander the hills without encountering the British brigands.

Faced with no alternative, his main concern was that the first Britons he encountered might simply kill him as soon as they found him wandering alone in their territory.

"You're a bloody fool," he told himself for the hundredth time since he had set off.

Even if he succeeded in his self-appointed mission, which seemed unlikely, he doubted whether anyone would remember the part he had played. And if he failed, few would mourn his passing. His men, of course, would drink to his memory and recount tales of his exploits, but a new man would take command and Macrinus would soon be forgotten. Flaccus would certainly not lose any sleep over his disappearance and, while Agricola might regret the loss of an able Tribune, the Governor would soon appoint someone to replace him.

"Not much of an epitaph," Macrinus grumbled. "He rode into the barbarian lands and nobody ever saw him again."

He shook his head, annoyed with himself. He was a soldier and had lived with the prospect of death for as long as he could remember. He was also, he knew, extremely good at staying alive. That was not boastful or big-headed. It was a statement of fact. Macrinus was confident in his own ability because he understood how men behaved, and he took care to reduce the chances of failure whenever he needed to take a risk.

Once he had been forced into undertaking this venture, he had changed into some old, civilian clothes and divested himself of all valuables except a few copper coins and a long knife. He would give nobody an excuse to rob him. Taking a sword would have served no purpose either. Macrinus was a big man, tough and skilled in combat, but there was no way he could fight off an entire war band of Britons. He had no intention of fighting anyone. What he needed was to survive the initial contact with the barbarians so that he could talk to them.

That would not be easy but if he could cross that bridge, his chances of finding Calgacus would be significantly improved. It was not as foolhardy a risk as some of his men had clearly believed. He spoke the local language as fluently as any non-native could and he understood many of their customs. He was relying on the fact that they would be curious about him and would suspend their hostility long enough for him to persuade them that he was harmless.

"If you can't do this," he muttered to himself, "nobody can."

He had not set off completely blindly. The first part of his journey had taken him to the east, to meet with young Togodumnus, Calgacus' son. The newly appointed chieftain of the remnants of the Boresti had been suspicious and uncommunicative at first, clearly believing Macrinus was trying to test his loyalty to the Empire.

"I have no idea where my father is," the young man had assured Macrinus. "I am a friend to Rome, as you know perfectly well."

"Are you telling me he has not been in touch with you at all?" Macrinus had asked.

Togodumnus' face had betrayed nothing, but Macrinus had not really been watching him. Instead, his eyes had flicked towards Togodumnus' wife, an anxious young woman who had been doing her best not to meet his gaze, even when handing him a mug of honey flavoured berry tisane. When he mentioned that Calgacus might have been in contact with them, she had stiffened and stared intently at the floor, her whole body tense.

Togodumnus had noticed Macrinus' knowing smile and had sighed in tacit admission.

"I really don't know where he is," he had insisted. "He came here once, but I sent him away. I want nothing to do with him."

"I understand," Macrinus had assured them. "I only want to know how to find him so that I can talk to him."

"Ride north and slightly west, the young chieftain had reluctantly revealed. "He has men watching the glens. It shouldn't matter which one you ride into. They'll find you and he won't be far away."

Macrinus could have worked that out for himself but it was good to have some confirmation before he set off blindly into the hills. It seemed that Calgacus was, for whatever reason, staying as close to his former home as he could. In another man, Macrinus would have considered that a mistake, but Calgacus had such a reputation for unpredictability that Agricola had been convinced he would not remain in one place for any length of time. Calgacus, it seemed, had fooled the Governor once again.

Armed with the information he needed, Macrinus had ridden north and west, heading always for the higher ground, picking a way through thick woodland and across open meadows until the hills had confronted him like a low, grey wall. Choosing his path at random, he had eventually found his way into a long, wide valley which had slowly closed in on either side, forcing him closer to the broad, shallow river which rushed over its rocky bed on its way to the valley mouth and the distant Tava to the south.

He looked to the sky once more, blinking away the rain drops and drawing one hand across his face as he tried to estimate the sun's position. It was a futile effort, for the clouds were so low that they obscured everything, even the hilltops.

Sighing, he guessed there were still two or three hours until sunset; plenty of time to find somewhere to shelter for the night if he did not encounter any rebels before then.

Not that there were many places to shelter. The valley he had entered had few trees, seeming to comprise mostly of expanses of grass, heather and rocks. On a better, brighter day it might have held a sort of majestic splendour but, to Macrinus on this dreary, rain-filled afternoon, it was as miserable a location as he could ever remember seeing.

He plodded on, letting the horse pick its own way along the glen, his thoughts becoming increasingly concerned with finding somewhere to shelter for the night. All around, the hills seemed to be closing in, forming rugged barriers which appeared even more threatening than the desolate, empty valley, while the grey blanket above him pressed lower and lower, tendrils of mist wisping along the hillsides as if ghostly fingers were seeking him.

Except that the valley wasn't empty.

Macrinus had to look twice when he caught a glimpse of movement off to his left. He instinctively tugged on the reins to bring his horse to a halt as he peered through the shimmering curtain of rain and stared up at the mist-shrouded hillside. It took a moment but he had been right. At first, he had thought it might be a small herd of deer moving down the slope to escape the cloying dampness of the cloud base, but he soon realised that what he had spotted were mounted men.

They were almost invisible against the dull brown of the hill, their drab clothing allowing them to blend into the background, but Macrinus had seen mounted men before and the movement was unmistakable. Thirty or more, he guessed, and coming towards him.

No, he corrected. Not all of the horses bore riders. Only around half a dozen men were mounted, the other beasts simply being led down the hill.

Realisation struck him and he instantly twisted round, scanning the valley floor. Even as he did so, dark figures rose from concealment, men armed with spears and swords appearing from folds in the ground or among clumps of thick, brown heather.

They formed a widely spaced cordon around him, and he guessed they must have been closing in on him for some time. Two of them, he noted with more than a touch of concern, held the collars of large dogs, wolfhounds trained to hunt down prey with savage ferocity. If he attempted to flee, his horse would not outrun the hunting dogs.

A glance across the river revealed another small group of men who were poised to intercept him should he attempt to flee that way.

They could not know that he had no intention of fleeing. Smiling softly to himself, Macrinus sat back in his saddle and waited.

He had come in search of rebels and he had found them.

Chapter X

The low clouds that had covered the hilltops for the past three days had lifted slightly when Calgacus rode back into the high crater where his new mountain refuge lay concealed.

The men with him were tired, wet and cold, and looking forward to a few days' rest. Their families came out to meet them, ushering them indoors as soon as the care of the horses had been passed to the village's boys.

Hanging their wet cloaks on wooden pegs hammered into the roundhouse walls and stamping the mud free from their boots, Calgacus, Runt and Adelligus gratefully accepted the fuss that was made of them when they joined their wives and children around the hearth fire.

"How was your trip?" Beatha asked as she distributed freshly baked bread and hot porridge.

"Good enough," Calgacus replied through mouthfuls of food. "We brought back around fifty Taexali families."

"As many as that?" Beatha enquired in mild surprise.

"They've had a rough time of it lately," Calgacus informed her. "Most of their chieftains were killed in the battle, so they have few leaders left. Worse than that, Roman cavalry patrols are roaming all across their lands and Roman ships are raiding the coastal areas, destroying any settlements they find. They'll be a lot safer with us."

"Where will they stay?"

"Further up the valley. I've sent orders to our warriors to help them build houses. They brought pretty much everything else with them. They even dug up their grain supplies, so food shouldn't be a problem for a while."

Beatha understood that this confirmed the Taexali were serious about moving their homes. When the harvest was in, surplus grain was often buried in deep pits. For some reason which nobody really understood, the food supplies remained fresh for many months. Only the outer layers would be spoiled when the pits were reopened. It was a traditional method of storing grain and it had the added advantage that Roman patrols could rarely find the food even if they did destroy every home in a village.

She said, "I will pay them a visit as soon as I can. We need to make them feel welcome."

"That would be a good idea," Calgacus agreed.

He was about to ask what had happened in the village while he had been away when his daughter, Fallar, let out a gasp of pain. She clamped her hands to her swollen belly and screwed up her face in distress. Beside her, Adelligus' expression grew alarmed.

"What is it?" he asked anxiously.

"I think the baby is coming!" Fallar gasped.

"Wait a while," Beatha told her as she patted her daughter's arm. "Let us see how quickly the contractions come. It may be a false alarm."

It was not long before all notions of a false alarm were banished and everyone knew that Fallar's time had arrived at last. Once she was satisfied that the contractions were increasing in regularity, Beatha promptly took control.

"Adelligus, help her up to the bedchamber," she ordered. "Go carefully."

While Adelligus held Fallar's arm and led her to the wooden steps leading to the upper section of the house, Beatha issued more instructions.

"Someone go and fetch Emmelia. I want water heated up and fresh cloths."

She turned her gaze on the men.

"And you can all go outside until this is over. This is women's business, and you'll just get in the way."

Calgacus and Runt dutifully gathered their cloaks and went outside, Adelligus joining them a few moments later. The young man's face was a picture of helpless agitation.

"What happens now?" he asked plaintively.

"We wait," his father told him, clapping a hand to his shoulder.

Calgacus cast an eye to the sky. The clouds still spread across the heavens in a blanket of grey, but the rain had granted them a temporary reprieve.

"We should keep ourselves busy," he decided. "Let's get a couple of practice swords and keep ourselves occupied."

Runt and Adelligus looked doubtful, but neither of them could think of any objections. Doing something, anything, was infinitely preferable to sitting around waiting.

They borrowed a couple of long, wooden swords from one of the neighbouring houses and walked to a small patch of open ground near the shallow loch which filled the deepest part of their mountaintop corrie.

Calgacus handed one of the wooden blades to Adelligus before turning to Runt.

"Do you want to take him on first?" he asked.

Runt shook his head.

"He's too good for me. Besides, I'm better with short swords than with those bloody great things."

Calgacus shrugged. Runt was one of the best fighters he had ever seen, equally deadly with a sword in either hand, yet his son, Adelligus, was, if anything, even better.

"Come on, then," he invited the younger man. "Let's see how good you are."

Adelligus gripped the practice sword with a half-hearted shrug as Calgacus faced him. The wooden weapons were made of oak, carefully carved into the shape of longswords although not as heavy as the iron weapons. Even so, they could deliver a hefty blow, which meant that broken bones were not unknown during practice bouts, especially when Calgacus was involved.

"Ready?" Calgacus asked.

Adelligus' mind was clearly elsewhere, but he adopted a fighting stance and nodded his readiness.

Calgacus attacked with blistering speed, swinging the long, wooden sword with frightening power, driving Adelligus backwards and making him stumble. As the young man lost his footing for a moment, Calgacus' blade lashed out, stopping at the last moment as the edge touched Adelligus' neck.

"You're dead!" Calgacus told him.

Runt put in, "Give him a chance, Cal. His wife is giving birth."

"I know. But sometimes we don't have the luxury of fighting when we want to. The Romans won't leave us in peace just because our women are having babies."

He stepped back, lowering his sword as he gestured to Adelligus to try again.

This time, the younger man's concentration was evident. He blocked every sweep of Calgacus' sword, the sound of the two wooden blades echoing across the water of the loch and bringing a small audience of young boys creeping out of their homes to watch.

Calgacus soon found himself hard pressed. His greater height and strength should have given him an advantage over the younger man, but Adelligus was able to counter every move he made and soon went on the offensive himself. Once, Adelligus almost got past his guard. He tried lashing out with his feet to kick the young man's legs from under him, but Adelligus was too fast, nimbly jumping aside.

Adelligus threw himself into the attack, forcing Calgacus back, driving him ever closer to the water.

Calgacus moved frantically, blocking and parrying, but Adelligus was remorseless, pressing home his attacks with animal ferocity. He used the advantages of youthful stamina and speed to keep Calgacus on the defensive as he slashed and cut with all his energy.

Just as Calgacus wondered whether he was about to get his feet wet, Adelligus suddenly switched his attack and delivered a stunning blow to Calgacus' sword, sending the wooden blade spinning out of his hand. In an instant, the edge of Adelligus' long practice sword was pressed against Calgacus' chest.

"You're dead!" Adelligus rasped, his eyes gleaming.

"Well done," Calgacus nodded. "How about the best of three?"

Runt had retrieved his sword for him. He was grinning hugely as he handed it over.

"He'll beat you again," the little man warned.

"We'll see."

Despite Calgacus' bravado, the third bout was over even more quickly than the first two. Adelligus caught him with a painful smack on his left leg and followed it up with an immediate blow to Calgacus' right side as he belatedly moved away from the first impact.

"You're dead again," Runt told him cheerfully.

"I slipped," Calgacus protested. "Let's try again."

They fought three more bouts. Calgacus managed to win one with a fortunate strike which caught Adelligus on the hand, forcing him to drop his sword, but he lost the other two convincingly, exposing himself in the final bout when, growing increasingly frustrated, he aimed a wild slash at Adelligus' head. The young man ducked, allowing the heavy, wooden blade to sail over his head, at the same time delivering a blow of his own that whacked into Calgacus' side.

Sweating and flushed, Calgacus extended his hand to the young man.

"Well done," he conceded. "Next time, I'll not be so easy with you."

"Any time," Adelligus smiled.

Calgacus laughed, then gave Runt a weary look of apology.

"You're right," he admitted. "He is too good for me."

They spent the next few hours with the young boys who had come to witness their bouts, allowing them to hold the heavy practice swords and teaching them the moves that would help them become warriors when they grew up. Then, as the dull day drew close to a damp evening, the rain beginning to spit down at them and the clouds closing in once more, they heard the sound they had been waiting for.

Adelligus looked momentarily bemused as the unmistakable cry of a baby could be heard from their house.

Runt could not help smiling broadly as he looked at Calgacus and said, "We have a grandchild."

They hurried to the house, tentatively peering inside as if to ask permission to enter.

"Come in," Beatha told them as she came to meet them.

She reached out to Adelligus and hugged him.

"You have a daughter," she told him.

"Can I go up?" he asked uncertainly.

"Of course."

Needing no other invitation, he hurried across the circular space and bounded up the steps to the upper level, with Calgacus and Runt following more sedately.

By the time they arrived at Fallar's bedside, Adelligus was holding a small bundle of cloth, peering down at it with wonder in his eyes.

"She's beautiful!" he breathed, presenting the child to Calgacus and Runt.

"Of course she is," Calgacus agreed. "She takes after her mother."

Fallar looked tired, her eyes heavy and black-rimmed, but she gave them a weak smile when she saw them.

"How are you?" Calgacus asked.

His niece, Emmelia, was sitting in the shadows beyond the bed. She was a tall woman, with angular features and a renowned sharpness to her tongue. Many people found her combative nature intimidating, but everyone acknowledged that she was an expert healer and herbalist. When it came to matters of health and medicine, nobody argued with Emmelia.

"She is very tired," she told Calgacus. "I do not want you to remain here too long. She needs rest, as well as time to get to know the baby."

Runt had appropriated his new grandchild, allowing Adelligus to squat down beside Fallar. He rocked the baby gently, crooning to it in a low, soothing voice.

Eventually, he relinquished his hold and passed the baby to Calgacus, who took her with some trepidation. It had been years since his own children had been born, and he was out of practice when it came to tiny infants.

The baby was small and delicate, with wrinkled skin and wisps of dark hair. She wriggled and squirmed in Calgacus' arms, letting out a soft squeal of protest.

"Do you have a name for her?" he asked.

Adelligus and Fallar exchanged a look. She nodded encouragingly at him.

He said, "We will call her Elaris."

Runt moved to embrace them both.

"Thank you," he said, acknowledging that the newborn girl had been named after his first wife, Adelligus' mother, who had died of fever several years earlier.

Baby Elaris continued to cry, prompting Emmelia to say, "You should go now. The child needs to be put on the breast."

Gently, Calgacus handed the baby back to Fallar, kissed his daughter's damp forehead and told her he was proud of her. Then he and Runt climbed back down the stairs, leaving Adelligus and the women to care for the child. Beatha and Runt's young wife, Tegan, joined the group around the bed, excluding the two grandfathers from the occasion.

It was a strange moment for both of them. They had known each other since boyhood, had spent their lives living and fighting alongside one another, but the newborn child was the first tangible link between them. The marriage between Runt's son and Calgacus' daughter had made this almost inevitable, but still the realisation gave a new perspective to their relationship.

"I bet I spoil her more than you do," Runt smiled happily.

"Probably," Calgacus agreed. "But girls are precious, so we will all spoil her."

"You're too bad-tempered to be a good grandfather," Runt pointed out good-naturedly.

"Probably," Calgacus agreed again.

"What's bothering you?" Runt asked. "Even you should be happy at a time like this."

Calgacus' lips twisted in a failed smile.

"Life goes on," he observed in a low voice so that his words would not carry to the upper level of the house. "But I can't help thinking this is a dangerous world she has been brought into."

"Life is always dangerous," Runt replied with a resigned shrug. "She will do well to survive beyond her fifth year. But she looks like a fighter and she has strong blood in her."

Calgacus nodded, but he had not been thinking of the usual rigours of childhood where disease and accident bore off more than half of the infants.

"It's not that," he sighed. "It's living up here in the mountains. Food will be scarce, the weather will be wicked and the Romans will be hunting us."

"There's a solution to all that," Runt told him easily.

"There is?"

"Of course. All we need to do is defeat the Romans and send them back across the sea."

Calgacus let out a snort of laughter.

"That shouldn't be too difficult," he said with a forced smile.

His words had come as an almost instinctive response but, for the first time he could remember, a small spark of doubt flared in his heart. Both Beatha and Togodumnus had warned him that the Romans would keep coming, no matter how many he killed.

His stubborn insistence on clinging to a promise he had made to his brother, Caratacus, had always sustained him in the face of such doubts. He had vowed never to surrender, always to continue the fight against the encroaching Empire. Now, for the first time in thirty years, the sight of his newborn granddaughter had forced him to reconsider.

He shook his head. Doubt was as deadly an enemy as a man with a sword. Too many people had put their faith in him for him to change his mind now.

He was about to suggest broaching a keg of heather ale to celebrate the baby's birth when the door burst open and Bridei bustled in, shoving back the hood of his cloak as he stepped into the warm house.

"There you are!" he beamed. "I wasn't sure if you'd be back. Come with me. I have something to show you."

"What is it?" Calgacus asked, reluctant to leave the house so soon after the birth of his granddaughter.

"Not what. Who. I found a Roman wandering in the hills. He says he knows you."

Chapter XI

Fastening their cloaks and pulling up the hoods against the drizzle, they made their way through the village, heading round the tiny loch towards a group of small huts which usually served as stores or as shelters for warriors returning from lengthy patrols.

Bridei asked, "Was that a new baby I heard?"

"That's right," Calgacus told him. "Fallar has delivered a daughter."

Bridei's smile was as fierce as ever.

"I'll bring her a birthing gift soon," he promised. "But don't expect me to hold the child. I've got enough brats of my own to worry about."

"How many children do you actually have?" Runt asked him.

Bridei shrugged, "I'm not exactly sure. Plenty women claim they've given me sons or daughters. I lost count a while back."

He grew a little more serious as he added, "But I am pleased for both of you. It's just as well you got back for the birth, I suppose. How was your trip to the Taexali, anyway?"

Calgacus explained about the additional families they had brought back with them.

Bridei nodded, "That's good, I suppose. A few more pairs of hands won't go amiss, even if they are only Taexali."

Calgacus shot him a warning glance which Bridei noticed and answered with a mischievous smile.

"Just kidding," he assured Calgacus. "We are all friends now. I have almost forgotten that the Taexali have been my people's enemies for generations."

"Good," muttered Calgacus. "We don't want any trouble between the tribes."

Still smirking, Bridei went on, "You won't get any trouble from me. I hardly ever think of them as murderous, scheming cowards any more. That's all in the past. I even paid a visit to Gabrain and his Venicones without picking a fight."

"How is Gabrain?" Calgacus asked, choosing not to respond to the Boresti King's cruel sense of humour.

"He's as happy as a pig in shit," Bridei assured him. "He and his lads raided another supply convoy last week. They went south, way past the new fort the Romans are building. It was bloody risky, but they got away with it. Got themselves royally drunk on the wine they liberated, too."

"Gabrain's still too reckless," Calgacus muttered. "One of these days he's going to get himself caught."

"One of these days we're all going to get caught," Bridei replied light-heartedly. "Until then, we each do what we can. Gabrain may take chances, but he's got the Romans running in circles trying to catch him. His only gripe is those messages you insist we all leave behind. He thinks his name should be written on them."

"Tell him it is," Runt suggested. "He can't read anyway, so he won't know the difference."

"Never mind Gabrain," Calgacus interrupted. "Tell me about this Roman you found."

Bridei explained, "I was on my way back here when some of the watchers told me they'd spotted him. He came riding into the glens all on his own. He wasn't wearing any sort of armour, but we knew he was a soldier. He has that look about him. I was tempted to cut his balls off and send him packing, but he spoke our language and he said he knows you."

"That narrows it down quite a lot," observed Runt. "Most of the Romans who know us are dead. And, of the ones we've allowed to live, not many of them speak our language."

Calgacus nodded thoughtfully. He had a fair idea who the man must be. But what would bring any Roman here alone?

"What does he want?" he asked.

Bridei shrugged, "He wouldn't say. Just that he has a message for you from the Governor."

Calgacus frowned as another thought struck him.

He asked, "Is there any chance he could find this place again? If it's who I think it is, he's a very clever and resourceful man."

Bridei chuckled, "I doubt it. We blindfolded him, although we probably didn't need to because the clouds were so low it was like riding through a permanent fog. Just to be sure, though, we took a very long way round. I knew you were away looking to recruit the Taexali, so there wasn't a rush to get back here. We found him only a few hours' ride from here, but we took two days to bring him in by a very long and winding route. Unless he's some sort of magician, he'll never be able to retrace the path. I probably couldn't do it myself, and I knew where we were."

"Good enough," Calgacus nodded approvingly.

"We've got him in one of these huts," Bridei explained, waving a hand to indicate one of the small shacks where a glimmer of light filtered out through the cracks around the doorway.

Bridei led them in, pushing open the door and stepping into a small open space with a central hearth fire around which sat half a dozen men, most of them armed with swords or spears. The men's conversation died away as soon as the three chieftains entered.

"Outside, lads," Bridei commanded cheerfully. "It's a lovely evening. Don't go far, but let us have a private talk with our guest."

Grumbling good-naturedly, the men picked up their weapons, donned their cloaks and pulled up their hoods before filing outside into the dreary murk. As they moved aside, allowing Calgacus to see the interior of the hut properly, he noticed another man sitting against the far wall, half hidden in shadow. The man stood, the dim light of the fire and a handful of tallow candles revealing that his ankles were hobbled by a length of iron chain connecting two thick shackles.

"Julius Macrinus," Calgacus said. "I thought it must be you. There's only one other Roman would dare come looking for me, and the last time I saw him he told me he was returning to Rome."

"Ah, you must be referring to Anderius Facilis. Yes, he left a few months ago, just after you decimated the Ninth Legion. That was quite brilliantly done, by the way."

Calgacus gave Macrinus a quizzical look.

"You don't seem to mind that we killed so many of your countrymen."

"I speak purely in military terms," Macrinus smiled. "I admire your skill as a leader. You caught us completely off guard and achieved what few have ever done. Storming one of our camps is a rare feat."

"I've done it before, and no doubt I'll have plenty opportunities to do it again," Calgacus stated stiffly. "But I'm sure you didn't come all the way here just to flatter me. So, let's sit down and talk."

Gesturing towards the iron bands around his ankles, Macrinus asked, "I don't suppose you could see your way to removing these?"

"No. You are much too dangerous for me to allow that."

Macrinus gave an easy smile as he shuffled over to the fire and awkwardly moved around one of the long benches which sat near the hearth. These crude seats had been made by simply splitting a small tree trunk lengthwise and fitting support legs to each of the sections using mortice and tenon joints, each tree producing two benches.

As Macrinus pulled his perch close to the low, flickering flames, the other men dragged two of the other benches into position and sat facing him.

"Have you been treated well?" Calgacus asked.

"Well enough," Macrinus nodded, casting a sharp look at Bridei. "Your painted friend there threatened to castrate me on several occasions, but the worst I got was a few punches and kicks from his men."

"There's still time," Bridei growled.

Calgacus observed, "You don't look as if the kickings did you much harm."

"I've suffered worse during training exercises," Macrinus responded dismissively. "An observation that goes for your food, too. You seem to eat very well."

"We gave you what we feed our dogs," Bridei assured him. "We eat much better than that."

Macrinus gave a low chuckle as he replied, "I like you, little man. But don't try to kid an old soldier. The men you set to watch over me ate the same as I did."

"I was punishing them," Bridei smiled jovially.

Macrinus laughed aloud before saying to Calgacus, "I could do with some wine, though."

"We would need to go and steal some from one of your supply bases," Calgacus explained. "It might take a while."

"Then I will stick to your beer," Macrinus shrugged. "There will be plenty of wine when I get back."

Calgacus eyed him curiously. He had met Macrinus twice before, once as an enforced ally, once as an enemy. They shared a mutual respect which would probably have grown to friendship had they not been on opposite sides, but he knew he could not allow his personal liking for the big German to cloud his judgement. Given his situation, Macrinus' confident manner was puzzling.

"You are assuming we will let you leave," Calgacus replied. "I like you, Macrinus, but you are an enemy of my people. I will do whatever is required to safeguard them, even if that means killing you."

Macrinus gave him a pleasant smile as he said, "I had heard you have a reputation for not killing defenceless men."

"Reputations can be exaggerated," Calgacus told him. "Besides, I have grown more ruthless as I have grown older."

Macrinus did not appear at all intimidated. He merely shrugged and went on, "Be that as it may, I think you will let me return when you hear what I have to say, even if it is only to take back a message that you are not interested."

"Interested in what?"

"Let me ask a question first," Macrinus countered.

"What question?"

Macrinus leaned forward, studying Calgacus intently as he explained, "When we met in Hibernia last year, I watched as that witch woman sacrificed your life and then brought you back. I'd like to know how she did that."

"Magic," Calgacus replied instantly. "Scota is a powerful sorceress, and her magic helped us defeat you."

"I'll not deny that," Macrinus agreed gruffly. "But I've never seen a dead man brought back to life before. How was it done? Really, I mean."

"You would need to ask Scota," Calgacus told him with a vague shrug.

He kept his expression blank as he faced the Tribune. Only Runt knew how the apparent sacrifice had been carried out. Scota, the sorceress, had stuffed the innards of a recently killed mule into a bag which she had hung around Calgacus' neck beneath a baggy tunic. Using sleight of hand, she had appeared to cut his throat, drawing a knife in front of him while splashing a smear of berry juice to mimic a spray of blood. Then she had slit his tunic and the bag, allowing the mule's intestines to spill out before genuinely sacrificing a goat and appearing to invoke some powerful magic to resurrect Calgacus. Carried out in the early half light of dawn at a distance from the Roman camp, the trick had obviously accomplished its purpose. Scota had terrified the Roman legionaries and now, more than a year later, Macrinus was still curious about it.

The German waited for a further explanation but, when Calgacus refused to say anything more, he shook his head.

"Ah, well," he sighed. "You look none the worse for it, whatever happened to you. But the magic did not help you at Mons Graupius."

"I am not one to dwell on the past," Calgacus told him. "What I want to know is why you are here."

Macrinus sat back, conceding that he would discover nothing about the mystery of Calgacus' apparent death.

"Very well," he sighed. "It is really quite simple. I am here to offer you a chance to discuss peace terms. That is why the Governor sent me here."

Runt made a derisory sound, but Calgacus merely held the Roman's gaze.

"I know Rome too well, my friend. Peace only comes when you have killed or enslaved all your enemies."

"That's not necessarily true," Macrinus protested. "The Empire has many allies and client Kings. The Governor, like me, respects a tough and resourceful opponent. He is prepared to offer terms which would see you as an ally of Rome."

"I may be a King," Calgacus replied carefully, "but my people, the Catuvellauni, were enslaved many years ago. I have no kingdom to rule. The place where I grew up is a Roman town now, and the only people I lead are those who followed me into exile. These days, I am merely a war Leader. Bridei here is the only true King in this region."

Macrinus regarded Bridei's tattooed torso with some distaste before returning his attention to Calgacus.

"You do yourself a disservice," he countered. "Everyone knows that, King or not, you are the one who leads the resistance to the Empire. Call yourself whatever you like, the other tribal leaders will listen to you. That is why the Governor wants to treat with you. He wishes to establish a formal frontier so that you and your fellow chieftains can rule in peace and security."

"Will he give me my lands back?" Bridei demanded brusquely.

Macrinus shrugged, "That is what negotiations are for. I cannot say what the Governor will agree to."

"The Venicones will want their territory restored as well," Bridei glared.

"As I say," Macrinus replied smoothly, "I am not authorised to agree to anything. I am merely here to broker a meeting."

There was a short silence, broken only by the soft crackling of the fire, while Calgacus considered the offer. Then he said, "Your Governor, Agricola, will return to Rome before long, won't he?"

"Who knows?" Macrinus shrugged. "He may be here for a few years yet."

"But, sooner or later, he will be recalled and your Emperor will send someone to replace him. Will that new Governor respect any treaty we agree?"

"If the Emperor orders it," Macrinus replied.

"Which is no guarantee at all," Runt observed darkly.

Macrinus persisted, "Then let me be blunt about this. If you do not agree, the Governor intends to resume his campaign in the spring. You must know you cannot defeat Rome. We smashed your army at Mons Graupius just a few weeks ago, and your war host is scattered. The Governor has the means and the will to hunt down each band, no matter how long it takes. You know he can do it. You have seen it done before. But you can avoid that fate and save the lives of many of your people. I know you do not wish to see your women and children taken as slaves. If you speak to the Governor, you could at least preserve peace for a few years. And, the longer that peace persists, the more chance there is of it continuing."

Calgacus sat very still, aware that Bridei and Runt were both watching him, waiting to see how he would react to Macrinus' impassioned appeal. The memory of his new granddaughter flashed across his mind, a powerful tug on his emotions. He wanted her to grow up free, the way he had done, the way his own children had done under his protection. Runt had a young daughter as well, while Bridei had several children who were now exiled from their homes. His decision would affect them all, and that was a heavy responsibility.

But how could he ensure their safety? He knew that everything Macrinus had said was true. Rome would never be deterred by the difficulty of a project. Once they had put their minds to it, they had the manpower to complete the subjugation of the free tribes, even in the mountain wilderness where he had made his new home.

Making peace was the obvious solution, and yet he had little faith in Roman honour, knowing the Empire's thirst for conquest and supremacy.

Aware that the others were waiting for him to respond, he sighed, "It is not a very tempting offer."

"It is probably the best you will get," Bridei grunted.

"It is the only one you will get," Macrinus corrected. "But the Governor is serious. Why else do you think I would risk my neck coming out here alone? The least you could do is agree to meet him."

"Waste of time," muttered Runt.

Bridei growled, "I agree. Just cut his balls off and send him back with that as our reply."

Calgacus gave no indication that he had heard them. He sat very still, keeping his eyes on Macrinus.

"You have not convinced me this is worthwhile," he told the Roman.

Macrinus leaned forwards, his elbows resting on his knees, his hands clasped together over the fire.

Staring intently at Calgacus, he said, "I know you are a warrior, but you are sensible enough to understand what is at stake for you and all your people. How many years have you been fighting Rome? You have had some successes, but still you have been forced further and further north. Now you have nowhere else to run to, my friend. Surely it would be better to make an honourable peace while you can. But even if I have not persuaded you, what do you have to lose by talking to the Governor for a while?"

"My life," Calgacus replied evenly.

Macrinus frowned, cocking his head slightly in enquiry.

Calgacus explained, "You are a good soldier, Macrinus. One of the best. I trust you, but I do not trust Rome. It occurs to me that this offer could well lead me into a trap."

Smiling, Macrinus sat up, spreading his arms in an admission of guilt.

"Of course it's a trap," he agreed. "But it is not of the Governor's making, and you do not need to walk into it unprepared."

Bridei bristled, "I knew it! You hold him down while I sharpen my knife."

Calgacus gestured the Boresti King to silence.

"What do you mean?" he asked the Tribune, puzzled by the Roman's response.

Holding out his hands in a gesture of conciliation, Macrinus explained about the arrival of the new Assistant Procurator.

"He sees a meeting as an opportunity to capture or kill you. That way, he can claim the credit when he writes to the Emperor."

"And Agricola is happy to go along with this?"

"The Governor has no choice, really. Besides, he wants an end to the war as soon as possible. Whether that's through you offering some sort of nominal surrender and a peace treaty, or by him cutting off your head, doesn't really matter."

"A true Roman," murmured Runt angrily, his hands moving to the hilts of his twin swords.

Impatiently, Calgacus waved a hand, signalling to his friend to remain calm.

"So," he said to Macrinus, "it is a trap, but you want me to walk into it anyway?"

"Oh, we can make it work better than that," Macrinus smiled. "If you agree to meet, it makes me look good. I can expect some sort of reward for having arranged the meeting at considerable risk to my person. And if Agricola can conclude a peace treaty with you, it will enhance his reputation with the Emperor. If, in addition to all that, you can foil the Assistant Procurator's plan to capture you, it will diminish his authority."

Calgacus asked, "And what do we get out of it?"

"That is up to you to decide," Macrinus replied. "You know how negotiations go. You ask for more than you are prepared to settle for, and hopefully end up with more than you need."

"But you can't guarantee anything?"

"Like I said, it will be up to the Governor."

Calgacus gave a slow, thoughtful nod.

He asked, "So how do I avoid falling into this snare your Assistant Procurator has set for me?"

"That's easy," Macrinus assured him. "I'll tell them that you only agreed to meet on condition that you were allowed to set the time, place and circumstances. All we need to do is arrange things so that there can be no prospect of treachery from either side. Then you can talk to the Governor and see what comes of it. If it's a peace agreement, all well and good for everyone concerned. If not, you have lost nothing."

"And your Assistant Procurator is made to look foolish whatever happens?" Calgacus enquired.

"That is a nice bonus which benefits us all," Macrinus agreed.

"Don't do it, Cal," warned Runt. "It's too dangerous."

"I agree," put in Bridei.

"So do I," nodded Calgacus. Then, grinning at Macrinus, he added, "But let's do it anyway."

Chapter XII

Four days after being blindfolded once more and led on a tortuous, wet and interminably long trek, Macrinus was again back in the Twentieth Legion's ever-growing fortress. Tired and hungry, he nevertheless reported the success of his mission to the Governor.

Oil lamps had been lit against the approach of evening as the senior officers gathered in the command tent to hear his account.

"Could you find Calgacus' camp again?" Flaccus demanded peremptorily, interrupting Macrinus' explanation.

"No," Macrinus replied instantly. "I am certain that they were leading me in circles much of the time, and I lost all sense of where I was. On the few occasions when the sun came out, I could tell I was often travelling in different directions, but I have no idea where they took me."

"So there would be no chance of sending in a small band of mounted men to catch him off guard?" Flaccus persisted.

"No chance at all," Macrinus answered emphatically. "Even if I knew where his camp is, he has men watching every approach. Not only that, they have dogs. They can smell us coming before we get close."

"But the mountain range is vast," Flaccus argued. "There must be some routes you could use without being seen."

"Not without a guide. Even then, Calgacus will have patrols scouring the hills to check for just that sort of thing."

Flaccus scowled at this news and lapsed into a brooding silence while Macrinus related his account of his meeting with Calgacus. The Assistant Procurator did not remain quiet for long, though, bursting into more loud protests when he heard the conditions Calgacus had stipulated for the proposed meeting with Agricola.

"He wants to meet the Governor alone?" Flaccus demanded incredulously.

"At a safe distance between our two groups," Macrinus confirmed. "I don't think he trusts us."

If Flaccus appreciated the jibe, he gave no sign.

"We should send some cavalry to the meeting place immediately," he declared. "They can set a trap and capture him as soon as he arrives."

"I'm afraid not," Macrinus replied, enjoying the opportunity to counter the young nobleman's suggestion. "We have no time. The meeting is to take place tomorrow and I'd guess Calgacus is already there and watching for signs of us trying anything. That's why they took so long bringing me back. They wanted time to arrange things so that we cannot spring any surprises."

Flaccus tutted, frowned, rubbed a hand over his face and then abruptly rose to his feet.

"If you will excuse me, I must think on this," he announced before giving the Governor a curt nod and stalking from the tent.

Once he was gone, Agricola regarded Macrinus with a meaningful frown.

Speaking softly, he observed, "This is a dangerous game you are inviting me to play, Macrinus."

"Yes, Sir," Macrinus agreed.

"And yet I confess that Gaius Popidius Flaccus is making my life more complicated than I would wish. He is keen to make a name for himself, but he understands little of the difficulties we face."

"I know, Sir. But, with luck, you may be able to thwart both him and the barbarians."

Agricola gave a slight nod of agreement before asking, "Can we trust Calgacus? It occurs to me that he might be setting a trap of his own."

"That is always possible," Macrinus conceded. "But he has a reputation as being a man of his word. And I believe we can take precautions against any treachery."

"How so?" the Governor asked.

"May I have a map of the local area?" Macrinus asked.

Agricola signalled to his secretary, Donnatus, who quickly produced a map of the northern part of Britannia. Macrinus was not surprised to see that vast swathes of the parchment were blank, for no Roman had travelled very far into the interior of the island. The map did, though, clearly show the two great rivers whose estuaries gouged great indentations in the eastern coast.

Macrinus tapped a grimy finger to the line marking the flow of the Tava, the northernmost of the two rivers, and the one which flowed past the fort currently being constructed around the Governor's tent.

"We control the river," Macrinus recounted. "Calgacus agreed that we could sail down to meet him. The meeting will take place here, before the river begins to widen. If we are afloat, there is little the barbarians can do to harm us."

"Yet he is a cunning devil," Agricola put in. "He might still try something."

"Indeed, Sir. Which is why I suggest we also take along a strong contingent of legionaries and a force of cavalry. It's a long march, but they could follow the course of the river."

Agricola nodded, then glanced at Piso.

"Can you spare one Cohort?" he asked.

"Of course, Sir."

Turning to Macrinus, the Governor said, "And as many of your Auxiliary cavalry as you can muster."

"Yes, Sir."

Agricola rubbed his chin pensively, but appeared satisfied with the arrangements.

"A show of force will not do any harm," he reflected. "If it is a trap, we stand to lose no more than one Cohort."

Piso ventured, "And one Governor."

"I shall take good care," Agricola smiled. "As Macrinus says, I can always climb aboard one of the galleys."

"I doubt that will be necessary, Sir," Macrinus assured him. "I genuinely believe Calgacus might be willing to come to terms."

Agricola looked at him in surprise.

"Really? His reputation suggests otherwise."

Macrinus explained, "But we are now in a position to offer him a deal which will benefit him."

"What sort of deal?" the Governor wanted to know.

"I did not go into details, Sir, but I know what his demands will be."

Piso snorted, "Barbarians do not make demands on Rome."

Macrinus ignored the Legate's intervention. Tapping his finger on the map to indicate the other great estuary on the eastern side of Britannia, he continued, "He wants us to withdraw at least as far as the Bodotria. That will allow some of the Kings under his command to reclaim their land."

"And what do we get in return?" Piso demanded gruffly.

"A quick peace settlement," Macrinus replied, meeting Agricola's gaze as he did so.

The Governor nodded slowly. Provided the terms were beneficial to Rome, obtaining a peace settlement would enhance his reputation while simultaneously rendering Flaccus' scheming unnecessary.

"Will that be enough, though?" he wondered aloud.

"We can save ourselves a few years of hard fighting for little gain," Macrinus said. "The truth is that there is little of value in the north. There are no precious metals to be mined, no great cities to conquer, no industries producing goods of high value. Why waste Roman lives conquering a place like that?"

"Because the tribes may not agree to submit to Roman rule," Piso suggested sarcastically. "The Kings would need to acknowledge their status as clients, and would need to provide hostages as well as tribute."

"Will Calgacus agree to that?" Agricola asked sharply.

Macrinus shrugged, "I don't know, Sir. But that is the point of the meeting, is it not? To negotiate."

"The point of the meeting," Agricola said slowly, "is to convince our new Assistant Procurator that we are doing something to end the war and complete the conquest of Britannia."

Macrinus decided not to remind the Governor that the conquest of Britannia had already been proclaimed. Instead, he answered, "Perhaps Calgacus can be persuaded to admit Roman traders to the northern territory. He might even agree to allow our Assistant Procurator to tour the new province to assess it for taxation purposes. That, after all, is what Flaccus says he is here to do. No doubt he would soon be able to confirm to the Emperor that there is nothing the barbarians possess that we can exploit."

Agricola continued to frown, but Macrinus could see that he was weighing up the benefits of concluding a treaty. Military glory was all that continued campaigning offered, and the Governor already had more than his share of such fame.

Piso, who had been firmly against anything other than complete conquest of the island, now gave a soft smile as he put in, "An unworthy thought has occurred to me. There might be another opportunity here."

"What might that be?" Agricola enquired sharply.

Piso shrugged, "Let us say the barbarians do conclude a treaty with us, and our Assistant Procurator carries out his mission to assess them for taxation. It seems to me that he is likely either to have his throat cut, or to stir up a revolt. In either case, we would have the perfect excuse to declare war again, and we would be rid of Flaccus."

Macrinus grinned, "He'd either be dead or have his reputation ruined."

Agricola held up his hand, silencing the brief moment of amusement.

"I do not wish to hear any talk of such a thing," he stated firmly. "I will carry out my duty as Governor, and Popidius Flaccus will no doubt carry out his duties as he sees fit."

Piso and Macrinus accepted the rebuke, but both of them knew that, while the Governor may not be able to agree with them officially, he was enough of a Roman to understand that there was more than one way to deal with a troublesome political opponent. For his part, Macrinus despised such intrigues, but he also despised Flaccus, and he silently vowed to back Agricola in any scheme which might remove the threat the Assistant Procurator represented. The man was a troublesome meddler, and Macrinus wanted him to go away. Whether that meant Flaccus died or merely returned to Rome was immaterial as far as Macrinus was concerned. All he wanted was to get on with soldiering without the need to constantly look over his shoulder to see whether Popidius Flaccus was watching him.

Agricola rapped his knuckles on the wooden table top, dragging Macrinus out of his silent reverie.

"The first thing to do," the Governor stated, "is discover whether we can come to an arrangement with Calgacus. I must admit I am curious to meet him."

Piso sighed, "And I suppose we are no worse off even if he does not agree a treaty. We can always crush him next year."

"Indeed we can," Agricola agreed.

Passing the map back to Donnatus, the Governor looked across the table. With his decision made, his mood had lightened considerably.

"Now, Macrinus," he said, "you had better go and have some food. And a bath. You stink like a barbarian."

Macrinus was feeling quite pleased with himself after a decent night's sleep, a shave and a cup of wine with his breakfast of porridge. By the time dawn began to illuminate the fort with dull, watery sunlight, he was fully dressed in his armour and plumed helmet, sitting astride his horse as he joined the procession waiting to leave the fortress on its way to the assigned meeting place.

The Governor, though more relaxed than he had been the previous evening, was in a sombre mood as he rode over to greet him.

"At least it's not raining," he observed as he cast a jaundiced eye at the clouds overhead. "Much more of it and we'd be sinking into the mud."

Macrinus could appreciate the sentiment. The rain may have eased off but the ground underfoot was still wet and inclined to turn to mud, especially under the thousands of feet and hooves which pounded inside the fort. The lull did, however, allow the legionaries to resume their construction work and the camp was already alive with the sounds of hammering and sawing.

"Is everything in hand?" Agricola enquired.

"I've sent out a cavalry screen, Sir," Macrinus reported. "They'll scout ahead and cover our flank while we march."

"Good," Agricola nodded approvingly. "The last thing I want is to be ambushed on our way downriver. You know how the Britons love to catch us on the move."

"They won't catch us this time," Macrinus promised.

At that moment, Flaccus appeared, wearing a highly decorative breastplate of polished bronze, sculpted to represent the musculature of a powerful man, with ribs and pectorals defined by exquisitely designed lines and ridges in the metalwork.

He also wore a soldier's traditional kilt of studded leather strips which left his legs bare, hobnailed sandals and a gleaming helmet with a red-dyed horsehair plume. A short *gladius* was strapped to his waist.

"Quite the hero," Macrinus muttered under his breath, wondering whether he should inform Flaccus that the *gladius* was far too short to be of any use to a man on horseback. Macrinus wore one himself because he often fought on foot, but he also had a long *spatha*, a proper cavalry sword, fastened to his saddle. Still, he had to admit Flaccus looked the part of a wealthy young nobleman going to war.

Flaccus rather spoiled the effect when his horse was brought to him. At a signal from the Assistant Procurator, one of his slaves immediately dropped to all fours on the muddy earth beside the horse so that Flaccus could use the man's back as a mounting stool.

"By Mithras!" breathed Macrinus. "He must think he's a Persian Satrap."

Agricola normally disliked open criticism of that nature, but he made no comment, merely sitting stiffly, his lips a thin line of disapproval.

Piso, who had come to see them off, remarked in a low voice, "My father once told me that one can best judge the character of a man by how he treats his slaves and others of lower class. I have often seen for myself that he was correct."

Flaccus' behaviour also attracted some ribald laughter from the ranks of the Cohort that was assembled behind the mounted officers. The men of the Twentieth were tough veterans who would not be impressed by shining armour and an officer who treated his slaves little better than beasts.

Macrinus could not help smiling, but his good humour evaporated when he saw Flaccus ride over to meet them. As he approached, the Assistant Procurator turned in his saddle and gestured to some men behind him. From the crowd came something Macrinus had not expected.

"Dogs?" he challenged. "What are they for?"

Flaccus gave a sinister smile as he answered, "A little surprise for our barbarian friend, that is all. You mentioned that he uses dogs, so I thought we should employ the same tactic."

Macrinus looked in alarm at the Governor, but Agricola's stern glare warned him to hold his tongue. If

Agricola countermanded Flaccus on this, his motives would certainly be questioned in the Assistant Procurator's next letter to the Emperor.

Macrinus looked again at the two handlers and the four dogs they held at the end of long, leather leashes, two beasts to each man.

The dogs were huge mastiffs, half as high as a tall man, with shaggy coats, thick, powerful bodies, large heads and wide, tooth-filled jaws. They were well trained but already straining at their leashes and occasionally snapping at one another as they crowded together. To add to their ferocious appearance, each animal wore a thick, iron collar which was studded with long, sharp spikes. Anyone who tried to fend off an attack from a dog's fangs would find any attempt to grip the hound's neck foiled when his hands were skewered by these needle-sharp points.

Apart from their panting, the dogs were virtually silent, but their very presence caused the horses to skitter nervously.

"Keep them back!" Agricola commanded, waving a hand to signal to the dog handlers. "Take them onto one of the galleys."

The handlers dutifully urged their charges towards the South Gate which led to the river where the two galleys were waiting to shadow the column's march.

"Time to go, gentlemen," Agricola declared.

He gave the order to depart. As the mounted officers turned towards the northern gate, Macrinus caught a glimpse of the expression on Flaccus' face.

He did not like what he saw.

Leaving the two galleys to follow the meandering course of the river, the column cut across country in order to reduce the distance they needed to cover. It was still a long journey because they moved only as fast as the legionaries could march, and Agricola did not want to tire the men in case they needed to fight a battle at the end of their long trek. As a precaution, the soldiers had stowed most of their equipment on the two galleys which shadowed their march, so all they carried were their weapons.

Macrinus had no option but to remain close to the Governor and to Flaccus, although he did his best not to become involved in their conversations. It seemed to him that Flaccus was too eager to spring a trap, while the Governor appeared unusually aloof and noncommittal. Macrinus hoped this was because Agricola was attempting to humour the Assistant Procurator in order to prevent any criticism of his actions being relayed to the Emperor, but he still worried that Flaccus might take things into his own hands if the Governor did not assert his authority.

There was the added concern that Calgacus may have fooled him, and might have set an ambush for the expedition. This provided Macrinus with an excuse to ride out to speak to the cavalry scouts who were patrolling ahead and to the side of the column. So far, there was no sign of any barbarians at all.

Whenever he was alone on these short forays, Macrinus wondered what he could do about the dogs. Flaccus' intention was clear. If Calgacus insisted on meeting in the open, with only himself and the Governor talking in a field between their respective forces, even mounted men would be hard pressed to capture him without provoking a response from Calgacus' warriors. But dogs could move even faster than horses over a short distance and, once the great mastiffs were released, nothing would prevent them ripping their prey to pieces.

Macrinus cursed himself for a fool but, try as he might, he could think of no way of sending a warning to Calgacus without being discovered. It was not that he wished to betray his own side, but he had arranged the meeting in good faith, and he detested the thought that Flaccus intended to betray the trust Calgacus had placed in him. As far as Macrinus was concerned, that was yet another reason for him to curse the Assistant Procurator, but silent curses were the only remedy for his predicament.

By the middle of the afternoon, they re-joined the river and made contact with the two galleys. A short time later, they passed beneath a ridge of cliffs which towered high above the plain, forcing them into a narrower gap. This was the most dangerous part of the journey, for the steep slope leading up to the cliffs was covered by dense forest where hundreds of Britons could have been lying in wait. The cavalry formed a protective screen between the trees and the marching infantry, while Macrinus insisted that the Governor should ride near the river bank so as to be close to the galleys which were moving slowly downstream, their oars almost idle as the ships' masters allowed the current to propel their vessels.

Macrinus remained on edge until they passed beyond the cliffs to where the plain opened out slightly and the distance between the river and the forest widened into grassy meadows that were dotted with scrub and isolated clumps of trees. Here, though, the ground became marshy, with reed beds blocking the approach to the river. These marshes were normally inhabited by several species of birds, but most had begun their long migrations, leaving only a few herons to stalk the reed beds, giving the place an empty, menacing air.

Recalling how Calgacus had trapped Jacundus' cavalry patrol by having men immerse themselves in a river, Macrinus kept scanning the tall reeds for any signs of an ambush.

At last, the reeds gave way to long grass, allowing the galleys to approach the bank once more.

To the left of the marching column, in a wide space between two outstretched arms of the forest, the ground was ridged and furrowed, the remnants of a ploughed field which was slowly being reclaimed by weeds. Beyond the abandoned field, around five hundred paces from the river, a dark patch of burnt ground marked where a roundhouse had once stood before Agricola's army had first passed this way at the beginning of summer.

"This is it," Macrinus announced. "He said we should remain by the river opposite the ruined farm."

"I don't like it," Agricola observed. "The ground is very marshy here. Horses can't operate well in this terrain. And those reed beds are a might too close for my liking."

The cavalry units were riding in, drawn by Macrinus' signal. As they drew near, he realised the Governor was correct. The animals' hooves were sinking into the muddy, boggy ground, hampering their movement.

"I suspect Calgacus knew what he was doing when he proposed this place," he informed Agricola. "He doesn't want us sending a quick cavalry charge as soon as he appears. But it works both ways. His horsemen won't be able to attack us easily either. That ploughed field bars their way. As for the reeds, I'll post one Century to watch them."

"Good enough," the Governor nodded resignedly.

Orders were shouted, the soldiers shuffled into position, and the cavalry took up its station on the right flank where the ground was slightly less marshy. The bulk of the legionary Cohort, each Century's standards held proudly aloft above the iron helmets of the soldiers, formed up facing inland, while the Century on the left of the line made a half turn in order to face the reed beds.

The entire operation took only a few moments, the legionaries moving with practised speed despite the cloying, clinging mud that threatened to suck them into the earth.

While the legionaries were deploying, the two galleys dropped their stone anchors and bobbed close to the bank, a wooden gangplank being shoved over the side of the nearer vessel to allow the dogs to disembark. After a long day confined on the narrow decks of the ship, the huge beasts were irritable and eager to be let off the leash. Macrinus, though, ordered them to take up a position near the rear of the Cohort's ranks where they would be well away from the horses.

"Now what?" Flaccus asked impatiently. "Where are the barbarians?"

He was doing his best to sound bored and impatient, but Macrinus thought his voice was thick with barely suppressed excitement. He supposed that, apart from the poor slaves who were thrown into the arena to face wild beasts, Flaccus had probably never seen a true barbarian.

"They are there," he replied, nodding towards the tree-covered hills which loomed darkly over the river plain.

"I don't see anything," Flaccus complained.

"You will."

It was several moments later that Macrinus realised there was something to see. Difficult to make out because of the distance and the dull browns and greens of the forest behind him, a solitary figure had emerged from the trees beyond the wrecked farm. The man was on horseback, plodding slowly towards them, crossing a natural hollow between the two arms of the forest which jutted out from the foot of the hills and which had once sheltered the farmstead from the worst ravages of the weather.

"It's Calgacus," Macrinus announced.

A ripple of excitement coursed through the small group of mounted men, and the harsh barks of Centurions could be heard, commanding their men to silence.

"He really is coming on his own?" Flaccus exclaimed in surprise.

Macrinus shot the man a derisory look as he said, "His bravery cannot be questioned. That is what makes him a great leader."

Flaccus returned a frosty glare as he retorted, "A leader who has no followers, it seems."

Agricola told him, "I expect he has a few men watching from the forest. He's keeping them hidden so that we don't know how many he has. Note, too, that he has woods to his left and right, as well as behind him, so he can quickly surround us if we try to attack him."

The warning in the Governor's words was plain, and even Flaccus understood that Agricola did not want the legionaries ordered forwards into a trap.

"He's dressed for a fight," Macrinus observed as Calgacus drew slowly nearer. "Chainmail coat, helmet and that bloody great sword he always carries on his back."

Calgacus kept moving until he reached the far side of the ploughed area. There he stopped, folded his arms across the front of his saddle and waited.

"He looks ridiculous on that tiny horse," Flaccus sneered. "His feet are almost touching the ground."

"He's a big man," Macrinus replied, finding that he wanted to defend Calgacus from Flaccus' caustic remarks. "But don't be fooled. Those little ponies are tough beasts. They can carry a heavy weight a long way before they get tired."

Flaccus merely snorted as if he did not believe the Tribune.

Beyond the ploughed earth, Calgacus waited patiently, apparently unconcerned that he was facing several hundred Roman troops.

"We should release the dogs now," Flaccus insisted eagerly.

Agricola shook his head.

"I'd like to see what he has to say. Keep the dogs under control unless I give you a signal to release them. Is that clear?"

Flaccus pursed his lips, but gave a surly nod.

"Good," Agricola stated. "Now, wait here while I go and talk to him."

With that, he nudged his horse into motion and rode to meet Rome's most famous enemy.

Chapter XIII

Calgacus watched the Governor ride slowly towards him. He could feel the tense watchfulness both of the distant Roman soldiers and the warriors he had concealed in the trees behind him, but he forced himself to sit still, his head held erect, occasionally patting his horse's neck to reassure it that there was nothing to fear.

Agricola also gave the appearance of being unaffected by the occasion. He rode slowly but confidently, exhibiting the air of a man out for a pleasant ride, as if he did not care whether Calgacus had men hidden in the trees to his left and right. He could have been entering the jaws of a trap, yet he kept his eyes fixed on Calgacus while his horse carefully negotiated the wet, clinging mud of the ploughed field.

What the Roman could not know was that Calgacus had brought very few men with him, and the forest, dark and forbidding as it appeared, was largely empty.

Bridei had warned against this approach.

"You can't trust the Romans," the Boresti King had growled. "We should take as many men as we can in case there's trouble."

"No," Calgacus had decided. "Taking a small army is likely to cause trouble. I don't want it turning into a battle in a situation where the Romans are ready for us."

"Even if it's a chance to kill their Governor?" Bridei had challenged.

"I've killed Governors before," Calgacus had shrugged. "They just send another one."

"So you are going to walk into a trap with only a few men?"

"If it is a trap, then a few of us will be able to slip away through the forest easily enough. We'll take a couple of dozen. No more."

The next argument was about who should go. In addition to Runt, who would not have stayed behind even if ordered to, Calgacus selected Adelligus and the two dozen trained warriors of his own bodyguard because he knew he could rely on them. He did not want anyone else placed in danger, but both Bridei and Gabrain insisted that they wanted to see the Governor. Calgacus, as War Leader, could have ordered them to stay away, but they were both Kings, important men whose support he relied on, so he reluctantly agreed that they should join the party. It meant that, if the Romans did intend treachery, all three of the rebel leaders would be in danger, but all Calgacus could do was hope that the precautions he had taken when choosing the location would be sufficient to ensure they could escape if necessary.

This spot, he reflected, was as good a location as any he could have thought of. The hills behind him were very steep, difficult for horses even if there had been no trees to force riders to keep their heads down. Apart from Calgacus, the others had left their ponies at the summit, making their way down on foot. Climbing back up the hill should be easy enough because the pine forest had little undergrowth beneath the trees' impenetrable net of interwoven branches, and the warriors should be able to climb more quickly than any mounted pursuit. They had taken other precautions against Roman treachery, but Calgacus hoped they would not be required.

By riding out alone, he hoped to convince the Romans that the woods were full of warriors who would surge out if he was threatened.

The few men he had brought, including Bridei and Gabrain, were behind him now, crouched low in the shadows of the woodland, clutching spears and swords, ready to rush to his aid if he needed them.

He looked beyond the approaching rider to where the Roman troops were assembled. He did not fear the legionaries because they were heavily armoured and, even though he was weighed down by his own chainmail coat and helmet, he would still be able to reach the sanctuary of the forest long before the Roman foot soldiers could haul themselves through the marshy ground.

The cavalry were a more dangerous proposition, he knew, but he had chosen this site because of the soft, boggy ground near the river and the rutted furrows of the old field which the days of rain had left muddy and difficult to cross. He was reasonably certain that the terrain would slow the horses long enough for him to reach the sanctuary of the trees should he need to make an escape.

"They probably won't try anything," he had assured his comrades.

He felt less confident now, exposed in the open as he was. Instinctively, he touched a finger to the iron buckle of the sword belt he wore looped over his shoulder as he whispered a prayer to Camulos, the deity who had watched over him throughout his life.

"Let me either gain an honourable treaty or escape this with my life," he implored the War God.

He was tempted to reach back to grasp the hilt of the massive longsword that hung reassuringly on his back, but he knew that such a move would be interpreted as a hostile gesture, so he stilled his hand and concentrated on keeping his expression serious. That, at least, was not a problem. Runt often chided him for being too serious, but there were times, like this, when it was essential to project an image of gravity and authority. That, he knew, was an attitude the Romans understood. Men of rank, accustomed to representing the greatest Empire the world had ever seen, regarded every non-Roman as their inferior. Calgacus knew it was important to let this Roman know that he did not consider himself inferior to anyone.

Then the time for reflection was over because Agricola had reached him. The Roman slowed his horse from its careful walk to a dead stop a mere three paces away. The animal tossed its head once, sniffed the air, then stood staring at Calgacus, its ears flattened. Agricola, sensing the animal's unease, clapped a hand to its neck and muttered some reassuring words.

Calgacus' own pony shifted its feet but, understanding the tightening of pressure he applied with his thighs, remained where it was.

The two men studied one another for a long, silent moment. Calgacus saw a well-built, lean man in his mid-forties, the iron helmet and cheek guards framing a typical Roman aristocratic face with its penetrating eyes and firm, clean-shaven jaw. Everything about the Governor, from the red-dyed horsehair crest of his polished helmet, through the matching scarlet cloak and the polished bronze leg greaves, to the iron hobnails of his expensive sandals, from the stern gaze of his eyes to the way he sat upright and formal in his saddle, radiated an image of power and authority. He was more than a man; here, in this remote part of the world, he was the embodiment of Rome.

Neither man made any effort to dismount. Agricola's horse was taller than Calgacus' war pony but, even though this meant the Roman was looking down at him, Calgacus was determined to let the Governor know that he regarded himself as an equal.

"You got my message, then," he said in Latin, his memory battling for the correct words.

Agricola gave a slow nod.

"Macrinus tells me you wish to discuss peace terms."

"He told me that was your idea," Calgacus replied gruffly. "I am happy to continue the fight."

"You must know you cannot win," Agricola asserted. "Your army was destroyed when we met a few weeks ago."

"No, it was defeated, which is not the same thing. But your army would have been destroyed had Macrinus not alerted you to our ambush."

"So you really do believe you can oppose Rome?" the Governor challenged, his tone expressing his incredulity.

Calgacus struggled not to let his annoyance show. He had not come to this meeting with any great expectations of success, but the Governor's superior attitude had already roused his anger.

"You should know by now," he rasped, "that we are a proud people. We like to live in peace, but we are not afraid to pick up our swords when anyone threatens us."

Agricola nodded again.

"I have certainly been in Britannia long enough to know the truth of that," he agreed. "Although the wisdom of it often escapes me."

"Wisdom has little to do with it," Calgacus assured him. "What do you expect us to do when an armed enemy marches in and steals our homes? Would you have us simply lay down and accept that we should be slaves?"

"I do not question your motives," Agricola replied. "Only the sense of continuing to fight when you know you cannot win."

"You think you can beat us?" Calgacus retorted with a bark of mocking laughter. "I destroyed a Legion when I fought with the Silures; I destroyed another one when my sister, Boudica, led the Great Revolt. Earlier this summer, I led the night attack which slaughtered hundreds of your men while they thought they were safe in their fortified camp. If you think you can march into these hills in safety, you are very much mistaken. You may defeat us eventually, but it will be at such a cost your Emperor will soon wish you had made peace with us when you had the chance."

"Well said," Agricola acknowledged with a wry grin. "But I think you need a peace treaty more than I do. You can hide in your hills if you wish, but you will find life hard when winter comes."

"Life is always hard," Calgacus replied. "Our people have lived in those hills for many generations. We know how to survive. It may be difficult, but it will be much worse for you if you come looking for us."

A faint smile touched the Governor's lips as he gave another slow, pensive nod.

"Rome does not baulk at difficulties," he stated.

"I know that well enough," Calgacus agreed. "But I also know that you like to see some return for your efforts. Spending time, men and money in conquering a huge area of what you deem a barren wilderness is hardly the best use of your resources, is it?"

"There is always the military glory of achieving a victory," Agricola reminded him.

Calgacus felt his irritation growing. From what Macrinus had told him, the Governor needed a peace treaty far more than the free tribes, yet the Roman seemed to have little desire for conciliation.

With an expansive shrug, Calgacus said, "In that case, we probably have little more to say to one another. Macrinus told me you wished to discuss peace, but if all we are going to do is exchange threats, insults and boasts, we may as well save ourselves that effort, too."

This time, Agricola gave a smile that was almost humorous.

He said, "I see you are as good at bluffing in negotiations as you are at devising military stratagems."

"I am not bluffing," Calgacus insisted. "I came here because Macrinus told me you wished to suggest a peace arrangement but, so far, you have offered nothing."

The Governor's horse was behaving skittishly, dancing from side to side, forcing the Roman to slap its neck and squeeze his thighs against its flanks. He was, though, an expert horseman, and he did not permit his mount's agitation to distract him.

Fixing Calgacus with a hard stare, he challenged, "Then tell me what it is you would want from such a treaty."

Calgacus felt a spark of hope. He began to suspect that the Governor's belligerent attitude might have been intended to establish his credentials as a tough negotiator who did not need to reach agreement. Of course, he might simply be attempting to end any discussion so that he could spring the trap Macrinus had warned of, but at least Calgacus now had an opportunity to state his terms.

What he really wanted was for the Roman legions to return across the sea, leaving the island of Britannia as it had been in the days of his boyhood. That, though, was an impossible dream, so he settled for asking for something more realistic.

Pausing to gather the words he had rehearsed, he recited, "All Roman troops must withdraw south of the Bodotria and Clota. Those rivers and the Great Moss between them mark a natural boundary. You may install a garrison on the rock at Giudi, but no troops will move north of there and none of your ships will sail further north unless invited."

Agricola's response was almost instantaneous.

"And what do we receive in return?"

"An end to warfare and raids," Calgacus promised.

"Can you guarantee that?" Agricola demanded. "You are a war Leader, not a King."

"There are only three Kings you need to worry about," Calgacus informed him. "Bridei of the Boresti, Gabrain of the Venicones and Bran of the Caledones. The other tribes either live too far north to bother you or they have lost their chieftains in the fighting. Of the three who matter, I have already obtained the agreement of two."

He wondered what Agricola would say if he knew that Bridei and Gabrain were lurking in the shadows of the forest only a few hundred paces away. It was probably as well that he didn't, Calgacus reflected. It was also probably for the best that neither of the two Kings was out here with him. Bearing in mind that Agricola was the man who had led the Legions into their territories, each of them was likely to draw a sword and attempt to kill the Governor, no matter the consequences.

Oblivious to the risk Calgacus had protected him from, Agricola persisted, "I need more of a guarantee than your word. We will require hostages."

"That would be pointless," Calgacus told him. "Either the Kings would send you people they disliked in the hope that you would kill them, or they would send you people who would not mind dying for the sake of their tribe. No, there is a more certain way to ensure that the peace will be kept."

"What is that?"

"The purpose of raids is to enrich those who carry them out. If you make it worth our while, the Kings would have no need to raid your province."

"Ah," smiled Agricola, "we come to the matter of payment. You want silver and gold?"

"Thirty talents of silver each year," Calgacus confirmed. "Ten for each of the three Kings."

The sum he had asked for was enormous, and he had expected the Governor to dismiss it out of hand, but Agricola merely asked, "Nothing for yourself? I had expected you to demand something. What is it you want?"

"I want you to leave our land," Calgacus growled. "Nothing would suit me better than never having to look on the face of a Roman ever again."

The sudden vehemence in his voice startled the Governor's horse and Agricola had to yank on the reins to keep the beast under control. When it had settled, he responded, "You ask a great deal and you offer very little in return. Your raids are little more than an annoyance. I do not see any compelling reason why we should give up so much territory, nor why we should agree to pay such extravagant bribes."

"The land you would be giving up is ours, not yours," Calgacus reminded him sharply. "Besides, are my terms any worse than the alternative? If you march into the hills, you will lose hundreds, probably thousands, of men. It will cost you your reputation and for what? If you agree to my terms, you can inform your Emperor that you have three new allied Kings and a peaceful, stable border without the need to waste your time conquering a worthless land."

"Will those Kings agree to become clients of Rome?" Agricola asked.

"No. Friends, perhaps, but not servants."

The Governor's mouth twitched in an expression of disapproval, but Calgacus hurried on, "This arrangement is, I believe, much the same as Rome has agreed with many German tribes. You would not be creating a precedent."

It was Macrinus who had told him about the German tribes, and Calgacus noticed the effect his comment had. The Governor stiffened slightly, and a flicker touched his eyes. Whether it was annoyance or merely surprise, Calgacus could not tell, for Agricola quickly recovered his composure.

"The Germans," he said carefully, "provide Rome with manpower. They join our Legions or fight alongside us as Auxiliaries. Will your men do the same?"

Calgacus shrugged, "I will not force anyone to do that, but if some men wish to join you, I doubt anyone will try to prevent them."

Agricola frowned, then gave a resigned sigh.

"It seems to me that you are not offering very much at all."

"On the contrary," Calgacus countered, "Is thirty talents of silver really too high a price for a guarantee of peace?"

He had expected the Roman to argue, to try to negotiate a lesser settlement, but Agricola merely snapped, "Are those your final terms?"

"Those are the terms the Kings demand," Calgacus told him, anticipating a counter offer.

Agricola surprised him once again by replying, "I will need time to consider whether to agree to what you ask."

The Governor's face was virtually unreadable so, for the sake of his newborn granddaughter, Calgacus made one final attempt to be reasonable.

He said, "I will order all raids to be halted for the next five days. If, at the end of that time, you wish to talk again, send Macrinus back to the place we found him last time."

Still battling to control his unruly horse, Agricola agreed, "Very well, Five days. If Macrinus does not come, you can expect my cohorts to come instead."

"I will be waiting, whoever comes," Calgacus assured him. "But you and I both know that a peace treaty is in everyone's interests."

The two men studied one another for a long moment, each weighing up the other and trying to assess whether to trust what had been said so far. For his part, Calgacus found it difficult to trust any Roman, but he sensed that Agricola, for all his haughtiness, was a man who was pragmatic enough to recognise when negotiation could achieve more than fighting.

His face still set in a stern expression, Agricola gave a final nod of farewell before turning his skittish horse and urging it into a trot as he headed back towards the river where his soldiers were waiting.

Calgacus watched him go, wondering whether he had achieved anything at all. Would the Governor really agree to withdraw his troops? Would he pay to keep the tribes quiescent? He would not know the answer to those questions for at least five days. It would depend on whether Agricola believed the price was worth more than the lives of his men, and on whether reaching a quick settlement would benefit his own career.

Despite himself, Calgacus found that he admired the stern Roman. Agricola was no fool, and he had more imagination than most Romans. Whether that meant he could be trusted was a separate matter.

As he watched, he noticed that Agricola was not riding directly back towards his troops but was following a curving route which would take him around the edge of the ploughed area. Calgacus supposed he wanted to keep his skittish horse out of the churned soil, but he frowned when he saw the Roman raise his right arm, then slash it downwards in a clear signal for some sort of action.

Calgacus was instantly alert, his eyes scanning the ranks of Roman infantry and cavalry as he looked for some movement.

But there was no response from the soldiers. Instead, what he saw made his heart skip a beat. From behind the armoured men, four huge war hounds had appeared. The handlers, urged on by another Roman officer, slipped the leashes, and the dogs barked eagerly as they bounded towards Calgacus.

Chapter XIV

Calgacus let his horse have its head, turning it round as quickly as it could manage and urging it into a gallop towards the distant trees which now seemed much further away than they had when he had left their shelter. He had reacted quickly, but horses take time to turn and to move from a standing start to the full gallop, and he knew without looking back that the four hounds must have covered half the distance between them and would be rapidly gaining on him. His pony was strong, capable of carrying his weight even with his full armour of chainmail, but it was built for stamina and endurance, not speed.

He cursed and swore as he leaned forwards, encouraging the pony to run faster.

Dogs!

That explained why the Governor had been so offhand. The discussion had been a charade, nothing more than an excuse to trap him, just as Macrinus had warned. They had discussed how to counter any threat Flaccus might devise, but they had never considered the use of dogs.

Calgacus had based his plans on facing men and horses, possibly even archers, which was why he had worn his full coat of chainmail. Now he was regretting that decision because the added weight was slowing his horse as it pounded across the uneven, boggy ground.

Dogs! And no ordinary dogs, at that. These enormous mastiffs were bred to kill. Once released, they could track a man for hours, only death or serious injury preventing them from hunting down their prey. Their massive jaws were so powerful that even his mail coat would be of limited protection if they managed to get a firm grip on him. And once they had him, they would drag him to the ground and tear him to pieces.

Cold sweat broke out all over his body as he imagined the huge hounds drawing ever closer. They were making no sound, their silence even more unnerving than a chorus of baying and howling.

Up ahead, he could see men emerging from the trees and hurrying to form a defensive line. Runt was there, as always, with the huge figure of Gabrain at one end of the line and Bridei at the other. In the centre, Adelligus, captain of Calgacus' personal guard, was shouting at the other warriors to advance. These men had been trained from boyhood in the art of war, not as most Pritani warriors were taught, but in the way of Roman combat. They wore chainmail, they carried large shields and were armed with Roman swords as well as heavy spears. They levelled those spears now as they began to hurry forwards, maintaining a close formation to present a hedge of sharp blades. This would normally serve to drive off cavalry but it would, Calgacus realised, be of equal benefit against the dogs.

All he had to do was reach his friends before the pursuing hounds caught him.

And then his horse fell.

It was so unexpected that he had no time to do anything except react instinctively. The panicking pony lost its footing and crumpled, flinging him over its head.

He threw out his arms and braced his legs as he crashed, face down on the wet, marshy ground, splashing into shallow puddles and sinking into the mud. The heavy hilt of his sword smashed into the back of his helmet before the weight of the weapon and the force of his fall slid it partially free from the ornate scabbard, leaving the metal cross-guard close to his left ear.

Dazed, he coughed and spat, pushing himself up just in time to hear a warning shout from Runt.

He twisted to his left, his right hand reaching for his sword. Grasping the hilt, he yanked it free as he surged to his feet, pivoting to his right and swinging the blade in one mighty movement.

He was only just in time. Two of the dogs were almost on him, the first one springing at him, jaws agape, a vicious snarl emanating from deep within its throat. The sword caught it full on the side of the head, the metal blade ringing as its lower edge crashed into the mastiff's spiked collar. The impact was so powerful that the beast was hurled sideways, colliding with the second dog which was preparing to pounce on Calgacus but had been forced to run wide by the larger animal.

Calgacus staggered, his feet slipping in the mud as the two dogs were sent sprawling, but he had no time to watch them because a third animal was coming for him.

He backswung his longsword, driving the beast off and forcing it to move wide to his left. It crouched, snarling and growling, its eyes red with malice.

The fourth hound joined it, circling further to Calgacus' left and then he heard the sound of the surviving dog from the first pair as it scrambled to its feet and came from his right.

He had nowhere to run. Struggling for footing, he kept turning, holding the great sword in both hands, presenting the blade first to one animal, then to the next, flicking it towards them to keep them at bay.

He tried shouting and lunging one foot forwards, but the dogs simply backed off, allowing one of the others to close in and forcing him to adjust his position.

He had no idea how long he stood there, but a loud shout, a war cry he recognised, distracted the beasts' attention.

"Camulos!"

He heard the sound of pounding boots, of splashes and wet grass being trampled by the approach of many men, and he laughed because his friends had come to rescue him.

One of the great dogs suddenly collapsed as a stone thudded into its skull, driving shattered shards of bones into the animal's brain. Runt, who had never lost his skill with a slingshot, yelled his delight at the accuracy of his throw.

The remaining two dogs hesitated uncertainly, so Calgacus took a step towards them, swinging his great sword in an attempt to drive them off. Both animals leaped aside, but the tip of the blade raked across the twisting body of the beast to his right, causing it to yelp in pain. The injury, combined with the arrival of two dozen armed men, persuaded it that this was a fight it could not win. It turned and bolted, tail down.

The last dog was either braver or less intelligent. It had circled away from Calgacus' attack and was slightly behind him. Growling malevolently, it made one last attempt to bring him down, leaping up at him with its mouth agape.

He spun round, trying to deflect the attack with the weight of his sword, but the mud sucked at his boots and slowed his movement. The edge of the blade caught the animal low down, just above its foreleg, but did not prevent it slamming its massive bulk into him.

He fell backwards, the dog snapping and snarling as it tried to rip his face off, only the pressure of his sword holding it away from him.

Then he slammed into the wet earth and the sword tumbled from his hands.

The dog had also lost its balance, scrambling awkwardly to his left, its foreleg useless as it struggled to leap back on top of him.

He saw it coming and raised his hands, crossing his arms in front of his face, hoping that the massive teeth would not be able to chew through the metal links of his chainmail and crunch his bones to useless splinters.

He was dimly aware of more yelling, but all his focus was on the gaping, drooling jaws of the great mastiff as it loomed above him. He could feel the warmth of its fetid breath, could see the red tongue and massive fangs within its wide mouth and he yelled, half in terror, half in an attempt to scare the animal away. Then, just as its jaws were set to clamp down on his upraised arms, the dog lurched violently and was thrown across him as it was punched aside by the impact of a spear being thrust into its body.

He heard the dog's growls change to a high-pitched whimper as it was pushed across his legs, and then it fell silent when a sword smashed its skull.

Calgacus lay back in the muddy grass, his breath coming in great gasps and his limbs feeling suddenly weak.

"You'd better get up, Cal," he heard Runt tell him. "The cavalry are coming for us now."

Hands reached down for him and he opened his eyes to see Adelligus yanking his spear free of the dead dog.

"I'm glad you didn't cut that any closer," he gasped.

"I didn't think you'd let a mere animal knock you over," Adelligus grinned.

"Remind me to knock you over for being so bloody cheeky," Calgacus grunted.

"Later!" Runt told him urgently. "We have no time. Come on!"

He thrust Calgacus' sword into his hands and tugged him away from the dead dogs.

As the warriors fell back, Calgacus looked over his shoulder and saw that the Roman cavalry, nearly two hundred of them, were churning their way across the ploughed field towards them, lances at the ready.

His own pony had fled, terrified by the dogs, so there was only one way he could escape this latest threat.

"Bugger!" he groaned as he dragged himself into as fast a jog as his trembling legs would allow.

Running men in the open were cavalry's favourite target, but Calgacus knew that two dozen men, even armed with long spears, could not hold off so many horsemen. If they stood their ground, they would die. Their only chance was to reach the trees before they were caught by the lances and swords of the charging horsemen.

He was amazed that he still had the strength to move, but a surge of excitement and fear sustained him as he followed his companions in the dash towards the forest.

Runt and Adelligus, both of whom could have outstripped him in a foot race, stayed close to him, offering encouragement by their presence. Despite the danger of their predicament, Calgacus felt pride rise within him. His friends had come to help him even though they knew they were putting themselves in mortal danger by doing so.

It was not only Runt and his son. Bridei, bare-chested as always, was whooping in delight at the madness of their predicament, and even red-haired Gabrain was there, clutching a spear and promising to kill any Roman who followed them into the depths of the forest.

The dull thunder of the horses' hooves grew louder, but the first men were already vanishing into the murky gloom of the dark pines. Calgacus was last, staggering and gulping for air, his sword heavy in his hand as he lurched between two tree trunks into the dark shade of the woodland.

"Nets!" yelled Adelligus, and the final part of Calgacus' plan was instantly brought into play.

Men hauled on ropes, running to left and right, drawing up large nets across the entrance to the forest. Normally used to trap birds, these nets were enormous and fine-meshed. The men pulling the guide ropes darted round trees, wrapping the ropes in place to hold the nets high like gates barring the way to the inner forest.

"Now run!" Adelligus shouted, and the flight continued.

There was no order to it. Each man climbed the steep slope as best he could. Calgacus paused long enough to shove his sword into its scabbard, frowning at not having enough time to clean the blade before he did so. Then he set off, scrambling up the slope, dodging between trees, hauling himself, almost on all fours, over rocks and tree roots as he climbed the steep slope.

Behind him, he could hear the frustrated shouts and yells of the Roman cavalry as they tried to hack through the nets or find a way round them. Not that it would do them much good, because their horses would struggle to climb the hill and the lowering branches of the pine trees would claw at the riders as they passed, blocking their view and slowing them.

Still, Calgacus would not feel safe until he reached the top of the hill where their own ponies waited. That would take time because he was close to exhaustion, and the hill was both high and steep. Breathing hard, he forced himself on, his fingers clawing into the soggy earth, his booted feet scrabbling for a purchase as he climbed.

Other figures were moving around him, difficult to make out in the shadowy gloom.

One of them was Bridei, still grinning happily, as if he had never entertained any doubt that they would escape.

"You cut that fine," he observed cheerfully as he drew alongside Calgacus.

"I wasn't expecting the dogs," Calgacus admitted breathlessly.

"I told you not to trust the bastards," Bridei rasped. "And you lost your horse. It's a long walk home."

"I'll take your horse," Calgacus gasped.

Bridei laughed, "Fine. Then, when you get back before me, you can explain to my lads how you lost their nets. We normally use them to catch game birds. It takes a long time to make a net as big as that, and we might go hungry this winter if we can't catch enough fowl."

"You could always go back down and collect them," Calgacus suggested.

Bridei chuckled, "Maybe later."

Sweating and breathing hard, they reached the top of the hill at last, locating their horses and preparing to leave. There was no sign of pursuit, but Calgacus did not want to remain there any longer than necessary. Still, he felt utterly drained by the desperate scramble up the hillside and he needed a few moments to recover his strength.

"Take my horse," Adelligus offered. "I'll hang on to a saddle."

Calgacus nodded his appreciation. Warriors often doubled up by one man clinging to the saddle horn of a rider, bounding along beside the horse as it moved at speed. He had done it himself once or twice in his youth, but it was too dangerous for a man of his more advanced years.

"Thank you," he said. "And thanks also for helping me back there."

The young man gave a curt nod as if to say that he had done no more than anyone would have done.

"At least we all escaped unharmed," he remarked.

"That's just as well," Calgacus replied. "Because I'd rather go and tackle those Roman horsemen than face Fallar if she gets angry with me for getting you into trouble."

"She's just as likely to be angry with me for bringing you back in a state like that," Adelligus replied, gesturing towards Calgacus.

"What do you mean?"

Runt laughed, "He means you look a mess, Cal."

Calgacus looked down at his tunic of chainmail and realised that it was caked in mud, the metal ringlets streaked with green slime and brown earth, along with a liberal spattering of blood.

"It will clean," he sighed, checking his palms and grimacing at the filthy mud that caked them.

He stamped his feet as he added, "And so will my boots, I suppose."

He was glad there was no polished mirror to show him a reflection of himself because he supposed his face must be filthy as well.

"We should go," Runt advised.

"In a moment," Calgacus nodded.

He reached back to draw his sword, frowning when he saw the dirt and blood caked to the blade. Whatever state his skin and armour might be in, his sword needed to be cleaned. He accepted a rag which Runt handed to him, and began wiping the metal clean, grateful for a chance to rest because he was still tired after the exertion of fighting, running, and climbing the steep hill.

"The Romans could be coming after us," Runt warned.

"All right. Let's go."

Calgacus shoved his sword away and wearily hauled himself into the saddle, signalling to the others to mount up. The leading warriors set off down the reverse slope, picking a meandering route through the forest, while Adelligus moved over to grasp one of the stiff, leather corner horns of Runt's saddle.

As Calgacus began the descent, Gabrain moved his pony to ride alongside.

Brawny and powerfully built, the young King of the Venicones was almost as big as Calgacus and, like him, dwarfed the tiny pony he rode, his legs dangling on either side so that his feet almost touched the ground. His broad, freckled face was set in a look of determination.

"No peace treaty, then?" he enquired gruffly.

"It seems not," Calgacus agreed, remembering that he had not yet had time to tell anyone what had passed between him and the Governor.

Gabrain, though, was not interested in the abortive conversation.

He said, "That's good. Does that mean I can carry on with my raids?"

"As long as you are careful," Calgacus agreed, reckoning that his offer to refrain from attacking the Romans for five days had been nullified by the attempt on his life.

"Seeing their ships gave me an idea," Gabrain informed him.

"What sort of idea?"

"I thought I might steal one."

Calgacus shot the young chieftain a look of surprise.

"What? Steal a ship?"

"That's right."

"Why? You can't do anything with a Roman galley."

"I could set it adrift and set fire to it," Gabrain suggested. "After emptying it of all the supplies it carried. They bring most of their food upriver, you know."

"I know. But how do you go about capturing one? We have no boats that are nearly big enough to attack a galley."

"Simple," Gabrain assured him. "We steal it when it's moored up for the night beside their fort."

Calgacus regarded the red-haired King with renewed respect. He had not thought Gabrain capable of devising such a daring plan.

Gabrain asked, "So, what do you think?"

"I think it's a crazy idea," Calgacus told him.

"Good. Runt always says you like crazy ideas. If there is to be no peace treaty, we need to show them what we are capable of."

Calgacus could not argue. He was tired, angry and annoyed with himself over nearly being caught. He wanted to dissuade Gabrain, but knew that the idea of attacking a Roman galley was just the sort of thing he would have attempted when he was younger.

"Work out a plan," he told the red-haired King. "Let's talk it over and make sure it has a good chance of success."

Gabrain's face lit up with savage delight.

"I'll make it work," he promised. "I'll teach those treacherous bastards what it means to betray our trust."

Calgacus gave a determined nod. He had gone to the meeting with few expectations, but a part of him had secretly hoped that he might have agreed a pact that would have left the world a safer place for his granddaughter. Instead, he had nearly died, and little Elaris' father, Adelligus, had been placed in danger.

"Yes," he muttered grimly. "Let's show them what it means to betray us."

Chapter XV

The stars blazed in a clear, cold sky, and a crescent moon cast a pallid, silvery light across the partly completed fort, creating ominous, dark shadows among the skeletal buildings and the rows of leather tents.

Julius Macrinus, hunched within the thick folds of his cloak, prowled the perimeter of the annexe where his auxiliary cavalry were billeted. They were kept apart from the legionary base because they were not citizen soldiers and because there was always a tremendous rivalry between the men who rode into battle and those who trudged on foot. Infantry and cavalry had been known to fight among themselves unless kept apart. Here, though, the Governor needed his best horsemen close at hand, so Macrinus' men were camped in a small, fortified rectangle that abutted the main fort.

Macrinus was not aggrieved over this discrimination. He had been in the army long enough to understand its methods. Besides, he reflected grimly, he had other things on his mind, matters that had kept him from sleep and resulted in him trudging the walls in the middle of the night.

He exchanged a few words with the patrolling sentries as he went.

The soldiers assumed he was checking up on them, as if the usual routine of the night duty were not enough to keep them alert. While on watch, each man was given a small, numbered token by the Tesserarius in charge of the sentries. They needed to complete their circuit of the walls and return the token within an allotted time, or face punishment. Knowing this, Macrinus did not delay any of the sentries as they walked the ramparts, merely giving a few words of encouragement to each man as he passed.

His presence would, he knew, add to his reputation as a man who took an interest in the ordinary soldiers but who could also be a stern disciplinarian when the occasion demanded. He did not attempt to disillusion them, not wanting to reveal the true reason for his nocturnal outing.

Normally, he had an old soldier's ability to sleep whatever the circumstances, knowing that the opportunity for rest should be taken whenever it presented itself. This night, though, sleep had eluded him and he had slipped out of the tent he shared with the other auxiliary commanders to begin a slow tramp around the circumference of the encampment, hoping to soothe his unfamiliar restlessness.

For what seemed the hundredth time, he ran over events in his mind as he slowly patrolled the ramparts.

It had been five days since the abortive meeting with Calgacus. There had been a great many recriminations afterwards, with Flaccus accusing the dog handlers of having trained their hounds inadequately, and then complaining that the cavalry had displayed sheer incompetence.

The Governor had insisted that the Assistant Procurator hold his tongue until they returned to their camp because it was unseemly for senior officers to be seen bickering in front of the men. Flaccus had grunted a grudging assent, but had brooded throughout the entire journey. Agricola, too, had been in an irritable mood, while Macrinus was also angry and confused. He had believed the Governor was genuinely interested in agreeing a peace treaty, yet Agricola had signalled for the hounds to be set on Calgacus. Macrinus had brooded over that decision all the way back to the fort, wondering what had driven the Governor to such treachery.

He had always admired Julius Agricola, and would follow the man into battle without hesitation, yet he could not ignore the fact that the Governor had deceived him. That knowledge stung Macrinus. Over the previous months, he had come to believe that being elevated into the Governor's inner circle of advisers had led to a mutual trust and confidence yet, when faced with a political problem, Agricola had used Macrinus for his own ends without any explanation. The sense of betrayal was almost too much for Macrinus to bear.

With everyone angry, frustrated or distrustful, it had been a long, grim march back to the fortress, and things had not improved when the senior officers met in the Governor's tent.

It was Flaccus who had seized the initiative and given full vent to his complaints.

"He was only one man," the Assistant Procurator had whined. "How could you fail to catch him?"

"The terrain slowed us down," Macrinus retorted, struggling to retain his temper in the face of the young man's accusations. "I told you it would."

"You could have chased them further," Flaccus persisted.

"Not into that forest," Macrinus replied testily. "We would never have caught them. Cavalry can't operate in wooded hills."

The Governor had been unusually reticent while the two men had bickered, but he eventually stepped in, saying, "Such things happen in war. No plan survives initial contact with the enemy. Calgacus was lucky, but he was also very skilful. I must confess I thought the dogs would bring him down. I've never seen anyone fight like that. One man should not have been able to fight off four dogs."

"You sound as if you admire him," Flaccus snorted accusingly.

Agricola gave a soft smile, one that showed a spark of his more normal strength of will.

He said, "Yes, I do admire him. I am glad I at least managed to meet him. He is a dangerous and difficult opponent, but now I know the sort of man I am up against."

"He is a barbarian," Flaccus grunted sourly.

"He is a fine leader of men," Macrinus put in, pleased that the Governor was taking his side in the argument. "Did you not see how his followers ran to help him even though we were charging at them?"

Flaccus muttered, "I think that merely shows how ignorant his followers are, not how good a leader he is."

"No," Macrinus insisted. "I have met Calgacus several times. He is a man who inspires loyalty. He is a 'Come on!' leader."

Flaccus' pale forehead creased in a perplexed frown. "What do you mean?"

With more than a hint of savage sarcasm, Macrinus explained, "Some leaders tell their men to 'Go on!', while others tell them to 'Come on!'. As a rule, soldiers admire a commander who leads from the front, and despise men who remain at the back."

It was, Macrinus knew, a jibe Flaccus could not fail to understand. The Assistant Procurator, having ordered the release of the war hounds, had then commanded Macrinus to lead the cavalry in pursuit of Calgacus, while he had remained with the legionaries, a mere spectator to the action.

"A General's role is to direct a battle, not to take part in it," Flaccus countered sarcastically. "Is that not so, Julius Agricola?"

The Governor gave a slight nod as he replied, "There are many commanders who believe that to be the best course of action. But Macrinus is also correct. A General who never shows his men that he is prepared to share the danger will soon lose their respect."

Flaccus, clearly irritated, rasped, "That may be so, but for a man to put himself in danger the way Calgacus did, tells me he is reckless."

Macrinus snapped, "Some would say it shows his confidence in his own ability. The way he tackled those dogs certainly made an impression on the men."

"What do you mean?" Flaccus scowled. "What sort of impression."

Agricola gave a soft, warning cough, stifling Macrinus' response and taking up the discussion himself.

"You must understand, Popidius Flaccus, that Calgacus is much more than a man in the eyes of most of our soldiers. He has been Rome's main antagonist for the past thirty years. He has evaded capture, led rebellions and stormed our forts, a feat which no other person has ever achieved."

"From what I understand," Flaccus said dismissively, "most of his achievements were long ago. He has spent most of the past fifteen years hiding up here in the north, has he not?"

Agricola sighed, "Nevertheless, he has defeated a Legion in battle at least twice and, though it pains me to admit it, he outwitted me earlier this year, and nearly destroyed the Ninth Legion in their camp. Things like that make a strong impression on soldiers. His reputation is such that our men fear his name. That is why those carved messages his warriors leave after every attack have such an impact."

"But he is just a man!" Flaccus protested, sitting up straight in his chair and waving his hands in exasperation.

"Indeed he is," Agricola agreed, shooting a warning glare at Macrinus to prevent him repeating the rumour of Calgacus' invulnerability. "But consider what our men saw the other day. He came alone and, when his horse fell, he fought off four of our fiercest war dogs. The way he used that sword of his was, even I must admit, impressive. If he had done something like that in the arena at Rome, the crowd would have been acclaiming him a hero and begging for him to be spared."

"And your men are as fickle as the Roman mob?" Flaccus challenged, his eyes hard and uncompromising. "They see him fight once and they think he is some sort of invincible demigod from legend?"

"He is no demigod," Agricola insisted, "but he has built an aura around himself by his deeds. Whether we like it or not, his reputation is such that we are facing the legend as much as the man."

"And how will you face him now?" Flaccus asked mockingly. "What will you do to defeat him?"

"As I explained when you first arrived here, we will need to do it the hard way," Agricola shrugged. "When the spring comes, we will march into the hills and find him. We will burn every farm and homestead, take every head of sheep or cattle, and plough salt into their fields. Calgacus will need to either fight us or starve."

"That may take a long time," Flaccus remarked coldly.

"It will take as long as it takes," the Governor conceded with rather less grace than usual.

For a moment, Flaccus said nothing, as if the Governor's sharp tone had shocked him. Then, unexpectedly, he seemed to relax, his shoulders lowering and his posture becoming more serene. Macrinus thought the man seemed almost pleased with himself, as if he had thought of something the others had completely missed.

As if to confirm this, Flaccus stood up and gave a perfunctory bow of farewell.

"I believe there is a better, faster way to accomplish victory," he informed them haughtily. "If you will excuse me, I have a letter to write."

His face was set in a sly, self-satisfied smirk as he left them.

After a long silence, Agricola sighed, "I suspect I will need to write a letter of my own. It is best that the Emperor hears both sides of the story."

"You think Popidius Flaccus will try to blame you for what happened?" Macrinus frowned.

"I think he will tell the Emperor that my plan for defeating Calgacus will take too long. He will probably recommend a younger, more dynamic Governor is appointed."

"Someone like himself," muttered Macrinus.

Agricola shrugged off that suggestion. With a resigned sigh, he confided, "In normal circumstances, I would not be concerned. I went along with Flaccus' plan because failing to do so would have given him a perfect excuse to criticise me. But we tried it, and it failed. Now my way is the only way we can suppress the rebellion. That is what I shall tell the Emperor. After that, the decision will be his."

Macrinus felt dismayed. He liked and admired the Governor, but now he realised that Agricola had never had any intentions of agreeing a peace treaty. He had always intended to go along with Flaccus' plan even though he despised the man himself. If the dogs had succeeded, the barbarians would have been shorn of the one man who held them together, but the failure of the trap meant that Agricola was now in a stronger position to ensure his own plans went ahead. He had been far more subtle than Macrinus had guessed, because the Governor won either way. And yet Macrinus felt a hollowness in the pit of his stomach when he recognised Agricola's subterfuge and how he had been duped into going along with the plan.

His expression must have revealed his disappointment, because Agricola went on, "If I had agreed to Calgacus' demands, we would have conceded a lot of territory which includes decent farmland. That would have given Flaccus good reasons to undermine me. Now, the failure is his."

It was, Macrinus reflected glumly, all about politics. He had been convinced that he had persuaded the Governor that a peace treaty could be concluded, but Agricola had sprung the trap because he could not afford to ignore a man who had as much influence as Popidius Flaccus.

But now all chance of a peace treaty had gone, because Calgacus would certainly never trust them again. It had not been Macrinus' doing, but he felt somehow tainted by association with the double-dealing and deviousness of the decisions which had brought them to this stage.

Now, as he stood on the walkway of the earth rampart surrounding the fort, Macrinus wondered what the future would bring. How long would it take for Flaccus' letter to reach Rome? Would the Emperor decide that Agricola had been in Britannia long enough? If so, how long would it be before his replacement arrived?

Macrinus had been a soldier all his adult life, joining the Roman Army as chieftain of a band of auxiliaries who had been sent in part payment of tribute to the Empire. Rome's thirst for men to feed its armies was insatiable, and taking recruits from neighbouring, subject tribes was common.

Macrinus had not minded. As the youngest son of a minor chieftain, his future would have been bleak if he had remained at home. Joining the Roman army had given him purpose.

And he had enjoyed the life. He had soon discovered a talent for war and leadership. Now he was a Roman citizen, having completed his twenty-five years' service. He could have gone home or perhaps retired to some sunnier part of the Empire, buying a farm and finding a young wife to bear him some sons. Then he could have spent his days with no worries apart from fretting over how hard his slaves were working in his fields.

He gave a soft chuckle as he tried to envisage the scene. Somehow, he could not make it appear real.

"That's not for you," he whispered to himself.

And yet, he wondered, what was the alternative?

He had stayed with the Army but he was now, for the first time, wondering what life would be like with a new Governor in charge. His career had prospered under Agricola, who had promoted him to command all the Auxiliary troops, but a new Governor might well want his own man in charge of such a vital component of his army. Macrinus had seen men forced out before, and he did not relish the prospect of being compelled to relinquish command and being sent away or demoted to some inconsequential role where his greatest challenge would be to avoid getting splinters in his fingers from handling dozens of writing tablets every day.

He came to a halt, breathing in the cool night air, filling his lungs and telling himself that he should shake off these morose thoughts. Agricola may have misled him, but the Governor was, at heart, a fine commander and a good man to serve under, even if his recent decision had shown that he was a politician as much as a General. Macrinus had always known he would move on one day. The transition to working under a new commander might be difficult, but Macrinus would cope with it. He was a soldier, nothing more, nothing less. He would accept whatever came his way because he knew no other way to cope with life.

What he needed, he told himself, was to get away from the intrigues of Popidius Flaccus. The man's constant criticisms were what was making him gloomy and introspective. Without Flaccus' intervention, Agricola would have pursued the war properly and methodically, disdaining snares and traps. Macrinus would have been content with that, but Flaccus had taken all the joy out of life with his secrets and treacherous stratagems.

No, Macrinus frowned, that was not entirely true. He was not above employing stratagems himself. What irked him was that Flaccus, a man with no experience of warfare, had assumed the unofficial role of military adviser and was using his relationship with the Emperor to compel older, more experienced men to do his bidding. The man was a menace and his interference was what Macrinus resented. There was, though, nothing he could do to alter the situation, a helplessness that only made him more depressed.

Sighing, Macrinus looked out over the ramparts. He had reached the southern edge of the annexe. Another sentry passed him by, giving him a silent nod of greeting as he trudged his way round the circuit of the walls. Up ahead, flickering flames showed where braziers had been set up near the gates to provide some heat and light for the men who guarded the entrance. Out beyond them was a wide expanse of flat grassland which was now covered by a miniature village of tents. This was the temporary home of many of the traders, merchants, unofficial wives and whores who followed the army, a gaggle of people who trailed wherever the soldiers went. Some of them had begun building more permanent homes, knowing that winter would soon be upon them, but the Army had first claim on the local timber and stone, so most of the camp followers would need to live under the leather or cloth shelters for some time yet.

The tented village was also home to the crews of the galleys which brought supplies upriver to the fort. There was a steady procession of these ships, three or four a day arriving with barrels of building materials, spare equipment and grain, along with the huge amphorae containing wine, olive oil or the potent *garum* fish sauce which was used to garnish so many Roman meals.

Macrinus' gaze swept further out, picking out a few details in the ghostly light of the quarter-moon. The trees and hills were virtually indistinguishable from the surrounding blackness except that their existence was marked by the absence of the blazing stars that lit the heavens. The river, though, barely forty paces wide at this point, was a dark ribbon against the ground, its inky surface occasionally sparkling with reflected starlight.

Only one galley was moored at the bank. It had been unloaded that evening, the sailors and soldiers combining to heave the stores ashore and transport them into the fort. With the evening approaching, the ship's Captain had decided to remain until morning before setting off on the return journey with a cargo of sick and injured men who were to be transported to bases further south.

The galley's crew were free men, not slaves. While their small contingent of marines would spend the night on board to guard the vessel, the rowers and other sailors took possession of some of the tents set up on the river bank to accommodate them. They were a rowdy, noisy lot; men who enjoyed singing and drinking, and the evening had been a lively one, with the whores finding plenty of customers. Things had settled down now, though, and only one or two fading camp fires dotted the rows of tents where the men now slept.

Macrinus was about to move on, determined to return to his own tent and snatch a few hours of sleep before dawn brought another busy day, when a barely audible sound caught his attention.

It had come from the south, somewhere near the river. It had been faint but, to Macrinus' ear, unmistakable. Someone had cried out in surprise or pain. The shout had been quickly stifled, but it had definitely been there.

He stared out into the darkness, seeking the source of the disturbance, straining his ears to catch any repetition.

There was nothing. The night was still. He could hear only the faint murmur of conversation from the guards at the gate, the stirring of the horses who were tethered in the lines below him, and the occasional rasp of a deep snore from within the fort. A bat fluttered overhead, but quickly vanished into the night in pursuit of its prey, leaving Macrinus with the feeling that he alone was awake and alert.

He looked to his left, towards the main fort, but all was quiet there.

Frowning, he turned his attention back to the area beyond the ramparts. There was no repetition of the sound, yet he had not been mistaken. Someone had cried out.

He told himself he was being overly anxious. It had probably been nothing more than one of the marines slipping or stumbling on the galley's deck.

But this was frontier territory, a dangerous place, and Macrinus had not risen to command by ignoring his instincts. He stood silent and still, listening for any further clues that might suggest something was not as it should be.

He was so intent on listening that it took a few moments for his eyes to register what they were seeing. He blinked, looked again and gaped in horrified amazement.

The galley was moving!

Slowly, almost imperceptibly, the ship was drifting away from the river bank and heading downstream.

Then he saw the spark of flame and heard muted shouting from the distant vessel.

"Sound the alarm!" he yelled to the men at the gates. "There's a barbarian attack!"

The response was instantaneous. No Roman soldier wasted time when danger threatened. The harsh, blaring call of a *buccina* echoed through the night air, calling the soldiers to arms. Moments later, the call was echoed by the legionaries within the main camp. They could not know what had caused the initial alarm, but they knew such a warning would not be given without good reason.

Macrinus ran to the gates, scampering down the wooden stairs that led from the rampart to ground level. To his right, the horses were waking, snorting their irritation at being disturbed. Beyond the horse lines, men were scrambling from their tents, grabbing weapons and struggling to don their armour in the dark.

He ignored the reaction his warning had caused, knowing the Centurions would soon impose order. They would have the men ready as soon as possible.

"Open the gate!" he ordered the half dozen men who manned the entrance.

The senior man shot him a quizzical look but did not argue. Opening the gates during an attack was completely against regulations, but Macrinus was a Tribune and, above all, a commander with a reputation for doing the right thing. The gate officer signalled to his men to obey the order.

"What's happening, Sir?" he asked.

"Somebody is stealing a galley," Macrinus explained hurriedly. "Now, stay here and close the gates as soon as I am outside."

"You're going alone, Sir?"

"That's right."

The soldier looked dubious but knew better than to argue. If the Tribune was daft enough to venture out into the middle of a barbarian raid on his own, that was his problem.

The soldiers removed the heavy locking bar and pull one of the timber gates back to allow Macrinus to slip outside.

He hurried through, the gate closing again almost before he had time to move beyond the entranceway.

He would not be alone, of course, because the inhabitants of the tented village were waking up, roused from sleep by the repeated calls of the horns. Not wanting to be delayed by anyone stumbling sleepily out of their tent to find out what was happening, Macrinus set off at a fast jog, cutting to his left and following the wall of the fortress until he reached the main gate of the legionary camp. Once there, he turned right and hurried down the main thoroughfare through the outer settlement, a wide path of trampled mud and earth that led from the fort to the river bank.

People were scrambling outside, the civilians fearful, the galley's crew picking up anything that might serve as a weapon. By the time Macrinus reached the river, nearly a score of men were jostling behind him, all of them demanding to know what was going on and where in Jupiter's name their ship had gone.

And it had gone. Already it was drifting towards a bend in the river, a dark bulk sitting on the silver-flecked smoothness of the water, with bright tongues of orange flame spurting from deep within its hold and a black plume of smoke rising lazily into the still air.

"They've taken our ship!" someone exclaimed in disbelief.

"They've set fire to the ruddy thing," growled a deeper voice.

Macrinus felt helpless. All he could do was watch as the galley edged slowly out of sight. As it went, though, he caught a glimpse of other, smaller shapes on the river.

"There they are!" he pointed.

All around him, men rumbled their anger, but there was nothing they could do. A gaggle of small river boats, the coracles of wood and animal hide used by the natives, was moving away from the burning galley, the occupants using broad, wooden paddles to make their way to the shore. They were less than one hundred paces away, but they knew there was nothing the ship's crew could do to catch them.

That did not prevent someone shouting, "Let's get them!"

"No!" Macrinus bellowed. "You'll never find them in the dark, and there might be more of them out there waiting for us."

"So what are we supposed to do?" the man next to him demanded angrily.

"Make your way to the fort. Get inside and stay safe until we know what's going on. It's too dangerous to stay out here."

His words brought a momentary stillness, then the crowd began to turn and scurry back towards the fort, jostling and stumbling in the darkness in their haste to escape the unseen threat of lurking barbarians.

Macrinus stood on the river bank for a little longer, rubbing his chin pensively.

He was about to make his way back to the fort when he realised that not everyone had followed his instructions. One man had moved closer to the water and had been slowly searching the river bank. He now turned and trudged back towards Macrinus, shaking his head in frustration.

He was a tall, rangy man with stooped shoulders and his voice held an aggrieved tone when he spoke.

"They cut the ropes," he complained bitterly. "Cut the ropes and stole my ship."

"You are the Captain?" Macrinus enquired solicitously.

"I was."

"What about the marines?" Macrinus asked. "They should have been on watch."

The tall man gave a sigh as he shrugged, "Most of them would be sleeping below decks. Only two or three would be on watch. They must have been taken by surprise, I suppose."

Macrinus nodded. He remembered the startled shout that had first drawn his attention. Had that been the cry of a sentry being attacked? If the barbarians had paddled their tiny craft across the river, or perhaps come downstream through the shadows by the riverbank, they could have swarmed over the decks, killed the sentries and then massacred the sleeping marines before anyone knew they were there.

"That's exactly what they must have done," the Captain agreed when Macrinus outlined his theory. Then he handed Macrinus a short, flat chunk of wood.

"I found this," he said softly.

It was too dark to read the message carved into the wood, but Macrinus knew what it said.

"Calgacus was here," he whispered.

"Is he still out there, do you think?" the Captain asked, jerking his head towards the dark, silent night.

"I think we would be dead by now if he was," Macrinus replied grimly. "Come on, we'd better head back to the fort. The Governor will want to know what we've found."

"I hope he can arrange for me to be given another ship," the Captain grumbled miserably as he plodded after Macrinus.

Macrinus did not reply. Obtaining a new galley for the Captain and his crew would be the least of Agricola's concerns after this latest, audacious raid. The loss of one supply ship was not important in itself, but it was an embarrassment, and what bothered Macrinus was how Flaccus would respond and, more importantly, how the Emperor would take the news when the Assistant Procurator's letter reached him.

Chapter XVI

A heavy overnight downpour of rain had washed away the dust and filth from the city's streets, but the sun was out once more and drying the cobbles, creating wispy threads of steam which fluttered around Flavia's feet as she walked.

She smiled to herself as two of her burliest slaves cleared a path for her, ploughing along the crowded roadway with a purpose that made people hurriedly step aside to let them pass. Behind her, her maid, Iusta, scurried along, struggling to keep pace with Flavia's determined strides, while two more slaves brought up the rear.

Flavia ignored them all. The rain had brought back memories of a time when she had been Cartimandua, Queen of the Brigantes. In those days, she had detested the rain, for it was usually cold, heavy and often seemed to last for days on end. The rains here in Rome seemed almost inconsequential by comparison, although she knew they could be every bit as torrential as anything Britannia could offer. Such downpours were, though, usually a welcome relief from the sometimes stifling heat of the city. Now that the approach of autumn had banished the fiercest temperatures, the rain had left a pleasant, warm morning which Flavia would normally have enjoyed. Much to her annoyance, though, the cooling rainfall had triggered other, less welcome memories of her former life.

Once she had been a powerful ruler, wealthy beyond the dreams of most people, feared and respected by all for her political skill and her ability to manipulate others into doing her will. She had ruled the troublesome and fractious Brigantes for nearly twenty years until the machinations of her former husband, Venutius, had forced her to flee to Rome.

She was still rich, probably wealthier than she had been in her earlier life, but Rome operated on a far grander scale than Britannia, and it had taken her some time to appreciate that she was a figure of far less importance here despite her friendship with the old Emperor, Vespasian. It had taken her a long time to cultivate her network of informants and clients, but she had enjoyed using her skills in a way that was even more subtle than the methods she had employed when she had been a Queen on the fringes of the Empire.

Now, though, her political acumen seemed to have deserted her. She had experienced a difficult few days, and her mood was resentful. The chance to walk the streets in the relative coolness of a wet morning was almost welcome, although the reason for her journey had initially irritated her.

Belinus had sent her a message, asking her to come to his shop. That was unusual in itself, for Belinus was a client of hers and should, by rights, have come to her. He was, though, a loyal and dependable man, not given to unnecessary panic, so she reasoned that the message, delivered by a most insistent slave, must be important. Wondering what lay behind the summons, she had called for Iusta and a protective body of slaves, and set off for Belinus' cookshop.

They passed the towering heights of the new Flavian amphitheatre, four magnificent tiers of arches and colonnades rising high above the tenements that surrounded it. It had been a stupendous achievement to construct such an enormous building out of stone, and even Flavia could not resist glancing at the breath-taking monument to Rome's power and glory.

There were no Games on today, but the place was always busy, the booths and stalls situated beneath the lower tier of arches always capable of attracting a crowd of potential customers. At night, Flavia knew, there would be customers of another sort because, when the stallholders packed up and went home at sunset, the city's prostitutes moved in to take their place. As a consequence, the area around the great amphitheatre was one of the busiest places in Rome at night as well as during the day.

Flavia permitted herself a wry smile as she passed the amphitheatre. It had been begun by the Emperor Vespasian, whose Flavian dynasty had ruled the Empire for twelve years now, a period of relative calm and peace or, at least, stability.

It had been Vespasian who had granted her asylum when she had first arrived from Britannia. She had been a long-time client of Rome, so it was theoretically his duty to do so although, as a new Emperor recently come to the throne after a bloody civil war, he could easily have turned her away or simply had her killed. There had been so many dead in those days that one more foreign princess would not have been missed. But Vespasian had been charmed by her looks and intelligence, and had readily granted her a home and an income. She had used both wisely, and had prospered, remaining friendly with the old Emperor until his death. She had taken her new name from his own family name, a sign of the respect she had genuinely felt for him.

Vespasian's son, Titus, had seemed set to emulate his father, but the young man's reign had been beset by the disaster of the eruption of the volcano, Vesuvius, and the destruction of the two towns of Pompeii and Herculaneum. Titus' reputation had suffered because of this disaster, a clear sign from the Gods that they were unhappy with Rome, but Titus had not suffered for too long because he had died shortly afterwards under circumstances which remained mysterious, thus allowing his younger brother, Domitian, to ascend the throne.

This was the same Domitian Flavia had promised Caratacus she would attempt to influence. The same Domitian she had been unable to get close to, not even to shout at, let alone speak to.

Her small entourage entered one of the narrow streets leading away from the amphitheatre. Here, the tall buildings left most of the roadway in shadow, so the cobbles were still wet and slippery. Flavia slowed her pace slightly, knowing they were approaching their destination and wanting to calm herself into the correct frame of mind for whatever problem Belinus was about to reveal.

The cookshop was busy, the morning's customers tucking in to freshly baked bread, warm sausage, cheese, olives and a variety of other dishes including, Flavia noted, sheep's brains. Belinus, it seemed, was trying to move upmarket.

Her slaves waited outside while she stood in the doorway, waiting to catch Belinus' attention. He was a tall, middle-aged, balding man, now hugely fat as a result of constantly sampling his own fare, although his bulky frame still held faint traces of the warrior he had once been.

He was bustling around behind the counter, apparently serving several people at once, chatting amiably to them while also maintaining a constant stream of instructions to the serving girls who were darting back and forth from the rear kitchen.

Ever attentive to new customers, Belinus looked up and glanced at the doorway. When he recognised Flavia, his features became momentarily stiff before reverting to their usual good humour.

"Praxus! Take over here," he called to a chubby young man who was clearing away empty platters from the half dozen tables in the main part of the cookshop. Hearing the call, the young man hurriedly took Belinus' place, and the proprietor waddled around the counter to greet Flavia.

"Thank you for coming, Domina," he told her, rubbing his hands on his grease-stained apron. "Please follow me."

He moved past her, heading outside. Flavia said nothing. She signalled to her slaves to wait while she followed the fat man.

He led her to the next property, a run-down tenement with gaping windows and peeling, graffiti-scrawled plaster on the outer walls. As they went into the dingy entrance corridor, an unwholesome smell made Flavia wrinkle her nose in distaste.

Belinus, glancing back over his shoulder, explained, "Most of the rooms here are empty during the day. The owner owes me a couple of favours, so I borrowed a room for a short while."

He paused slightly before adding, "I thought it best to bring him here rather than into my own place. There is less chance of anyone seeing him."

"Him?" Flavia asked.

"He refused to leave until he had seen you, Domina. I am sorry. I know you did not want to meet him, but he insisted. I thought it would be better not to create a scene, so I sent for you."

Flavia sighed. She knew now who Belinus was talking about.

The cookshop proprietor led the way up a flight of uneven, stone stairs to the second level. Here, a narrow corridor led the way to four doors. Belinus headed for the third one.

Approaching the room, he rapped his knuckles on the door before pushing it open. Stepping aside as it swung into the room, he turned to face Flavia.

"I will wait at the bottom of the stairs," he said.

Flavia nodded her appreciation of his discretion, then stepped into the room.

It was a tiny chamber, with a straw-filled mattress lying on the floor beneath a narrow window through which filtered a bright stream of dust-laden sunlight. A quick glance confirmed that, apart from a bucket for night soil and two other mattresses which had been stacked against the wall to her left, there was no other furniture. Like so many rooms in Rome, it was used only for sleeping. She guessed it might accommodate as many as half a dozen people. During the day, they would remain outdoors, doing whatever work they could find, and eating at establishments like Belinus' cookshop.

There was, though, one person in the room.

He was standing beside the window, turning slowly to face her as if she had interrupted his contemplation of the outside world.

"Hello, Cartimandua," said Caratacus.

"I told you we should not meet again," she replied harshly.

"You also told me you would send news via your fat friend out there, but I have heard nothing from you for several days."

"That is because I have nothing of importance to tell you," she snapped irritably.

"And why is that?" he demanded, inching closer to her. "Have you decided against helping me?"

Flavia exhaled a sound of irritation.

"You were always impatient," she said disparagingly. "These things take time."

"How much time?" he challenged.

She gave a slight shrug.

"I cannot be certain."

"Is that because you have had no luck in finding a way into the Imperial Palace?" he asked, his blue eyes boring into her.

Flavia was not one to be cowed by anyone, not even as imposing and forceful a character as Caratacus. She held her ground and retorted, "One does not simply turn up at the door and demand to see the Emperor. There are certain barriers to be passed."

"But you have not even passed the first one," he declared. "Tell me why."

Flavia stood silently, considering whether to confide in him. After some thought, she took a deep breath before letting the air out slowly.

"Very well," she sighed. "I do not like to admit it, but my network of clients and patrons is not as well connected as I had believed. I have not yet been able to find anyone who could introduce me to the Emperor in such a way that would result in a private conversation."

"I thought you knew everyone," Caratacus frowned.

"Hardly. I had hoped I knew enough of the right people, but it seems I was mistaken. You must appreciate that a new Emperor has his own circle of close acquaintances. Domitian cares little for the Senators who might be prepared to help me. He has his own cronies, and I have not yet been able to bring any of them into my own circle."

"There must be someone!" Caratacus exclaimed.

"Of course, but I must be careful about this. Emperors are always suspicious of anyone who seeks to gain their friendship. I need to find a believable reason for an introduction."

"That could take too long," Caratacus said sharply. "Can you not simply have one of your Senator friends take you to the Palace?"

"On what pretext? They have wives of their own, so they could not take me without it being remarked upon."

She paused as if an idea had come to her, then asked with deliberate scepticism, "I don't suppose you would care to ask your son-in-law, Annius Persus, to effect the introduction?"

Caratacus' eyes flashed dangerously as he snapped, "No!"

"I didn't think so," she scoffed. "So, you see my problem. Most Senators are very unwilling to draw attention to themselves. They are happy to avoid the Emperor unless they have no alternative."

Caratacus gave a morose nod as he muttered, "That sounds like the Domitian I knew. Persus rarely mentions him in my presence because he knows how I feel about the man, but I expect the whole Senate can see he is becoming a tyrant."

Flavia nodded, "Sadly, that seems to be true."

Caratacus balled his right hand into a fist and punched it against the palm of his left hand.

"He was always an unpleasant little sod," he snorted angrily. "I should have let him die on the Capitol that day."

"You never did tell me the whole story about that," Flavia remarked. "It was during the civil war, wasn't it?"

Caratacus gave a grim nod.

"A batch of us took refuge up there when Vitellius' soldiers decided to do away with anyone who supported Vespasian. We held out for a couple of days, but it was always a hopeless prospect. When they broke through, the temple of Jupiter was on fire, and the whole of the Capitoline Hill was in chaos. I was up there with Persus. I managed to get him out but, unfortunately, I also rescued Domitian. I wish I'd left the snotty little shit up there."

"Life is full of regrets," Flavia commented drily. "But you got him away and now he is the Emperor. But if he owes you your life, why do you not simply go to him yourself?"

"We had some disagreements," Caratacus admitted. "Also, Domitian is not the sort of man who likes owing favours to anyone. Things became ... complicated."

"Which is why you faked your own death?"

"It seemed like the best way to remove myself from his attention."

"So, it is up to me to deal with him?"

"Yes, but how are you going to do that?"

Flavia regarded her tall companion with a secretive smile.

"It seems my initial plan will not work, so I will try another way. Like everything else in Rome, doors can be opened if you have the right keys."

Caratacus frowned, "What are you talking about? What keys?"

"Money," she replied with a broader smile. "If my political connections will not grant me access, a few bribes might accomplish the desired result. It is merely a case of identifying the correct person and making the right approach."

"Have you identified the right person?"

"I think so. You must know by now, Caratacus, that slaves are not the dumb, silent brutes many Romans regard them as. My slaves have been speaking to slaves of the imperial household. Minor ones, to be sure, but it has suggested a possible way in."

"You can't just bribe the door slaves to let you in," he grunted.

"Of course not. But there is someone I know who knows someone in the Palace. With a little exchange of silver, that someone might be prepared to make an introduction to someone else."

Caratacus began to pace the room, shaking his head in frustration.

"It all sounds very vague," he muttered, shooting her a dark look from beneath furrowed brows. "How long will this take? I cannot wait much longer."

"Give me another few days," she told him.

He ceased his pacing and stood facing her, his expression grim and threatening.

"Three days," he stated, holding up a hand with three fingers extended. "After that, I will take matters into my own hands."

"Six days," she countered instantly, calmly ignoring his aggressive attitude.

"Four."

"Five."

"Four," he repeated obstinately.

"Very well, four days. Now, I must go. Please wait at least an hour before you leave. I do not want anyone knowing we have met."

Caratacus gave a reluctant nod.

"I suppose I have put up with the stench in here for most of the morning as it is. Another hour won't hurt. Tell me, though, who are you going to see?"

"It is probably best that you do not know any names," she said enigmatically. "But, if you think about it, who do you speak to about matters of finance?"

Caratacus gave her a puzzled look as he shook his head.

Flavia smiled sweetly as she informed him, "You see a banker, of course."

Chapter XVII

Flavia was feeling less confident when, later that day, she stepped out of her litter at the door to the home of Decimus Sulpicius Firmus. This was a large, imposing property occupying almost an entire block of a street just off the main Forum. She had travelled in her litter, carried by her four biggest slaves, because this mode of transport portrayed an image of a wealthy, important personage. Such an image was important when dealing with financiers like Firmus, she knew.

Except that she wouldn't be meeting Firmus. The slave she had sent to inform the banker that she would be paying him a visit had returned with the news that the old man had died suddenly from heart failure four days earlier.

"His nephew says he will be happy to speak to you," the slave had reported.

Flavia was uncertain what impact Firmus' demise would have. She had never liked the old man, regarding him as devious and unscrupulous. That had made him easier to manipulate, but she had never enjoyed her dealings with him. At another time, she might have regarded his unexpected death as a minor blessing but, as far as her current plans were concerned, it presented a potential problem. She had never met his nephew; in fact, had not even known he had a nephew, another gap in her knowledge which had served to add to her growing vexation.

The need to deal with a new, unknown individual added to her difficulties. Firmus would have been easy to handle. Payment of bribes was second nature to the sly old crook. He would have taken a cut of the amount she would pay and would have handled all the arrangements for her. Now, she reflected grimly, she would need to be careful how she dealt with his nephew until she could gauge whether the man could be bribed into being discreet. But time was against her, Caratacus' deadline only four days away, so she could not afford to take too long.

Not that she normally had much difficulty in persuading men to do her bidding. She had been born with a face that would usually allow her to get her own way. In Rome, though, a pretty face was not always a guarantee of success, and Flavia was realistic enough to know that her looks were more mature than they had once been. Still, she reckoned that old Firmus' nephew was probably around the same age as herself. That might make things easier. Unless, she reminded herself, he was happily married, or was one of those who preferred boys.

She shook her head in irritation. She would need to take things carefully, to play a part and try to tease information out of the man in order to judge how much she could tell him, but the need to do so would make her visit a more difficult meeting than she had anticipated.

She was met at the door by a smartly dressed slave, a serious-looking young man who led her into the coolness of the large property, directing her to one of the rooms near the atrium. The atmosphere within the house was calm and quiet, but it did not escape Flavia's notice that the first open door she passed led to a small chamber where two large, muscular men watched her as she followed the door slave. Firmus' nephew, it seemed, took security seriously.

"The lady Flavia to see you, Master Facilis," he informed the room's only occupant as he stood aside to admit Flavia.

She swept past him, a polite smile fixed on her face, stepping into a large, rather gloomy room that was devoid of decoration, the wall panels being painted a uniform, dull, reddish-brown, and the floor consisting of plain, unadorned tiles. A large, mahogany desk which bore several stacks of imposing ledgers, was situated opposite the door, with two padded chairs facing it, while long, rather uncomfortable-looking couches occupied the space to her left beneath a row of tiny windows which admitted the room's only illumination.

She supposed the room's austere atmosphere was intended to portray an image of sobriety, but she found it more than a little depressing. Still, she managed to maintain a smile as she entered the dreary, cavernous chamber.

The man behind the desk rose to his feet and moved round to greet her. He was, as she had guessed, in his early fifties, of average build, with thinning, brown hair and a face that wore a worried, serious expression that matched the room's gloom. Whether his demeanour was as the result of Firmus' recent passing, or whether it was the man's normal manner, she could not yet tell.

Determined to stick to her plan of action, Flavia treated him to her warmest smile, made sure that she was standing tall and erect, with her shoulders back and her travelling cloak parted to provide him with the best possible view of her still full and shapely figure.

It was a ploy that had rarely failed her, but it did so this time. Instead of faltering while he gazed at her in open admiration, he returned her smile in a friendly, welcoming manner. It was, though, his words which astonished her because, when he spoke in greeting he did not do so in Latin but in Brythonic, the language of the Britons.

"It is a pleasure to see you again after all these years," he said.

Flavia stopped in her tracks, for once caught off guard and almost flustered. Only years of rigorous self-control enabled her to regain her composure. Wonderingly, she shook the man's hand and studied him more closely as she gave a rather formal reply in the same language.

"I am sorry," she said. "When did we meet? I'm afraid I do not recognise you."

"It was a long time ago," he told her. "Please sit down and I will explain. Would you care for some wine?"

"I think I would," she agreed, still feeling slightly disconcerted.

The man named Facilis already had two goblets and a small jug. He poured large measures and passed one goblet to Flavia before taking his seat and sipping at his own drink.

"Alban," he informed her. "My late uncle's favourite, although he rarely shared it with others. I found this particular one in his wine cellar and thought it would be as well to try it. If I have watered it too much, I can mix you a stronger cup."

"It is fine as it is," Flavia assured him, still puzzled as to how he knew her. That was an unexpected complication, and she needed to be wary until she understood who this man was and how much he knew about her former life.

Smiling, he said, "Allow me to formally introduce myself. My name is Anderius Facilis."

"I am pleased to meet you. I am Flavia Alba."

He gave a thoughtful nod of acknowledgement, his eyes studying her closely as if he were trying to summon his memories.

Choosing her words cautiously, she observed, "You speak the language of Britannia extremely well. I presume that is where we met?"

He nodded, smiling as if enjoying his secret.

"I served with the Army for many years," he explained. "I visited your home in Isuria a long time ago, when Ostorius Scapula was Governor. I'm afraid I was under orders to deliver something of an ultimatum."

Flavia closed her eyes, searching her memory. Slowly, she nodded, then took another sip of wine as if feeling the need for some fortification.

"We were both very young back then," she remarked. "But I must apologise. I remember the occasion, of course, but I would not have known it was you."

"I am hardly surprised," he smiled. "It was a brief meeting. But I have never forgotten that day."

"Neither have I," she admitted. "It was the day that sparked events that shaped many lives."

Her memories were flooding back now. She had been barely eighteen years old, newly come to rule the Brigantes after her father's death. She had followed his advice about maintaining a fragile peace with Rome, but the message Facilis had brought to her that day had threatened everything.

The occasion was burned into her memory and yet she could not picture Facilis as the young Roman officer who had stood in front of her in her hall that day. All she could recall were his doom-laden words.

A Roman girl, the daughter of a Legate, had been kidnapped by raiders, Facilis had informed her, and he was there to convey the Governor's ultimatum, a demand which was being issued to the rulers of all the northern tribes; return the girl unharmed, or Rome will wage war on you and destroy you.

Flavia, or Cartimandua as she had been in those days, had been desperate to preserve peace, but matters had been complicated by the arrival of Caratacus, who had come to her after his latest defeat in an attempt to urge her to take up arms against the Empire. With him had been his younger brother, Calgacus.

A faint smile crossed her lips as she recalled that brief span of days when she and Calgacus had been lovers. Young and passionate, he had tried to persuade her to join the war, but she had refused. Caught between two diametrically opposed arguments, she had decided to follow the path of caution in order to save her people from destruction at the hands of the Empire.

At the time, she had managed to convince herself that Calgacus had fallen under her spell and accepted her decision. When the Roman girl had been captured, he had told her he would help find her. He had been almost as good as his word, but when he located the girl, he had hidden her away, hoping to engineer the war that would force her to rouse the Brigantes into action.

Calgacus had been thwarted by her other suitor, Venutius, who had tracked him down and rescued the girl.

When Cartimandua discovered Calgacus' betrayal, she had seized Caratacus and handed him over to the Romans along with the Legate's rescued daughter.

So many lives had been shaped by those traumatic events. Cartimandua had retained her throne and kept her people out of a war they could not win; Calgacus had returned to the south-west and become the leader of the resistance to Rome, a greater War Leader than even his more famous older brother. Caratacus had become a prisoner of the Empire and had never returned home. As for Cartimandua herself, she had married Venutius and then suffered an even greater betrayal when he had plotted against her in an attempt to seize power for himself.

And everything could be traced back to that fateful day when Anderius Facilis had marched into her hall and demanded the return of the Roman girl.

Flavia was not one to regret past mistakes, but she had often wondered what would have happened if she had accepted Calgacus' proposal, married him and joined the fight against Rome. With Calgacus and Caratacus to aid her, might they not have won? Instead, she had chosen Venutius, imprisoned Caratacus, and spurned Calgacus.

And yet it had been Calgacus who, ultimately, had saved her life when Venutius turned against her. Life, she reflected, was full of difficult choices but, whichever path one chose, the Gods seemed to take mocking delight in twisting the threads of the future so that the past returned to haunt you.

Now it had returned again, in the shape of Anderius Facilis.

Despite herself, Flavia could not avoid uttering a deep sigh.

"I remember it all," she told him. "Perhaps better than you can understand."

Facilis nodded, his features reverting to a more serious expression.

"A great deal has happened to both of us since then," he agreed. "I must admit I was very surprised when I discovered who you were. When I heard you were coming, I checked my uncle's records and discovered the truth of your identity."

"It is no secret," she informed him. "It is just that I prefer to be known as Flavia these days. Most people in Rome have forgotten all about Cartimandua."

"Not all of us," he assured her.

Flavia shifted in her seat, determined to move the conversation on and learn more about the man sitting opposite her.

"What about your uncle?" she asked. "I was sorry to hear he had passed away. I understand his death was sudden?"

Facilis' mouth twisted in a grim smile as he replied, "Yes, very sudden. He simply collapsed one evening after dinner. As for being sorry about his death, you would probably be one of the very few who feel that way. He was not a pleasant man and, as I have discovered, not entirely honest either."

Flavia was surprised at Facilis' candour, but confined herself to raising her eyebrows and remarking, "I hope his dishonesty did not extend to embezzlement."

"No," Facilis assured her. "Your money is quite safe, although I must confess that, had I been administering your investments, I would not have taken quite as large a share of the profits as my uncle did by way of commission."

"I see. So, my money has helped pay for this ..." She waved a hand, taking in the room.

"In part, I suppose." He placed his goblet on the desk and leaned forwards. "You understand, what I am telling you is not something I would tell any of my other clients."

"I appreciate that. You have assumed control of your uncle's business, then?"

"He has no other relatives," Facilis replied. "Still, I was very surprised to learn that he had named me in his will.

I only returned from Britannia a few weeks ago and, reluctantly, I came to work for him because I had no other options."

"A happy coincidence," Flavia observed.

Facilis sat back in his chair as he gave her a knowing look.

"I am sure others will think it more than coincidence," he told her. "I expect there are already rumours that I poisoned the old fraudster in order to get my hands on his money and his business."

He shrugged as he went on, "There is nothing I can do about that except to say I have always tried to be honest and open with people, and murdering anyone, even my uncle, is beyond me."

"Even though you clearly disliked the man?"

"Even so. He exploited my mother's vulnerability for years, earning a fortune for himself while keeping her in virtual poverty. I never forgave him for that. But I never entertained any thoughts of hastening his death. One thing life has taught me is humility, and I was content to work for him in order to earn a living."

"Things seem to have turned out well for you, all the same," Flavia commented.

"Yes," he admitted. "Especially because my uncle disliked me. However, he disliked virtually everyone, so there is nothing remarkable about that. As for the inheritance falling to me, it seems that he made his will many years ago, before we fell out, and had never got around to altering it. If he had, I do believe he would have left his estate to some distant acquaintance simply in order to spite me."

"Then I will toast your good fortune," Flavia smiled, lifting her goblet to her lips.

"Thank you. But I am sure you are not here to discuss my uncle. Perhaps you should tell me what I can do for you."

They were still conversing in Brythonic. Flavia briefly considered reverting to Latin because the British tongue was sometimes inadequate when it came to discussing concepts of finance, but she decided it would be better to keep their conversation as private as possible. After all, one never knew whether a slave was loitering outside with an ear to the door.

"First of all," she began, "can you tell me how much ready cash I have at my disposal?"

Facilis picked up a small parchment scroll and unrolled it on the desk. She could see it was covered in columns of dates and figures.

After a moment, he informed her, "The precise figure is one hundred and twenty thousand, four hundred and fifteen denarii. A significant sum, if I may say so. You also have considerably more invested in properties and businesses throughout Italy. If you want to know the value of those investments, I can give you an estimate."

"No, it is the cash I am interested in. You keep it all here?"

"We have a secure room deep in the basement, but we also keep some in various temples throughout the city and, indeed in neighbouring towns. That way, we avoid too great a loss if we were to suffer some unforeseen disaster like a major fire."

"A wise precaution," Flavia nodded approvingly. "Your uncle was a prudent man, it seems."

"Actually, this is a recent decision," he said modestly. In fact, we have only just begun moving some of the coinage to other locations. My uncle had not considered the potential for loss until I reminded him of the great fire during the reign of Nero. He was fortunate then because this part of the city was spared, but he eventually took my point and agreed to relocate some of our customers' valuables."

"So how much of my money is still here and readily available?" she enquired.

"All of it. The dispersal of actual coins does not affect your money. It would only be an issue if every one of our customers came here to withdraw all their funds on the same day."

"I see."

"How much is it that you want?" he asked.

"I am not sure. Several thousand at least. Perhaps twenty thousand."

Facilis gave a slow, thoughtful nod.

"Might I ask the purpose? Not that it is really my business, but if it comes to making a payment to a third party, I might be able to assist by issuing a payment promise to that person's banker. We would then exchange the actual money later."

Flavia smiled apologetically.

"It is confidential," she told him. "But I might need the money at short notice."

"That will not be a problem," he assured her with an easy smile.

"Excellent."

There was a brief, awkward silence. Facilis looked as if he wanted to say something but was unsure how to articulate his thoughts.

For her part, Flavia found herself warming to Facilis. She had decided that he was a fundamentally honest man, a fact which made her reluctant to broach the subject of paying bribes. That, she decided, was a matter she would need to attend to herself. It was an unwanted complication, but she could see no alternative.

She was tempted to make her excuses and leave, but the soldier turned banker intrigued her and, knowing she would need to have more dealings with him in the future, she decided she should learn more about him.

"You mentioned that you were in Britannia for many years," she remarked politely. "How long, exactly?"

After a moment's thought, as if he were not sure how much to reveal, Facilis nodded, "Some would say too long. I have spent much of the past thirty years there, although I did have a few years back here between my spells with the Army."

"Oh? What tempted you to return? Did you like Britannia so much?"

A brief pang of hurt flashed across his eyes as he gave her a sad shake of his head.

"My home was in Pompeii," he said softly.

Flavia pursed her lips.

"I am sorry. You lost a great deal?"

"Everything," he confirmed, clearly struggling with his emotions. "Everyone."

"I am sorry," she repeated and, for once in her life, realised that she genuinely meant it. The lives of other people rarely affected her, but Facilis' plain honesty and genuine pain over his loss tugged at her heart.

Pompeii and his dead family were obviously difficult subjects, so Flavia quickly returned to his time in Britannia.

"So you went back to the Army?"

He nodded.

"It was a mistake. I should never have gone back. It was supposed to be a nice, safe administrative role but, as things turned out, I was lucky to escape with my life."

"I have heard there has been some terrible fighting," Flavia prompted.

"There has indeed."

"Is that why you came back a second time?"

"Partly. But, strange as it may sound, I was persuaded to come back after spending some time as a prisoner of the Britons."

"A prisoner?" she frowned. "You were fortunate indeed. Most tribes would kill a captive Roman."

"I was very fortunate," he acknowledged. "The experience altered my outlook considerably. I found that my sympathies lay as much with the Britons as with my own people. Then, just after the assault on the camp of the Ninth Legion, I returned a favour to the leader of the rebels. When I spoke to him, I realised that I had seen enough killing and that it was time to return home for good."

Flavia was more intrigued than ever. She leaned forwards, holding his gaze as she asked, "You spoke to the leader of the rebels?"

"Yes. A man named Calgacus. As you must know, he is rather famous in Britannia."

Flavia was astonished at the coincidence. She could feel her heart beating faster and her legs trembling with barely suppressed excitement. Had fate brought her another ally?

"You met Calgacus?"

He gave her what she interpreted as a shy smile as he confirmed, "Yes. Several times, in fact. I spent quite a long time with him, and I must admit I like him, even though he can be rather intimidating."

Flavia nodded absently as Facilis went on, "I met his wife, too. I like her a lot. She is very clever as well as being quite striking in appearance."

"I have never met her," Flavia said, surprised to find that she felt a pang of jealousy at the thought of Calgacus having another woman in his life. Chiding herself for such an irrational response, she continued, "although I suppose she must be remarkable to have caught Calgacus' attention."

Facilis was smiling broadly now, his expression softened by his memories.

"She is very remarkable indeed," he agreed.

"But what about Calgacus?" Flavia persisted. "How well do you know him?"

"He saved my life," Facilis shrugged. "I will always be grateful for that. I partly repaid the favour, but I feel I still owe him a great debt."

Flavia could not suppress a smile of her own.

"I, too, owe him a great deal," she admitted as she leaned even further over the desk, closing the distance between them. "In fact, that is part of the reason I am here."

Facilis looked at her in wonder.

"It is?"

She nodded, still smiling.

Lowering her voice to a seductive whisper, she asked him, "How would you like to help me repay the debts we both owe to Calgacus?"

Chapter XVIII

Gabrain, King of the Venicones, was drunk. He had consumed several large mugs of heather ale in the celebrations to mark his achievement in stealing and burning a Roman galley from under the noses of the legionaries, and he could feel the effects of the alcohol swimming in his head. All around him, men and women were laughing and talking loudly, music was playing and more and more ale was being passed around. He should have been immensely pleased with himself, yet the more he drank, the more sullen he became.

Memories made his mood darker. Raised in a royal family, he had been taught from a young age that he was special, that he had a great destiny. He had lived with the hand of fate on his broad shoulders for as long as he could remember. His wild, red hair and his imposing physique had always set him apart from other men. His size and strength meant that men feared him and women admired him, which was as it should be for a King.

Yet the past year had been a difficult one. When the Romans had threatened his tribe, he had challenged Calgacus for leadership of the alliance, and had been humbled in front of the other chieftains when Calgacus had easily defeated him. That had been hard to bear, but Gabrain was not a fool and he knew that the Venicones needed the aid of the other tribes if they were to withstand the invasion. So he had swallowed his pride and agreed to follow Calgacus' orders. That had been difficult, especially when, despite their success in storming the camp of the Ninth Legion, they had been forced further northwards, abandoning the Venicones' territory to the enemy and seeking refuge in the hills.

Then there had been the failure of Calgacus' battle plan and the scattering of the alliance. With nowhere else to go, Gabrain and his warriors had made new homes high in the mountain glens, but his heart ached with the need to regain the lands where he was King.

What was a King without land of his own? He ruled as long as he had people who followed him, but the harsh mountains, where cattle struggled to feed and where crops would grow only reluctantly, were not the same as the wide, fertile lands where his ancestors had ruled.

His dissatisfaction had been tempered by the raids they had carried out but now, in the moment of his greatest success, his mood had darkened again. His standing was as high as it had ever been among the tribes, but still he was regarded as the most junior of the tribal leaders, and that knowledge rankled.

What made matters worse was that, even though this celebration was being held to honour him and his men for their startling success, it was Calgacus who remained the focus of attention.

Even while drinking to mark Gabrain's triumph, men sought Calgacus out, wanted his praise and grinned like idiots when they received it. Worse, to Gabrain's mind, was that, although men respected Calgacus and few would dare oppose him in a fight, the main fear they held was losing his respect. A word of praise from Calgacus was, it seemed to Gabrain, more highly prized than any gift of gold or silver.

Even the magical pieces of carved wood they were supposed to leave behind after every raid were marked with Calgacus' name. It was Calgacus the Romans feared, despite his having lost the battle; it was Calgacus the warriors of the free tribes looked to for leadership even though he had led them only to their hilltop fastnesses.

Gabrain's resentment was growing, but he was not so blinded by it that he would challenge Calgacus again. What was left of the alliance would disintegrate if he did that, and he knew there would be no prospect of the Venicones ever regaining their homes without the aid of the other tribes. No, there was only one thing he could do to alter the balance of power and claim his place as the true leader of the resistance.

He mulled over the idea all evening, keeping his thoughts to himself. By morning, with his head pounding from the effects of the heather ale, he had convinced himself that his plan of action was sound.

"I'm going on another raid," he told Calgacus.

"What do you have in mind?" the War Leader asked.

"We'll cross the river at night," Gabrain replied. "Well downstream, out in the estuary. They don't have enough men to watch the entire shore. Then we'll lay up for a day or so before cutting inland and ambushing anyone we find on their overland supply route. They must have messengers and wagons coming up all the time. If we can't find any luck with that, we'll destroy a few of their outposts. They'll have waystations and minor forts all over the place."

"Attacking forts is difficult," Calgacus reminded him.

"We've done it before. I know how to do it properly."

Calgacus nodded pensively, his brow furrowed in a deep frown.

He said, "It would be better if you were on horseback. They'll have cavalry patrols out. If they catch you on foot, you'll be cut to pieces."

"They won't catch us," Gabrain insisted. "We know how to move and how to hide. That is my tribe's territory. My men need to show that they are able to fight for it."

"It's too dangerous," Calgacus warned.

"You can't stop me," Gabrain asserted, his face flushing.

"I am the War Leader," Calgacus reminded him gently.

"And I am the King of the Venicones. I don't need your permission to enter my own lands."

Calgacus held the younger man's gaze for a long moment before giving a reluctant nod.

"Very well. But if you insist on doing this, let us at least give you a chance of success. You need to find a specific target. If you are on foot, you cannot roam around simply hoping to find some vulnerable Romans to attack.

Then, when you have selected a target, we will agree a day on which you will make your attack, and we will make some raids north of the river to distract the Romans' attention."

"That sounds good," Gabrain agreed, giving a satisfied nod.

What he did not reveal was that he had no intention of crossing the river simply in order to burn a few outposts or ambush a handful of wagons. He had something far more ambitious in mind, but he knew Calgacus would seek to prevent him if he learned what it was, so he continued the pretence and sent some scouting parties across the river to seek out suitable targets.

Four days later, he reported to Calgacus, "There's a small fortlet near the south shore. It's close to one of our larger villages, but it only holds around a dozen Romans."

Calgacus nodded. Just as they had done with the watchtower near his own former home, the Romans often placed small garrisons near larger settlements as a reminder to the local population that they were under military control.

"Is it fortified?" he asked.

"Naturally. But if I take enough men, we can overcome that, especially if we attack at night. We can cut down trees and use them to bridge the ditches, then scale the walls with ladders."

Calgacus smiled. He had once made a similar attack on a Roman fort.

"That's a lot of tree felling you will need to do," he observed.

"I'll take two hundred men," Gabrain replied. "That will be enough to do the work quickly."

"You don't have enough boats to carry so many across the river," Calgacus objected.

Gabrain grinned, "I've had men building more curraghs for the past few days. We'll have enough to transport at least a hundred men. We can get the rest across in a second journey."

Calgacus pursed his lips. One river crossing was risky enough. Two increased the dangers significantly.

"Best do it in one crossing," he advised. "Especially if you need to get back across in a hurry. You don't want to abandon half of your men on the far shore."

Gabrain frowned but gave a reluctant nod.

"All right. A hundred men should be enough anyway."

They spent the rest of the day discussing the details and working out timings, then Gabrain called his war band together and set off for the coast. As part of their equipment, he made sure that each man carried an axe along with enough food for three days, their weapons and, most importantly, their boats. These small, lightweight vessels were constructed from wooden frames covered by treated animal hides to make them waterproof. The smaller coracles and curraghs were light enough to be easily carried by two men, and even the larger ones could be transported overland without much difficulty by fastening them to pack horses.

Evading Roman cavalry patrols was the most challenging part of the journey, but Gabrain and his men were experienced fighters now, accustomed to avoiding being caught in the open and keeping well below the skyline. Following little known paths and travelling late in the day, they were able to use the cover of darkness to mask the final part of their journey, reaching the northern bank of the Tava three hours after sunset.

They squelched their way across the marshy ground and clambered aboard their flotilla of small boats. The river was almost two hundred paces wide here, just beginning to open out into the broad estuary, but the water was ebbing slightly away as a low tide revealed stretches of mud and rock beyond the grassy bank. It was not an ideal place to cross, but moving further downstream would have meant that the watchtower on the northern shore would have had a clear view of their crossing.

The boats pushed off, paddles were thrust into the water, and men began to row energetically, driving the bobbing vessels to the other side, using the faint reflections of the waxing moon to guide their way.

Gabrain felt unusually anxious, remembering another raid he had led across a river which had ended in near disaster. This time, though, the Romans could have no idea where they were going to strike. Still, he was grateful when the curragh he was in crunched ashore, allowing him to step onto solid earth again.

Moving as silently as they could, the warriors dragged their flimsy boats into the cover of a nearby woodland, turning them upside down to provide shelters into which they crawled to snatch a few hours' sleep.

Gabrain smiled to himself. They had accomplished the first part of his plan. In the morning, they would set to work.

Including himself, Gabrain had one hundred and fourteen men. They moved inland, well away from the river, to a large, dense woodland that some of the men who had once lived in this region were familiar with. Here, after posting sentries the way Calgacus had taught him, Gabrain divided the others into working groups who set about gathering wood and cutting down three large trees.

It was exhausting work, but Gabrain kept them at it all morning and well into the afternoon. By then, two of the trees had been transformed into climbing poles, with the outer sections of their branches hacked off to leave stumps which would provide hand and foot holds when the crude ladder was placed against a wall. The other had been fashioned into a rudimentary battering ram. While this work had been going on, the rest of the men had picked up or cut hundreds of long branches, including those chopped from the fallen trees, which they tied together with leather cords, making the bundles as large as possible.

"If you can put your arms around the sticks and make your hands meet, they're not big enough," Gabrain told them, using his own massive reach to demonstrate that some of their efforts needed yet more work.

"Make some more, then we'll rest up for a while and have some food," he ordered.

The day was dull and overcast, a good day for such strenuous work, but they still had a long way to travel. They would need to carry their heavy creations with them, but there was no help for that. They could not have cut the timber close to the village or the Roman fort for fear of discovery, so they were faced with a long, tiring march through the night.

This was the part of the plan which had occupied much discussion with Calgacus. A long march across country, weighed down by their storming implements, was not good preparation for an immediate attack on the fort. The alternative, though, was to find another place to conceal all the men for an entire day within easy reach of the enemy and, moreover, in close proximity to the village. Shepherd boys or farmers might stumble across them, dogs might smell them out, or simple bad luck might reveal their presence to the Romans.

"It's too risky," Gabrain had insisted. "We'll make the long march and attack just before dawn. The lads will be tired, but the prospect of a fight will soon give them energy."

Calgacus had been concerned, but Gabrain had assured him that he would make the plan work. Now all he had to do was prove it.

They set off while the sun was sinking below the horizon, although the day remained so dull that it was difficult to gauge exactly where the sun was. The layer of clouds also concealed the moon and made the night darker than Gabrain would have preferred. Knowing they could not afford to become lost, he sent out the local men to guide them on their way.

Slipping and stumbling under the bulky, heavy burdens, they slowly trudged eastwards, following a course running roughly parallel to the great river estuary.

The march seemed to take forever. Gabrain reckoned it was well past midnight before word filtered back that they were close to their target. They had wandered slightly off course in the darkness, but had come near to the fort on its southern side.

"That's good," Gabrain assured his men. "They won't expect an attack from that direction. All right. Rest for a while, then we'll go at them just before dawn."

He crept to a low rise, little more than a slight undulation in the ground, and peered cautiously towards the fort. It was further away than he had hoped, perhaps eight hundred paces, its location marked by the tiny, dancing flames of the burning torches at its southern gate. Worse, there was nothing except open ground between him and the fort.

"Let's hope their sentries are sleeping," he muttered to himself, knowing it was unlikely.

The fort was a small thing, little more than twenty paces square, with a solitary wooden building at its centre, a high perimeter wall of earth topped with pointed, wooden stakes and surrounded by a double ditch. There were only two gates, to north and south, each entrance blocked by double doors of thick oak. There were no more than fifteen men inside, he knew, so his much larger force should be capable of storming the place, but taking Roman forts was never easy, even small outposts like this one. They were always sited in such a way as to offer excellent views of the surrounding countryside, and their deep ditches and high walls were designed to provide maximum protection for the garrison. A small group of determined men could hold off many times their number from such a fort.

A few of Gabrain's men remained awake, but most lay down to snatch a few moments of uncomfortable sleep, wrapped in their thick cloaks against the chill of the night.

Gabrain was pleased at their calmness. Most of these warriors had fought in much larger engagements than the one facing them now, and he had chosen them for their ferocity and love of combat. However tough it might be to storm this small outpost of the Empire, Gabrain knew his warriors would not fail due to lack of effort.

Gabrain could not sleep. He sat hunched against the growing chill, wishing dawn would come soon. Inadvertently, he started when a fox called out somewhere in the darkness nearby, the sound reminiscent of a woman screaming for help.

Gabrain swore under his breath, hoping nobody had witnessed his reaction. The last thing he could afford to do was appear anxious about their chances of success. Wrapping his cloak more tightly around his shoulders, he settled down again.

Overhead, the clouds which had cast their veil across the sky all day began to dissipate, allowing the moon and stars to blaze down on the slumbering war band. Gabrain cursed the change, for the additional light would make it easier for the Roman sentries to spot their approach. The weather gods, though, held a surprise for him. The temperature dropped as the clouds reluctantly gave way to clearer skies, and a mist began to rise, soft and gentle at first, then damp and clinging. Soon, it had reduced visibility to less than a hundred paces and masked the sky as effectively as the clouds had done.

Uncertain as to how near dawn might be, Gabrain began to kick and nudge his warriors awake, telling them to prepare. Some grumbled when they saw the mist, but most realised that it would prove more of a help than a hindrance.

"Borrum, God of the Winds, has blown away the clouds and sent us this protective mist," Gabrain told them. "The Romans will not see us coming."

Quietly, they readied themselves, picking up spears and swords, testing the points and edges on their thumbs. Then, at a word of command from Gabrain, they gathered up their bulky bundles of sticks, their ladders and the large battering ram.

The problem now was to make sure they did not miss the fort. The last thing Gabrain wanted was to walk past it in the mist. He spread his men out in a ragged line, keeping the ram at the centre, then waved them forwards.

The sky was already lightening, a mere hint of brightness away to his right, just visible through the mist like a lantern held behind a veil. He clucked his tongue and urged his men onwards, passing his commands in hoarse whispers.

The mist seemed to amplify the sound of their tramping footsteps and the swishing of the long grass as they walked. Gabrain thought they were making far too much noise, but was more concerned that they had not reached the fort yet. It felt as if they had covered more than twice the distance, and still he could not see it.

Then a brief flicker of sputtering flame caught his eye and a dark shape loomed out of the mist some hundred paces ahead of him. Sword in hand, he continued his steady advance.

Moments later came the warning shout as one of the Roman sentries noticed them.

"Run!" Gabrain yelled, pointing with his sword.

Instantly, the entire war band broke into a run, most of them managing little more than a fast jog due to the heavy, awkward burdens they carried, but they did not have far to go and, almost before Gabrain realised it, they had reached the south gate, a wide pathway providing a route across the ditches.

He could hear shouts and cries of alarm from inside. A javelin lanced down, missing him by an arm's length and thudding into the ground where it stood, quivering for an instant before being knocked flat by the men carrying the battering ram as they charged towards the wooden doors that barred the entrance to the fort.

"Break down the gates!" Gabrain screamed unnecessarily as the dozen men heaved the long, heavy tree trunk forwards.

Theirs was a dangerous task, for the gates were the weakest point in the fort's defences and therefore the place the Romans would send most of their troops. To counter that, the rest of Gabrain's warriors hurled their bundles of sticks into the first ditch and jumped down onto them before scrambling up the embankment to the second ditch. This had been Calgacus' idea, a way to cross the deep ditches without being impaled on the sharpened stakes that lined the foot or becoming stuck in the filth and slime that filled the bottom of the trenches. The crude bundles filled the ditch like stepping stones, allowing the men to scramble over them and reach the wall of the fort. It was slow, difficult work because the ditches were broad and deep. Even with their fascines of bundled wood, the warriors still faced a drop into the dark trench and a steep climb up the other side. More than one man slipped or stumbled and fell into the trench where he struggled to escape. Most, though, leaped or even crawled across, passing yet more bundles of wood to be hurled into the second ditch.

Beside Gabrain, the battering ram struck the double doors of the gateway with a dull, reverberating thump. The thick oak timbers withstood the blow with little more than a slight tremor, but the warriors dragged themselves back, then heaved again, smashing the tip of the heavy tree directly onto the gap between the two doors.

Javelins came down, felling one man and wounding another, but there were only a handful of Romans on the ramparts beside the gates because whoever was in command had seen the warriors crossing the ditches and had sent defenders to oppose them. Other Romans, Gabrain knew, would be manning the walls on the other side of the fort in case a second attack came from that direction. Which meant that his hundred warriors faced only around eight or ten men at most.

The first of the makeshift ladders, hauled over the ditches by relays of warriors, was at the walls now, and men were scrambling up the precarious ascent. The leading climber fell back, screaming, as soon as he reached the top, his face ruined by a vicious thrust from a sword, but others followed, and the second ladder was slammed against the wooden ramparts.

Still the battering ram hammered on the doors. Gabrain sheathed his useless sword and grabbed for one of the short stumps that provided a grip. Wrapping one arm under the tree, he joined his warriors in the next surge.

"Go!" he yelled, and the ram smashed into the doors again.

This time there was a visible gap as the doors were forced back, and he heard the creaking protest of timber under stress.

"Again!"

He drove all his massive strength into the blow, and the ram thundered into the double gateway, smashing the locking bar which held the doors shut and flinging both gates aside.

"Go!" Gabrain yelled. "Kill them!"

The ram was dropped and he was forced to leap nimbly aside to prevent his foot being crushed by its dead weight as it thudded to the ground. He clawed for his sword, rasping it free of its scabbard, then he chased after the leading men who were already storming through the open gates.

The first men died, met by four Romans who held a line with large shields and short, stabbing swords. They were, though, outnumbered and easily outflanked as Gabrain's men swarmed around them. The Roman line soon disintegrated into four individual soldiers who were quickly surrounded and hauled or battered to the ground by screaming, battle-crazed tribesmen.

It was the same story on the walls. The Romans had put up a good defence, but there were simply too few of them to hold back the assault. Gabrain's warriors, many of them bare-chested, their torsos decorated by dark tattoos of powerful animals, howled and laughed as they surged over the palisade and hunted down their enemies.

"To me!" Gabrain yelled, furious that his own sword was as yet unbloodied.

His men ran to him, their faces alive with excitement and the lust for blood.

"Let's find the rest of them!" he shouted.

The Romans who had manned the far wall had gathered in a knot of six men in the lee of the northern gate. They stood nervously determined, their shields presenting a wall of painted wood and studded iron, their swords jutting from the gaps between the metal-rimmed shields. This time, there was no way to surround them because the protruding buttresses of the gateway protected them on both flanks.

Gabrain, though, had more than twenty men with him, and other warriors were running round the ramparts or jumping down to scour the fort of any defenders. Some men smashed their way into the central building, a long wooden-framed hut of white-plastered wattle and daub with a thatched roof.

Gabrain ignored them. If there were any Romans inside the building, they had nowhere to run. His attention was on the defenders at the gate.

He did not need to issue any orders. He simply pointed with his sword, and his men charged alongside him.

Howling their war cries, they smashed into the Roman line, battling with one another in their eagerness to reach the foe. The Roman swords jabbed, men screamed, swore, grunted and yelled as they battled furiously.

Gabrain used his massive reach and his bulk to drive back the man facing him, swiping his sword high to make the soldier duck, then crashing his shoulder into the man's shield.

It was a dangerous tactic. The Roman could have stabbed him, but the man was knocked off balance so that his attack missed Gabrain's unprotected body. The Roman staggered, stumbled back, and Gabrain fell on top of him as both of them tumbled to the earth.

He landed on top of the man's shield, pinning it between them. The Roman's helmet caught him a nasty blow on the forehead, but he used his left arm to reach up, grab the man's face and smash his head back against the earth in a succession of hammer blows.

He could feel and hear fighting all around him. Someone stamped on his leg, another man tripped over him, catching him a blow on the side as he fell, and the soldier beneath him was punching his left side as he struggled to shove Gabrain off. If the Roman had not dropped his short sword, Gabrain would have been dead.

They sprawled and wrestled for several long moments while screams and shouts surrounded them. At last, Gabrain's repeated thumping of the man's head against the hard ground had an effect, and the Roman ceased struggling.

Fumbling for his own sword, Gabrain pushed himself up.

The fight was over, the Romans dead. Seven of his own men lay on the ground, three of them dead, the others nursing wounds.

"Are there any more?" he called, looking in all directions for signs of a threat.

"They're all dead," came the response.

His surviving warriors were already hacking at heads to take back as trophies of their victory. Gabrain let them argue over who had killed which Roman. He did not care. They had done what few men had done, and he felt elated despite the aches and pains from his protesting head and body.

The Roman he had grappled with was quickly despatched by a man wielding a long dagger.

"His head is mine," Gabrain told the warrior with the knife.

The man grinned, nodded, yanked off the dead soldier's helmet and began the grisly process of hacking off the Roman's head.

Gabrain left him to it. Striding to the centre of the fort, he bellowed for everyone to gather. As the warriors came to him, he counted them. Of the one hundred and thirteen men who had begun the assault with him, eighty-seven answered his summons. Several of them bore wounds which they were attempting to bind with ragged strips of cloth hacked from the clothing of the dead. The success had come at a price, but Gabrain had always known their task would not be easy.

"Gather all the supplies you can find," he told them. "Bring food, blankets and weapons. Cooking pots and lamps if you can, but don't weigh yourselves down too much."

Jabbing a finger at one man, he ordered, "Run to the village and tell them we have wounded men here. Any who can't walk will need to be taken there and tended as best the villagers can manage."

Nodding, the man hurried off, mouthing a prayer of thanks to the War God, Belatucadros, that he was not among the wounded. Even being taken to the village was no guarantee of safety. There was a good chance that the Romans would search every home and kill any wounded warrior they found.

Gabrain fretted over the delays. While some men raided the fort's small store of food, others searched the fallen and gathered the badly wounded Venicones together outside the fort. Gabrain went to talk to these men, not because he wanted to, but because he had seen Calgacus do this, and he knew that the men respected a leader who cared for his injured comrades.

There were twelve badly wounded men. Several of whom were beyond saving because their bellies had been ripped apart by the vicious blades of the Roman short swords. These men would die slowly and painfully, and they knew it, but still they gritted their teeth against the pain and tried to smile when Gabrain spoke to them, assuring them of a place of glory in the Underworld.

One man had broken both legs when he had fallen from the ramparts, another was bleeding to death from a savage wound in his neck. Gabrain steeled himself to speak to each man before returning to the fort to check on the warriors who remained fit.

The mood here was more to his liking, the men laughing and joking with one another as they gathered bundles of plunder and searched the dead Romans for any valuables.

The sun was up and burning away the mist by the time a handful of nervous villagers arrived. Most of them were elderly men or young boys, but a couple of women had also come to see what had taken place during the raid. All of them looked appalled when they saw the devastation of the fort and the headless corpses that lay strewn all over the wrecked camp. Their fear increased when Gabrain told them he wanted them to care for the wounded who were unable to walk.

"Hide them in the woods if you must," Gabrain told the villagers. "But they are your fellow tribesmen and they deserve your protection."

The villagers looked uncertain, clearly in two minds about the consequences of aiding the raiders.

"What about this place?" asked one of them, an old, grey-haired man who walked with the aid of a carved stick.

"We are going to burn it," Gabrain told him.

Gazing at Gabrain with rheumy eyes, the old man said, "The Romans will take revenge on us for this."

"Why should they?" Gabrain countered. "Tell them it was Calgacus who came here. They will believe that."

"But if they find the wounded men ..."

"Make sure they do not!" snapped Gabrain.

The old man gave a surly nod which led Gabrain to suspect the villagers might well slit the throats of the wounded men as soon as he had gone. There was, though, nothing he could do to alter their fate. Two more had already died and were being carried into the fort's barracks hut where they were placed alongside the other dead Venicones.

"I want horses," Gabrain told the old man.

The village elder's eyes widened in surprise.

"Horses?"

"You know. Animals with four legs, manes and tails. You ride them."

The old man bit back a retort, knowing he was addressing his King. He simply replied, "We have no horses. The Romans took them all."

For a moment, Gabrain stared at the man with a disbelieving expression. His eyes scanned the other villagers who merely nodded mute agreement.

"You have no horses at all?" he queried, feeling his plans begin to unravel.

"We have two mules," the elder told him. "Would they serve?"

Gabrain's mind was racing, forming and discarding ideas in a torrent of frustration, but he shook his head, attempting to disguise his confusion. It would not do to let these peasants see him being anything other than confident. Still, the lack of horses was a bitter blow. Part of his plan had involved sending riders to neighbouring settlements to call for men to join his war band. Without horses, though, the chances of rallying support were non-existent.

"It doesn't matter," he muttered. "But I want you to tell every able-bodied man in your village to find a weapon and join us."

The elder gave him another bemused look. Gesturing to the others who had accompanied him, he said, "These are all the able-bodied men we have."

Gabrain blinked as he surveyed the small group of grey-haired, stoop-shouldered men and beardless young boys.

The old villager continued in a reproving tone, "Our young men went to join your war host earlier this year. None have returned."

Gabrain felt his temper fraying. He recalled that, when he had tried to find men among his war band who knew this area, only a handful of them had any knowledge of the surrounding locality, and only one had actually come from this village. That man's corpse was now lying in the barrack block. He had assumed that the lack of men from this region was because many of them had returned to their homes. Now, this grey-haired cripple was trying to tell him that was not true.

Gabrain thrust a furious finger at the man's face.

"We are fighting to protect you!" he shouted angrily. "The least you can do is help us."

"And will you help us when the Romans come back here?" the old man shot back, unbowed in the face of Gabrain's temper. "Or are you going to stay here and fight them all?"

The prospect of seizing the fort and using it as a rallying point for local tribesmen to join had briefly crossed Gabrain's mind, but he had dismissed the idea because he knew the folly of attempting to defend a fixed position against the Roman army. The small fortlet had not been able to withstand his assault with a crude battering ram, so he could never hope to hold out against ballistas and catapults.

His reason for abandoning the fort were sound, but the elder's accusation stung him, rousing his anger even further.

He moved close to the villager, thrusting his face forwards as he rasped, "One day, the Romans will be gone. When that day comes, I will remember who has helped me and who has not."

The man stared back, unblinking and uncowed, his silence as eloquent as any words. It was evident that he did not believe the Romans would ever leave.

Gabrain snorted angrily, turning his back on the villager.

"Time to go!" he shouted, waving his arms in signal.

Hurriedly, his warriors poured oil from the Romans' store over the building, splashing yet more of the liquid onto the gates and as much of the wooden upper rampart as they could.

"Set it alight," Gabrain ordered as most of his men trooped out, carrying away all the food and weapons they could find.

The village elder looked at him quizzically.

"A fire will bring the Romans here more quickly," the old man observed.

"I know," Gabrain replied. "That is what I want. Now, take the wounded and hide them as best you can."

The old man frowned, but did not argue. His villagers had already brought small carts onto which they had loaded the severely injured warriors. Now, he turned and hobbled after them, not looking back.

"I will remember you," Gabrain promised under his breath as he watched the old man go.

Then it was time for him to leave. As the first flames leaped up, hungrily devouring the oil and setting their fury to the wood and plaster, he strode through the gates and led his men away to the north.

His mood was bitter and angry. He had held such great plans for this raid, but those dreams were now in tatters. He had hoped to gather men to join him, had expected to send messengers riding all across the region to rouse the local population, but now he was left with fewer than ninety men, and every one of them was on foot. He knew they should return to the river and locate their boats so that they could cross back to the northern bank as soon as night fell, but his pride would not let him do that. He had not come here simply in order to burn one small fortlet. His men seemed happy enough with what they had accomplished so far, but Gabrain wanted more.

He halted their march as soon as they were out of sight of the village and the burning fort. Behind them, only a dark column of smoke denoted the place they had left.

He quickly divided the men into two groups. The first, fifteen of them including the wounded who could walk, were given the task of transporting the bulk of the booty back to the place where they had hidden their boats.

"Wait there," Gabrain told them. "If we are not back by tomorrow evening, go back and tell Calgacus what has happened."

The men looked puzzled, some of them exchanging frowns.

One asked, "What are you going to do?"

Gabrain shot him a savage grin. Leadership, he knew, was about making decisions. Now he revealed the decision he had made before the raid had begun and which he had concealed from Calgacus. His plan may not have worked out as well as he had hoped, but that was no reason to abandon it entirely.

"We are going to kill some more Romans," he informed his bemused warriors. "One little fort is not enough glory for the Venicones. We are going to do a lot more damage than that."

Chapter XIX

The camp was alive with the usual bustle, the sounds of sawing and hammering having begun as soon as the morning meal of porridge and dark bread was finished. Macrinus, after making a brief inspection of the work his auxiliary troops were carrying out, and visiting the infirmary to check on the men whose ailments left them unfit for duty, made his way to the Governor's tent.

Even as he reached the entrance, he knew that something unusual was happening. Men were scurrying urgently in and out of the large tent which served as the temporary Principia, their faces set in serious expressions. In moments, the horns were sounding, calling the men to arms.

Macrinus pushed through, heading for the inner sanctum where he found Agricola and Piso standing over a map which was spread on the Governor's table, while Flaccus, wearing a richly embroidered cloak over his purple-striped tunic, stood to one side, his hands clasped behind his back, his eyes studying the two officers as if waiting to pounce on any slip they might make.

Macrinus did his best to ignore the man but the Assistant Procurator's presence unsettled him.

Agricola looked up as Macrinus gave him a hurried salute.

"Ah, there you are, Macrinus. Have you heard the reports?"

"No, Sir. What is happening?"

The Governor's eye held a gleam of excitement as if the prospect of danger had momentarily lifted the burdens of command and the added pressure of Flaccus' presence.

Tapping the map, he explained, "The barbarians are attacking one of our forts at the mouth of the nearest valley. The garrison spotted them and sent a signal by flag."

Macrinus frowned. The outlying forts were manned by his auxiliary troops, and his initial reaction was one of concern for their safety. He glanced at the map. The fort in question was several miles away, but a chain of signal stations had been set up so that messages could be quickly relayed back to the Governor's Headquarters.

"How many?" he asked.

"We are not sure. The message claimed the fort is in danger, which suggests a large number of attackers."

Macrinus nodded, scratching pensively at his cheek. He knew that the messages, transmitted by large, brightly coloured flags, could provide only very limited information.

"Fabianus is not a man given to unnecessary panic," he observed, referring to the commander of the fort in question. "Which means it could be a major attack."

"I agree," Agricola nodded. "However, another message came in from the south-east. One of our signal stations reports a possible attack on a small fort further to the east. They have sighted smoke."

Agricola tapped the map again, indicating a spot on the southern side of the Tava estuary.

"We think it could be this one. The officer at the signal station has sent out a cavalry patrol to investigate."

"It could be nothing," Piso offered, clearly repeating an argument he had already made to the Governor. "Farmers burning stubble. A native house on fire because someone was clumsy with a candle."

"Or it could be the fort," Agricola shrugged. "If it is, we have two separate attacks to contend with."

"One is probably a feint," Macrinus declared.

Agricola smiled as he nodded, "Yes, but which one?"

Stabbing a finger on the map at the location of the smaller fort, Piso asked, "Why would the barbarians attack that place? There is nothing there of strategic importance. Only a scattering of villages and farms."

"It's a small fort," Macrinus replied. "Which makes it vulnerable. The rebels might have gone for an easy target where they could snatch some supplies."

"Or it might be more serious than that," Agricola countered. Placing a finger on the map, he went on, "If the barbarians have managed to send a sizeable force across the river, the first thing they would need to do is destroy that fort to prevent word of their arrival from being sent to us."

"Then why burn it?" Piso argued. "That gives the game away."

"As you say, someone might have been careless with a candle. But it could also be the first sign of a general uprising. Perhaps the assault from the north is merely intended to draw our attention away from the real threat."

Macrinus rubbed at his stubbled chin.

"Yes," he agreed. "That is the sort of thing Calgacus might try. If he can gather a large enough force there, we would be caught between two barbarian armies and could find ourselves cut off from the south."

"Then we must deal with that one first?" Piso asked with a frown.

Agricola shook his head.

"We do not have enough information. Crossing the river with a large war band would be a bold move, but we know Calgacus is both bold and unpredictable. However, it is a long way from here, and we face what could be a major attack much closer to home. On balance, I think you are correct, Piso. This southern fire is either nothing to worry about, or it is designed to draw troops away from facing the main attack."

"So we ignore it?" the Legate asked.

"I can't afford to do that either," Agricola replied. "But the main threat is the attack from the hills on our northern fort. I want you to take three cohorts and half the auxiliary cavalry to reinforce the fort and drive off the attack."

Piso nodded, "It will be a pleasure."

Agricola held up a cautionary hand.

"Don't go chasing the barbarians into the hills. You know how Calgacus loves to draw us into traps. All you need to do is drive them off and make sure the fort is safe."

"I will see to it," Piso promised.

Agricola looked at Macrinus.

"I'd like you to take the rest of your cavalry and check that fire to the south-east. It's a long ride, I'm afraid, and it may be a wasted journey, but a reconnaissance in strength won't do any harm. I'd like you to impress the locals with a show of power. And if it does turn out to be a genuine revolt, send me word as soon as you can. Above all, though, don't go riding into a trap."

"With respect, Sir," Macrinus complained, "I would prefer to join Hordonius Piso in relieving the northern fort which we know is definitely under attack. The men there are under my command."

Agricola shot him a stern look as he answered, "No, Macrinus. Piso and his legionaries can deal with whatever needs doing there. But I need a fast moving unit of cavalry to check on what is happening to our rear, and I want you to command it. Is that clear?"

"Yes, Sir."

"Good. I'll order a couple of war galleys to patrol the river in case the barbarians really are moving men south."

He looked at each of them in turn, his expression calm but determined.

"Thank you, gentlemen. Please move out as soon as you can. Oh, and if you can capture a few rebels, bring them back here. We can crucify them outside our walls. That ought to send a message to Calgacus."

Macrinus rode at the head of one hundred and sixty heavily armed horsemen. Some of them wore chainmail armour, while others sported breastplates on their chests and greaves on their legs. All of them wore iron helmets and carried brightly painted oval shields, long lances and straight-bladed, heavy swords. The sound of their passing was like a distant thunderstorm, a reverberating rumble caused by the drumming of hundreds of hooves, the jangling of harnesses and the clanking of metal.

They headed south at a brisk canter, setting a pace the horses could maintain for a long time before needing a rest. By alternating this with periods of slower trotting or walking, Macrinus knew his troop could cover the distance more quickly and effectively than if they set off at a gallop. There was no point in dashing into what might be a war zone only to arrive with the mounts exhausted and unable to carry the men into a fight.

The early morning mist had cleared, leaving a crisp, bright, cloudless day with a yellowing sun crawling in a low arc across the blue backdrop. Its light reflected from every bright surface, dazzling the riders and making Macrinus squint through half-closed eyes as he rode.

Despite his concern for the men in the besieged fort, he felt relieved to be away from the camp and with his own command again, even if the number of troops he led was relatively small. Soldiering was what he was good at, not the political intrigue Flaccus had brought with him.

There were stratagems in warfare, too, but Macrinus understood these. The more he considered the news of the twin attacks, the more he came to suspect that there was more to this fire he had been sent to investigate than Piso had guessed. The attack on the northern fort might appear serious, but was it really the main danger? Calgacus had little to gain except prestige from the destruction of one fort. A major assault would have involved attacks on all parts of the chain of defences the Governor was constructing. The more Macrinus thought about it, the more he suspected the attack from the hills was a mere diversion and this alleged raid to the south-east could well be something more than a simple house fire.

Or perhaps that was merely wishful thinking, simple justification for an excuse to spend time away from the machinations of Flaccus.

Macrinus recalled how the Assistant Procurator had been unusually quiet during the discussion about how to deal with the latest situation. The man had remained uncharacteristically silent throughout the briefing, contributing nothing at all. In some ways, that had been more disconcerting than his normal habit of interfering in military matters.

It had seemed to Macrinus that Flaccus had been smiling, as if amused at some private joke known only to himself.

Perhaps, Macrinus thought glumly, Flaccus was merely taking satisfaction from watching Agricola struggle with the difficulties of the campaign when he knew that the Governor's fate had already been decided by his letter to the Emperor.

If that were the case, Macrinus told himself, Flaccus' self-congratulatory gloating was premature. There was no way he could have received a reply from Rome so soon. Yet he was, in Macrinus' opinion, up to something, and that something would probably be unpleasant.

Macrinus shook his head and tried to dispel all thought of the Assistant Procurator. He had a task to carry out, and it required his full attention. If Calgacus was setting a trap, he could not afford to blunder into it through lack of concentration.

He led his long column of riders towards some high, towering hills which formed a barrier south of the river. One of these was crowned by an ancient hillfort, a ring of earth and heavy stones surrounding the home of some long-dead chieftain. The Governor had evicted the few barbarians who still clung to their homes on this hilltop refuge, and had placed a signal station and watchtower on the summit. It was this station that had sent the warning message about possible trouble to the east.

Macrinus left most of his men at the foot of the hill, ordering them to rest while he led a small party, including the troop's standard-bearer, up to the watchtower.

When he reached the top of the hill after a long, slow climb, an Optio of auxiliaries met him with a concerned expression on his young face.

"It's good to see you, Sir. The lads are growing worried."

"What's going on?" Macrinus asked as he swung down from the saddle to stretch his legs and back.

"We saw a column of smoke at first light," the Optio explained, pointing eastwards, along the southern bank of the Tava which stretched into the distance on Macrinus' left, broadening out as it flowed towards the sea, dividing the land in two.

He followed the direction of the Optio's finger, seeking signs of trouble. From this high vantage point, he could see for miles, the land laid out beneath him like one of the Governor's maps, except that the greens and browns were vivid under the sun's glare, and the hills and forests rose like bumps formed by some giant lying beneath a spread blanket.

He could make out the occasional farmstead and a cluster of roundhouses forming a tiny village near a stream which meandered through the lowlands on its way to join the Tava. He could see the fields and meadows, the wild grasslands and the vast expanse of woodland which covered much of the terrain.

And there, perhaps twenty miles distant, rising from behind a wide expanse of trees, was a faint smudge of dirty brown smoke that could only have come from a large fire.

"I sent out a small patrol," the Optio explained. "Only four men." He looked sheepish as he added, "They have not come back. I only have a small garrison here and no more horses, so I couldn't send anyone out to look for them."

"Probably just as well," Macrinus told him. "How many men do you have here now?"

"Seven, including me."

Macrinus gave the young man a wry smile as he said, "Don't worry. From up here you can see anyone coming to attack you. If they come this way, pack up and clear out as quickly as you can."

"Yes, Sir," the Optio frowned, clearly not relishing the prospect of trying to march all the way to the Governor's half-built fortress while being pursued by a band of bloodthirsty savages.

"You think there is trouble coming?" the Optio asked nervously.

"The fact that your patrol has not returned is worrying," Macrinus admitted. Then he shot the young man a confident smile as he told him, "Don't worry. We'll go and check it out. It's probably just a minor raid. If it was anything larger, you'd have seen more signs by now."

"Yes, Sir," the Optio answered dutifully, although the look in his eyes suggested he did not fully believe Macrinus' assertion.

Leaving the nervous Optio and his tiny garrison, they rode eastwards. This time, though, Macrinus prepared for trouble. Instead of riding in a long column four abreast, he split the formation into three long lines of around fifty horsemen each, with fifty paces between each rank. This way, if trouble threatened, at least two-thirds of his men should be able to avoid it because, unless there were several hundred raiders marauding across the river, there was no way they could attack all his men simultaneously.

Spread out as they were, they rode steadily on, keeping well clear of woodlands wherever possible even if that meant they were forced to trample through village fields and meadows. The crops had been gathered by now, the fields left only with standing stubble which the cattle would feed on over the winter, so their passing caused little actual damage although many of the villagers and farmers fled when they saw the riders coming. Macrinus could not blame them. Most of them would have seen the pillar of smoke and known that it foretold trouble. The sight of so many Romans riding across their land must have terrified them.

As for the smoke itself, it had largely dissipated into ethereal mist, leaving barely a trace of its origin. Macrinus, though, was reasonably confident that he would find the location of the fort. All they needed to do was keep riding eastwards, staying clear of the patches of forest that dotted the land. All Roman forts were sited in clear ground, with excellent views of the surrounding countryside. By sticking to open ground, they would find it before too long.

The route they needed to follow took them past yet another wide expanse of trees on their left, the beginnings of a forest which covered much of the terrain south of the Tava. The world they were passing through was one of browns and greens. A few of the trees were showing the first signs of turning to autumnal colours, but most retained their full, verdant foliage. Against this drab backcloth, a flash of red stood out from a considerable distance. Macrinus saw it as soon as he crested a low hummock and entered a wide, grassy bowl that was bordered on its northern side by the forbidding trees. He held up a hand, calling for the pace to slow while he studied this unexpected sight.

It took only a moment for his eyes to make out the shapes of four horses tethered at the edge of the woodland. Brown coated, wearing polished leather saddles, they were difficult to make out against the trees, but the bright red of their saddlecloths stood out like beacons.

He drew his troop to a halt while he scanned the surrounding terrain. There was nothing except the stillness of the grass, the shallow depression of the arena-like bowl and the wall of trees to his left, around two hundred paces away.

And four horses.

Four tethered, anxious horses. Their ears were pricked up, their limited movements agitated. They had clearly sensed the arrival of their stable-mates, but they were unable to break free of their tethers.

"That," Macrinus announced to his men, "looks like a trap."

He did not delay his next move. Hesitation, he had learned long before, could be fatal in hostile territory. Holding up his right arm, he gave a signal and led his men off to the right, climbing out of the dip in the land and heading away from the trees. He half expected to find a small army of barbarians concealed beyond the rising ground, but there was nothing except more grass, more low hills and yet more stretches of woodland.

He reined in again once his entire troop had moved beyond the ridge and out of sight of the trees. Then he signalled to one of his Centurions who nudged his horse to stand next to Macrinus.

The Centurion was named Sdapezi, a man from the eastern provinces who had joined Macrinus' unit only a few months earlier. He was an experienced man, quiet and softly spoken, and he was not what Macrinus would describe as a charismatic or inspiring leader. He was, though, a good horseman, thorough, conscientious and, above all, reliable.

"I want you to stay here with one *turma*," Macrinus told him. "Go back and sit up on the rim of that dip so that the barbarians in the trees can see you. Let them know we know they are there, but don't engage in combat. They might attempt to lure you down by sending out a small group of men. Resist the temptation."

Sdapezi gave a curt nod.

"Where will you be?" he asked.

"I am heading on to the fort to see what happened there. I'm also going to visit the local villagers. If the barbarians in the forest make a move, send word to me. Keep trailing them, but don't get too close."

Macrinus was pleased that Sdapezi did not question how he knew there were barbarians hiding in the woods. Four Roman cavalrymen would not leave their horses unattended but, although the Centurion understood this, he did have one question.

"What do we do if they have kept those four alive? They might bring them out and begin torturing them to mock us."

"They might," Macrinus agreed. "But the only reason they would do that is to tempt you into going down there. You are not to do that under any circumstances."

"Let's hope they killed the poor buggers quickly," Sdapezi observed with the dry lack of emotion old soldiers reserved for such occasions.

"I'd like to go down there and find out," Macrinus admitted. "But we don't know how many rebels there are and, even though I'm no woodsman, I can tell those trees aren't pines. There will be lots of tangled undergrowth in there, and we can't operate on horseback in that sort of terrain. If we had a cohort of infantry, I'd send them in, but our lads aren't used to fighting on foot, so it's too risky until we know a bit more."

The Centurion surprised him by saying, "I agree. The trees, by the way, are mostly oak, ash, lime and hazel. I think there are holly and rowan as well. Moving among that lot is not easy."

"Then we'll need to find a way to flush them out," Macrinus said. "In the meantime, stay here and stay safe."

Leaving the Centurion and thirty men to watch for the raiders, Macrinus led the bulk of his force onwards, reaching the smouldering remains of the ruined fort half an hour later.

Cautiously, he split his force again, sending two groups in wide sweeps of the surrounding countryside and encircling the fort before he dismounted and approached the wrecked ramparts.

With half a dozen men acting as guards, he walked towards the smashed gates, noting the abandoned battering ram and the bundles of sticks the raiders had cast into the ditches, along with fallen climbing poles which had toppled away from the wooden palisade when it had crumbled under the devouring flames. Some sections of the wooden wall still stood, the wood too weather-worn and damp to catch fire properly, but great swathes of it had burned down to nothing more than charred stumps protruding from the top of the earth rampart like blackened, rotting teeth.

Inside, the devastation was even greater. A black and grey mass of ashes and burned timbers was all that remained of the barracks building. There were other charred lumps among the debris which he recognised as burnt corpses, the distinctive smell of cremated flesh still hanging in the calm air.

There was no sign of human activity, but there were some other living creatures within the confines of the earth walls. As the men moved into the fort, dozens of crows squawked their protest and rose in a barrage of beating wings from their interrupted feeding.

"Mithras!" whispered one of the soldiers when they saw what the carrion birds had been pecking at.

"They've taken all the heads!" exclaimed another when he stepped closer to the nearest bodies which were obviously those of the Roman garrison, abandoned where they had fallen, and stripped of their armour and valuables.

"It's what the Britons do," Macrinus replied, swallowing hard and gritting his teeth to prevent his own bile rising. "Come on, we've seen enough here."

Hurrying back to their horses, they headed for the nearby settlement. Macrinus' anger had brewed to a simmering resentment by the time he reached the village. His men spread out in a long arc, cordoning off the widely spaced houses. Lances ready and faces grim, the men were keen to exact revenge on whoever had massacred the fort's garrison.

Macrinus rode to the edge of the village where he stopped and bellowed in the local language, "I want to speak to the head man. Now!"

He had to shout a second time before a small gaggle of villagers were brave enough to peer out at him from the spurious shelter of their doorways. Eventually, an elderly man appeared, hobbling slowly towards him with the aid of a knobbled length of wood with a rounded handle. Macrinus waited patiently until the man limped to within five paces.

"What happened at the fort?" Macrinus demanded.

The old man gave a shrug.

"Men came. We did not see them coming. They attacked at dawn. The first we knew was when the fort was set alight."

Macrinus guessed the old man was being less than truthful. The raiders would not have ignored the village entirely.

"How many?" he snapped.

Another shrug greeted the question.

"I cannot say."

"More than I have with me?" Macrinus persisted, waving an arm to encompass his watching horsemen.

"Perhaps, yes."

The old man had not even glanced beyond Macrinus before answering. His blinking, watery eyes suggested that he could barely see further than the length of his arm.

"Fewer than I have?" Macrinus demanded.

"Perhaps, yes."

Macrinus leaned forwards in his saddle and fixed the grey-haired Briton with an iron stare. Speaking slowly and clearly, he said, "Listen to me, old man. I want to know how many raiders there were. You are going to tell me. I have already picked up their trail, and I will catch them soon. When I do, I will know whether you have told me the truth. If I find that you have lied, I will come back here and burn down every house in this village. That's if I am in a good mood. If I am angry, I'll either kill or enslave every last one of your people. Do you understand me?"

The Briton's Adam's apple bobbed as he swallowed nervously. He nodded his head.

"Good," grunted Macrinus. "Then tell me how many there were."

"It is difficult to say," the villager replied miserably. "They were moving around, not standing in one place, and I did not see any reason to count them."

"Give me a rough idea," Macrinus growled impatiently. "And do it quickly or I'll start the killing right now."

Looking utterly wretched, the Briton replied, "At least four score. Perhaps more than a hundred. But there may have been others I did not see."

"Let us hope for your sake that you saw them all," Macrinus snorted. "One way or another, I will be back. You can count on that."

So saying, he yanked on his horse's reins and wheeled it round, holding up his arm to summon his troop to follow him.

One question had been answered for him. Unless the village elder was lying, or unless Calgacus had divided his forces, this was only a large raiding party he had to deal with. That made his life simpler and also helped fuel his anger. Including the four men sent to investigate the column of smoke, at least twenty of his Auxiliaries had been killed. That was an act which required a swift and thorough response.

Macrinus had work to do.

Chapter XX

Calgacus lay on his belly, keeping his head low as he watched events in the valley far below. Beside him, Runt swore softly, his voice angry and disappointed.

"They're not falling for it!" he complained.

"They must be learning at last," Calgacus replied with a sigh. "It's only taken them thirty years or so."

He turned, rolling onto his side to look back at the expectant horsemen gathered on the slope behind him. With a shake of his head, he waved an arm, signalling that they would not be taking part in any action.

"It was worth a try," he told Runt as he resumed his observation.

Off to his left, he could see the squat, wooden towers of the Roman fort which lay near the entrance to the glen where it blocked the approach to the open land to the south. It was one of several such fortified camps the Romans had constructed to guard their new frontier, and it was a prime target for Calgacus' rebels.

He had told Gabrain that he would launch a diversionary attack on the fort in order to draw men away from the Venicones' raid. That idea had, though, developed into something more ambitious.

"If we're going to make it look good," he had explained to his friends, "we might as well use the chance to kill a lot more Romans."

Bridei, as usual, had been all for it. The Boresti King had led six hundred warriors in an attack on the fort. In keeping with the plan, his men had made sure that they had been seen approaching so that the garrison had time to send a message for help. Then they had hurled javelins at the walls, rushed at the gates, and even thrown bundles of sticks into the ditches to aid attempts to cross them. Flaming brands had been tossed high to arc over the ramparts, adding to the spectacle, even though they knew the Romans always left a wide open space beyond the walls so that nothing combustible would be set alight. The whirling, sparking torches did no more than cause some momentary alarm, just as the ferocious yells and war cries of the Boresti were designed to terrify the defenders and persuade them that the attack was in earnest.

A handful of warriors had actually managed to traverse the deep, steep-sided ditches and scale the wooden walls. One or two had leaped down inside the fort, but they had not reappeared and Calgacus knew they must have been killed. He had frowned at their over-zealous charge, but their sacrifice must have made the attack seem a genuine threat to the fort.

For a long time, though, Bridei and his men had been able to achieve little more than surround the fort, rattling their swords and spears against their shields in raucous drumbeats, calling insults and flinging javelins. In return, the Romans hurled their own javelins and even threw some large rocks from a small ballista. As the attack turned into a noisy siege, the defenders must have realised that there was little chance of the Britons storming their walls. Even though there were fewer than two hundred men inside the fort, they could easily hold off Bridei's warriors thanks to the formidable defences of their camp. All they needed to do was hold out until help arrived.

That assistance came in the shape of more than a thousand Roman legionaries, the heavy infantry of the Empire's army, supported by nearly two hundred cavalry. They came marching up from the Governor's fortress, giving up a loud shout to help drive off the attackers.

Bridei had been watching for them. He had given the signal to withdraw, and his men had run back up the valley, scattering widely as if in panic, hoping to lure the Romans into pursuit.

That was the trap Calgacus had planned. He had known the enemy would send a relief force, and he had wanted to cut it off in the valley, surround it and annihilate it. He had gathered nearly three thousand horsemen who were concealed beyond the crest of the hills overlooking the fort, waiting for a chance to swoop down and catch the Romans unawares.

But the Romans were not prepared to fall obligingly into his ambush. The relief force halted when it reached the fort, the cavalry venturing only a little further as if to make sure that the Britons really were fleeing.

"Damn them!" Runt muttered. "We lost some good men drawing them out and it's all for nothing."

"Maybe not for nothing," Calgacus remarked thoughtfully.

"What do you mean? They aren't going to come any further, and we can't attack them in the open. They'd cut us to pieces."

"I know that. We can't do anything today, but maybe another day. Look at how many men they sent to drive us off."

Runt looked down again, frowning as he studied the ranks of metal-clad soldiers arrayed beside the fort. They were too far away to distinguish individuals, but there were other means of judging their numbers.

"I'd say three cohorts from the looks of the standards they're carrying," he observed.

"Which means, with all the men they have manning the forts and watchtowers they are setting up, the Governor only has around fifteen hundred or maybe two thousand men at his main fort."

Runt turned, giving his friend a look of alarm.

"You're not thinking of attacking the legionary camp?"

His face fell as he sighed, "By Toutatis, you bloody are, aren't you?"

"It's an idea," Calgacus admitted.

"It's a bloody crazy idea," Runt murmured darkly. "It's a permanent fortress, not a marching camp."

"I know that. We probably wouldn't be able to storm the place, but we could drive all his men inside which would give us a chance to destroy their quarry works and perhaps set fire to any boats docked at the river. We could certainly come away with the cattle they keep in the fields near the fort."

"I've always said you were crazy," Runt grumbled. "What with you, Bridei and Gabrain, I think I'm the only sensible person here."

"You probably are," Calgacus agreed with a wry laugh. "But being sensible will only get us so far. Every now and again, we need to do something bold that the enemy doesn't expect."

"He certainly won't expect you to go walking up to the doors of the largest fortress he's ever built in the entire island," Runt grunted. "It's a daft idea, Cal. You should forget it."

"You can't unthink something once you've thought of it," Calgacus replied. "But we won't rush into it. Let's talk it over with Bridei and Gabrain when they get back."

Runt sighed, "Bridei will do whatever you tell him. The man's as mad as you are. As for Gabrain, he's wild by nature. One of these days, he's going to do something that will land him in trouble. That's if he hasn't done it already."

At that precise moment, Gabrain might have agreed with the sentiment because he was seriously regretting his decision not to cross the river and return to the safety of the hills.

When he had first conceived his idea of crossing into his old territory, he had held dreams of raising a full scale rebellion. Common sense had soon persuaded him that this was an impossible dream, but he had nevertheless retained the idea of using the burning fort as a lure to ambush a Roman relief force.

He had entertained visions of returning to the mountains with a larger war band than he had begun with, and with his warriors laden down with booty. The lack of horses had put paid to that idea, so he had been forced to reconsider his plans. Essentially, though, his intention of ambushing a Roman column remained his principal goal. He might have fewer men at his disposal than he had hoped for, but there were still enough of them to tackle an equal number of Romans.

At first, he had believed that his plan was working because the four Roman horsemen sent to investigate the smoke from the burning fort had ridden straight into his war band, lured by the sight of half a dozen bodies apparently sprawled lifeless on the grass near the forest. The Romans had been caught completely unawares when the corpses had sprung to life as soon as the riders reached them. Dozens of other Venicones had surged out of the woods to surround the horsemen, grabbing at bridles to prevent the horses bolting, and dragging the men from the saddles.

It had all seemed so easy, but it had presented Gabrain with yet another difficult decision. He now had a few horses, but the village elder's warning about the lack of available young men to join his war band had given him second thoughts about sending messengers to summon more help. After a long period of doubt, he had decided that it would be better to use the horses as bait for the next group of Romans who would inevitably come to investigate.

What he had not counted on was that so many cavalry would appear, nor that their commander would ignore the bait Gabrain had set out.

"Why didn't they come near us?" one of his warriors asked in a perplexed tone.

"They know we are here," Gabrain muttered in reply.

The Romans' behaviour puzzled him. The horsemen had thundered away over the ridge, but some of them had then returned, spreading out in a widely spaced cordon along the crest of the skyline. Gabrain had tensed, passing the word to his men to be ready for a fight but nothing else had happened. The troopers had simply sat on the rim of the bowl and waited.

Gabrain was puzzled. What were they waiting for? Were the others still hiding beyond the ridge? Were they trying to tempt him to attack, just as he had been attempting to lure them close to the trees? Or were they circling round the forest to launch an assault from the rear? He did not know and was unsure what to do.

His self-doubt angered him. He was a King, the man his warriors looked to for guidance and leadership. He had brought them here with the promise of plunder and glory, but now he was faced with a problem. He spent a long time considering his options before eventually making up his mind.

"We are heading back to the boats," he informed his men, keeping his expression confident. "Without horses of our own, we can't get close to those Romans. They may outnumber us, but they'd just run off if we tried to attack them, and we'd never catch them. But they won't come to us. Horsemen can't fight in woodland like this, and they know it. So, I reckon they're waiting for their infantry to arrive. If we stay here, we'll find ourselves trapped, so we're going to sneak away and leave them sitting up there watching an empty forest. By the time they figure out we've gone, we'll be back across the river and half way home."

Most of the warriors saw the sense in what he was saying. Tackling superior numbers of Romans did not overly concern them because they had little fear of death. If they were killed in battle, they would be welcomed as heroes in the Underworld. Even so, there was no sense in throwing away their lives for little purpose, so Gabrain's decision was greeted with only a few, muted grumbles from a handful of the more aggressive tribesmen. Within moments of Gabrain giving the order, the warriors spread out and slowly made their way northwards, heading towards the further edge of the woodland.

The going was not easy. There were some open spaces among the trees, areas where the sun dappled through the overhead canopy onto lush grass, but in other places the way was blocked by dense scrub of bushes, brambles and fallen trees. This was ancient woodland, rarely visited by humans, and their progress was slow.

"It won't take long to get through," Gabrain insisted. "Then we'll have a quick march across open ground to the woods where we left the boats."

It sounded simple and so it should have been. The Gods, though, were not smiling on them this day. Just as Gabrain was congratulating himself on making the Romans look foolish, he heard a succession of loud noises from his right where some of his men were picking a cautious way through the tangled undergrowth.

The first indication that something was wrong was a low, rumbling snuffling sound which was instantly followed by a snort, shouts of alarm, then a scream of pain and yet more yelling.

Every head turned. Gabrain drew his sword and ran towards the noise, forcing a way past men and trees until he came to a small open space where several of his warriors were gathered around two shapes that lay on the blood-stained grass.

One figure was a young warrior, his face pale and creased with agony, rocking from side to side as he lay on his back, his hands clamped to his thigh where blood had soaked his woollen trousers. Lying only a couple of paces away was the body of a wild boar, a spear jutting from its side and its neck slashed by a vicious wound that could only have been inflicted by a sword. Its curved, wickedly sharp tusks were stained red with the blood of the man it had gored.

"Damn thing came out of nowhere!" one of the warriors told Gabrain apologetically.

The stillness of the forest had been shattered by the commotion. Overhead, birds were circling above the treetops, squawking in protest at being disturbed while, on the ground, the murmur of men's voices had grown to an alarmed chattering as they came running to see what had happened.

"It's the mating season," one man told Gabrain. "The boar are especially temperamental at this time of year. That looks like a young male. Probably looking for someone to fight, and we just stumbled onto him."

Gabrain nodded absently. As a King, he had hunted boar often enough. The specimen on the ground was not a large one, but its tusks were sharp, and he knew that size had little to do with aggression when it came to boar.

He frowned, looking down at the injured man whose pale face was contorted in agony, low whimpers of pain escaping his lips. He was a young man, barely sixteen years old, on his first raid. Gabrain tried to recall his name, but it would not come to him.

"Bind his leg and carry him," he told the closest men.

Whirling, he waved at the gathering crowd of warriors who were clustering into the tiny clearing, many of them peering over others' shoulders as they tried to see what had happened.

"Get back!" he ordered. "Spread out and keep moving. And try to keep quiet."

Once he was satisfied that the crowd was dispersing, he turned back to the men who had encountered the boar. One of them walked over to the dead animal and tugged at the spear, placing a foot on the beast's body and yanking the blade free.

"We should take this as well," he observed, casting a look at Gabrain as if to ask approval. "It will feed us tonight."

"If you can carry it, you can take it," Gabrain shrugged.

He waited while the wounded man was tended to. The bleeding gash was hastily bound with strips of linen, but Gabrain caught the eye of one of the older men who shook his head in an unmistakable signal. The wound, it seemed, was likely to prove fatal. Still, two men hoisted the injured youngster up and struggled off in pursuit of the main group. Two others lashed the boar's feet together over a spear and lifted it onto their shoulders before following their comrades.

Sighing, Gabrain sheathed his sword and went after them.

The wood was larger than he had guessed and it was growing late in the afternoon by the time he was able to make out clear daylight up ahead. His men had gathered at the edge of the trees, waiting for him. One who would not wait was the youth who had been gored. He had bled to death at some point during the trek, so his friends had laid him down at the base of a tall birch.

"We should bury him," one of them suggested.

"We cannot spare the time," Gabrain told them. "Come on, we still have a long walk ahead of us, and I'd like to reach the boats before nightfall."

He moved to the fringes of the woodland, looking up at the clear, blue sky like a man stepping from the confines of a prison. Checking to left and right, he raised a hand in signal.

"All clear! Come on!"

They moved out into the grassy meadow, heading slightly west of north, knowing they had a clear route now. The ground was relatively flat, with only a few low undulations which restricted their view of what lay beyond. Glancing at the sky once more to check on the position of the sun, Gabrain reckoned they had around two hours before sunset. It should be more than enough. He strode on, glad to be able to walk more swiftly now that they were out of the forest.

Then the world turned to chaos.

Several men shouted warnings simultaneously, pointing and drawing their swords or hefting their long spears. Up ahead, a long line of horsemen had appeared over the crest of a low incline. They were moving at a fast trot which they were already pushing into a canter. They were two hundred paces away and would soon raise that canter into a gallop as they rode down the exposed Venicones.

Frantically, Gabrain spun round, seeking some refuge, but they were in the open, every patch of scrub or woodland too far away. Worse, as he turned, he saw yet more Roman cavalry emerge from beyond the nearest clump of trees behind him. They, too, were winding up their mounts into a charge.

Gabrain felt dismay almost overwhelm him. What should they do? What could they do?

Men on foot could not outrun horses. Cavalry liked nothing better than to hunt down fleeing victims. Spearmen could hold off the riders if they formed a tight, defensive formation because horses will not charge home at a close-knit group of armed men, but even if they gathered together in a huddle of spears and swords, cowering like a hedgehog against the attack of a fox, he knew they could not escape. The Romans would simply surround them and cut off all avenues of retreat. Sooner or later, they would need to either run or surrender.

"Run!" Gabrain yelled, waving to his right towards a distant stretch of pine trees. They were too far away, he knew, and pine trees offered more scope for horsemen to pursue them even if they were able to reach the wood, but it was the only hope any of them had. With luck, some of them might escape and make their way back to the boats.

Everyone was running now. Some men threw away their spears and shields to lighten their load and allow them to run faster. The two who had been carrying the boar dumped their booty and pelted along with the rest of them.

Gabrain laboured after them, arms pumping and breath coming in great, ragged gasps. He could hear the drumming thunder of the horses and another, strange, eerie wail which he vaguely recognised as coming from a "dragon", an emblem often used by Rome's auxiliary cavalry. It was a carved head of a mythical monster, its body and tail formed by flumes of coloured ribbons which fluttered wildly in the air behind it when the rider carrying it broke into a gallop. In the carved beast's long, fang-filled snout were reeds which created a whistling, moaning sound as the wind passed between them. It was a similar idea to the great carnyx horns used by the Britons, but even though Gabrain understood that it was merely a man-made creation, the sound filled him with terror because it represented Roman cavalry on the hunt.

And, this time, he was the prey.

The first group of riders were on them now, galloping with well-drilled precision as they rode into the fleeing tribesmen. The air filled with the pounding thud of horses' hooves, and Gabrain saw lances held high in overhand readiness, then watched them being stabbed downwards as the horsemen ploughed into the scattered ranks of the Venicones. Men screamed as they were sent tumbling, blood spurting from their wounds, and the horsemen galloped on, hunting down their next victims. Other riders wielded the long-bladed, heavy swords, the *spatha* that could chop a man almost in two when backed by the power of a charging horse. Hacking to left and right, the horsemen carved a swathe through the helpless Venicones.

Gabrain knew he would never reach the trees. Men ahead of him were being cut down by the riders who were pouring in from his left, while the sound of dull thunder from behind told him that he had only moments to live before a lance ripped through his body or he was trampled to death by the charging horses.

Skidding to a halt, he spun round, yanking his sword from its scabbard. Only days earlier, he had seen Calgacus perform the same feat to drive off a pack of war hounds. Now it was his turn, but he did not hold out any hopes of survival because the enemy facing him was just as deadly but far more numerous.

He was only just in time. A line of riders, widely spaced to give each man room, was almost on him. One trooper let out a savage yell of delight as he nudged his mount to run at Gabrain. The man held a lance over his head, ready to plunge it down into Gabrain's unprotected body.

The panting, snorting horse swerved slightly, intending to pass Gabrain on his right. As it did so, the rider braced himself against the high rear panel of his saddle and stabbed viciously down, aiming his razor sharp lance at Gabrain's broad chest.

Gabrain swayed back, swinging his sword in a desperate attempt to knock the lance aside. For the first time that day, luck was with him, and his heavy iron blade smashed into the wooden shaft just behind the lance's metal tip, deflecting it sufficiently that the edge of the blade raked across his bicep before the horse's momentum carried it past him. His own swing drove his sword on, crashing into the rider's saddle with a jarring impact which caused the horse to whinny in panic and yanked the sword from Gabrain's hands as horse and rider sped past him.

The frantic move had spun him almost completely around, and he staggered as he struggled to regain his balance. Tottering like a drunk man, his eyes desperately darted all around, striving to find his sword.

There! It lay on the grass several paces away, thrown like a leaf in a strong wind. The trooper had ridden on, struggling to regain control of his frightened mount, and having lost all interest in Gabrain. The other riders had charged past in a torrent of sound and shaking earth, eager to cut down other tribesmen, and Gabrain had a sudden thought that, against all expectation, he might yet escape.

His right arm was burning with the sting of the cut the lance had made, and he could feel the hot stickiness of blood, but he knew it was only a superficial wound. Ignoring the pain, he decided to run to gather up his sword and then to try to reach the trees by dodging through the Roman cavalrymen who were now scattered and as disorganised as the tribesmen they were hunting.

His hopes died almost as soon as they had formed.

"Stand very still," a voice commanded.

He disobeyed, instinctively spinning round. More horsemen had come up on him, more sedately than the first line. He could not imagine how he had failed to see or hear them, but they were crowding around him now, swords drawn and ready to hack him down. The man who had spoken to him in his own language was looking down at him, a satisfied smile on a grim face that was framed by a plumed helmet with iron cheek guards.

Gabrain whirled his head from side to side, seeking a way out, but the horsemen were crowding all around him, pressing close to pin him in place.

"We are not going to kill you," the man in the plumed helmet told him. "But that doesn't mean we won't hurt you if you do anything foolish."

Gabrain was tempted to try something foolish anyway, but a sudden, blinding blow to the top of his head made him stagger. Stars exploded in front of his eyes and he knew that he had been struck by the heavy, iron pommel of a cavalry sword. Penned in on both sides by sweating, stinking horseflesh, he was unable to fall until one of the beasts shifted aside and he lurched drunkenly. Even as he did so, he felt strong hands yank his arms back as someone expertly tied his wrists together before kicking his feet from under him.

He hit the ground like a felled tree, only dimly aware that his ankles were being hobbled by a short length of leather cord.

He heard the officer issuing calm, confident commands in Latin, the words a reminder of his complete failure. He was dimly aware of movement around him, of faint shouts and screams, of laughter and the sound of foreign voices, but his pounding head left him virtually blind.

By the time he recovered sufficiently to prop himself into a sitting position and look around, the slaughter was over. He could see dismounted Roman troopers moving among the fallen, searching the bodies, finishing off the seriously wounded with their daggers, while their horses lowered their heads to chomp on the grass. The bodies of his warriors were strewn all across the ground, and it seemed to him that none had come close to reaching the sanctuary of the forest. Around a dozen were still alive, some wounded but all capable of walking, and these men were being ushered over to join him, their faces drawn tight in expressions of bewildered despondency.

"A decent enough haul," the Roman with the plumed helmet observed as he rode back to stand over Gabrain. "I take it from that torc around your neck that you are the leader?"

Gabrain looked up, giving an ungracious nod.

"Excellent. The Governor does like it when we capture chieftains. I'm sure he'll grant you the privilege of being the last to be crucified."

Chapter XXI

Macrinus was feeling pleased with himself when he returned to the Governor's camp two days later, even though his satisfaction was tempered by the knowledge that he would once again be forced to endure the company of Popidius Flaccus. Still, as he clattered across the narrow pontoon bridge which the Legion's engineers had constructed a little way upstream of the fort, he was confident that he could not be faulted for anything he had done since being sent on his mission.

The capture of a dozen Britons had created a slight problem in that they slowed the speed at which he could move. He was also concerned that there might be other rebels still roaming free.

"What makes you think that?" Centurion Sdapezi had asked when Macrinus had voiced the opinion.

"There is hardly any plunder here," Macrinus had informed him. "They were carrying a dead boar, but very little from the fort. We know they took weapons and armour, and they must have helped themselves to most of the food supplies, but this lot have nothing with them except the heads of the men they killed."

Sdapezi had looked around the field, nodded gravely, then muttered, "I suppose we'll need to find the others, then. But how?"

Macrinus had made up his mind quickly. After despatching two riders to take a hastily scribbled message to the Governor to inform him of what had happened, he had sent Sdapezi and half of the troopers back to the ruined fort with the prisoners, giving instructions that the dead of the garrison, reunited with their heads, should be buried in a mass grave.

"Put them in one of the ditches, then cover them by demolishing the rampart," he ordered.

Leaving Sdapezi to carry out this task, Macrinus had led the rest of his men to the river bank, then made a sweep along the shore, looking for signs of any place the Britons might have concealed their boats. It was a fruitless search because the riverbank was a maze of trees, reeds and swamps. The Britons he was seeking might already have crossed to the northern bank, or they might be lying in concealment, completely unseen even though Macrinus and his troop could be passing within twenty paces of them.

Unwilling to risk his troopers in such unsuitable terrain for horses, he had returned to the fort to claim a portion of the roast boar which Sdapezi's men had cooked on open fires. They had then spent an uncomfortable night in the open before heading back to the Governor. On the way, he had left Centurion Sdapezi and one turma of troopers at the watchtower to provide some reassurance for the anxious young Optio, giving instructions that Sdapezi should continue to carry out patrols for the next few days in case a handful of rebels had decided to remain in the area.

Now, as he led his wretched gaggle of prisoners through the wide gates of the Governor's fortress, he was confident he had done everything that could be expected of him.

The Governor himself, alerted by the sentries, came to meet him, accompanied by Hordonius Piso, the Twentieth Legion's Legate, and, inevitably, the stalking shadow of Popidius Flaccus.

Other men were crowding round too, soldiers streaked in sweat from labouring at the construction of the buildings they would need to complete before winter set in, along with a handful of the slaves and freedmen who served the senior officers, with Flaccus' more extensive retinue forming an inquisitive gaggle behind the Assistant Procurator.

Agricola clasped Macrinus' hand warmly as he stepped forwards to meet him.

"You have done well," he declared, speaking loudly and looking beyond Macrinus to include the Tribune's troopers in the praise.

"I fear a few of the raiders may have escaped," Macrinus confessed. "But these are all that is left of the ones we were able to find."

Flaccus was at the Governor's elbow in an instant, his nose twitching in distaste as he cast a jaundiced eye over the prisoners who stood in a miserable huddle, their wrists bound together, with Macrinus' men at their backs.

"A sorry looking lot," he commented loftily. "They don't look terribly dangerous."

"They were dangerous enough to storm a fortified camp and massacre the garrison," Macrinus pointed out, finding his temper already rising.

Flaccus opened his mouth to speak, but Agricola cut over him.

"We will crucify them tomorrow," he announced. "That will show the locals what it means to oppose Rome. No doubt word will reach Calgacus soon enough, especially if one of them is a chieftain."

Macrinus pointed to the large man at the head of the column of weary captives.

"The big, red-haired one," he said. "He won't tell me his name, but the others defer to him. He is certainly a man of some importance."

Macrinus suspected the big Briton was more than a mere chieftain because the man had worn a golden torc around his throat, the symbol of royalty. That torc now nestled in Macrinus' pack, his share of the plunder taken from the captives, but he saw no reason to reveal its existence. Agricola would know the Auxiliaries would have helped themselves to the best of the loot, but he would ask no questions as long as Macrinus deposited a reasonable quantity of rings, arm bands and brooches with the Governor's treasury.

Flaccus had other priorities. His eyes lit up as he once again butted in.

"If I might ask a favour?" he said to Agricola.

The Governor gave a cool nod.

Flaccus declared, "I think I have a better idea than simply crucifying all of them. May I suggest we put on some entertainment for your men? Caesar's loyal soldiers deserve a little fun."

Agricola gave a casual shrug.

"This is why you sent for your new acquaintance?"

Flaccus smirked as he confirmed, "Precisely. But, not only can we have some entertainment here, I believe I have a way to bring about Calgacus' downfall."

Macrinus gave a puzzled frown. He could see that Agricola was not best pleased, but was once again being forced into a corner by the Assistant Procurator.

Behind Agricola, Piso caught Macrinus' eye and gave an almost imperceptible shake of his head, warning the Tribune not to become involved.

Agricola waved a hand.

"Very well. What is it you wish to do?"

"By all means crucify most of them," Flaccus grinned. "But keep the chieftain alive for a little while. Plus one other."

He said to Macrinus, "Ask the chieftain who is the best fighter apart from himself."

Macrinus bit back the temptation to ask why Flaccus wanted to know this. The Assistant Procurator clearly had some devious scheme in mind, but there was, Macrinus realised, nothing to be gained by arguing when the Governor had already acceded to Flaccus' demands.

Still bemused, Macrinus turned back to the prisoners and approached the red-haired barbarian leader. The man gave him a surly, defiant look.

"The Governor wishes to know which of your men is the best warrior," Macrinus said to him. "Apart from yourself, of course."

"Why does he want to know?" the big man shot back, suspicion flaring in his eyes.

"I do not know for certain, but I expect it will determine the manner of his death."

The other Britons were listening intently, some fearful but others suddenly interested.

One tall, well-built man growled, "My King, let me face whatever death the Romans wish to inflict."

"So you are a King?" Macrinus asked the chieftain. "I thought as much."

"Does that make any difference?" the red-haired giant asked.

"I doubt it. Certainly not in a good way. But you could tell me your name."

"Gabrain of the Venicones. Son of Urgist, son of Barrix, son of —"

Macrinus held up a hand as he interrupted, "Spare me the litany. I understand your pride in your lineage, but that is not important right now. I asked you to tell me who is your best warrior."

Gabrain sighed as he jerked his chin to indicate the man who had volunteered.

"Durren is as good as any of us," he said dully.

Macrinus signalled to one of his troopers.

"Bring that one."

He returned to the Governor and Flaccus who were maintaining a safe distance from the prisoners.

"This one claims to be the best," he informed them, keeping Gabrain's identity to himself for the time being. He decided he might inform the Governor later, when Flaccus was not able to hear. That would be a petty victory, he knew, but he could not bring himself to willingly provide any information that might aid the Assistant Procurator.

Flaccus beamed at the Governor.

"Might I suggest a show at sundown? That will give my man time to prepare."

"As you say," Agricola agreed. Turning to Macrinus, he said, "Have the others kept under guard. We'll crucify them tomorrow morning."

"Apart from the leader," Flaccus interjected. "Keep him safe and secure."

"Apart from the leader," the Governor echoed, attempting to retain a vestige of authority.

Agricola made perfunctory excuses, then strode away, heading towards his tent. As soon as he did so, the Legion's Centurions began barking at the soldiers to resume their interrupted work. Slowly, the watching crowd dispersed as men went back to their duties.

Flaccus, obviously delighted with himself, made a more sedate departure. As he headed towards the barrack block that had been set aside for him, most of his retinue scurried after him, but one man remained standing very still, watching the British warrior named Durren.

This man, clearly a civilian, was a stranger to Macrinus. He was of average height, his torso bulky, his arms and legs displaying heavy muscles, although he gave the impression of running to fat. He was in early middle-age, his hair trimmed very short, his face tanned yet somehow appearing unhealthy. It was his eyes, though, that caught Macrinus' attention. Set in a hard, expressionless face, they were as cold and chilling as any the Tribune had ever seen.

The man studied Durren for a long time, then glanced at Macrinus, holding his gaze with what Macrinus could only think of as insolent contempt, before casually turning and strolling away.

Piso edged close to Macrinus, lowering his voice so as not to be overheard by the soldiers who were moving nearby, ushering the prisoners away.

"An unpleasant character, don't you think?" the Legate enquired.

Macrinus was tempted to ask whether Piso was referring to Flaccus, but decided against the joke. Piso was an aristocrat. He may have disliked Flaccus, but he would not countenance someone of a lower social order openly criticising the Assistant Procurator.

Instead, indicating the departing stranger with a nod of his head, Macrinus merely asked, "Who is he?"

"I'm sure you have heard of him. They call him Serpens."

"The Snake? Not a very nice nickname. No, I don't think I've ever heard of him."

"Really? He is very famous. Or, at least, he used to be. He's a gladiator."

Understanding dawned on Macrinus. The man's bulky build should have provided the clue. Many gladiators tried to develop layers of fat and muscle to protect their vital organs from shallow sword thrusts.

"I take it he must be quite good," he remarked.

Piso replied, "He is still alive, which is no mean feat after more than a dozen years in the arena. I dare say he is not as fast and nimble as he once was, but I wouldn't like to go up against him, that's for sure."

"None of us is as fast or nimble as we used to be," Macrinus smiled.

"True. In The Snake's case, though, I suspect his slowest move would still be significantly faster than our best."

"I suppose so," Macrinus conceded. "Although I have heard of groups of gladiators being drafted into Army service and not doing too well."

"Ah, yes. That happened during the last civil war," Piso confirmed. "Vitellius, who lost the war as you know, was rather desperate for troops, so he offered some gladiators their freedom if they would fight for him. They agreed, but they were sadly ineffective. They were roundly defeated the first time they met up with the Legions."

"I thought they were supposed to be extraordinary fighters," Macrinus frowned.

"They are. But only as individuals. They are trained to fight one on one. They have no concept of teamwork or fighting as a unit. Arena combat is very different to the sort of warfare you and I are accustomed to. Still, like I said, I wouldn't bet against him if he's facing a single opponent."

"And the Briton, Durren, is to be his opponent in a show this evening?"

"So it would seem. The lads will appreciate it, of course. A show like that will be good for morale."

"I'm sure Popidius Flaccus did not bring him here just to improve our morale," Macrinus observed drily.

"I suspect not," Piso agreed.

"Then why is he here?"

"That, I am afraid, is known only to Flaccus. But you heard what he said. He clearly has something in mind."

"He can't be thinking of sending a gladiator to challenge Calgacus," Macrinus scoffed. "The man wouldn't last a day once he ventured into the hills."

"I quite agree," nodded Piso. "No doubt our Assistant Procurator will reveal his plan in his own good time. Who knows, it may have more success than his last effort."

Macrinus grunted sceptically. One thing the gladiator's presence did explain was the letter Flaccus had promised to write. He had not sent it to Rome, after all. Instead, he had summoned Serpens to this northern outpost.

But why?

Macrinus had still not worked out what lay behind Flaccus' machinations by the time evening arrived. He was tempted to ask the Assistant Procurator when they gathered for the entertainment, but decided against it because he doubted whether Flaccus would tell him, and he could not bear the thought of the man's smugness when he refused to divulge his plan.

Shaved, washed, and wearing clean trousers, tunic and cloak, Macrinus went to join the audience for the promised entertainment. There was a buzz of excitement in the air as the soldiers gathered to watch the promised show. A small area had been roped off near the Principia, at the intersection of the camp's two main roads. Where the *Via Principalis*, running north to south, crossed the east–west *Via Praetoria*, was a wide, open space that was usually used for parades. Now, the soldiers crowded all around the edge of the cordoned section, many of them sitting on hastily arranged tiers of benches that were supported by wooden scaffolding normally used in the construction of the fort's buildings.

The scene was lit by dozens of burning torches attached to the tops of high poles that had been set up all around the improvised arena. Their flickering, orange light added additional excitement to the occasion, and the sound of voices and ribald laughter echoed all across the camp.

The senior officers had their own seats, set up on a raised platform in the manner of a tribunal which was usually reserved for formal matters such as disciplinary hearings, but which would now serve to provide them with a grandstand view of the combat.

Macrinus took his seat beside Piso who, as Legate, sat at Agricola's right. Flaccus, Macrinus was pleased to note, was on Agricola's left, which kept him far enough away for Macrinus to relax. His mood was aided by a drink of wine which the Governor's slaves served to the senior officers, and was further boosted when he heard Flaccus complaining of a sore throat and blocked nose.

To be fair, the Assistant Procurator looked a little unwell as he took his seat, but colds were an everyday occurrence in Britannia, where keeping warm and dry was virtually impossible. The fort's infirmary dealt with more cases of colds than anything else, including the eye infections that were a constant feature of military life. Flaccus, for all his coughing and spluttering, received little sympathy.

Macrinus felt a perverse pleasure at seeing the man suffering, but he soon dismissed the Assistant Procurator from his thoughts and turned his attention to the impending spectacle.

"It's not often the lads get to see a genuine gladiator," he remarked to Piso.

"I hope they aren't disappointed," the Legate murmured in response. "An untrained man doesn't stand much chance against a gladiator. It might all be over before we can enjoy the show."

"I'm sure Durren won't object if he lives a little longer," Macrinus replied.

"Durren? Oh, the barbarian. You sound as if you know him."

"I had to translate while he was being prepared. I explained what was going to happen."

"I expect he nearly wet himself," Piso chuckled.

"No. He seems to be looking forward to it. I don't think he believed me when I told him about gladiators. Among the Britons, the upper classes are trained to fight as part of their upbringing, you see."

"That savage is one of the upper class?" Piso sneered. "It is so hard to tell with these barbarians. They all look like peasants."

"Not upper class, perhaps, but he's a warrior," Macrinus replied. "He is one of the chieftain's personal bodyguards. He'll fight well enough."

"He won't be up to the same standard as Serpens," Piso asserted.

"No. But Durren doesn't care. He said he only wishes to win or to die well."

"It's a better death than being crucified, I suppose," said Piso.

Macrinus, who had often observed the painful punishment reserved for criminals, could not agree more.

Their conversation was ended by a fanfare of horns which brought a roar of acclaim from the crowd and heralded the arrival of a man who emerged from one side of the square. He was dressed for combat, carrying a shield on his left arm, and wearing an iron helmet with a face guard.

A section of the rope was untied to allow him to pass, then refastened once he was inside the square.

"Impressive," murmured Piso.

Serpens' face was invisible, the mask of his helmet having holes to aid breathing and vision, but obscuring all sight of his features. His torso was largely bare, but he had thick, linen cloths bound around his belly which were topped by a metal girdle. His right arm was swathed in more layers of cloth from wrist to elbow, and a metal guard protected his right shoulder, while two bronze greaves covered his shins. The bare skin of his back, chest, arms and legs, gleamed with oil which was intended to make it difficult for an opponent to grab hold of him, but it had the additional effect of reflecting glimmers of the firelight, giving him the appearance of a man who had bathed in flame.

All of this, though, was standard for a gladiator, Macrinus knew. What was unusual about this man was his shield. Against a dull, plain background, it bore the image of a green snake, coiled but rising up with gaping mouth and huge, venomous fangs. Its eyes seemed to stare out from the rectangular shield, radiating menace.

Yet even this was not what struck Macrinus most as he studied the man. He could not help noting the relaxed posture, the ease with which Serpens moved, the self-assurance in every step and in the way he held his head. He had the air of a man who had complete confidence in his own ability.

The gladiator waited calmly, standing like a statue while the soldiers cheered him and shouted encouragement. It was as if he were oblivious to everything around him. Then he shifted expectantly as a second man arrived in the arena.

Durren, the Venicones' champion, ducked under the encircling rope before standing upright and peering all around. Boos and hisses greeted him, taunts and jeers which he could not fail to understand even though they were shouted in Latin. He snarled his own insults at the crowd, a gesture which only raised louder catcalls from those nearest to him.

Two more men made their way under the ropes, two big, burly soldiers who had been assigned to watch the captive Briton. Now they handed him his weapons.

Durren was bare-chested, wearing only long trousers of wool and a pair of old boots. He had discarded his ragged tunic, displaying a torso that was lean and hard, yet pale against the brown of his face and arms. His long, unkempt hair gave him the appearance of every Roman's impression of what a wild, heathen barbarian ought to look like.

He was handed a rectangular shield, identical to the one Serpens carried except that it was painted in a bright shade of red with a yellow circle surrounding its central boss. This device was used by many legionaries because the central circle sometimes acted as a target. Enemies were inclined to unconsciously aim for the shield rather than aim at the man carrying it. From what he had seen of Serpens so far, though, Macrinus doubted whether the gladiator would fall for such a simple ploy.

Finally, one of the soldiers handed Durren a short sword, the standard *gladius* used by Rome's infantry. The Briton took it with a curious expression, hefting it and testing the needle point against his left hand, drawing a tiny speck of blood.

The two soldiers stepped back as if expecting him to attack them. They drew their own swords both as a precaution and as an incentive to him to fight properly.

They need not have worried. Durren turned away, ignoring them, and faced his opponent.

Serpens moved at last, drawing his own sword and turning to the tribunal where the senior men were seated. If he spoke the words of the traditional greeting, nobody could hear them over the tumult of shouts and yells from the spectators, but he raised his sword in salute before turning again to face Durren.

The Briton was already moving, light on his feet and going directly for the gladiator. He held his sword high, the blade over his right shoulder, bringing yet more raucous jeers from the watching soldiers.

"He's more used to a long blade," Macrinus observed when Piso joined in the laughter.

"He'd better be a fast learner, then," the Legate chuckled as he sipped at his wine and sat back to enjoy the spectacle.

Durren's unusual tactic almost caught Serpens by surprise. The gladiator was forced to raise his shield to ward off the hammer blow which the Briton delivered as he ran at his opponent, using his own shield as a battering ram intended to knock Serpens off his feet.

Serpens' own sword flicked out but merely glanced from the edge of Durren's shield as the gladiator was forced to dance away from the attack.

Durren swung round to follow, but the ground was uneven and he lost his footing momentarily. In that instant, Serpens stepped forward and rammed his own shield into Durren's right side with enough power to numb his arm and make him drop his *gladius*.

Again, Serpens' sword thrust at the Briton, but Durren staggered back, off balance, and the blade missed him by a hand's breadth.

The crowd groaned at the ease with which the fight had been ended. An unarmed man could not hope to last longer than a few heartbeats against a trained gladiator.

"I told you," Piso murmured.

But the fight was not done. To everyone's astonishment, Serpens took a step back, then retreated further as he gestured to Durren to retrieve his sword.

"Arrogant sod, isn't he?" Macrinus muttered to nobody in particular.

The soldiers loved it. They laughed and applauded as Durren carefully edged over to his fallen weapon and, keeping a careful watch on the gladiator, picked it up.

The two men faced one another again. Macrinus expected Durren to be more cautious but, after a moment's consideration, the Briton hurled himself at Serpens, blocking the gladiator's attack with his shield and hammering blows on the Roman's own snake-bedecked defence, hoping to use his longer reach to keep Serpens at bay.

It was the way the Britons fought, Macrinus knew. He had stood in the line facing them often enough to know that they fought without fear, without any concern for their survival. He guessed Serpens had never faced such an opponent before because arena combat between trained gladiators was a formalised, almost ritual contest in which both combatants knew they might survive if they fought well enough. Durren, on the other hand, knew no rules other than to attack with reckless disregard for his own safety. This made him extremely dangerous because a man who is not afraid to die is the most deadly enemy of all.

Durren's assault was a torrent of quick, often clumsy, attacks, using both sword and shield to drive Serpens back. Yet the Briton, too, faced an unusual opponent. When the two sides normally met in battle, the Roman line would not yield. The soldiers stood side by side and protected one another, using their combined strength and training to hold the Britons at bay. If a legionary had retreated the way Serpens did before Durren, the Venicone would have shattered the Roman line, but Serpens fought alone, and had no qualms about stepping back.

For all Durren's efforts, the gladiator maintained his balance, kept moving and countered every blow with apparent ease.

"He's bloody playing with him," Piso observed with a hint of disapproval. "The barbarian will tire himself out before long."

Macrinus nodded in agreement. Serpens was prolonging the show, giving a display of defensive footwork that the professional soldiers could appreciate. He kept moving, never still for an instant, and always seeming to be sure-footed.

Then his own sword flashed, almost too fast for the spectators to see what he had done. Durren had overextended his reach with a succession of ferocious hacking blows which knocked slivers of plywood from Serpens' shield. As he leaned slightly too far forwards, Serpens' blade raked across the inside of his forearm, the razor-sharp edge drawing a red line across Durren's arm.

The Briton leaped back, but blood was pouring from the wound, and the pain was evident in his expression.

"Hoc habet!" roared the audience as one. "He has that one!"

The fight was over. Everyone knew it. The wound was not deep, but it had severed several veins and arteries, and blood was pumping from Durren's arm, running down to his hand and making his grip on his sword too slick to maintain. The *gladius* fell to the ground at his feet as he drew his left arm across, vainly attempting to clamp his left hand over the cut.

Serpens began circling, the tip of his sword weaving invisible patterns in the night air. Durren turned, keeping his face to him, then letting out a defiant roar and charging at him, holding his shield in front of him and lowering his head like a bull on a rampage.

Serpens was a bulky man, but he moved with incredible lightness, dodging aside at the last moment and lunging with his sword to plant the blade in Durren's body just below the ribs as the Briton plunged past him.

"Hoc habet!"

The tip of Serpens' blade was stained dark in contrast to the polished gleam of the rest of the sword. It had not buried itself too deeply, but it was enough. Three fingers' depth was often sufficient to deliver a fatal blow.

Durren, though, was not dead yet. He had fallen to the earth, blood now running from two serious wounds, but he forced himself up, reeling like a drunk man, and gripped his shield in both hands. He launched himself into a staggering, lurching run as if to try the same tactic again, but this time he waited until he was only two paces from Serpens and then threw the shield at the gladiator's head.

Serpens would have been less than human if he had not flinched as the iron-rimmed shield came at his face. His helmet's mask would have saved him, but he instinctively tried to duck out of the way, allowing the flying shield to flash over his head. As he did so, Durren grabbed the edge of the gladiator's own shield and yanked hard, attempting to either wrench it from Serpens' grip or haul the Roman to the ground.

It was a brave move, a desperate last bid to snatch some sort of victory before his wounds overcame him, but it was in vain.

Serpens might have been caught by surprise, but his reactions were impossibly quick. He dug his left heel into the ground, flung his right leg forwards and spun his body in to meet Durren's driving attack. This time, the sword found a vital spot, driving deep into Durren's belly.

All the strength ebbed from the Briton. He lost his grip on Serpens' shield, and slowly slumped to his knees, his hands clasped to his belly, blood covering his fingers as his head drooped.

Serpens did not waste time seeking approval from the Governor to deliver the killing stroke. Durren was a dead man anyway.

Serpens released his grip on his shield, letting it clatter to the ground. Then he stepped close to Durren and, in one easy move, planted his left fist in the Briton's hair, yanked his head back, and drove his sword into the man's exposed throat. For a long moment, he held the Briton in place, staring down at the dying man's face as if to ensure that Durren's last sight was of the impassive face mask of

Serpens' helmet. Then, as if losing interest once life had fled from his opponent's eyes, he yanked the blade back, released his hold on the dead man's hair, and turned away before Durren's corpse had hit the ground.

The crowd cheered wildly as Serpens recovered his shield, turned to salute the Governor with his bloodied sword, then strode from the arena to loud applause.

"You were right," Piso said to Macrinus. "The Briton fought well."

"Yes, but Serpens doesn't have a scratch on him, and I don't believe he's even sweating."

Flaccus had overheard. He was moving from his seat to pass behind them, probably on his way to congratulate the victor.

"He is impressive, is he not?" he sniffed hoarsely. "He could have finished it much sooner, of course, but I told him to put on a decent show. I think the men appreciate it."

The cheering and applause was only now subsiding, with the hero having departed.

The Governor was on his feet too, turning to face Flaccus.

"I am sure this will be spoken of for many days yet," Agricola remarked. "But perhaps you could tell me how this gladiator will help us defeat Calgacus."

Flaccus had an audience. All the senior officers were standing nearby, most of them still smiling after witnessing Serpens' victory. There was, Macrinus knew, nothing a man like Flaccus appreciated more than a receptive crowd to witness his cleverness. The Assistant Procurator produced a linen handkerchief and ostentatiously blew his nose, making a great show of letting everyone know that he was unwell. Then he spoke as loudly as his rasping throat would allow.

"It is very simple," he explained. "We will challenge Calgacus to come and fight Serpens."

There was a moment's stunned disbelief before Agricola said calmly, "Even you must know that Calgacus will never do anything as foolish as that. Why would he accept such a challenge?"

"He will accept if he is forced to," Flaccus replied dismissively.

"And how do you propose to compel him?"

Swallowing to clear his throat, Flaccus said, "I believe Calgacus has a son. A man who lives not far from here."

Macrinus felt a cold shiver run down his spine at the Assistant Procurator's words. He wanted to argue, but the Governor made his protest for him.

"Young Togodumnus is under my protection," Agricola stated firmly. "I appointed him King of the Boresti, and I have no wish to remove him."

"I am not talking about removing him," Flaccus stated. "Merely using him to bring Calgacus to us."

"He will not fall for that," Macrinus managed to rasp through dry lips. "Togodumnus may be Calgacus' son, but they are estranged."

"You misunderstand me," Flaccus informed him. "I merely wish him to convey a message to his father. They may be estranged, but I am certain he will find a way of communicating if there is sufficient need."

Macrinus could not argue with the Assistant Procurator. After all, he had come to the same conclusion himself, and proved the truth of it when he had visited Togodumnus.

"Perhaps you could enlighten us as to what you intend to do," the Governor requested impatiently.

"It is very simple," Flaccus replied airily. "Serpens will visit various villages, where he will kill whoever is deemed the local champion. Each time, we will issue the challenge that Calgacus comes here to fight him. Sooner or later, he will either agree, in which case he will die, or the barbarians will come to view him as a coward, in which case he will lose his place as leader of the rebels."

The officers exchanged mystified looks, some shaking their heads, others frowning while they considered Flaccus' plan.

After a moment, Piso ventured, "Wouldn't it be easier simply to threaten to execute a few men from each village?"

Agricola growled, "I want the locals to support us. Executing them will not achieve that."

"Neither will setting a gladiator on them," Macrinus argued.

Flaccus flapped a hand at him in a gesture of irritation.

"The aim is not to kill the locals," he insisted. "It is to shame Calgacus into accepting the challenge. We shall begin by putting him up against that red-haired barbarian chieftain you brought in. If Calgacus is truly a man of honour as everyone claims, we should not need to pick on anyone else in order to goad him out. If he really is a noble spirit, how can he refuse?"

The last words were directed at Agricola who understood the thinly veiled inference. How could he, a loyal Roman, forbid this plan? Flaccus, the Emperor's friend, had proposed a way to defeat Rome's greatest enemy in Britannia. As with the plan to use war dogs, if Agricola denied him the chance, Flaccus would soon report his obstinacy.

Agricola stood dumbfounded, resignation etched on his face.

"I suppose we have nothing to lose," he admitted wearily.

Flaccus coughed, wiped his nose again and told them, "We will wait a few days for my cold to improve, and then we shall put this plan into motion."

With that, he turned and strode hurriedly away, heading towards the relative warmth of his room.

The other officers stood uncertainly. Even the Governor seemed at a loss for words.

Macrinus was the only one who felt any conviction about anything, but that certainty felt as if it would choke him. In his heart, he knew Calgacus would accept the challenge. He was not the sort of man who would let others die for him unnecessarily. He would probably come as soon as Flaccus' pet gladiator had killed Gabrain.

Which meant that Calgacus, too, would die under Serpens' sword.

Chapter XXII

Flavia forced a sensuous smile to her lips as the naked man beside her reached over to run his hand over her breasts.

"You really are very beautiful," he breathed admiringly. "Have you discovered the secret of eternal youth?"

She had to concentrate very hard not to let him see that his touch made her skin crawl. It was as well, she reflected, that she had spent a lifetime mastering her emotions and presenting other people with the image she wished them to see.

"I fear not," she replied. "The Gods have been good to me, that is all."

"Venus has, at least," he leered, squeezing her breast.

She smiled to let him see that she appreciated his praise and did not object to his rough fondling.

"Perhaps," she said. "But I have also been very fortunate. My life has been such that I have been spared the hardships faced by most people. I have never needed to perform menial tasks, nor have I ever had children, so my body has not been subjected to the same rigours that other women suffer."

"You were quite rigorous a little while ago," the man laughed. "Or should I say, vigorous?"

"As were you, my Lord."

He was pleased by that compliment, she could tell. She maintained her false smile as she continued, "If you wish to resume, I am at your disposal."

"Perhaps later," he sighed, at last removing his groping hand from her flesh. "Regrettably, I have other duties to attend to now."

"Affairs of state cannot be ignored," she agreed. "I know that only too well from my own experiences."

He had been on the point of leaving the bed, but he stopped, leaned up on one elbow and looked down at her with a thoughtful expression.

"My father always admired you," he told her. "Not just because of your beauty, either. I remember he told me your mind was your best feature."

"Your father was always very generous to me," Flavia simpered artfully.

"Did you ever sleep with him?" he asked, his tone conversational but with a faint echo of jealous danger lurking behind the words.

"No," she replied, "although I would not have objected. But he was always more interested in the advice I was able to give him on affairs in Britannia."

He relaxed slightly, nodding pensively. Seemingly deep in thought, he rolled from the bed, stood up and went to retrieve his clothing.

Flavia watched him, careful not to let her mask of adoration slip. Domitian, Emperor of Rome, was reputed to be suspicious of everyone, his paranoia allegedly giving him the habit of glancing in mirrors or other reflective surfaces to check on what people behind him were doing. It would not do for him to see any signs of the revulsion she felt at the sight of him.

He was a tall man, with skinny legs, but a body showing the signs of luxuriant living, his belly having expanded considerably since he had become Emperor. He was only thirty years old, yet his hair was already thinning, a trait he was known to dislike.

As he pulled on his underwear and found his tunic, Flavia recalled some of the stories she had heard about him. In public, he often presented the image of a kind and considerate ruler, throwing extravagant shows for the people of Rome. Chariot races, arena combats, theatre shows and lavish public feasts were all designed to demonstrate his largesse.

He was also making a name for himself as an improver of public buildings, having ordered the renovation of many old and crumbling edifices, although some people had commented that it was Domitian's name which appeared on the new dedication tablets, with all mention of the original founder being omitted. That, she knew, was a sign of his vanity. Still, the works were in the public interest, and his reputation had been enhanced as a result.

In private, though, things were very different. Like many people, he was a man of contradictions. He could, she knew, be very generous to his friends and yet be extremely cruel. Criminals appearing before him for sentencing were now becoming wary of kind words. The more conciliatory Domitian's opening remarks, the more harsh the punishment was likely to be.

He was also showing signs of impulsive cruelty. Several Senators had already been banished or even executed for relatively trivial, and occasionally imagined, offences. Domitian's own cousin, Flavius Sabinus, had been put to death because, when he had been elected consul, the public crier's proclamation had inadvertently referred to Sabinus as Emperor. The unfortunate verbal slip had thrown Domitian into a rage and his cousin had been executed despite his protestations of innocence. How many more such executions would the Emperor order in the coming years, Flavia wondered?

It was not a question she wished to have answered while she was close to him. Proximity to Emperors could, she knew, be fatal. She had liked Domitian's father, old Vespasian, who had been a canny, humorous man with an understanding of how to run an Empire. His elder son, Titus, could have been another such ruler, but Domitian had begun plotting against his older brother as soon as Vespasian had passed away. Domitian had even gone so far as to claim that he should have been co-ruler of the Empire but that his father's will had been forged. Titus, good-natured as he was, had refused to punish his younger sibling even when plots were uncovered, but Titus had not lived long enough for his rule to count for anything. Many people accepted that Domitian had been responsible for his brother's sudden and mysterious death, but such things were never spoken of in anything other than whispers and, even then, only outside the Palace. Nobody close to Domitian would dare utter such thoughts, even though he himself had proclaimed to the Senate that he had been responsible for winning the Empire for his father and brother and that they had now returned it to him. It was an outrageous claim, of course, because Domitian had been a teenage boy when his father had come to power at the end of the disaster of the civil war. Indeed, she knew from speaking to Caratacus, that Domitian had spent much of that war in hiding, emerging only once his father's army had captured Rome from the usurper, Vitellius.

    He was, then, a complex character and one she needed to be careful with. She had heard that he was prone to brooding, often remaining in his chambers alone, not even permitting a slave to be present. Some said he spent his time catching flies and sticking pins through them. If true, it was a bizarre and slightly disturbing hobby.

    He seemed to be brooding now, his ruddy face creased in a frown. Once he was dressed, he turned to face her.

    She lay still, conscious of his eyes wandering up and down her naked body. One thing everyone knew about him was his lust for women. He was married, of course, but his wife had recently been banished. Nobody was quite sure why. Some said it was because their only child, a boy of two years of age, had died earlier that year. According to speculation, this had left Domitian angry that his wife had not produced more children. Having met him, Flavia considered that explanation unlikely. From what she could see, Domitian cared for nobody other than himself, so the lack of an heir was not liable to trouble him.

    Other whispers suggested Domitian had exiled his wife because he was carrying on an affair with his niece.

That, Flavia guessed, was more likely, although she doubted that a man like Domitian would bother exiling his wife simply to prevent her interfering in his love life; he was perfectly capable of carrying on an affair without concern for who knew about it, and both his wife and his niece must have known there were other women. Young or old, Domitian did not mind. If a pretty face came near him, it was quite usual for him to insist on the owner of that face joining him in his bedchamber.

That, Flavia thought to herself, was what had made her own arrival here inevitable once she had managed to gain access to the Emperor. She had always been able to hook men if she wanted to, but Domitian had needed very little encouragement. At their first meeting, arranged thanks to several hefty bribes placed by Facilis, the Emperor's eyes had lit up at the very sight of her. It mattered nothing to him that she was twenty years his senior. She was still an attractive woman and, just as importantly, she had let him know that she was more than willing.

Flavia had always enjoyed sex, and had taken many lovers in her time. Usually, she had chosen men whom she found attractive but, once or twice, she had used her body to snare a man who could be useful to her. Sleeping with Domitian was very much in the latter category. For all his conquests, he was not a great lover, and she had needed to employ her best acting skills to convince him that she had enjoyed what was, in truth, more of a chore than a delight.

Her next move would be more difficult, though. She dared not push things too far because he might become suspicious. Yet he was so fickle that he might never agree to see her again. Now that he had bedded her, his attention could easily move onto other prizes.

"Do you wish me to leave or should I stay here?" she asked, ensuring that her words implied what would happen if she stayed.

Domitian blinked as if coming out of a dream. Then he gave a sly smile as he replied, "Stay. In fact, dress yourself and come with me. Perhaps you will be able to advise me in the same way you gave counsel to my father."

"I thought you were going to the Senate," she replied, languidly stretching her limbs to provide him with a better view of what he would enjoy once his business was done. "Women are forbidden from attending the Curia."

"I have more private matters to attend to first," he informed her. "Letters, despatches, petitions; that sort of thing. I thought you might enjoy sitting with me while I attend to those."

Which meant, she realised, that he would enjoy impressing her with the extent of his power. He was the ruler of the civilised world, the most powerful man on Earth, whose word was law for millions of people, yet he was still insecure and vain enough to want to show off to his latest lover.

"I would be delighted," she smiled. "Although I am not sure that I will be able to offer much guidance. I have lived away from politics for more than ten years."

"Come anyway," he told her brusquely.

She rose from the bed, picked up her discarded clothing and dressed hurriedly. Finding an ivory comb on his dressing table, she hastily tugged it through her long, dark hair. She quickly piled up her tresses and shoved some hairpins in to hold them roughly in place. The result, she could tell from a glance in the mirror, was less than satisfactory, but a high class Roman lady never wore her hair down in public.

It would, though, have to do. Domitian was fidgeting impatiently by the time she turned to him.

"Come," he commanded peremptorily.

He led her through the thick, oak door to an antechamber which served as his private office. His secretary, a middle-aged Greek freedman, was waiting patiently, standing near the main door which led to the Palace's maze of public rooms. He held a bundle of scrolls cradled in his arms. Flavia idly wondered how long he had been there and what sort of terror Domitian must impart for the man to stand holding the scrolls for so long without daring to sit down.

The Emperor took a seat at a large desk, gesturing to Flavia to seat herself on a padded armchair to one side. She did so, noticing that the secretary ignored her. No doubt he was accustomed to seeing strange women in the Emperor's company and knew better than to make any sort of comment.

"What do you have for me today, Epaphroditus?" Domitian asked with an air of weary boredom.

The secretary laid his bundle of scrolls on a small table on the far side of the desk. Lifting up one of these, he unrolled it and passed it across to the Emperor.

"A report from Silius Barbicus on the construction of the Rhine defences you ordered, Caesar."

Domitian glanced at the neatly inscribed handwriting on the scroll, clearly doing little more than scanning it.

"Is there anything of importance in it?" he asked.

Epaphroditus, obviously expecting such a question, replied, "Only that the local Germanic tribe, the Chatti, are displeased at the works."

"They would be," Domitian grunted. "When the defences are complete, they will no longer be able to raid our territory."

"Silius Barbicus reports that the more peaceful tribal leaders see the *Limes* as a barrier to trade," the secretary explained.

"The *Limes* are intended to be barriers," Domitian scoffed. "That is their purpose. When confronted by ditches, ramparts and fences, they will be forced to enter Roman territory through controlled gateways. What they are really objecting to is having to pay taxes on their goods rather than smuggling them across an open frontier."

"Yes, Caesar," Epaphroditus dutifully acknowledged.

Domitian picked up the manuscript again, reading the relevant section more closely. When he was done, he tossed it casually back to the secretary who caught it, rolled it up and placed it back on his small table.

Domitian said, "Draft a reply to Silius Barbicus. Tell him I intend to visit Gaul to inspect the *Limes* for myself."

The secretary revealed no surprise at this sudden announcement. As he scribbled a short reminder to himself on a wax tablet, he said, "Yes, Caesar. Shall I give him any indication of when he might expect you?"

"When it is convenient for me," Domitian snapped. "Tell him also that these ... what tribe did you say?"

"The Chatti, Caesar."

"Yes, the Chatti. Tell him that he should keep a close eye on them. If they give any trouble, I will deal harshly with them."

"Yes, Caesar."

"What else do you have for me?"

Picking up another scroll, Epaphroditus said, "A further petition from the people of Ephesus, Caesar. If you recall, they wish to erect a statue of you in the main Agora in their town. Their delegation is waiting outside in the hope of presenting the formal document to you."

"So they are back again?"

"Indeed, Caesar. You ordered them to return today. If you recall, their proposal was for a statue constructed of bronze. You indicated that was not acceptable."

"Ah, yes. I remember. What do they propose now?"

"A statue of marble, Sire."

"Not good enough," Domitian frowned. "Tell them to come back tomorrow with a better proposal."

"Of course, Caesar. Would you like me to give them a suggestion as to which material would be acceptable?"

Domitian snorted, "If they cannot work that out for themselves, tell them to take a stroll around the Forum and look at my new statues there."

"Yes, Caesar."

Flavia sat silently as she watched the exchange, marvelling at Domitian's vanity. New Emperors always had statues erected because it was a way of reminding the people what their ruler looked like. Sometimes, for reasons of speed and economy, existing statues simply had the heads removed and replaced by images of the new Emperor. Domitian, though, had decided that the Imperial Treasury he had inherited from his father and brother could be put to better use, and had insisted that all new statues of him should be made from gold. The people of Ephesus, far away in Ionian Greece, had clearly not heard about this decree. Flavia pitied them, knowing that Domitian was amusing himself at their expense. His apparent forgetfulness was, she recognised, a ploy to convince her that he was so busy he could not recall their earlier visit. That was patently untrue, but she dutifully blinked in wide-eyed amazement at the Emperor's workload.

"What else?" Domitian asked his secretary.

Another scroll was passed over.

"A report from the borders of Dacia, Sire. It seems the Dacians are proving troublesome again."

"When are they not?" the Emperor sighed. "What is it this time?"

"Nothing specific, Sire," Epaphroditus replied. "There are suggestions they may refuse to pay tribute. There is nothing official, but merchants returning from Dacia say the mood of that people is becoming increasingly hostile."

"Damn them!" Domitian exclaimed, hurling the scroll down on his desk. "They need to be taught a lesson."

He shot a dark look at the secretary as he demanded, "How many Legions do we have near their border?"

"Only two at present, Caesar."

"Write letters to the Legates informing them to make a show of strength on the border. They are not to cross into Dacian land, but to make sure the barbarians know they are capable of doing so should the need arise. And prepare a list for me of suitable senators I could send out there to take command of an expedition."

"Very good, Caesar," Epaphroditus nodded as he jotted down another note on his tablet.

"Bloody Dacians," the Emperor muttered. "Is there anything else needing urgent attention?"

The scribe still had several untouched scrolls, but he replied, "I am sure most of these could wait until a more convenient time, Caesar."

Shooting a knowing glance in Flavia's direction, Domitian asked the secretary, "Is there anything from Britannia?"

Epaphroditus nodded as he rifled through the scrolls, handing one across the desk.

"This is a report from Julius Agricola in Britannia, Caesar. He seeks despatches of new recruits to bring his legions up to strength following his recent campaign."

Domitian gave Flavia a smug smile as he quickly read the scroll. She knew he was showing off, but her interest was piqued nonetheless, especially because his arrogance might just have presented her with the opportunity she had been hoping for.

"He does not seem to say very much about the current state of affairs on the island," Domitian observed sourly. "Do we have anything from Popidius Flaccus?"

"Not for some time, Caesar," the scribe explained. "His last letter suggested that, despite Julius Agricola's claims to have conquered the entire island, there is still considerable resistance to our control of the northern regions."

Domitian sat back in his chair, the fingers of his right hand drumming a pensive rhythm on his knee while he made a great show of considering this news. Eventually, as she had known he would, he turned to Flavia.

"What do you think?" he asked her. "Agricola claimed the island was under our full control following his recent easy victory. Now he wants reinforcements."

Flavia shot a meaningful glance in the direction of the secretary before raising her eyebrows to Domitian in a silent question.

"You may speak freely in front of Epaphroditus," the Emperor confirmed.

"Very well," she replied with apparent reluctance. "In my opinion, Julius Agricola is a fine commander. I have no doubt he genuinely believed he had won a decisive victory after what has been a very long and arduous campaign. However, the northern tribes are renowned for their stubbornness, so it does not surprise me that they continue to resist."

She hesitated, as if unwilling to say any more.

"But?" Domitian prompted expectantly.

With a hesitant sigh, Flavia explained, "Quite frankly, Caesar, the northern parts of Britannia are hardly worth the effort of conquering. There are endless tracts of mountains, lakes and forests, but nothing of real value. I believe there is some coal, but there are no important minerals. As for the people, their tribes are widely scattered, each village constantly at war with its neighbours. Controlling such people would certainly require a great many troops. In that respect, I can understand why Julius Agricola has requested reinforcements."

She could see that she had Domitian's full attention. Offering up a silent prayer of thanks to the Gods for presenting this unexpected opportunity, she went on, "Julius Agricola is, of course, a highly experienced commander. He has worked wonders in Britannia since he arrived there."

"Go on," the Emperor nodded.

"Well, my Lord, I confess that I did not believe it possible for even the might of Rome to conquer Britannia. The land is too wild, the people too fierce. Most of them would rather die than surrender. Yet Julius Agricola has accomplished this almost impossible feat. I do believe that, if you send him more troops, he might actually be capable of subduing the place. Whether the financial rewards will make that worthwhile remains in doubt, but his victory would certainly add to the glory of Roman arms."

"That is not something to be lightly dismissed," Domitian observed pensively.

She gave a slow nod of agreement, hoping she would not need to be more obvious in her comments. She wanted him to grasp the wider implications of what she had said. His father, she knew, would have recognised her implied warning without needing to be told, but Domitian, it seemed, was not quite as subtle as she had hoped. Yet she was uncertain whether she dared express the thought openly.

Gesturing towards the pile of scrolls, he added, "And you see from these other reports that barbarians must be taught to fear and respect Rome."

"Indeed," she agreed, mentally furious with him. It appeared that he needed more of a prompt.

She made a show of brightening her face, as if an idea had struck her.

"May I make a suggestion, my Lord?"

He frowned for a moment before apparently remembering that he had asked her to accompany him in order to provide advice.

"What is it?" he asked.

"You were seeking the names of men who might command an expedition to Dacia. Why not Julius Agricola? He has been in Britannia for several years, and is perhaps overdue a triumphant return. He is the most successful General under your command. The victories he has achieved in Britannia are little short of remarkable. Surely he is the perfect choice to bring more glory to Rome by defeating the Dacians? That would be of greater service than battling a few disaffected rebels in the wilds of northern Britannia."

This time, she saw, her unspoken message got through to him. A look that might have been fear or horror, or perhaps jealousy, flashed across his eyes.

"Thank you, my Lady," he said softly. "Your advice is, as my father told me, worth listening to."

He turned back to his secretary.

"I want another list prepared. Find me men who could be sent to replace Agricola as Governor of Britannia."

"Yes, Caesar. Do you wish me to draft a letter to Julius Agricola informing him that he is to command in Dacia?"

"Certainly not!" exclaimed Domitian. "I want him recalled to Rome. I will still need someone else to go to Dacia."

The secretary did not question the Emperor's apparently contradictory commands. He merely nodded and said, "Very good, Caesar."

"Now," Domitian declared, "I have no time for any more of this. The Lady Flavia and I have other business to attend to before I go to speak to the Senate."

Epaphroditus' face was an unreadable mask as he nodded, "Yes, Caesar."

Without saying another word, he gathered up the scrolls and hurried from the room.

When he had left, Domitian held out his hand to Flavia and helped her to her feet.

"Your mind is as excellent as my father told me," he smiled. "But not, I fear, as subtle as my own."

"Naturally," she said, putting on a perplexed frown. "That is why you are Emperor. But may I ask why you do not wish Julius Agricola to command your troops in Dacia?"

She knew the answer. She had, after all, planted it in his mind, but she also understood that she could never let him know. He needed to believe that he had found the solution for himself.

He grinned happily.

"I confess I have overlooked Britannia since I took my rightful place as Emperor," he admitted. "However, now I see that I have allowed Agricola too much time to build up a power base for himself. A General with three Legions who are loyal to him, and with a track record of many victories, is not a man I can afford to ignore."

Flavia put a hand to her mouth and widened her eyes in mock horror as if she had only just realised the implications of what he was saying.

"You think he could be a threat to you?" she asked breathlessly.

"All successful men are a threat to an emperor," he confided. "They are jealous of me, you see. And Generals with Legions backing them are sometimes inclined to take action once their jealousy takes hold."

She nodded, giving him a smile.

"Then it is as well that you realised the threat. What will you do about him?"

He shrugged, "I have not decided. I will probably award him some triumphal honours, then pack him off somewhere he can do no harm."

A malicious smile curved his lips as he added, "Or I might do something more permanent."

In her former life as Cartimandua, Flavia had been renowned for her ruthlessness, but she would never have ordered the execution of an obviously loyal subordinate simply out of suspicion, and she felt a tinge of regret at the casual way Domitian spoke of killing a man who had served him well. Agricola, though, was not her main concern.

She regarded the Emperor with an admiring smile as she said, "You are very cunning, my Lord. But perhaps I could make another suggestion?"

He was in a good humour now. Taking hold of her hand, he moved in close, kissed her on the lips, then breathed, "Of course you may."

This time she abandoned subtlety. Maintaining her false smile, she planted his hand on her breast, holding it in place.

In low, seductive tones, she suggested, "Whoever you send to Britannia to replace Agricola should not be given the same opportunity to build victories for his own glory. As I told you, there is nothing but wilderness and savage people in the north. They are not worth expending time and troops on conquering. It might be better to consolidate the southern part of the island in order to extract what riches it has. That way, the province might begin returning a profit for your treasury."

Keeping his hand firmly in place, he cocked his head to one side, thinking long and hard. Then he grinned and nodded, pulling her close to him and squeezing the soft flesh of her breast while his other hand snaked round to plant itself on her buttock.

"My father was most definitely right about you," he told her as he pulled her close. "For a woman, you have a most remarkable mind."

"Thank you, my Lord."

"But he was also wrong."

Flavia could feel the hardening in his loins as he pressed against her. Her own hand slid down to caress him as she maintained her false smile.

"Oh?" she breathed softly. "In what way?"

"He should have taken you to his bed," Domitian informed her. "For all the cleverness of your mind, it is your body I desire now."

Flavia put her arms around him and reached up to kiss him passionately. Somehow, she managed to conceal her revulsion as she whispered, "I am at your disposal, my Lord."

Chapter XXIII

Iusta was waiting for her when she left the Imperial Palace. The maid scurried over to greet her, with the slaves bearing Flavia's litter struggling in her wake.

Iusta said nothing, simply guiding Flavia to the curtained litter and helping her step inside.

"Take me to the nearest bath house," Flavia commanded. "I feel the need to wash."

It was mid-afternoon now, the sun at its hottest, still warm despite the waning season. The streets were as crowded as ever, the litter bearers needing to battle their way through the noisy crowds as they carried Flavia to the bath house.

Inside the litter, she lay back on the soft cushions and closed her eyes, feeling pleased with herself despite the cost to her pride. It was not the first time she had slept with a man in order to make him do what she wanted but, somehow, it had left her feeling dirty. Still, she had achieved her goal far more quickly than she had dared to hope, and that was something to be grateful for.

The bath house was a large affair, its outer walls lavishly decorated with statuary and brightly coloured murals. Flavia stepped out of the litter and hurried to the door, enjoying the coolness of the lofty entrance room with its marble-tiled floor and tasteful decoration.

It was the time of day when both men and women could bathe together, so Flavia was required to pay a higher entrance fee than normal. As a woman, it was expected that she would be able to more than make up for the additional cost by having men pay her for sex. That was the last thing she wanted, but she needed to cleanse herself, so she paid the attendant the fee, stripped off her clothing and left it with Iusta to watch. Donning a pair of the heavy, wooden clogs that would prevent the heated floor from scalding her feet, she wrapped a towel around herself and proceeded through the doors to the first chamber.

The bath was busy, as it usually was. This was one of the more select establishments, but everyone in Rome visited the baths on a more or less daily basis, and there was no escaping the crowds, especially when joint bathing was permitted.

She did not normally mind the attention she received from the male bathers, but today she found their presence irritating. Domitian, it seemed, had affected her more deeply than he should have.

She could have waited until the time when the baths were reserved for women, but the need to feel clean was too strong to resist, so she resigned herself to coping with the mixed bathing.

She slid the sandals from her feet, dropped the towel and stepped down into the cold pool, feeling her body tense as she lowered herself into the water. Undeterred, she ploughed on, going deeper and even ducking her head underneath the surface. The cold water served to refresh her, soothing every pore as she resurfaced, took a breath, and began to swim.

The pool was not large, and there were too many other bathers for her to make more than a few strokes, but the effort eased the tension in her muscles. Turning, she swam back to the side of the pool where she beckoned one of the slave attendants to pass her some soap. Most people scrubbed themselves in the warm pool, but Flavia felt the need to cleanse herself with the chill of cold water. Briskly, she washed herself, not caring who was watching. Many men, she knew, visited the baths in order to watch the naked women as much as to wash. Some of the women were there to exploit that fact and perhaps earn some extra coin, while others, especially the younger ones, simply enjoyed the attention and made great play of showing off. Flavia could understand that but, for her own part, she had never felt the need to vie for anyone's attention. She was already aware that some of the men were casting appreciative looks in her direction, but she paid them no heed. *Fools*, she thought to herself as she finished washing and climbed out of the pool, feeling the delicious chill of the air on her wet skin. She towelled her dripping hair, then, shoving her feet into the heavy sandals and wrapping the towel around herself once more, she proceeded towards the hot pool.

Fingers of steam wafted across the surface of the dark, soapy water, and the heat struck her like a physical blow as she went through the doors into the hot room. Large windows admitted warm sunlight to add to the sensation, and her skin reacted with a flush of warmth.

"Good afternoon," said a deep, male voice.

A portly, middle-aged man, naked apart from a towel wrapped loosely around his waist, was smiling at her.

"Would you care to sit with me?" he asked, gesturing to one of the side alcoves where cushions covered stone benches and where many couples could retire to a place with an element of privacy.

Flavia shook her head.

"Perhaps another day," she replied politely.

The man gave a regretful shrug, inclined his head in a slight bow, then moved on in search of some other companion.

Flavia smiled to herself. No, she need not worry about competition from younger women. She could still attract male company if she wished, although whether the chubby man would have been her chosen partner was debatable. In the baths, all men were supposed to be equal, no signs of status visible. Yet the man had a certain bearing about him, a sense that he was, if not important, then certainly wealthy. Such a man might prove useful to her in the future but, for today, she wanted no company, not even one of the strutting young bucks who paraded around naked like peacocks, proudly displaying their manhood for all to see.

Not that the alcoves were used solely for sex; sometimes people merely sat and relaxed, enjoying the hot, steamy atmosphere of the pool. In the baths, there was something for everyone. In another part of this complex, Flavia knew, was a library and, outside, a games yard where men lifted weights or threw balls to one another, keeping a score of who caught the most throws and who would be buying the drinks later.

Inside, as she slowly walked along the edge of the pool, she took in the other amenities. Some patrons were lying on tables, being massaged or having oil rubbed on their bodies by the slave attendants who used strigils to scrape the oil away, cleansing the pores more thoroughly than mere soap and water could achieve. That was a treat Flavia decided to indulge later. First, she required the soothing comfort of immersing herself in heated water.

The hot pool was busy, but she found a space near the far end. Again, she divested herself of the towel and stepped down into the water, luxuriating in its welcoming warmth. Making herself comfortable on one of the stone seats beneath the surface, she closed her eyes and relaxed, enjoying the soft, caressing movements of the constantly circulating water.

She felt detached, as if half asleep, almost able to cut out the raucous noise and chatter all around her, the splashing and horseplay of the younger couples and the distant shouts from the games yard beyond the windows.

"There you are," said another deep voice.

She was aware of movement as someone settled down beside her, but it took a moment for her to realise that he had spoken to her. Opening her eyes, she turned to see a familiar face.

"Caratacus!" she hissed in surprise.

"Relax," he told her, leaning close so as to speak without raising his voice.

"I am trying to," she retorted. "You have interrupted that. What are you doing here? I thought I told you we should not meet in public."

"It is quite safe," he assured her. "Nobody followed you."

"Apart from you, it seems," she shot back.

"Not just me," he grinned, raising a hand out of the water to signal to a second man who moved, a little self-consciously, from behind her and dropped into the pool to her left, sitting so that she was between the two men.

"Facilis?" she frowned.

He gave her an apologetic half-smile.

"We were worried about you," he explained.

"We? Since when have you known Caratacus?"

"Since yesterday," the Briton interrupted. "Although, to be fair, we met some years ago. Just after you handed me over to the Romans. Facilis was among the Governor's aides at the time."

Flavia ignored the reminder of her role in Caratacus' capture. It was in the past, and she had done what she believed to be right at the time. She would do it again in the same circumstances. Caratacus, though, rarely wasted an opportunity to cast it up to her, which only served to increase her irritation at his unwanted presence.

"And you just happened to bump into one another yesterday, I suppose?" she challenged.

"Absolutely!" chirped Caratacus.

Flavia turned to Facilis, raising an interrogatory eyebrow.

He shifted, his eyes refusing to meet her accusation.

"He came to see me," he admitted. "It seems he followed you to my home."

"I see," she sighed. "So you both followed me to the Palace, I suppose?"

"Something like that," Caratacus agreed. "But your love struck friend there is correct. We were worried about you. We knew his bribes would gain you admittance to the

Emperor, but we had no way of knowing what would happen once you met him."

Flavia was never one to miss an unsubtle reference. She turned her head again, studying Facilis who seemed to have taken an interest in the frothing water bubbling around his chest. His face was slightly flushed, perhaps because of the heat. Or perhaps not, she realised as she became more acutely aware of the proximity of their naked bodies under the surface of the water and, unaccountably, felt unusually self-conscious about it.

Facilis, it seemed, was even more conscious of their closeness since he refused to look at her, or to allow their arms to accidentally brush against one another.

Before she had time to consider Facilis' feelings, though, Caratacus continued, "So, tell us what happened."

Flavia shook her head slowly, wondering at the twisting, unpredictable currents of fate. She leaned back but, aware that the move had exposed the curve of her breasts above the dark water and increased Facilis' embarrassment, sat forwards again.

Gathering her thoughts, she told them, "I think I was successful. Fortunately, he is an arrogant man. He could not resist discussing the situation in my homeland, and I think I was able to persuade him of the futility of waging war in the north. He intends to recall ..." She hesitated, not wishing to mention anyone by name in case they were overheard. "... the General to Rome, and to order the withdrawal of his troops from the north."

"Yes!" exclaimed Caratacus, bunching his fists in triumph.

His unexpected shout brought one or two looks of surprise from nearby bathers, causing Flavia to shoot him a warning scowl.

"Sorry," he mumbled as he settled back, grinning sheepishly.

"You must have been very persuasive," he chuckled once the rest of the people in the pool had gone back to ignoring them.

"I hope so," she sighed. "Even so, it will be some time before word reaches the far north."

"How long, do you think?" Caratacus asked.

She shrugged, "Three or four weeks, at least. Perhaps longer. It is difficult to be certain about such things. Imperial messengers use relays of fast horses, but there can always be delays. It also depends on favourable winds for the ships."

"A lot can happen in that time," he muttered, a frown of concern adding to the wrinkles on his forehead.

"There is nothing we can do about that," she replied. "We must hope that ... our friend can survive long enough. But there is another potential problem."

"What is that?"

"The, ah ... man I saw today is unpredictable. He may change his mind before he signs the letters."

"Then you had best return tomorrow and make sure he does not," Caratacus told her.

Flavia was looking at the elderly Briton, so she could not see Facilis' face, but she could almost feel his imploring eyes burning into the back of her head.

"I would prefer not to," she said simply. "He is a dangerous man. Not to mention unpleasant."

"We cannot be sure unless you do," Caratacus pointed out.

"I know."

"And it would look odd if you did not go back."

"I know that, too."

"Then you will return tomorrow?"

"I suppose so."

"Good," Caratacus nodded approvingly. "We should meet here afterwards."

"Not here," she told him. "Belinus' cookshop would be better."

"Fine. We will come after you again to make sure nobody else is following you."

Flavia gave a nod.

"Until tomorrow then," Caratacus said, pushing himself up out of the water and turning to leave.

Flavia watched him, noting the lean toughness of his body, slightly wrinkled by age, yet still displaying the physique of a man twenty years his junior.

He half turned, grinned and winked at her, knowing she had been watching him. Then, with a curt wave and a nod of farewell, he picked up a towel, shoved his feet into a pair of heavy sandals, and clopped away round the pool, occasionally pausing to chat with a pretty woman as he passed.

Flavia sighed, "He is a most irritating man, don't you think?"

For almost the first time, Facilis looked at her.

"He is a difficult man to oppose," he said by way of agreement. "Very forceful."

"Yes, that is a good word to describe him."

"I am surprised he never attempted to return to Britannia," Facilis remarked with a pensive frown. "He spent so many years fighting us, yet now he lives among us."

"He has a daughter and grandchildren here," Flavia informed him. "I believe he did intend to return to Britannia after the Civil War, but his son-in-law is a Senator, and he refused to help."

Facilis' frown deepened, then he smiled as understanding dawned.

"The Senator and his family would have been implicated if the infamous Caratacus had turned up in Britannia once again."

"Exactly," Flavia agreed, delighted to discover Facilis' ability to understand the complexities of Roman political life.

"He is an intriguing character," Facilis mused. "He likes you, despite what happened in the past."

For once, Flavia was surprised.

"I doubt very much whether he likes me at all," she replied with a shake of her head.

"Perhaps it would be more accurate to say he respects you," Facilis conceded.

With a soft smile, Flavia admitted, "For all his many faults, I respect him, too."

"Is that why you agreed to help him with this … venture?"

"Partly, I suppose. Mostly it was because I know how much I owe Calgacus, but I must confess that it was also partly because I was growing bored. Caratacus provided me with a challenge."

She had not meant to reveal so much of her private thinking, but she found it was easy to confide in Facilis. He, though, regarded her with a concerned expression.

"It is a challenge which has placed you in danger," he reminded her.

She assured him, "I am not reckless, Lucius. I have lived with danger for most of my life, but I have always planned my actions to minimise the risk."

He hesitated, diverting his eyes from her once again. At first, she thought this might be because she had embarrassed him by addressing him by his *praenomen* rather than his more formal *cognomen*, and she was surprised to find that she found his reaction endearing. But when he spoke, she realised his response was due to a more serious concern.

Still unable to look at her, he said softly, "I must tell you that I find it difficult to think of you with ... the man you met earlier. I know what you must have done to persuade him."

"If it is any comfort," she told him, "I did not enjoy a single moment of it."

"But you will go back to see him again tomorrow?"

"I must. You know I must. It would look very suspicious if I did not."

"And you will sleep with him again?"

"Probably," she admitted.

He took a deep breath, closing his eyes.

"I find the thought of that hard to bear," he said in a low whisper, barely audible over the tumult of the pool.

Flavia reached out her hand to place it gently on his arm, seeing the quickening of his heart in the expression on his face as she did so.

"I appreciate your feelings, Lucius," she told him. "You need not worry. I can deal with him. He will soon forget me. He is that sort of man. But I must go back or he might suspect my motives. Besides, I need to be sure he has signed the letters."

Facilis gave a reluctant nod.

"I understand," he said.

They sat in silence for a moment, each of them deep in thought. Then Flavia slowly stood up. He turned to look at her, and she smiled when she saw him swallow nervously at the sight of her body rising out of the water like one of Neptune's sea nymphs.

"I think I will go home now," she told him.

Holding out her hand to him, she added, "Why don't you come with me?"

Chapter XXIV

Flavia returned to the Palace the following day, arriving just before midday. The servants and guards let her pass with virtually no comment when she asked to speak to Epaphroditus. The secretary, ever discrete, welcomed her politely then led her to Domitian's private chambers.

"Caesar is expecting you," he informed her, using the same matter-of-fact tone in which he probably announced that dinner was about to be served.

He pushed open the door, closing it behind her as soon as she stepped into the bedchamber.

Domitian was indeed expecting her, lying naked in his bed, reading a scroll of Herodotus' Greek Histories which he tossed carelessly to the floor when she entered the room.

"I had hoped you would arrive earlier," he complained peevishly.

"My apologies, my Lord. I was not certain that I would be welcome."

"You are always welcome," he replied. "But I do not like to be kept waiting."

She began pushing aside the shoulders of her dress as she kicked off her sandals.

"I'm afraid that it takes me longer to apply my makeup than it used to," she smiled sweetly. "I wanted to look my best for you."

"You look magnificent," he assured her as she tugged the hair pins from her head and allowed her long, dark tresses to cascade around her bare shoulders.

Feigning delight, she quickly joined him on the bed, arcing one leg over him to straddle him.

"Thank you, my Lord," she teased. "And now, I will do my best to make up for my tardiness."

As before, their lovemaking was quick, enthusiastic and almost brutal. Domitian referred to it as "bed wrestling", and did his best to ensure it lived up to that name. By the time they were finished, they were both sweating and tired, collapsing side by side on the rumpled bed.

"You really are magnificent," he told her in a lazy whisper.

"As are you, my Lord."

"So I have been told," he admitted without a shred of irony.

"Do you have another busy day ahead of you?" she enquired, snuggling close to him and draping her leg across his hips.

"Every day is busy," he confirmed.

"And will you require my advice on Britannia again today?"

"No, that is all taken care of. I signed the letters this morning."

"I always admire decisive men," she purred, nibbling at his ear.

He lay still, his eyes half-closed, sated after their energetic coupling. This, she decided, was the right time to make her final play.

Running her hand across his hairless chest, she said softly, "I hope I have been of service to you, my Lord."

"Yes, you have," he agreed dreamily.

"Then might I seek a favour in return?"

His eyes snapped open and alert as he turned his head to look at her.

"A favour?"

"The matter on which I originally came to see you yesterday. We never had time to discuss it."

He stared at her for a moment before saying, "Everyone wants something from me. Did you know that?"

"That is because, as Emperor, you have authority over everything."

"That is true," he sighed. "Very well, what is it you wanted to discuss?"

She leaned up on one elbow, moving close so that he could feel the warmth of her body and be in no doubt that she had been a willing partner.

"It is a small matter to you, Caesar, but important to me. You see, although your father awarded me grants of land, I find myself temporarily short of cash, and my creditors are pressing me for payment. I was hoping that, knowing your generosity to those who serve you well, you might see fit to award me a small bounty so that I need not sell off my landholdings in order to pay my debts."

A sneer twisted the corner of his mouth as he asked, "Money? Is that what you want? I should have known. Everyone wants money, power, or fame."

She adopted a slightly hurt expression as she replied, "I have no interest in fame, Caesar, and, as for power, I have experienced that before and have had my fill of it. I have no ambitions other than to live quietly and in a measure of comfort. Unfortunately, it is not always easy to maintain even that modest lifestyle when you are a woman alone in a man's world."

"How much?" he asked tersely.

"A mere ten thousand denarii," she said in what she hoped was a hesitant whisper.

He lay very still for a long moment, making her wonder whether she had overplayed her request. Yet it had been necessary. Sooner or later, he would have wondered why she had wanted to see him, and what it was she wanted from him. As Emperor, he would know that most women would agree to becoming his lover in the hope of gaining power. She could not afford for him to think that of her, but greed was an equally plausible motive.

Abruptly, he moved away, sliding from beneath her leg and sitting up on the edge of the bed.

"Is something wrong?" she asked. "Have I offended you?"

"You are just like all the others, aren't you?" he complained, not turning round.

"I am sorry, my Lord. It is just that the sum is so insignificant for someone in your position, yet it is a considerable burden to me, and your divine father always told me that he would ensure I need never worry about such things."

"Is that why you came to my bed?"

"I came because you asked me, Caesar. I hope I have not disappointed you in that."

His shoulders heaved as he let out a loud sigh.

"No, you have not disappointed me."

He stood up, moving to a nearby couch where he had laid his clothes. As he began to dress, he turned to look at her.

"Very well," he said, his voice holding a harder edge than she had been accustomed to hearing. "Since you have played the part of a street prostitute, it is only right that you be paid. I will speak to Epaphroditus and have him authorise a payment from the Imperial Treasury."

"Thank you, Caesar."

She spoke softly, blinking and managing to force a trickle of moisture from her eyes. She hoped he would believe his insult had hurt her.

"Should I come back tomorrow?" she asked, stifling a mock sob.

"Perhaps," he shrugged. "I am very busy. I will send for you if I require you."

"Of course, Caesar. I shall await your summons."

A summons she knew would probably never come. Her request for money had offended him, and she was sure that he would turn his attention to other conquests. He might perhaps call for her if he ever needed advice on events in Britannia but, other than that, she doubted whether she would ever see him again.

Even that would be too soon, she reflected sourly.

"I must go to address the Senate now," he informed her. "Do not be here when I return."

She did not have time to reply. He strode to the door, flung it open and stalked out, leaving her alone.

She lay still for a long time, listening to his receding footsteps and his petulant complaints to his secretary as they moved away into the Palace. She half expected him to order some of his slaves to throw her out of the palace, or perhaps have his guards do away with her, but there was no sound other than the fading slap of sandals and Domitian's querulous grumbling.

Breathing a sigh of relief, she rose from the bed and retrieved her clothing. Dressing hurriedly, she moved to face the mirror that stood on his dressing table, regarding her reflection as if trying to examine her own soul. The past two days, she thought, had been as eventful as any she had ever experienced.

Had it been worth it, she wondered?

Yes, her reflection silently answered. Everything had worked out almost exactly as she had hoped. In fact, better than she could have dreamed.

Caratacus would now leave her in peace and, more importantly, would not attempt to assassinate Domitian.

And she had met Facilis, who would no doubt be like an eager puppy when he saw her. The thought of him made her smile even more broadly. How strange that, after so many years, she might have found a man she genuinely wanted to spend time with.

It was odd how much she liked him. He was not big, or tough, or strong in any physical sense, the way most of her lovers had been. Yet he was clever, resourceful and talented, and had spent his life around men of more authority but lesser intellect. He understood power and how it could be used, and she already felt that he could simply look at her and know exactly what she was thinking. For someone who had spent a lifetime ensuring that nobody could read her mind, his uncanny empathy made her feel vulnerable in a way she had never experienced. Even more surprising was that this feeling of vulnerability did not make her want to push him away but, instead, to be close to him.

It was a strange feeling, one that made her heart skip happily, as if she were once again the eighteen-year-old Queen of the Brigantes. That, she recalled, was the last time she had felt like this. When she had first met Calgacus.

Calgacus.

That was who this had all been for. She would never see him again, and he would never know what she had done, what she had sacrificed, to help him. Somehow, the thought of him did not hurt quite as much as it usually did. Perhaps that was because she could do no more for him, or perhaps it was because meeting Facilis had softened the memories.

"You are becoming old and maudlin," she scolded her mirror image.

The woman in the mirror looked back at her with an amused smile. With her long, dark hair hanging loose, she looked more like Cartimandua than Flavia, a reminder of past times and lost futures.

"I am no longer you," Flavia told her silent double as she gathered up her hair and jammed the long pins in it to hold it in place.

"Goodbye, Cartimandua," she told her reflection.

Then she strode from the room, making her way to the outer world and the rest of her life.

Chapter XXV

Togodumnus sat by the hearth fire, deep in thought, cradling a bowl of vegetable broth which Thenu had proudly served from the pot that sat bubbling on the hearth stones.

"Are you not hungry?" she asked, her face wearing a look of hurt disappointment at the thought that the soup might not meet his expectations.

"I am sorry," he told her with a smile as he spooned a mouthful from the bowl. "The broth really is very good."

"I spent all afternoon preparing it," she explained.

"I know. It is very good."

She gave a tentative smile, as if unsure whether to believe him, so he ate the soup with obvious enjoyment, letting her see that he appreciated her hard work.

Thenu never seemed to relax, he realised. She was on edge all the time. Even when they made love, she clung to him as if terrified that he might abandon her. Those feelings seemed to almost overwhelm her when he did leave, as he had done the day before when he had visited the Governor again. Thenu always seemed to suspect that he might not return from those trips, and her face had been a picture of relief when he had ridden back into the village earlier that afternoon.

Her loneliness made him feel guilty, but he did not know how to overcome her sense of insecurity because he was partly to blame. He knew that she was finding it difficult to mingle with the other villagers. Some of the women were wary of her because she came from another tribe and had been a prisoner of Rome for many months. She was shy, nervous and terrified of offending anyone, so she rarely spoke which often gave the impression that she was aloof and felt superior to the other villagers. As wife of the head man, a man who had himself been appointed by the Romans, she was regarded with more than a hint of suspicion by the few Boresti who remained in their little settlement.

In some ways, he knew, it was for the best. The less she mingled with the other villagers, the less chance of their shared secret being revealed. While Togodumnus wished he could do something to alleviate her feelings of isolation, he was only too aware of the dangers of including others in his clandestine activities. It did not concern him too much that he, too, was regarded as a man apart, because it had been that way most of his life. When growing up, he had rarely fitted in with the other boys of his age, a situation that had continued as he grew into manhood. He had been alone all his life, with only his family to provide any sort of comfort. Even then, with two sisters who had little in common with him, and a father who, despite his recent admission to the contrary, had tended to regard him as a failure, the only person he really missed was his mother. Yet even that separation was not total because, in recent weeks, Beatha had assumed the role of go-between, meeting Togodumnus in secret to exchange news and accept small supplies of food which she would take back to the rebels' mountain hideaway. He treasured those brief assignations because they were a link to happier times. They helped him cope with the sense of isolation, but in some ways they added to his feelings of guilt because he knew that Thenu had nobody apart from him.

There was, though, nothing he could do to change things. At least, not if he intended to continue aiding the rebels. His decision meant that it was necessary for him to appear friendly towards Rome, to speak to the soldiers in the watchtower, to visit the Governor, and to entertain any officers or officials who passed through their little settlement.

The people, he knew, resented Rome and wanted nothing to do with their overlords, but he dared not reveal his true feelings. Many of the villagers were plain, simple folk who might inadvertently betray too much. That was a risk he was not prepared to take, for their own sakes as much as for himself and Thenu. Rome, he knew, could be a harsh master, and that knowledge was weighing heavily on him just now.

"What is wrong?" Thenu asked him once he had finished his meal.

He looked at her across the fire, saw the concern in her face and knew that she was able to read his moods.

He sighed, "I saw some unpleasant sights at the Governor's camp."

She moved around the fire, pulling her chair close to his and reaching out to take his hand.

"Tell me," she encouraged. "You have nobody else you can talk to. You should not keep such things to yourself."

"It will not make pleasant listening," he warned.

"Tell me anyway."

He sighed again, squeezing her hand to let her know he was grateful for her support.

"The Romans caught a batch of raiders," he explained. "They crucified ten of them."

For a moment, she sat very still. Then she said softly, "I have heard of this punishment. It sounds awful."

"It is. They set up the crosses outside their fort, facing the hills. Ten of them in a row. Then they forced all the local villagers to come and watch the men die."

"You as well?"

He nodded.

"I missed the beginning, when they nailed them to the wood. I am glad of that. But they made sure I went to see the result."

He felt a chill run through his bones as he recalled the sight.

"When I arrived, they had been hanging there for two days. Most were dead, but a couple still clung to life. The Romans were laughing about it, placing bets on who would be the next to die. It seems the rain showers had helped keep some of the men from dying of thirst, but it is suffocation that kills them. Hanging there like that, they cannot breathe once their arms can no longer support their weight."

"It sounds awful," Thenu breathed. "How can anyone survive that long?"

"Men cling to life," he shrugged. "The soldiers boasted about how some of the men had screamed when the nails were hammered into their hands and feet, but they also said some barely made a sound. I don't think I could ever be that brave."

"It will not happen to you," she assured him, gripping his hand more tightly.

"I hope not. It is a horrible way to die."

"Who were the men? Raiders, you said? Your father's warriors?"

"I suppose so. I did not recognise any of them. That is one thing I am grateful for."

"You should not dwell on it," she told him.

"It is difficult not to," he replied, trying to force a smile to his lips. "We run a risk every time I pass information to my mother."

"Nobody knows about that," she insisted. "You always ride well out of the village to meet her."

"That is no guarantee of safety," he said. "And I am afraid that it puts you in danger as well."

"I have been in danger before," she reminded him. "When I was a hostage in the Roman camp, I was under the threat of death every day. Now, I am free and I have you. I can put up with a little danger."

"It is far more than a little," he insisted. "If it was only my life at stake, I would not be so concerned, but I am worried about putting you in peril."

"You are doing the right thing," she insisted. "You are helping our people in the best way you can. You have often admitted you would be of no use as a warrior, but nobody else could do what you are doing."

He looked into her eyes and saw no recrimination in her expression. She knew his failings as well as his strengths, and she did not judge him simply because he had no skill in the arts of war that were so vital in the eyes of most people.

"Are you sure?" he asked. "I will stop if you want me to."

"Do not place your burden on me like that," she smiled sadly. "We both know you must carry on. I don't think either of us would be content if we did nothing to help. I have felt trapped and powerless before and, believe me, it is far worse than this."

He squeezed her hand again, leaning in to kiss her.

"You are as brave as you are beautiful," he told her.

That brought a bashful smile to her face, lighting up her eyes.

"And you worry too much," she replied. "Perhaps the Romans will be satisfied now that they have done this."

"I'm afraid not," he confessed.

"What do you mean?"

Reluctantly, he explained, "Some new official has arrived. I did not speak to him because he is unwell. They say he has caught a fever. But the Governor was very cautious when mentioning him, and that big soldier who came to see us, Julius Macrinus, told me all about him."

"Who is he?"

"His name is Popidius Flaccus. They say he's a friend of the Emperor. Worse, Macrinus warned me that he is out to trap my father."

"How can he do that?" Thenu frowned. "No Roman has ever been able to catch him."

"I don't know. All Macrinus said was that they have another prisoner, a chieftain of some sort. He said this Flaccus has a plan to use him to lure my father into a trap."

"Why would he warn you?" she wanted to know.

"I think he wanted me to pass the news to my father. But I need to know more, and all Macrinus would say was that I should expect a visit from Flaccus once he recovers from his fever."

Thenu leaned towards him and put her arm around his shoulders, drawing him close and hugging him tightly. Her earlier determination wavered in the face of this new information.

"Do you think he was telling you to run away and join your family?" she asked in a hoarse whisper. "Are you in danger?"

"No. Macrinus told me that much. He says the Governor won't let Flaccus harm me."

She relaxed slightly, but still held him as if to be certain that he really was sitting beside her.

"But you should warn your father," she said. "What will happen if they catch him?"

"Like you said," he replied, giving her a smile of confidence which he did not truly feel, "nobody has been able to catch him yet."

"I will pray to all the Gods that you are right," she whispered.

"As will I," he agreed. "As will I."

Togodumnus was too busy to spend much time worrying about Popidius Flaccus and his mysterious plan. Autumn was a busy time in every settlement, and his tiny village was no exception. There was firewood to be chopped and stacked for winter fuel, stone dykes to be repaired, roofs to be patched up to withstand the gales, rain and snow. Cattle and sheep must be slaughtered, the meat salted or smoked to preserve it, the skins dried and treated so that they could be used to make clothing. The harvest was in, but the grain needed to be separated by threshing, then stored in deep pits where it would be covered with earth to preserve it. Ovens needed to be checked for cracks and repaired with fresh clay, beer and heather ale must be brewed, and sea water gathered in broad, iron pans to be heated until it evaporated, allowing the salt to be harvested.

There was so much to do and so few people to do it. Apart from Togodumnus himself, there were only four men aged between fifteen and sixty because all the others had gone to join Calgacus' war host. Of those four, Ardoc had a club foot which made him walk with a pronounced limp, while Cedd had such weak eyes that he could barely make out a person's face unless he was so close he could reach out to touch them. This meant that most of the heavy work was done by Togodumnus and the other two men, with the women and children doing nearly everything else.

To add to the burden, Togodumnus insisted that the empty homes must be maintained as far as possible. Many villagers had abandoned their houses to flee to the mountains, but Togodumnus, who knew how severe the winters could be, expected some of them to return when conditions became too bad. The homes might be empty for the moment, but he refused to let them collapse due to lack of care. Which meant plastering the walls with fresh daub of mud and dung, and using the stalks of their harvested wheat, oats and barley to repair the thatched roofs.

As a result, the steadily shortening days were so busy that nobody had time to rest. At nights, they stumbled to their homes, warmed themselves by their fires, ate their evening meal, then went to bed in the hope of resting their weary bodies enough to allow them to repeat the process the following day.

Despite his weariness, Togodumnus had secretly met Beatha at a spot high in the hills overlooking the river valley, and he had relayed Macrinus' warning about a plot to entrap Calgacus. Without details, though, the message served no real purpose.

"I will tell you more when I hear anything," he had promised his mother.

More than a week had passed since then, an exhausting, busy span of days during which he had little time to spare to gather information. The few conversations he held with the soldiers who manned the watchtower provided nothing of any real importance, only rumours of distant wars and the news that the Governor's fort was taking shape. It was all so inconsequential that he was seriously contemplating missing the next meeting which was planned for three days' time, on the morning after the next full moon.

    He was busy stacking firewood against the side of his house, having spent most of the morning chopping the long chunks into shorter logs, an exercise he had not enjoyed for it required better coordination of hand and eye than he possessed. His arms and shoulders were aching with the effort of wielding the axe, and his back was protesting at the constant bending and twisting it was being subjected to as he piled the irregular lumps of chopped wood.

    He took a moment's respite, stretching his back muscles and wiping sweat from his forehead, when he heard a shout from a high, piping voice and turned to see two young boys, no older than seven years of age, scampering towards him, waving their arms excitedly and pointing over their shoulders.

    "Romans!" they cried as they drew close. "On horses!"

    Togodumnus' first reaction was to glance at the long-handled axe that he had left stuck in one of the logs. He dismissed the idea of picking it up. Even his father would not have attempted to fight off a troop of Roman cavalry single-handed.

    "Go to your homes," he told the boys. "Tell everyone to stay indoors."

    They ran off, breathlessly shouting their warnings, while Togodumnus walked slowly towards the centre of the widely-scattered village where an open space was reserved for public meetings and festivals.

    Thenu came out of the house, her face showing the exertion of a day spent grinding corn into flour, her hands dusty white from scraping the flour from the quern stones and scooping it into clay storage jars.

    "What is it?" she asked anxiously.

    "I don't know. Best you stay indoors."

She ignored him, moving to stand just behind him, although he could practically feel her fear.

The horsemen were close now, two outriders entering the village, their heads constantly turning as they watched for any signs of danger. When they reached the wide space at the centre of the village, they separated, moving to either side, having first cast a quick glance at Togodumnus and then dismissing him as no threat once they saw he was unarmed.

The rest of the column pounded into the village, at least sixty horsemen, most of them wearing armour and carrying their long lances. At their head, Togodumnus recognised the big, broad-shouldered figure of the German Tribune, Julius Macrinus, his bulk emphasised by his crested helmet, red cloak and armour of segmented iron plates protecting his upper body.

The Tribune rode up to him, giving a grim nod in greeting as he tugged his horse to a halt.

"Please summon your people," Macrinus said without observing any of the usual formalities.

"Why? What is going on?"

"Popidius Flaccus is here, as I warned you would happen," Macrinus informed him stonily. "You have nothing to fear, but I suggest you do as I say. Quickly."

Togodumnus turned to Thenu, nodding his acquiescence.

"Go and fetch everyone," he told her.

She bit her lip, eyeing the Roman cavalrymen nervously, but turned and hurried away to call the villagers together.

Macrinus swung down from his saddle as his troopers spread out, forming a barrier across one side of the village green. As they did so, other men dismounted and came forwards. Togodumnus' eyes were drawn to them because they were most definitely not ordinary cavalrymen.

One was a Briton, a big man with a mass of tangled, matted, red hair hanging around a face that bore the bruises and swellings of recent beatings. He walked reluctantly, prodded on by two guards who shoved him in the back to keep him moving. His hands were bound together, but he held his head high, and the set of his shoulders showed no sign that he felt defeated.

The second man, lurking behind the others, was dressed in a plain tunic, walking with an air of indifference to his surroundings. He was of average height, slightly plump, and had the coldest, cruellest eyes Togodumnus had ever seen.

But it was the third man who demanded his attention. Slight, with dark hair, he was wrapped in a thick cloak which occasionally billowed open as he walked, revealing that he wore a fine, white tunic with a broad purple stripe. His face appeared pinched, his nose slightly red as he wiped it with a piece of fine linen and sniffed disapprovingly as he gazed at Togodumnus.

"This is him?" the man demanded, his voice slightly hoarse and nasal. He spoke in Latin, the accent refined and polished, sounding odd when compared to the soldiers' speech Togodumnus was more accustomed to hearing.

"This is Togodumnus," Macrinus confirmed. "Son of Calgacus, and the new King of the Boresti."

Giving Togodumnus a warning stare, he said to him, "May I introduce Gaius Popidius Flaccus, Assistant Procurator and friend of His Imperial Majesty, the Emperor Domitian."

Togodumnus held out his arm to offer a formal welcome but, after one disdainful look at his grubby hand, Flaccus pointedly ignored him.

"Where are the rest of them?" he demanded, although the question lost some impact as it developed into a violent bout of coughing.

Macrinus waited patiently until Flaccus had recovered, then calmly replied, "They will be here soon."

Flaccus sputtered something incomprehensible as he coughed once more before sneezing into his linen handkerchief.

Togodumnus caught Macrinus' eye and thought he detected a hint of amusement at the Assistant Procurator's apparent misery.

"Popidius Flaccus has only recently arrived from Rome," the Tribune explained. "It seems the change of climate has induced a rather bad cold."

"We have some local remedies to help that," Togodumnus informed them.

"I will rely on Roman medicine," Flaccus grunted ungraciously.

Togodumnus shrugged, deciding he had made all the effort he could to appear friendly. Flaccus was clearly in no mood to reciprocate so, in an effort to discover what had brought them here, Togodumnus addressed Macrinus.

"What is this all about?" he asked.

"Popidius Flaccus wishes you to take a message to your father," Macrinus replied.

Togodumnus could hear the unspoken warning in the big German's voice.

He said, "You know I have not spoken to my father for many months. He is a rebel, hiding out in the hills somewhere."

He waved a hand in the general direction of the inland mountains.

"Nevertheless," Macrinus said, "you have more chance of finding him than we do. I have no wish to risk my life by venturing into the mountains on my own again, and if we go in force, we are likely to be met with a less than friendly reception."

Togodumnus sighed, "I suppose you are right. But, if I do happen to find him, what message am I to give him?"

He was surprised at how calm his own voice sounded, and amazed that his knees were not trembling. There were so many Romans, all of them armed, all of them capable of cutting him down where he stood, of destroying his village and murdering every person there. Macrinus had told him there was no danger, but he could tell that it was Popidius

Flaccus who was in charge, and one look at the Assistant Procurator was enough to tell Togodumnus that this was a man perfectly capable of ordering a slaughter.

There was a slight distraction as a soldier came down from the watchtower to find out what was happening. Flaccus sent him back again with a curt warning to mind his own business. By the time the chastened soldier had turned tail, Thenu had returned, bringing a gaggle of nervous villagers trailing behind her.

"Tell them to stand over there," Flaccus commanded, pointing to the side of the village green opposite the ranks of Roman horsemen.

Once the Boresti had huddled together in the appointed place, the horsemen spread out, forming a widely spaced circle around the entire open area. The villagers watched nervously, expecting to be attacked, but Macrinus repeated his assurance that they were perfectly safe.

"We are merely making sure that our prisoner does not make a run for it," he informed Togodumnus.

Togodumnus relayed the assurance to the villagers, but even he felt nervous, not entirely convinced that the Romans would keep their word.

Once the riders were in position, Flaccus nodded to Macrinus.

"Make the announcement," he ordered.

Macrinus took a few paces towards the villagers. Switching to the local language, his voice, accustomed to bellowing orders over the noise of battle, boomed out.

"This man," he said, indicating the red-haired Briton, "is Gabrain, King of the Venicones. He was captured two weeks ago when trying to raid Roman territory. His men are all dead, but he is about to be given a chance to win his freedom."

The villagers stood mute, staring blankly at Macrinus as if they could not understand him.

Undeterred, he continued, "All he needs to do is fight our champion and win. If he does that, he goes free."

Gabrain was clearly as surprised as any of them to hear this news. A grin spread across his bruised features when he heard that he had a chance to gain his freedom through skill in arms.

His hands were untied. He rubbed at his chafed wrists, flexing his fingers to force the blood back into them. Then he was bundled to one side of the open space where he was handed a shield and sword by one of the soldiers.

Togodumnus felt Thenu grab his arm and cling to him.

"What is this all about?" she hissed in a terrified whisper.

All he could do was shake his head. It was obvious what was about to happen, but he still could not comprehend why. What was the purpose of this staged combat, and what message was he supposed to take to his father?

Then he saw the man with the cold eyes.

He had stripped off his tunic and was wearing only a loincloth, his bronzed skin paling in the chill air. In his right hand he held a short sword that was the mirror of the one Gabrain now clutched. On his left arm he carried a large shield painted with the image of a green, rearing snake.

"This is Serpicius," Macrinus announced. "Also sometimes known as The Snake. He is our champion."

Flaccus, beaming broadly, called in a throaty rasp, "Begin!"

Gabrain did not need to speak Latin to understand the command. He gripped the unfamiliar short sword and moved forwards to meet Serpicius who was edging close to him, moving lightly on the balls of his feet.

"I have heard of Gabrain," Togodumnus whispered to Thenu. "He is reputed to be a fearsome fighter."

As he studied the two men, he thought the fight seemed fairly evenly matched. Gabrain was a head taller than Serpicius, and much broader in the shoulders. The Roman, though, had muscles to match and seemed utterly confident. He was also clearly well fed and fit, while Gabrain had been in captivity for two weeks and had obviously been badly treated during that time.

Togodumnus caught Macrinus' eye and raised his eyebrows in a silent question. In response, the Tribune gave a small shake of his head as if to suggest that Gabrain had no chance of gaining his freedom.

"The Snake is a gladiator," he explained in a soft murmur.

Togodumnus' heart sank. He had heard tales of these trained killers who fought to entertain the Roman mob. The stories of their skill were legendary. Yet Gabrain, too, was a trained warrior, a man born to be King, who had spent his life learning the art of combat. Perhaps he had a chance.

The two men circled one another warily, neither rushing in. Gabrain made a few, tentative jabs with his short sword which Serpicius easily blocked with his shield or parried with his own blade.

Gradually, Gabrain began to warm to his task, jabbing faster, thrusting harder, swinging his large shield to force the Roman backwards, attempting to use his greater strength and reach to overpower the gladiator. Serpicius, though, seemed to dance away from each attack, constantly on the move, his own sword darting in quick, threatening jabs whenever Gabrain presented an opening.

Those openings were all too evident. Gabrain was both strong and skilful, but the Roman possessed phenomenal speed. Gabrain's attacks became more ragged as he attempted to close with his opponent, never quite able to land a decisive blow.

The shields clashed, the swords rang in the air, but neither man seemed capable of breaching the other's defences. Gabrain's greater reach kept Serpicius at bay, while the gladiator's skill foiled every assault from the Briton.

The two men moved like dancers performing a ritual, their concentration locked on one another.

Even the onlookers were silent, the Boresti because they had never witnessed anything quite like this, and the

Roman cavalry because their role was to act as guards, not as an audience. Only Flaccus occasionally let out a cry of acclamation whenever Serpicius performed some clever manoeuvre to slip away from one of Gabrain's ferocious lunges.

Then, without warning, the gladiator struck. Having fended off a frustrated thrust by the Briton, he suddenly leaped forwards, crashing his snake-emblazoned shield into Gabrain's plain one. The sound of the impact echoed across the village green, the force of the blow enough to make Gabrain take a half step backwards.

Serpicius was already moving, spinning round to his right, momentarily exposing his back to his foe, but whirling so quickly that Gabrain, pushed back by the blow to his shield, had no time to take advantage of the opening.

Serpicius kept turning, the move so fast that his blade had struck Gabrain's right arm almost before most of the watching crowd realised that he had begun his pirouette.

Gabrain let out a stifled gasp of pain as dark blood spurted from the wound. He withdrew his arm, stepping back again, but Serpicius was after him now, crouching slightly, shield held high, sword jabbing as he sought to capitalise on his advantage.

"Hoc habet!" barked Flaccus admiringly as Serpicius pressed the attack.

The gladiator darted low, blocking Gabrain's sword with his raised shield, and sweeping his own *gladius* in a lightning arc, the tip grazing Gabrain's left leg, searing a bright gash across his shin.

Again Gabrain tried to pull back. Again the gladiator pursued him. This time, the Briton was slower, hampered by his wounds and by shock at the speed with which Serpicius had dodged past his defences.

Serpicius' next strike caught him on the side of his waist, a raking thrust which opened the skin as the razor edge of The Snake's sword lanced past Gabrain's guard.

Togodumnus heard Flaccus shout in approval and Thenu gasp in horror as Gabrain, slower with every moment, was hunted around the open arena, unable to block the vicious thrusts and slashes of Serpicius' sword. Cut after cut appeared on his body; rents flapping in his tunic as blood ran from wounds on his shoulder, his arm and even his back when Serpicius forced him into a desperate spin and still somehow managed to dance around him, lash out and draw blood.

None of Gabrain's wounds were fatal, but he was losing blood and growing tired. Realising he was beaten unless he tried something desperate, he roared in anger and defiance, attempting to frighten the Roman with the sheer ferocity of his next attack. He ran forwards, blood spraying from half a dozen cuts, trying to batter the gladiator to the ground.

Serpicius was ready for him. He waited until the last moment, then ducked aside, using his shield to help deflect Gabrain's mad rush, swung his right arm so quickly that many of the watchers missed it, and neatly hamstrung the Briton as he lumbered past.

For the first time, Gabrain let out a yell of pain. He had suffered every other cut with barely a sound, but the savage blow to his left leg was too deep and too serious to ignore. He staggered, should have fallen, but somehow managed to stay on his feet, his left leg barely able to support him. He still held his sword ready and he tried to hold his shield in place, but he could no longer react quickly enough to avoid Serpicius' next attack.

The gladiator's sword flicked like the biting fangs of the snake pictured on Serpicius' shield, drawing blood with every thrust. Gabrain's tunic was ripped in several places, blood soaking through the material and drenching every limb. Hopping on one leg, he was virtually helpless.

"Finish him!" Flaccus shouted.

Serpicius gave no indication that he had heard the Assistant Procurator, but his next blow shattered Gabrain's forearm, forcing him to drop his sword. The Briton tried to huddle behind his shield, but the gladiator skipped around him, forcing him to turn too quickly. Gabrain lost his balance, dropping to his knees. Even as he struggled to raise himself, using his shield as a prop, Serpicius was behind him, sword thrusting deep into his back, aiming expertly for his kidney.

An involuntary gasp went up from the watching villagers as Gabrain stiffened, his head arcing back, mouth open in a silent scream. Then Serpicius was yanking his blade back, twisting it to avoid trapping it between the Briton's ribs, and Gabrain slowly toppled to the ground.

A stunned silence fell across the village. The only sound was the crying of some terrified and shocked young children who clung to their mothers, hiding their eyes from the spectacle.

Serpicius, still holding his bloody sword, strolled over to face Flaccus.

Togodumnus heard the gladiator say, "I hope Calgacus is more of a test than that. This is little better than some light training."

Togodumnus could not tell how much of the statement was bravado, but hearing the gladiator speak his father's name filled him with a sense of dread.

Flaccus signalled to Macrinus.

"Tell them. Make sure they understand."

Macrinus gave a resigned nod before turning to face the villagers. He singled out Togodumnus.

"You will take a message to your father. Tell him we expect him to come to the Governor's fort. He will fight Serpicius. If he does not come, we will visit every settlement north of the river, and Serpicius will kill men one at a time until Calgacus accepts the challenge. Do you understand?"

"No," Togodumnus replied, shaking his head. "Why are you doing this?"

"Isn't it clear enough?" Macrinus growled, his tone angry, although his rage seemed to be directed as much at himself for being involved in the threat than at Togodumnus' wilful lack of understanding. "Serpicius is here to challenge your father to single combat. If Calgacus is too much of a coward to accept, then others will die in his place. One at a time, every ten days until there is nobody left to fight."

Togodumnus was horrified. His eyes darted to the prostrate and bloodied figure of Gabrain lying on the trampled grass, and his own blood ran cold.

Macrinus stepped close, leaning in to speak more softly.

"I am sorry, boy. I would help if I could, but I cannot. I know your father is a man of honour. Tell him it would be best if he accepts the challenge, because Flaccus is determined to carry out his threat. You will be forced to stand there and watch every man in your village slaughtered like that."

"The Governor—" Togodumnus began.

"Can do nothing!" Macrinus interrupted, jabbing a finger at Togodumnus' chest to emphasise his words. "Flaccus has the Emperor's ear. Tell your father he has no choice. Everywhere The Snake goes, people will be told Calgacus can prevent this from happening." The Tribune stepped back, his face once again becoming grim.

"Do you understand now?" he asked.

Togodumnus found himself nodding his head, but his voice was lost somewhere deep inside his aching chest.

"Good enough," Macrinus said. "Ten days. He has my word the fight will be fair. Tell him to wait outside the camp with one other man. I will accompany Serpicius myself, and I promise there will be no trap."

Again, Togodumnus nodded dumbly.

Macrinus turned, striding away to his waiting horse. Flaccus and Serpicius were already mounted, the gladiator having pulled on a tunic and cloak, the Assistant Procurator still sniffing and spluttering through his cold but managing to grin with satisfaction.

"Ten days!" Macrinus called as he hauled his horse around, holding up his arm and signalling to his men to withdraw.

The horses rumbled away, throwing up clods of earth from their hooves as the troopers rode away. In their wake, they left a shocked group of villagers, a bloody corpse and a promise of more deaths to come.

Unless Calgacus faced an unbeatable foe.

Chapter XXVI

Clouds had once again descended on the hilltop village, shrouding everything in a ghostly, concealing mist. Rain pattered steadily, turning every trip outside into a damp and potentially dangerous venture as the opaque whiteness hid all features from view.

"This could last for days," muttered Bridei as he sat beside the comforting warmth of Calgacus' hearth fire, noisily chewing on a cutlet of lamb.

Grease ran down his chin and he wiped it with the back of his hand before taking another bite.

"It's bad weather for going anywhere," he opined. "Even folk who have lived in the mountains all their lives don't go out in this sort of fog. It's too easy to get lost, and if you lose your footing you can fall a long way."

"We need to do something," Calgacus replied, needing to raise his voice over the tumult in the crowded roundhouse. While he, Bridei and Runt sat around the hearth fire, several women were chattering noisily as they worked at spinning yarn from the freshly gathered wool plucked from the sheep that had been slaughtered. Others operated a large, wooden loom, turning the yarn into woven garments with a rhythmic clatter. On the opposite side of the house, Fallar sat nursing a crying Elaris while Adelligus sat awkwardly beside her, unable to help but unwilling to abandon her.

All around them, small children ran and dodged, shouting and screaming in high pitched voices which set the dogs barking and yapping, while the constant patter of rain on the overhead thatch provided a noisy background accompaniment.

"There's nothing we can do until the weather lifts," Bridei asserted with a cheerful grin.

Carelessly, he tossed the bone to the nearest dog, chuckling when other hounds tried to battle for it.

Runt said, "The weather closed in quickly. You know it can clear just as quickly."

Calgacus gave a brooding nod.

"We need to do something," he repeated. "Something to show the Romans we are not going to be put off just because they crucified some of our lads."

"You're still thinking of attacking the main fort?" Bridei enquired sceptically.

"Madness," Runt advised. "The best we could hope to achieve is kill a few of them and maybe burn their village outside the fort. We won't accomplish much of importance. That won't sit well with the lads. Not after what happened to Gabrain's raid."

That was the hardest thing of all; a dark cloud that hung over them just as certainly as the grey, wisping murk that enveloped the world beyond the door of the roundhouse.

"Gabrain wasn't among the men who were crucified," Calgacus pointed out. "We know that much."

"Which means he was probably killed during the raid itself," Runt argued.

"The locals say the Romans have a prisoner," Calgacus countered.

"Could be anyone," said Runt dismissively.

Bridei stood up, wandered to the side of the house and, carefully negotiating his way back past three young children and a large dog, placed another block of peat on the fire. It sizzled and hissed as it momentarily smothered the flames, wisps of smoke rising from its edges to add to the cloud that hovered in the rafters high above their heads.

"Whatever happened," he stated firmly as he sat back down on the log bench, "Gabrain is gone. The Venicones will need to elect themselves a new King. Let's hope they choose someone who is prepared to carry on fighting. If they decide to give up and make peace, we will lose nearly half our war host."

"I've already spoken to them," Calgacus informed him. "I think most of them will stick with us."

"Fair enough," Bridei shrugged. "But there are other things we need to watch."

"Such as?"

"We are beginning to wear paths on the hillside. If that carries on, any Romans who come into the valley will see where we are. All they'll need to do is follow the trails."

"Then we prepare defences," Calgacus replied. "We can't stop men and animals taking the easiest route uphill. So, let's make sure the Romans walk into a trap if they come the same way."

"It would be better to stop them before they get this far," Runt remarked.

"We can do that," Calgacus agreed thoughtfully. "This valley has several narrow sections. There are trees and there are also rocks, which means we have plenty of places to conceal an ambush."

"That might work," Bridei nodded thoughtfully. "But we are a fair distance from the nearest Roman fort. How do we lure them into this particular glen?"

"That's easy," Calgacus grinned. "Someone needs to betray us and lead them here."

Bridei and Runt looked at one another as if to make sure they had heard correctly.

Twirling a finger beside his temple, Bridei chuckled, "You are right, my little friend. He is crazy."

"It would work," Calgacus insisted. "The Romans want me dead, but they've never known where to find us. If they discover where this village is, they'll come in force."

"What about our families?" Runt asked, sweeping his gaze around the busy house.

Calgacus followed his friend's eyes. They were all there, the people he had worked so hard to protect. Beatha, Fallar, Adelligus and little Elaris; Runt's wife, Tegan, with their daughter, Sorcha; Calgacus' niece, Emmelia, with her husband and children. Then there were Bridei's womenfolk, their status never quite defined, along with several children whom Bridei generally acknowledged as his own.

"We needn't put them at risk," he told his friends. "The intention is to bring the Romans into this valley, not necessarily up to this settlement. There are a few farms further along on the lowland beside the river, as well as the new homes the Taexali refugees are building for themselves. Our traitor could lead the Romans there."

"The Taexali will love that," Runt muttered.

"Only if we let the Romans get that far," Calgacus answered. "Like you said, it is better to stop them before they reach us. As for our families, we can always move them further into the hills."

Bridei shrugged, "We were always likely to have to move at some point."

"It might not be necessary to move if we do it right," Calgacus stated emphatically. "If we can draw their army into the glen, we can surround them before they reach any of our homes."

"All right," Runt agreed reluctantly. "It's a better idea than trying to attack their main fort."

"Yes," Calgacus agreed. "It's always best to fight on terrain of our choosing."

Runt shot him an aggrieved look.

"Why do I have the feeling that you only suggested that other plan so that this one wouldn't sound quite so crazy?" he challenged.

"Would I do something as devious as that?" Calgacus asked innocently.

"Yes, you bloody would."

"Maybe," Calgacus admitted with a grin. "But you must admit it's a good idea. If we can time it right, we could bring them into the hills in winter."

"There's less cover for us to hide during winter," Runt objected.

"I know. But if we wait until spring, that gives them too much time to prepare for next year's campaign. Besides, there's more chance of our traitor convincing them to make an attack during winter if they think they can catch us unprepared."

"It's worth a try," Bridei agreed.

Runt shrugged his acceptance before asking the most important question.

"So, who is going to betray us?"

Calgacus smiled, "Not you, anyway. You are too well known as my shield-bearer. The Romans would never believe you."

Bridei offered, "I'm sure I could find a volunteer."

"It's a death sentence," Runt informed him. "Whoever goes to them will be forced to act as a guide. They'll be under guard the whole time, and they'll be killed as soon as we spring the trap."

"I can still find plenty volunteers," Bridei insisted. "My lads are willing to die if it means beating the Romans."

"I know that," Calgacus nodded. "But whoever goes to the Governor will need to be convincing. Your lads are tough, but can they act the part of a disenchanted warrior or someone who is prepared to betray his people for a reward of gold and silver?"

Bridei frowned uncertainly.

"That makes it a bit trickier," he confessed.

"It also needs to be somebody we trust implicitly," Calgacus told them. "That narrows it down quite a bit."

Runt swivelled his head, looking around the noisy gathering.

"We can't send anyone from here," he ventured. "That big bugger, Macrinus, would probably recognise them."

"I know," Calgacus agreed. "I wasn't thinking of asking anyone here to do it."

"Then who?"

Calgacus sighed deeply before responding, "There is one person they would believe. He wouldn't even need to act the part of a disenchanted traitor."

He paused, lowering his voice as he spoke the name.

"Togodumnus."

Runt let out a low whistle as he shook his head.

"Are you serious?"

"I'm afraid so. He's the best person for the job. The Romans already think he's on their side."

"They'll soon change their minds if he leads them into a trap," Runt pointed out.

"I know. Once we spring the ambush, we'll need to make sure we rescue him before they realise he's on our side."

"Now you are thinking crazy," Runt scoffed. "How do you propose we do that?"

"I haven't worked out all the details yet," Calgacus admitted. "But I'm going to go and talk to him as soon as the weather clears."

"Have you mentioned this to Beatha?" Bridei asked, his expression one of innocent enquiry.

"Not yet. I thought I'd speak to Togodumnus first. I can always tell her it was his idea."

"I'd like to listen in when you're explaining that one to her," Runt murmured.

Calgacus had intended to join Beatha when she went to see Togodumnus for their planned meeting two days later, but he saw his son sooner than expected. A breathless warrior, his hair sparkling with moisture, arrived at the roundhouse with the news that Togodumnus was on his way to the village.

"What for?" Calgacus asked over the buzz of excitement this news engendered.

"He has brought Gabrain," the warrior explained. "His body, anyway."

The house emptied at the news as everyone flooded out to meet Togodumnus. His arrival was, though, delayed because the long trek up the steep hill was even more dangerous than usual thanks to the clinging mist. Eventually, though, several dark shapes materialised out of the murk as the guide led Togodumnus to the house.

He was not alone. Beside him, looking frail and vulnerable in a thick, hooded cloak, was Thenu, the young woman he had rescued from Roman captivity. He also led a pony which carried a cloth-wrapped burden draped over its back, the shape unmistakable.

Beatha hurried to embrace her son, kissing him and hugging him tightly before moving to greet Thenu with the same warm fervour.

Calgacus' greeting to his son was more formal, an extended hand which Togodumnus grasped with obvious trepidation.

"You have brought Gabrain?" Calgacus asked, nodding towards the figure slung over the pony's back.

"Yes. I didn't know what else to do with him. He's a King, so I thought it best to bring him to his own people."

Bridei, who had fought the Venicones for most of his life, stepped forwards to take the reins from Togodumnus.

"I'll have him laid out in my house," he said gravely. "I'll send word to the Venicones to collect him."

Togodumnus nodded his thanks, obviously glad to be rid of his self-imposed burden.

Calgacus asked him, "What happened?"

"It's a long story," Togodumnus sighed wearily.

Beatha, holding Thenu's hand in one of her own, wrapped her other arm around her son's waist.

She said, "Then come inside and tell us. There is hot food and plenty to drink."

They filed back indoors, the children quickly returning to their play, while Togodumnus and Thenu were kept busy as the rest of his family gathered round, each of them eager to welcome him. Shaking off their cloaks, the two visitors were ushered to the fire, where everyone clustered around, squeezing together on the long, log benches that bordered the hearth. Beatha organised food, serving bowls of steaming broth, while Togodumnus held his niece, baby Elaris, for the first time, smiling warmly as he congratulated his younger sister on becoming a mother.

Thenu was silent and shy, but Beatha sat beside her and chatted in a friendly way, asking about their journey and remarking how difficult it must have been once the weather closed in.

"I was lost as soon as we left our village," Thenu admitted with a nervous smile. "It wouldn't have made much difference to me whether the clouds were low or not, but it was not too bad until we began climbing the last hill to get up here."

While Beatha did her best to make the young woman feel welcome, Calgacus sat impatiently, waiting for Togodumnus to eat his broth. When Bridei re-joined them, he could wait no longer.

"Tell us what happened to Gabrain," he demanded. "How did you come to find him?"

Togodumnus sighed, taking a deep breath before replying. Then, speaking slowly and clearly so as to be sure that everyone could hear, he recounted how Macrinus and Flaccus had brought the King of the Venicones to their village and forced him to fight the gladiator.

"He never really stood a chance," he told them. "The man, Serpicius, was unbelievably fast. Gabrain didn't so much as scratch him."

Bridei growled, "I was no great friend of Gabrain, but he was a fine warrior. Nobody could dispute that. How could anyone defeat him so easily?"

Beatha put in, "I never saw an arena combat, but I have heard all about these gladiators. They are extremely skilled. They do nothing but practise fighting."

"We practise too," Adelligus put in.

"Not all day, every day," Beatha replied.

Togodumnus agreed, "I am no swordsman, as you all know, but I have watched most of you during your own practice bouts. Believe me, this gladiator was far more skilful than anyone I've ever seen."

"He must be good," Bridei shrugged grudgingly. "Gabrain's body has half a dozen wounds on it."

"Macrinus was part of this?" Calgacus asked his son.

Togodumnus nodded, "He wasn't happy about it, but he didn't have much choice. The man from Rome, Flaccus, was behind it."

"But what was the point of it?"

Togodumnus hesitated, shooting a look at Thenu who lowered her eyes. Aware that everyone was watching him, he gave a mournful shake of his head.

"It's not good news," he said softly.

"Just tell me," Calgacus growled.

Togodumnus looked up to meet his father's gaze.

"He issued a challenge. He says you must go to the Governor's fort to fight The Snake. If you don't, he will simply carry on killing people and blaming you for being a coward."

A hush fell over the seated gathering, disturbed only by the chattering of the children and the yapping of the dogs. Everyone looked from Togodumnus, to Calgacus and back again, all of them thinking the same thing.

Beatha, her face pale, urged, "Cal! You can't even think of it. This man will kill you."

He gave her a slow, sad smile.

"Would you prefer I stayed safe up here while others died in my place?"

"That's not what I meant!" she protested.

"Then what would you have me do?" he asked.

Beatha shook her head, holding back tears. When he looked around the faces of the others, nobody had any suggestions.

"Then it looks as if I will need to fight him," he announced. "I'll just have to make sure I win."

"How?" Runt challenged.

"I don't know yet," Calgacus admitted. "If anyone has any ideas, I'll listen."

They discussed the problem late into the evening. Togodumnus recounted everything Macrinus had told him, his words providing some comfort that the big Tribune would ensure no secret trap would be sprung, but it did not answer the fundamental question of how Calgacus could defeat Serpicius. Even Emmelia, who possessed one of the shrewdest minds of them all, had little to offer.

Most of the talk centred on what Togodumnus and Thenu had seen of the gladiator, with Bridei, Runt and Adelligus firing questions on his technique and ability. Togodumnus did his best to answer them but could offer little insight.

"All I can tell you is that Gabrain couldn't get close to him. He moved so quickly, light on his feet, and his sword was so fast he seemed to strike at will."

In the end, it was Calgacus himself who came up with a suggestion.

"It sounds like this man is unbeatable," he breathed. "If you think about it, why else would this Roman, Flaccus, bring him all the way here? He knows I can't beat him in a straight fight, just as he knows I won't let others die for me. Which leaves us only one choice."

"What is that?" Beatha asked, her voice a mixture of hope and fearful resignation.

"Not to fight him at all," Calgacus grinned. "Earlier on, we were chatting about a plan to draw the Romans into a trap. Perhaps we need to adapt that slightly."

He explained his idea to lure the Romans into an ambush by sending someone who would claim to have some sort of grievance which made him willing to betray the location of Calgacus' base.

"If we can destroy their army, they'll have no choice but to withdraw to the south," he declared. "The problem of this gladiator goes away with them."

"You want someone to pretend to betray us?" Beatha asked. "Who?"

Togodumnus spoke before Calgacus could respond.

"Me," he told her.

Beatha looked aghast, but Togodumnus went on, "I am the obvious choice. The Governor knows me and trusts me as much as he trusts any of our people. Is that not correct, Father?"

Calgacus gave a slow, deliberate nod.

Beatha's body was rigid with disapproval, but Togodumnus continued, "It might work. If I go back and tell them you have refused to accept the challenge no matter how many people The Snake kills, the Governor might decide it's worth making a quick strike to catch you."

Runt frowned, "Agricola's not a fool. Do you really think he'll believe you?"

Togodumnus replied, "I can say that you called a meeting of all the tribal chieftains who decided the challenge must not be taken up because they do not want to risk losing their War Leader."

"That's true enough," grunted Bridei.

Runt looked doubtful, as did many of the others, but Togodumnus went on, "If they don't fall for that, then you still have the option of facing the gladiator. We lose nothing by trying, and we gain a lot if this succeeds."

"It is too dangerous for you," Beatha told her son, receiving a look of glad support from Thenu.

Togodumnus said, "I need to go back whatever you decide to do. They will want to know that their message has been delivered."

"No," Beatha argued, her cheeks flushing. "Stay here. Let them wonder what has happened to you."

"And let Serpicius keep killing people?" he shot back. "They'll keep sending other messengers, and more of our people will die. Not warriors like Gabrain, but older men, or people like Cedd, who wouldn't be able to see an attack coming, or Ardoc, who can barely walk without tripping over. We should be looking after these people, not leaving them unprotected."

Tears gleamed in Beatha's eyes as she wrapped her arms around Togodumnus, holding him close.

"I am so proud of you," she whispered.

Embarrassed, he eventually prised himself free of her embrace, pleasantly surprised to receive a nod of approval from his father.

Bridei muttered, "By all the Gods, the lad will make a better King than any of us."

"There is still a good chance it won't work," Togodumnus reminded them. "Agricola will be wary of walking into a trap. However, Flaccus might overrule him if I can convince him that an all out attack will catch you."

"Then that is what you must try to do," Calgacus nodded. "We need to destroy their army. Ambushing a few of them achieves very little in the long run."

"Can you defeat their entire army?" Togodumnus challenged.

"Nothing is certain in war," Calgacus told him. "But do you remember when Bridei killed that bear last year?"

Togodumnus frowned as he nodded, "I remember. But what has that to do with our current problem?"

Bridei grinned as Calgacus explained, "You don't kill a bear by standing in front of it holding a spear. You do what Bridei did; you lure it into a trap."

Bridei gleefully took up the story.

"That bear had made its home too close to one of our villages," he informed the young man. "It was too dangerous to leave it unmolested, but using hounds and horses against a bear is tricky work. You can lose too many good hunting dogs that way. So we taunted the beast until it came after us. But we'd dug a deep pit and covered it with branches and heather. The bear's weight broke the covering and it fell into the hole. We'd planted some spikes so that its own weight killed it when it landed on them."

"We'll do the same with the Roman army," Calgacus declared confidently. "All you have to do is persuade them to walk into our pit."

"I'll do my best," Togodumnus promised. "But there is one big problem I can foresee."

"What's that?"

"Macrinus. He knows, or at least suspects, that we have been keeping in touch. He came to me when he wanted to find you the first time. I have always tried to maintain that we fell out years ago, but I am not sure that he is entirely convinced."

Calgacus frowned, "Aye, Macrinus is a clever man. But I don't see that we have any choice but to take the risk and hope you can convince him that you are prepared to betray me."

Togodumnus gave a wan smile as he said, "There is one way we might be able to prove to him that I am serious."

"What is that?" Calgacus asked him.

Togodumnus gave a soft sigh as he replied, "You are going to have to beat me up."

Chapter XXVII

Morning brought a bustle of activity, even though the clouds still clung like leeches to the mountaintops and the village remained cocooned in an ethereal, ghostly mist. The rain had moved on, though, leaving only residual outbreaks of drizzle to dampen the spirits of the villagers.

Calgacus sent messengers to the neighbouring valleys with instructions to call a war host together. These men set off early, braving the dangers of the wispy fog, spreading the word far and wide that another attempt was to be made to destroy the Roman Legion before winter set in.

Bridei was preparing to journey down to the lower ground to warn the recently arrived refugees from the Taexali that their homes might be under threat. First, though, he and Calgacus solemnly handed Gabrain's corpse to the care of a group of men from the Venicones who had come to collect their dead King.

"We will bury him beneath a cairn," they vowed. "Once our lands have been recovered from the enemy, we will take him back to where he belongs."

Calgacus thanked them for their assurances that they would fight to avenge Gabrain, but their absolute certainty that the Romans would be driven back made him appreciate just how much was riding on the success of his plan.

That plan had been discussed long into the night. He knew the chances of drawing the Romans into a trap were not high, but he also knew that they must make the attempt. If he meekly accepted the need to face the gladiator, a mood of apprehension would have gripped every settlement, lowering the morale of the people. It was better, he knew, to give them a goal, to keep them occupied and to hope that Togodumnus could convince Agricola that a fast strike could lead to Calgacus being captured or killed.

Runt was, as ever, sceptical of their chances, but Togodumnus himself was almost eager to see the plan through.

"I want this war to end," he told everyone who would listen. "I think this is the best way to accomplish that."

There was, though, a price he would need to pay, and that confronted him once Calgacus had attended to the rest of the day's matters. By late morning, though, they could no longer put off the inevitable.

"Are you sure you want to do this?" Calgacus asked again as he and his son left the roundhouse and walked a few paces to an open area of trampled earth.

They had an audience of friends and family who were watching with expressions of mixed apprehension and curiosity. Under their concerned eyes, Togodumnus had little choice but to keep his promise.

"Just make it look good," he sighed. "Use a stick if you must. I need plenty of bruises in as many places as you can leave them."

Calgacus gave a reluctant shake of his head but Runt put in, "Your face is the obvious place. A couple of black eyes and a broken nose would look convincing. But your back would be good as well. That way, your ribs will protect anything vital from being damaged. Legs and arms are trickier because they can break more easily, but a few bruises there wouldn't do any real harm."

"Thanks for the sympathy," muttered Togodumnus. "Should I remove my cloak and tunic?"

"No. We should make it authentic, as if you really did have a fight."

"Let's get it over with, then," the younger man declared.

Calgacus still hesitated.

"I've never hit you before," he frowned. "Not even when you were a young child. Not much more than a smack on your backside, anyway."

"You could look on this as catching up on missed opportunities," Runt suggested, fetching a stout cudgel which he passed to Calgacus.

"You are not helping," Calgacus told him.

"You want me to do it?" Runt offered.

Calgacus shook his head.

"No. He needs to be able to truthfully say I did it to him. The fewer lies he tells, the more chance there is of them believing him."

"That's right," Togodumnus agreed. "So can you get on with it, please? I want this over and done with."

Calgacus still hesitated, standing two paces in front of his son, the long cudgel held in his left hand but dangling uselessly at his side.

Togodumnus shot a look to his mother who was watching with a drawn face, her eyes damp with concern. Beside her, Thenu was chewing her lip so fiercely he thought she might draw blood.

He looked back at his father who had still made no move.

"All right," Togodumnus sighed. "If you won't start it, I will."

He raised his hands, fists bunched, and stepped forwards, directing a jab at his father's chin. It was an awkward punch because he had no experience of fighting and Calgacus stood a head taller than he did. Still, he put all his effort into it, grunting as he threw the punch.

His fist never landed.

Calgacus swept up the stick in his left hand to knock Togodumnus' arm aside, delivering a blow that landed with an audible smack on the young man's forearm.

Togodumnus leaped backwards, cursing with pain, gripping his injured arm in his left hand.

"Don't you know better than to punch someone on the chin with your bare hands?" Calgacus chided angrily. "You could break your fingers doing that. Jaws are hard, you know."

Giving out a wild angry yell, Togodumnus launched himself forwards again, this time attempting to grab his father's waist and wrestle him to the ground.

It was like hitting a rock wall. Togodumnus grunted as he almost bounced off his father's torso. He struggled for a grip, hands groping for a hold, his feet scrabbling on the muddy earth. Then his head exploded in pain as Calgacus slammed a fist into his left eye, sending him reeling, dazed and blinded. He tried to stay on his feet, but he slipped on a patch of wet grass and fell to the ground.

"That's the stuff!" Runt called approvingly. "Now give him a few kicks in the ribs."

Togodumnus pushed himself onto his hands and knees, but the first kick landed before he could gather his wits, smashing into his ribcage and almost lifting him from the ground.

He shouted aloud in pain and surprise, barely evading another kick which caught him on the left thigh and another that thudded into his side, adding to the agony.

He lay sprawled and panting on the muddy ground, tears filling his eyes, unable to move, and dreading the next attack. It did not come because Calgacus backed off, giving his son some respite.

"Don't stop now," Togodumnus groaned. "You have barely started."

"You're going to have a beauty of a black eye," his father told him. "Maybe we should stop at that."

"No. Keep going. You haven't even used the stick on me yet. Hit my back a few times."

He pushed himself up onto all fours, closing his eyes as he heard Calgacus come closer. Then the cudgel landed with an awful thud, driving him face down on the damp, filthy ground once again. Twice more it whacked into his back, then again on his buttocks. Two more kicks to his left side left him breathless and gasping in agony.

"That's enough," Calgacus decided.

Togodumnus could not protest. His body ached from several places and, as he forced himself up, he realised that his nose had struck the ground hard and was bleeding prodigiously.

Calgacus helped him to his feet. He stood unsteadily as others ran to aid him. Beatha was there, with Thenu, both of them voicing their concern, with Beatha also managing to scold Calgacus for being so rough.

"I'm fine," Togodumnus insisted despite the evidence to the contrary.

Calgacus said, "There are no broken bones. I tried my best not to hurt him too much."

Togodumnus snorted blood as he tried to laugh.

"That makes me feel a whole lot better," he sputtered.

"Let Emmelia take care of you," Beatha advised, guiding his unsteady feet back towards the roundhouse. "And we need to get you cleaned up."

"No," Togodumnus protested. "If this had been a real fight, I wouldn't have had someone tend my injuries. I'd leave straight away."

"At least hold your head back and pinch your nose," Beatha told him. "You're bleeding all over the place."

He did as he was instructed, allowing them to guide him back inside the roundhouse. Here, Emmelia took charge, chasing the others away and insisting that she be left to check his injuries.

Many people, including Togodumnus, found Calgacus' niece intimidating. Her manner was often brusque and her reputation was fearsome. Togodumnus had heard many stories about her early life. He was never very sure how many of them were true, but if even half of them were accurate, Emmelia was not averse to bloodshed. He recalled how, as a boy, he had heard her outline the fastest way to kill a man with a single stab from a small knife. As if that were not enough, he had once heard her claim that, to be a good healer, one needed to know how a human body worked, and that the best way to learn that was to cut one open to see what lay inside.

Now, though, she tended him with gentle, probing fingers, lifting his muddy and blood-spattered tunic to check on his side and back.

"You will have some lovely bruises soon," she informed him. "Nothing broken though. I expect it will be painful sitting on a horse."

"I will need to put up with it," he replied through the discomfort of his bleeding nose.

"I will give you something for the pain," she told him in a tone that invited no argument.

"That would be good. I feel like I've been trampled by a bull."

"You are lucky," she chuckled. "Most men who fight your father don't escape so lightly."

By the time his nose had stopped bleeding, he felt weak and dizzy, pain throbbing from his side, back and buttocks. His nose felt swollen, his left eye was almost closed, his arm ached and he was not at all sure he would manage to ride all the way to the Governor's fort.

Emmelia called for a beaker of hot water which Thenu nervously brought to her. Togodumnus attempted to give his wife a reassuring smile, but his face ached when he tried to move his lips.

Emmelia demanded his attention again, passing him the pewter cup and then showing him a small, leather pouch, barely larger than a broad thimble. Untying the drawstring, she poured a small quantity of dark, grainy powder onto her palm.

"Watch carefully," she instructed. "This is the right amount. Do not be tempted to take any more at any one time. Do you understand?"

He nodded, feeling his skull throbbing with the effort.

She tipped the powder into his mug, wiping her hands clean, then used a small stirring stick to dissolve the powder in his drink.

"Hot water is best," she told him, "but cold will do just as well, although it takes slightly longer to stir in. You must make sure it is thoroughly mixed. Understand?"

"Yes."

"Now, drink it all. It will ease the pain."

"What is in it?" he asked as he took a first, hesitant sip, surprised to find there was hardly any flavour to the drink beyond a faint hint of tart bitterness.

"It is a concoction of my own," she replied vaguely. "Now, listen very carefully. I showed you the right amount. You may take that three times a day. A drink just before you go to sleep is particularly effective. You should also take one in the morning and another just after midday."

He gave a more careful nod this time.

She went on, "There is enough in that pouch to last you several days, although you shouldn't need to take it for more than three or four. You are young and your bruises will soon heal, although they will be painful for a little while. But be careful not to take too much."

"One large pinch diluted in water, three times a day," he recited.

"Very good. Don't forget it."

"Dare I ask what happens if I take too much?" he enquired as he took another long drink of the hot liquid.

"You'll never wake up again," she smiled. "It is quite lethal."

Thenu let out a shocked gasp, while Togodumnus regarded the half-empty beaker with nervous respect.

"Drink it," Emmelia commanded. "In those quantities it is an extremely effective painkiller."

He held her gaze for a moment, then put the mug to his lips and drank the rest of the brew, giving her a smile as he passed the empty cup back to her.

"Very good," she told him as she handed him the small packet in exchange.

He fingered the drawstring, made sure it was secure, then put the powder in his belt pouch.

Still aching, he pushed himself up and announced, "I will go now. It is a long ride. I'd like to get there before dark."

Thenu came to hug him, as did Beatha and Fallar. Then the men clasped his hand, wishing him well. Even Adelligus, who had often teased him when they were both young boys, made a point of saying farewell.

"Good luck to you," Adelligus told him. "May Camulos watch over you."

"Him and all the other Gods," Togodumnus replied.

There were more handshakes, more embraces, and a tearful farewell from Thenu.

"Stay here," he told her. "My family will look after you until I return."

"Promise me that you will come back," she whispered.

"I promise."

Disentangling himself from her arms, and gently passing her to Beatha with a silent injunction to take care of her, he went out to where a pony was waiting, already saddled and bridled.

"I'll help you up," Calgacus offered, cupping his hands into a step so that Togodumnus could mount the beast.

He groaned aloud as his bruises protested at the movement, then gasped as he sat wedged in the saddle, its four pommels, front and rear panels holding him in place. The stiff, thick leather of the seat sent screaming lances of agony shooting up from his battered backside.

"I don't think your powder is working," he told Emmelia through gritted teeth.

"Give it time," she grinned. "And don't be tempted to take any more until this evening."

He nodded, giving a final wave of farewell to his family before tugging on the reins to turn the pony.

"I'll walk with you a way," Calgacus told him, placing one hand on the bridle and leading man and horse towards the rim of the bowl in which the village was hidden.

Grey mist swirled around them, forcing them to tread slowly. There was a path of sorts, winding its way between trees and boulders, steep and difficult, treacherous with patches of slippery mud, and knotted with tree roots. With the added difficulty of navigating through the surrounding fog, Togodumnus was grateful for his father's guiding hand on the reins.

"Do what you can," Calgacus told him, chatting almost conversationally. "The Romans will be wary of coming up here. It will be difficult to convince them."

"I know. You told me that yesterday."

"It is worth repeating," Calgacus said calmly. "Be careful of appearing too desperate. If they think you are too eager, they will know it's a trap."

"Yes, you told me that yesterday, as well. What you didn't tell me was what you would do if I fail."

"Don't think about failure," Calgacus advised.

"You know the chances are little better than even," Togodumnus persisted. "What will you do if the Governor refuses to bring his army up here?"

"You let me worry about that," Calgacus told him.

"You cannot ignore the possibility!" Togodumnus protested.

"I won't ignore it, but you should. You have a difficult enough task as it is."

"Don't try to change the subject," Togodumnus complained. "I know you don't want to let other people die if you can prevent it, but you can't beat this gladiator."

"No man is invincible," Calgacus shrugged.

"No, and that includes you."

"True enough," Calgacus sighed as he went on, "All right, if it makes you feel any better, I've already started making plans just in case I do need to face the man."

That news surprised Togodumnus but did nothing to reassure him.

"What do you have in mind?" he asked.

"It's probably best you don't know," Calgacus told him.

"In case I am tortured, you mean?"

"No, in case you inadvertently let something slip. The less you know, the better. It's one less thing you need to concern yourself with."

"Yes, Father," Togodumnus replied with mock surliness.

Calgacus turned his head, taking his eyes away from the path for a moment as he brought the pony to a halt.

"I am sorry," he said gently. "I know you are a man. You proved that today, if you hadn't proved it often enough. But you are still my son. When I look at you, I still see the little boy I once knew."

He looked away, seemingly embarrassed, and tugged the horse into motion again.

"I worry about you," he went on. "That's what parents do."

Togodumnus felt slightly ashamed. His father had always been so grim and stern, so disapproving, that it came as a shock to realise that he might actually care.

"You had a strange way of showing your concern," Togodumnus remarked, using his pain to fuel his angry words.

"Yes, I suppose I did," Calgacus admitted. "I can't deny I always wanted a son who would be like me."

"I am sorry I could not live up to your expectations," Togodumnus grunted.

Again, Calgacus turned to look at him. He asked, "You don't understand, do you?"

"Understand what?"

"You haven't only met my hopes, you have exceeded them. I have thousands of warriors, but not one of them can do what you are capable of. That is why I am so proud of what you are doing for us."

"I haven't done anything yet," Togodumnus managed to say through the sudden lump that had risen in his throat.

"It is enough that you are making the attempt," Calgacus assured him. "If it works, be sure to make a run for it as soon as our attack begins. I don't want you caught up in the fighting."

"Neither do I," Togodumnus agreed.

Calgacus stopped again, turning to face his son and extending his hand. After a moment, Togodumnus took it.

As they clasped forearms, Calgacus sighed, "I expect we will always argue. We are too different in temperament. But I wanted you to know that does not mean I don't respect you as a man and love you as a son."

Togodumnus could not find any words. He swallowed hard, nodded again, then, looking around, realised that they had emerged into grey daylight below the level of the cloud cover. Ahead of him stretched the long, winding valley where he was to lead the Roman army into a trap.

"Go on," Calgacus told him, slapping a hand to the pony's rump. "Go and bring me some Romans to kill. That's what I am good at."

The pony lurched into a trot, sending more sharp shards of agony up Togodumnus' back. He was so sore and stiff that he could not even turn to look back. All he could do was raise a hand in farewell as he negotiated the final stretches of the slope and headed south towards the valley mouth and the Roman territory beyond.

It was only when he had passed out of the mountains and entered a more gentle landscape that he realised his father might have been saying a final goodbye.

Chapter XXVIII

Togodumnus sat, exhausted and aching all over, clasping a goblet of wine in his hands, wishing he could pour some of Emmelia's powder into the drink. Pain was throbbing down the left side of his face and all across his side and back. The hard, wooden stool he sat on did nothing to ease the protests from his rear end but, bizarrely, it was his left thigh that hurt the most, its sharp ache reminding him of just how hard his father had kicked him.

"You were fortunate he did not kill you," Agricola observed as he studied the young Briton from across his desk.

"I think he believes I am not worth killing," Togodumnus spat, reciting the words he had rehearsed during his long ride down from the hills.

It had taken until dusk for him to reach the Governor's fort, the last part of the journey undertaken at a dangerously fast pace as he strove to reach the camp before full darkness fell. Even with the numbing effects of Emmelia's potion, the long ride had caused him considerable pain as he bounced on the pony's back, every movement adding to his agony. The pain did, though, help him sound bitter towards his father when he recounted his story to the Governor and the senior officers.

Piso, the Legate of the Twentieth Legion, was there, as was Macrinus. So, too, was Popidius Flaccus, although the Assistant Procurator was in a miserable mood, complaining about the cold he could not shake off, coughing and spluttering between his dry, acerbic words.

"You say he refuses to fight Serpicius?" Flaccus demanded again, waving a hand to indicate the gladiator who stood silently to one side, part of the meeting and yet remaining aloof and detached.

"That is correct," Togodumnus repeated for at least the third time. "He was persuaded by the other chieftains that his life is too important to risk on such a one-off combat."

Flaccus took a sip of his own wine, a drink that had been mixed with warm water which he insisted would aid him fight off the cough that still assailed his chest. One of the slaves standing at the edge of the command tent's main meeting area kept a pot of water heated over one of the braziers which provided the tent's inadequate warmth.

Most of the men were wearing their cloaks against the night's chill, Macrinus even having gone so far as to don a pair of trousers. Togodumnus suspected the Tribune might have done that as much to irritate Flaccus as to keep himself warm. Flaccus certainly disapproved of such un-Roman dress. His own legs were bare beneath the folds of his cloak, a stubborn affectation that no doubt contributed to the occasional shivers that coursed through his body.

Flaccus' eyes flashed towards Macrinus with an expression that combined scorn and self-righteous triumph.

"You said he would not be able to refuse the challenge," the Assistant Procurator complained accusingly.

Macrinus shrugged, "I didn't think he would. It's not like him."

"That's what I told him," Togodumnus put in. "I accused him of being a coward."

He sighed, pointing a finger to the side of his face where he could feel a livid bruise. "That's why he did this to me. And a lot more. I feel black and blue all over."

"Which is why you are willing to betray him?" Agricola asked sharply, the question loaded with overtones of anticipation and suspicion.

Togodumnus snorted, pulling a face.

"It is hardly betrayal. My father and I have never seen eye to eye. You know that. It was why I chose to remain as a friend of Rome when I could have joined him. I do not agree with what he is doing. I do not want any more of my people to die simply because he refuses to see the futility of continuing to oppose the Empire."

"And you can lead us to his base?"

"Yes. Now is the ideal time to attack him. He has summoned all the tribal leaders in order to plan a major attack on you. If you strike now, you could capture or kill all the important men among the rebels."

"How accessible is this place?" Agricola persisted, apparently unswayed by Togodumnus' appeal.

"I am no soldier," Togodumnus replied with what he hoped was a casual shrug. "But the valley is long and narrow, with steep hills on either side. There is only one way in unless you wish to climb the mountains, which is very dangerous at this time of year."

Pulling a sour face, Piso put in, "Which means they will see us coming. How many men does he have there?"

"No more than five hundred at the moment," Togodumnus assured him. But that number will increase to several thousand once the war host has gathered."

"Why so few?" Flaccus demanded to know.

"Because they cannot feed their entire army if they stay together. Calgacus normally keeps his warriors spread out over a wide area."

Agricola asked, "I presume they maintain a watch on the approaches?"

"Yes. They have sentries and relays of messengers to warn of any approach."

"And how far is the actual camp from the mouth of the valley?"

"Around five Roman miles," Togodumnus answered.

"Which would give Calgacus plenty of warning. He could escape into the mountains long before we reached him."

"Not necessarily," Togodumnus replied, glad that his father had forced him to go over this part of the plan so many times. "You see, he has several smaller camps established along the floor of the valley. His warriors are based in these small, fortified villages, spread out like I said. It means you need to get past them to reach him but, just as importantly, it means he is more likely to come to join them if he thinks they are under attack. His reputation as War Leader would be destroyed if he simply ran away and left his men to die facing your attack."

"Five hundred men to get past, then?" Agricola enquired.

"About that number, I believe," Togodumnus confirmed. "But, as I say, only for a few more days."

"And how well fortified are these encampments?"

"Standard ditches and ramparts with a wooden stockade," Togodumnus answered. "They are small, though, no more than six houses in each one."

"But a quick cavalry raid against Calgacus' own home is out of the question?"

"You would need to get past all the other camps first," Togodumnus agreed.

Macrinus clucked his tongue disapprovingly, and Piso shook his head.

"I don't like it," the Legate remarked. "They will have plenty of warning of our approach, and it sounds difficult to reach the ultimate target."

Togodumnus, careful not to appear too anxious, argued, "No. It is possible. If you made a night march to reach the valley, you could enter it at dawn. With enough men, you could sweep the first defenders aside and be well into the valley before the rest have time to rally. Calgacus will come to see what is happening, and then you can launch your cavalry against him before he has time to summon reinforcements."

"You would be happy to see him die?" Flaccus coughed.

"After what he did to me?" Togodumnus grunted. "I want an end to this war. The only way I know how to achieve that is for my father to end his resistance. If that requires his death, so be it."

"Patricide is a crime," Flaccus observed with a faint sneer.

"Under Roman law. Not among the Pritani, at least not in the same way. Besides, I do not intend to kill him myself, merely to aid you in achieving that goal."

Flaccus regarded him coldly for a long time, as if attempting to read his innermost thoughts. Togodumnus kept his own face impassive and hard, doing his best to convince the Assistant Procurator of his determination.

At last, Flaccus turned to Agricola.

"Could this be done?" he asked.

"It is possible," the Governor nodded slowly. "But nothing is certain in war."

Piso ventured, "I am not convinced we could move the Legion quickly enough to prevent the barbarians learning of our approach."

"That is the most obvious flaw in the plan," Agricola agreed.

Togodumnus made his final attempt to convince them. Leaning forwards and clasping his hands together, he told them, "If you decide not to do this, you may still end up with a battle on your hands. My father is planning a major assault. I do not know where he intends to attack you, but I imagine your forts and watchtowers are the obvious choice. I overheard him mention something about luring your reserves out like the last time. Does that mean anything to you?"

Piso nodded, "He knows what we did when he attacked that fort a few weeks ago. If he does the same again and we respond in the same way, he could then launch other attacks against weaker positions which we would not be able to reinforce."

Togodumnus saw Agricola give a slight nod of agreement, so he pressed on, "Would it not be better to fight on your own terms? If you attack now, you could destroy the rebel alliance. Even if they see you coming and decide to fight, you have the advantage of taking the initiative rather than waiting for them to attack you. The worst that could happen is that my father and all the leaders run away, but that will destroy their standing among the tribes."

Agricola sat back, running a hand through his short hair.

"I will think on this," he decided at last. "If we can work out a way to achieve it, I think it might be worth attempting. After all, if Calgacus is not going to come out to fight Serpicius, we will need to deal with him another way."

Flaccus stated, "Serpicius will continue to fight other Britons until Calgacus is forced to accept his challenge. That was always the plan."

"Agreed," Agricola smiled smoothly. "But it seems your plan will not work quite as quickly as you had hoped. If we have another method of capturing or killing him, we should at least consider it. That is what I intend to do."

"Then I will leave you to your musings and bid you goodnight," Flaccus replied, holding out his goblet for one of his slaves to take.

He stood, gave a slight bow of his head in farewell, then strode to the exit, his attendants hurrying after him. After a moment, Serpicius also left, giving nothing more than a curt nod to the Governor.

There was a notable easing of tension once the Emperor's spy and his hired killer had departed, but Agricola cut short any further conversation by indicating that he, too, wished to retire although he gave one final instruction to his secretary, Donnatus.

"Can you find some accommodation for our guest?" he asked, gesturing towards Togodumnus.

Donnatus nodded, "There is one spare room in the block being used by Popidius Flaccus," he replied, quickly adding, "At the far end from the Gentleman's own quarters. It is being used as a store, but we can surely make enough space for one person."

"I'll see to it," Macrinus offered, rising from his own chair and sweeping one hand towards the tent's entrance in invitation.

Togodumnus stood up, grimacing with the effort. He said his farewells to the Governor and the Legate, then, walking slowly and stiffly, followed Macrinus out into the night.

The camp was settling down. Overhead, dark clouds obscured the night sky, but flickering torches and glowing braziers illuminated the interior of the camp. By their dim light, Togodumnus could make out the bulk of several large buildings arrayed in neat rows.

"Your construction work is going well," he observed as Macrinus led him along the wide pathway of the *Via Praetoria*.

"The granaries are complete," Macrinus confirmed. "As are most of the barrack blocks. We need to start on the infirmary and workshops next, but Piso is confident the camp will be finished before winter sets in."

Togodumnus could not help but admire the Governor's methods. The granaries, built with elevated floors to aid the circulation of air, and patrolled by the Legion's cats to prevent mice and rats consuming the precious grain, were the most important buildings. With the food supply secure, barracks blocks for the troops provided warmth and shelter from the weather. Only once the other administrative buildings had been completed would work begin on the Governor's own quarters. That way, the soldiers would see that their commander was looking after their welfare ahead of his own.

The same process did not apply to Popidius Flaccus, who had no qualms about taking over the legionaries' accommodation.

They could hear him now, complaining loudly as his slaves ran to fetch more hot water for him. Light spilled out from doorways as they bustled between Flaccus' large quarters at one end of a barracks block and the next door in line.

Macrinus grinned as they passed, explaining the layout to Togodumnus.

"Popidius Flaccus has the Centurion's rooms at this end. There are four more, smaller rooms in the block. The first is where his freedmen are billeted, the next for the slaves who do his cooking. There are no connecting doors, though, so they need to keep running up and down after him."

Togodumnus had once been imprisoned in a block identical to this one, so he knew the layout well enough. Not wanting to disillusion Macrinus, though, he asked, "Am I in the third room?"

"No, that's where Serpicius sleeps, along with his own slaves. You're in the last one."

"I thought Flaccus would need all the rooms," Togodumnus remarked. "He seems to have rather a large retinue."

"Oh, the rest of his slaves are in the next block. It's not too far away because an important man like Flaccus needs dozens of slaves close at hand to take care of him."

"What about the soldiers who were supposed to occupy these rooms?"

Macrinus waved a hand towards the dark shapes of several leather tents.

"Still there," he said, his tone indicating what he thought of the arrangement.

"That must make him popular," Togodumnus observed with a wry grin.

"I couldn't possibly comment," Macrinus replied, the dark of the night concealing any hint of mockery in his expression.

When they reached the darkened door of the last room, the Tribune said, "Wait here. I'll get someone to bring what you need."

He moved off into the darkness, leaving Togodumnus standing alone by the door. He turned, looking back along the building, noting the glimmers of faint light escaping from the gaps in the crude, wooden shutters of the windows. He looked at Serpicius' door, wondering what was going on behind it. Did the cold-eyed killer relax and smile as other men did?

Somehow, he doubted it. He was glad the door was shut because he had no wish to come face to face with The Snake. Even unarmed, the man was intimidating in a quiet, brooding way that made Togodumnus feel inadequate.

The next door was open, light from oil lamps spilling onto the ground, slaves still bustling to and fro as they carried jugs and pots to Flaccus' quarters at the far end. To judge by all the activity, it seemed the Assistant Procurator was having a late supper. Togodumnus was hungry himself, having had no more than a few mouthfuls of bread and cheese in the Governor's tent. Most of all, though, he was tired and very, very sore. All he wanted to do was take some more of Emmelia's medicine and sleep until the pulsating pain had gone away for good.

Macrinus returned, marching jauntily from the direction of the rows of legionary tents. He had two soldiers with him, each of them with their hands full. One, he saw, held a faintly glowing oil lamp.

"Here we are!" Macrinus grinned. "All the comforts of home."

"Not quite," Togodumnus grimaced, thinking of Thenu.

Macrinus ignored the remark, heading purposefully for the wooden door.

It was unlocked, as were all doors within the fort. Togodumnus followed the soldiers inside, peering around at the gloomy interior by the light of the tiny lamp which had been placed on top of a pile of wooden crates.

"Bit of a mess, isn't it?" Macrinus remarked cheerfully. "Right, lads, get some of that stuff shifted and make up a bed for our noble guest."

The room itself was small and square, only four or five paces on either side. What space there was would have been crowded in normal circumstances, three walls being lined by four sets of bunk beds, while the fourth wall, at the front of the building, had a small, clay oven and an open, brick-lined hearth space. There was no kindling or firewood, so the room had a damp, musty feel about it.

The worst thing, though, was the clutter. Crates, trunks and boxes were piled everywhere, including on the beds.

"That pompous bugger has a lot of luggage," Macrinus commented softly while the two soldiers set about clearing the nearest bed and piling the boxes to one side.

Togodumnus could tell that they had heard the Tribune's comment because both men were grinning as they heaved the boxes aside. Once they had cleared the bed, they shook the straw-filled mattress, then spread some blankets across it.

"There you go," Macrinus smiled. "There's a jug of water and a cup beside the lamp. We'll have a fire going soon."

"No need," Togodumnus informed him. "I'm going straight to sleep."

"Suit yourself. I'll have a word with Flaccus' head freedman and arrange for the slaves to bring you food in the morning."

"Thank you."

"Don't mention it. Right, lads, you can go now. I'm sure the King would like some peace."

Togodumnus gave the Tribune a smile of thanks. He had never felt less like a King in his entire life, but he realised that Macrinus' words would soon be all over the camp, thus affording him a measure of respect from the soldiers. It was a small kindness, but one for which he was grateful.

The two soldiers left, but Macrinus did not follow them. Moving to the door, he closed it, then turned to face Togodumnus.

"Are you sure you are all right?" he asked, his voice suddenly full of concern. "You don't look well at all. I can send for a medical orderly if you wish."

Togodumnus shook his head.

"I have some medicine of my own. I'll take it and try to get some sleep."

"Your father must have been rough with you."

Togodumnus realised that Macrinus was looking for confirmation that his tale of being beaten was not an exaggeration. He reached up, unfastened his brooch and slung his cloak over the top bunk behind him. Then he tugged up the side of his tunic and shirt, revealing a mass of purple and yellow blotches that covered the left side of his ribcage.

"Ouch," Macrinus tutted, leaning forward to peer at the injuries. "That must hurt."

"Not as much as my back," Togodumnus told him. "It feels a lot worse."

"Then I'll leave you to rest," Macrinus said, moving to the door and giving a nod of farewell.

Once the Tribune had left, Togodumnus moved to the table. He picked up the pitcher, poured a cup of water, then added a pinch of Emmelia's powder from his pouch. With nothing to use to stir the liquid, he stuck his finger in the cup and swirled it around. Then he drank it all at one go. Snuffing out the lamp, he felt his way to the bed. After tugging off his boots, he eased himself carefully under the blankets, not bothering to remove his clothes.

He ached all over but soon felt the numbing calm of the medicine creeping through his tortured body. Alone and sore, shivering and feeling miserable, he closed his eyes and fell asleep.

He was left to his own devices for most of the following two days. Macrinus was as good as his word, arranging for Flaccus' slaves to bring food to his room. Whether Flaccus himself was aware of this arrangement, Togodumnus did not know and did not care to ask. All he knew was that the slaves would arrive twice a day with his breakfast and evening meal. They asked no questions, offered no information, and left as soon as he gave them leave.

One of them, he was astonished to see, was a Nubian, a young man with skin as black as night. Togodumnus had heard of the dark-skinned Nubians, but he had never expected to see one of them in Britannia. It was difficult not to stare at the man, but he appeared perfectly normal in every respect other than the colour of his skin, and he understood Latin well enough. His presence, though, was another reminder of the power of the Empire which could uproot people from their homes and transport them to the opposite end of the known world. That, Togodumnus reflected, was a sobering thought.

He spent most of his time resting and sleeping, doping himself with Emmelia's painkillers, noting how he felt more light-headed as the pain from his injuries lessened and the powder needed less potency to dull the aches.

He ventured outside once or twice, but the camp was full of soldiers engaged in completing construction work, practising arms drill, or hurrying on other obscure business. Nobody had much time for him, so he spent most of the day in his room, thinking about Thenu and wondering whether he would ever see her again.

Macrinus popped in once or twice to check on him, but the Tribune was busy with the day to day running of his Auxiliary units, most of whom were based in outlying forts and watchtowers, resulting in him making long trips each day. When he did appear, he had no news of Agricola's decision.

"As far as I know, he hasn't made up his mind yet," he informed Togodumnus when he was asked whether the Romans were going to attempt to attack Calgacus' camp.

On the third day, Togodumnus felt a lot better. He decided to venture outside for a longer walk than he had attempted before. He managed a complete circuit of the huge camp, feeling no more than a little stiff from the effort.

As he returned to the barracks block, he noticed that the door to the central room, the one occupied by Flaccus' slaves, was open. On a whim, he went inside.

"Master?" a young man's voice asked in surprise.

It was the dark-skinned Nubian, regarding him with wide eyes which seemed startlingly white against the blackness of his face. He held a spoon with which he had been stirring the contents of a small pot which was placed over a tiny, flickering open flame.

There were two other slaves in the room, teenage boys who were hurriedly rising from beds where they had been resting. Togodumnus waved them back down, realising that the chances of gaining any respite from the demands of catering for Flaccus' every whim must be rare.

He turned back to the Nubian, smiling to relax the young slave's apprehension.

"I was wondering whether you might be able to give me something to eat," Togodumnus smiled.

The slave's face resumed its normal blank expression as he replied, "Of course, master. Just give me a moment and I'll get something for you."

"A little of whatever is in the pot will do," Togodumnus assured him.

"Oh, no, Sir. This gruel is just for us. It's not nearly good enough for you."

"I'm not looking for anything fancy," Togodumnus said. "I've eaten plenty of gruel in my time."

Noticing the flicker of agitation in the slave's eyes, he leaned closer to peer into the pot.

"How many of you is that supposed to feed?" he asked.

"Just the three of us, Master."

Togodumnus guessed the pot contained barely enough to fill a reasonably large bowl.

"Are you on short rations?" he asked.

"The Master insists we don't waste his stock of food," the slave explained, looking slightly embarrassed at making the confession.

Togodumnus looked around the room. There were boxes piled high between the bunk beds, labelled in dark ink with legends such as, "Olives", "Figs", "Peppers" and "Oranges". There were also several large amphorae marked, "Wine", "Vinegar" and even "Garum", the potent fish sauce which was an essential part of Roman cuisine. Sacks bulged with what he presumed was flour or grain.

"How would he know what you've used?" he enquired, giving the man a knowing wink.

"Gracchus, the Master's chief freedman, comes and checks every day," the slave explained.

Togodumnus felt a deep sense of injustice welling up inside him as he regarded the plentiful supplies stacked within easy reach, and then considered the meagre quantity of gruel in the pot.

"You must get fresh bread and meat from somewhere," he observed, not sure why he was so obsessed by Flaccus' treatment of his slaves.

"Gracchus purchases that from the Quartermaster," he was informed.

"I see. But what about the food you've been bringing me? Is that accounted for?"

"Oh, yes, Sir. We are always allowed to prepare an extra dish for you, by order of the Governor."

"No doubt your Master is recompensed for that out of the Army's pay chest," Togodumnus remarked sourly.

"I wouldn't know, Sir."

"But if I ask for food now, how can you give that to me if everything is rationed?"

"I will tell Gracchus and he will no doubt ask you to confirm it, Sir."

"No doubt. Well, I am very hungry indeed. What can you give me? I want a large plate, full as you can make it."

"Yes, Sir."

Still managing to keep one eye on the pot of gruel, the slave quickly reached up to a high shelf and pulled down a wooden platter. Togodumnus noticed that, in addition to piles of plates and cups, the shelf also bore a silver tray bearing a jug and goblet.

"Is that your Master's wine?" he asked as the slave busied himself rummaging in boxes and pulling out various items.

"Yes, Sir. We must always have a jug ready for him."

"Might I have a cup?"

The slave shot him a nervous look, and he was aware of an expectant stare from the two boys who had given up all pretence of trying to sleep in order to listen to the conversation.

"Of course, sir," the slave answered after only a moment's hesitation.

He busied himself cutting slices of dark bread and smearing them with honey. Then he chopped portions of cheese from a block unwrapped from within a linen cloth, placed some dried grapes and figs on the plate alongside a peeled orange and some sliced sausage and peppers.

"Here you are, Sir," he said, handing the plate to Togodumnus.

"Thank you."

The slave took down Flaccus' jug and poured him a cup before asking one of the younger lads to help him refill the jug from one of the heavy amphorae. Once this was done, he resealed the jug and replaced it on the silver tray.

"What's your name?" Togodumnus asked.

"Felix, Master."

Togodumnus guessed that Felix was in his early twenties, about the same age as himself, although the slave's face bore more worry lines than it should for someone of his years. Life, it seemed, had not been kind to him, making a mockery of his name which meant, "Lucky".

"You are from Nubia?"

It was a silly question, but he could not help asking it.

Felix gave a nod of confirmation.

"Yes, master."

Togodumnus wanted to know more. He wondered how Felix had come to be a slave. What had Fate done to him to bring him here, so far from his home?

But the slave resumed his task of stirring the pot, clearly reluctant to engage in conversation, and Togodumnus felt too embarrassed to probe any further.

Instead, he concentrated on his food, chewing on some sausage. He spent a few moments picking at the plate, eating some cheese and a slice of the honeyed bread, followed by a piece of the succulent orange. Then he laid the plate down on the small table beside Felix and took out his little bag of medicine. He sprinkled a few grains into the wine, swirled the glass a few times, then drank it, surprised at how much better it tasted than the standard fare the Governor usually provided.

He noticed that the slaves were watching him carefully, even though Felix was making great play of concentrating on stirring the gruel.

Replacing the empty cup, Togodumnus said, "Thank you for the food. No doubt I will see you later."

Felix shot him a puzzled look.

"But, Master, you've hardly eaten anything."

Togodumnus looked down at the plate of food.

"I don't seem to have been as hungry as I thought. Still, you'd better not waste it. Have it with your gruel. I'll tell Gracchus I ate it all."

Felix gave him a broad smile, revealing an array of perfect, white teeth, his eyes sparkling with delight. The other slaves were up on their elbows, looking incredulous but eyeing the plate hungrily.

"Better be quick," Togodumnus advised. "Eat it before Gracchus comes checking."

Felix grinned, "Thank you, Master."

Smiling happily, Togodumnus left the room, feeling pleased with himself, and hoping that the three slaves would not waste the opportunity he had presented to them.

When he returned to his own room at the end of the block, he lay on his bed and stared up at the wooden boards of the upper bunk above him, reflecting on the life of a Roman slave.

Not every Roman treated their slaves as Flaccus did, but a great many of them did and some, he had heard, were even harsher. While slaves could earn their freedom, most of them faced a life of endless servitude. Some, he had discovered, would be worked until they were no longer capable of carrying out their duties due to ill health or infirmity, then would be sold off to whoever would take them. When a slave fell sick, most were simply left to die.

Slavery was not unique to the Romans, of course, but, as in so many other aspects of life, they had turned it into an industry on a massive scale. Among the tribes of the Pritani, slaves tended to be war captives taken from other tribes, but even that habit was fading as the various peoples spent less time fighting one another and devoted their efforts to opposing Rome. Whichever way he looked at it, though, he could not help thinking how he would feel if he were in Felix's shoes.

"You were right, Father," he told the empty room. "Freedom is worth fighting for."

Gracchus, Flaccus' freedman, was an older man, in his fifties, with thinning, grey hair and a pock-marked face. His small, close-set eyes seemed to offer a threat as he arrived with Felix when the young slave brought Togodumnus' evening meal. Togodumnus took great pleasure in explaining how hungry he had been after the exertions of his walk, and confirmed that he had consumed a large plateful of food.

Felix took pains to keep his face blank, but Gracchus seemed almost deflated when he heard Togodumnus list everything he had eaten.

"Thank you, Sir," he growled indignantly as he left, chivvying Felix out of the door.

No sooner had they departed than Macrinus arrived, looking tired and wearing the unmistakable expression of someone bringing bad tidings.

"What is wrong?" Togodumnus asked the Tribune as he stood to greet him.

Macrinus gave him a grim shake of his head.

"I'm sorry, lad," Macrinus sighed. "I came to tell you that the Governor has decided against your suggestion. He's going to follow Flaccus' plan and have Serpicius continue to fight your folk until your father accepts his challenge."

Togodumnus felt his heart sink. He slumped back down on his bed, looking up at Macrinus as if the tribune might alter his story.

"But why?" he asked. "If he misses this opportunity, my father will launch an attack of his own."

"He decided it wasn't worth the risk," Macrinus explained. "One Legion isn't enough to go marching into those hills, and we don't have time to call up the other Legions. Besides, we need to make sure we finish building this fort before winter arrives."

Togodumnus struggled for words. Shaking his head, he muttered, "One Legion would be more than enough against a few hundred tribesmen. I thought the Governor was a man of action."

"He is," Macrinus said. "But he's not been the same since your father destroyed the Ninth Legion. That, and the death of his son, hit him pretty hard, I think. He knows another military defeat will mean the end of his career. This idea of yours was just too risky."

Togodumnus felt empty and numb. He had always known that his chances of success were slim, but he had convinced himself that he had done enough to persuade Agricola to march into Calgacus' trap. Now, the only thought in his mind was that he had failed.

Which meant his father would have no choice but to face the gladiator in a fight he could not hope to survive.

Chapter XXIX

"They're not coming."

Runt swore, pushing up his woollen cap to scratch at his balding head, his frustration plain for everyone to see.

"They're not coming," he repeated angrily, his foot kicking out to lash at a clump of brown heather.

"It certainly doesn't look like it," Calgacus agreed.

"It's been seven days since Togodumnus left," Runt told him.

"I can count."

"Which means your ten days are up tomorrow."

"That's right."

"They would be on the way by now if they were coming," Runt persisted.

"Yes."

The two men were standing on a high hilltop which provided a view of the terrain to the south. It was notoriously difficult to make out marching men amidst the patchwork of trees, streams and meadows of the autumn, but a Roman Legion was hard to miss. They had been waiting and watching for the past four days, but had seen no sign of any enemy soldiers. The scouts who had patrolled far to the south and west had brought back no news at all. The Romans, it seemed, were staying in their forts.

"So what are we going to do?" Runt asked.

Calgacus did not answer. He stood, his eyes staring out across the landscape, his thoughts dark and brooding. All his plans seemed to have gone awry recently. His ambush which should have destroyed the Roman Legions had been thwarted, his attempt to lure Cohorts into a trap by attacking a fort had failed, Gabrain's raid had been a disaster, and now his final attempt to trick the Governor into marching into the hills had also failed. Agricola, he realised, had learned how to neutralise him.

"Well?" Runt persisted. "We need to do something."

Calgacus spread his hands in a gesture of helplessness as he shrugged, "I suppose I'll need to go and fight that gladiator."

"Cal! You can't do that. Didn't you hear what Togodumnus said? The man slaughtered Gabrain easily. You know you had to cheat to beat Gabrain yourself."

"I know."

"So how can you even think of going up against this killer?"

"Because I intend to cheat again."

Runt shot him a baffled look.

"Cheat? How?"

Calgacus gestured towards the brooding figure of Bridei who continued to stare into the distance as if willing the Roman Legion to appear.

"Do you remember that bear Bridei killed last year?"

"You can't dig a pit for a gladiator to fall into," Runt snorted.

"Not a literal one," Calgacus agreed. "But that's not what I meant. Bridei is having a new tunic made for me."

At that, the Boresti King turned his head and treated them to a broad grin.

"It's ready," he informed them.

"A new tunic?" Runt scowled. "What good will that do?"

"It's made from bearskin," Calgacus told him.

Bridei put in, "I've been using it as a bed cover, but it's big enough to make a decent jerkin."

Runt looked from one man to the other, shaking his head.

"You two are as mad as each other," he sighed. "It may have escaped your notice, but a bearskin coat won't protect you from a Roman sword."

He shot a scathing look at Calgacus as he went on, "You've never believed that nonsense about the skin of an animal lending its properties to the wearer. Even when we

365

were boys, you used to argue with the druids about that sort of stuff."

"I know," Calgacus grinned. "But what I believe isn't important. It's what others believe that matters."

Runt waved his hands in despair.

"The Romans believe in the power of their swords!" he exclaimed. "The gladiator won't be put off by a mangy bearskin! He will know it can't stop his gladius."

Bridei let out a loud laugh.

"This particular bearskin might surprise him," he chuckled.

"What are you talking about?" Runt demanded.

Taking pity on his friend, Calgacus explained what he had in mind. Runt's expression remained dark even when he heard the plan.

"You really are crazy," he told Calgacus.

"Maybe. If you can think of a better idea, let me know soon. I'll need to leave in the morning because my ten days are up tomorrow."

"We should go back to your plan of storming their fortress," Runt suggested.

"I thought you said that was a daft idea?"

"It is, but it's better than this latest plan."

"We'll find out tomorrow," Calgacus said, rubbing his hands together to warm them. "Come on, let's head back home. I have a new tunic to try on."

They turned away from the slope, heading back to where Adelligus and a handful of warriors were waiting with their ponies. All of them wore expressions of deep concern, realising that Togodumnus' mission had failed.

The mood had not lightened by the time they returned to their hilltop sanctuary. The evening meal was plentiful, but the atmosphere was muted, with no music and little conversation. Almost instinctively, people sat in their individual family groups, leaving Calgacus and Beatha a spurious privacy.

Beatha echoed Runt's views on Calgacus' proposal for defeating the gladiator but, like Runt, she had no other suggestions to offer. She was also beset with concerns for her son.

"Why has Togodumnus not come back?" she wanted to know.

"Because it would look suspicious if, having gone to the Governor with an offer to betray me, the first thing he did when his suggestion was ignored was to come running back to tell me."

"You don't think they have harmed him?"

"Why should they? He's on their side as far as they are concerned."

"Poor Thenu is miserable," Beatha observed.

"Then go and reassure her. Tell her Togodumnus will be back soon enough."

Beatha fixed him with her blue eyes, refusing to allow him to ignore her.

"You had better come back too, Cal. I don't want to lose either of you. Losing both of you would kill me."

"We'll both come back," he promised.

She tried to smile, but her eyes remained anxious.

Most of them climbed the stairs to bed early. As part of an unspoken pact, Beatha and Calgacus engaged in quiet lovemaking, knowing this could be their last night together. The threat of imminent death had always aroused this passion in them, a need for a shared physical reassurance which the passing of years had done nothing to diminish. She clung to him with a fierce hunger as he moved rhythmically on top of her but, once they were spent, they knew that others had taken the opportunity for intimacy. The soft sounds of love floated through the roundhouse as the other couples sought comfort from one another. Even Fallar, who had so recently given birth, was heard to cry out in the darkness.

Only one adult slept alone that night.

"Poor Thenu," Beatha whispered as she snuggled in beside Calgacus.

He did not answer because he was already asleep.

It was still dark when he was abruptly woken. A hand shook him and he heard a frightened, tearful voice imploring him to wake up.

"Papa! He's gone!" Wake up! He's gone!"

"What?" he muttered groggily as he was roused from a deep sleep. "Fallar?"

"Papa! You must stop him!"

"What? Who?"

She was a mere shadow in the gloom, a faint silhouette outlined by the feeble glow from the dying embers of the hearth fire on the lower level. Calgacus' sleep-filled eyes struggled to make her out at all, but he could not mistake the anguish in her voice.

Beatha was awake now, sitting up and reaching across him to clasp Fallar's hand.

"What is it?" she asked her tearful daughter. "Who has gone?"

"Adelligus!" Fallar blurted, sniffing back her tears.

Calgacus was awake now, and so were others. He heard someone scrambling down to the lower level and soon saw the flare of a candle.

"Where has he gone?" he asked, reaching out to reassure Fallar.

"To fight the Roman," the girl sobbed.

Runt was edging towards them now, holding the guttering candle carefully to avoid the flame setting light to anything. Tegan was sitting up, clutching her blankets to her chest, her eyes wide with shock. From further round the house, Thenu was hurrying round to find out what was going on. Soon, the space around Calgacus' bed seemed crowded, the moment caught by the dim candlelight and disturbed when baby Elaris began to cry.

The sound of her daughter's wail set Fallar off again as she twisted uncertainly. Her confusion was calmed when

Tegan picked up the baby and carried her over so that Fallar could hold her.

"Tell us what is going on," Calgacus said, struggling to keep his own anxiety from adding to his daughter's distress.

Fallar took a deep breath, wiping tears from her cheeks with the back of one hand while she clutched Elaris in the other.

"He said something last night," she explained. "He told me he didn't think you could beat this Roman gladiator. He thought he would have a better chance because he defeated you in your practice fights the other week."

"Are you sure that's what he's going to do?" Calgacus asked.

Fallar could only nod her head.

Runt scrambled over to the sleeping chamber Adelligus and Fallar shared. When he came back, he was shaking his head in consternation.

"His sword and armour are gone," he reported. "I'll go and check his horse."

He grabbed up his cloak as he headed for the stairway once again.

Everyone was shivering in the cold gloom of the early morning. The women clustered around Fallar, trying to offer reassurance or provide some alternative reason for Adelligus' absence.

"I didn't hear him go," she whispered miserably. "I just woke up and he was gone."

Calgacus pushed himself from the bed and began dressing.

"What are you going to do?" Beatha asked him.

"I'm going to find the boy," he told her.

By the time he was dressed, Runt was back, frowning and looking angry.

"His horse is gone," he said. "I checked with the men on watch and they say he left a couple of hours ago."

Calgacus frowned, "He can't have got far. It's bloody dark out there."

"Far enough," Runt replied. "What do we do?"

His concern for his son was etched on his face, his eyes holding a silent plea.

"We know where he's going," Calgacus decided. "Go and wake our lads. Then send messengers to the rest of the war host. Tell every man who has a horse to join us as soon as they can."

Runt nodded as Calgacus added, "I'll go and fetch Bridei. He's got my new tunic. It looks as if I'm going to need it."

Runt was fretting by the time the sun rose a short while later. He paced up and down, constantly checking his horse's saddle and bridle, then taking out his twin swords and examining them as if they might have become blunt since the last time he had looked at them.

"We should go now," he told Calgacus. "It's light enough to see where we are going."

Calgacus, wearing an enormously bulky jerkin of bearskin, the fastenings made of the great beast's teeth, looked even larger than he normally did, his shoulders high and broad, his torso massively bulky. He wore his huge sword on his back, but had disdained his coat of chainmail. His frown made him resemble the bear his new coat had once adorned, but he was fully awake now and able to think about what they must do.

"It's almost a full day's ride to the Roman fortress," he reminded his friend. "That's in a straight line. To get there, we need to pass several watchtowers and at least two forts with cavalry garrisons."

"So does Adelligus," Runt argued.

"A man on his own can sneak past relatively easily," Calgacus replied. "If we take even twenty men, we'll either need to make long detours to get round the forts, or be prepared to be challenged by the Roman horsemen. Either way, we won't be able to catch up with him. He's got too much of a head start."

"So we wait for the entire war host?" Runt challenged. "That could take another hour or more."

"We'll wait until we have enough so that the Romans won't be tempted to try to stop us," Calgacus told him in a tone that brooked no further argument.

Runt turned away, kicking out angrily at an imaginary target.

They had ridden down to the valley floor, partly because it was the best place for the mounted warriors to assemble, and partly because it did not prolong the agonies of watching Fallar's distress. She blamed herself for not warning Calgacus the previous evening, and then for not alerting him sooner. She had thought at first that Adelligus might simply have ventured outside to answer a call of nature, but she had grown worried when he had not returned. That delay, she was certain, might prove fatal.

"He can't get far in the dark," Calgacus had assured her. "Once it is light, we'll soon be able to catch him."

He had spoken the words confidently, but Runt knew the truth of the matter. Even in the dark, Adelligus could rely on his horse to find a safe route for him. He would be well on his way by the time the sun rose.

"He'll wish he had just gone for a piss when I catch him," Runt had sworn.

As the grey light expanded across the sky and slowly flooded into the valley, more and more men came in answer to the call. Calgacus had gathered his entire war host in anticipation of ambushing a Roman Legion, but now he would use them for another purpose. They might not be able to cause any damage to the Governor's main fortress, but they would certainly terrify the garrisons of the other, smaller Roman outposts.

Riders appeared from further along the glen, coming at a fast canter. Others crested the hills to east and west and came flooding down the steep slopes to join the growing war band. Sooner than Runt had forecast and Calgacus had expected, nearly three thousand riders had gathered on the valley floor, with more streaming in with every passing moment.

"We'll go now," Calgacus decided. "The rest will need to catch up with us if they can."

He raised a hand, shouted a command, and jabbed his heels to his pony's belly, urging it forwards. In a thunder of sound, his warriors followed him.

They maintained a steady pace, knowing it was pointless to tire the horses by galloping the whole way. A fast canter, interspersed with short periods of walking and trotting, allowed them to cover the ground as quickly as any mounted army could. Horses have tremendous stamina and can maintain a fast pace for a long time, but Calgacus was wary of reaching the Roman fort with his mounts exhausted. He did not know what might happen when they arrived, but the last thing he wanted was a war host that could not fight.

Against that was the overriding need to catch Adelligus before he reached the fortress and issued his challenge to The Snake.

"The boy's a bloody fool," he muttered repeatedly as he rode.

They swept across the rolling countryside, by-passing Roman watchtowers with barely a glance at them, seeing the warning flags being waved and knowing word of their approach would reach the Governor long before they saw the walls of the fortress.

The other forts, positioned to block the entrances to the plain, were more of a hazard but Calgacus rode on, trusting to the sheer size of his army to keep the garrisons within their ramparts. That part of his plan, at least, was successful because not a single Roman ventured out to meet them. He could hear bugles and shouts of alarm as his vast horde rode towards the forts and he saw the shapes of men gathering behind the wooden palisades, but he led his riders past the fortifications and rode on.

They made only a few, brief halts to let the horses drink and eat some of the fodder they had brought in nets strapped to their saddles. The warriors chewed on stale bread or salted meat, swigging ale from the leather skins they carried, then they mounted up and rode on.

And still there was no sign of Adelligus.

The sun was always low in the sky at this time of year, its glare obscuring much of what lay ahead of them, but none of them could make out any signs of a lone rider blazing their trail.

Runt began to fret even more as the morning passed into afternoon, and the autumn sun began to descend towards the western hills.

"We're not going to catch him!" he spat vehemently.

Calgacus did not answer. He had no answer that could comfort his friend because there were barely two hours of daylight left and the fort lay just beyond the next line of low hills. Unless they could see Adelligus when they crested that rise, they were already too late.

Gritting his teeth, Calgacus urged his horse into a gallop.

Chapter XXX

Togodumnus had suffered bouts of mental anguish for days. He had failed to persuade the Governor to march against his father, a failure which meant that either Serpicius would embark on a killing spree, or that Calgacus would come to face the gladiator in single combat, a fight he could not hope to win. That knowledge weighed heavily on the young Briton, but the worst part was that he could not afford to let anyone see how much it affected him. As a consequence, he spent most of his time in his room, brooding silently or reading some of the Latin books he had borrowed from the Governor's secretary. Togodumnus had developed a passion for books as a boy, when his mother had taught him to read, but even these fascinating scrolls could not hold his attention for long.

When he did venture outside, he tried to avoid talking to anyone. For the most part, that was not too difficult since the soldiers were too busy with their construction work or guard duty to pay any attention to him. More difficult were the meals he was invited to attend with the Governor where he pretended that his injuries were still causing him pain so that he had an excuse for his dark mood.

"Tomorrow is the tenth day," Flaccus reminded everyone at dinner one night. "If Calgacus does not come, we shall visit the nearest settlement the following morning, and Serpicius will fight their champion."

"They won't have a champion," Macrinus muttered. "All their warriors are up in the hills with Calgacus. All that will be left are old men and young boys."

Flaccus gave an unconcerned shrug.

"As long as one of them dies and word reaches Calgacus, that is all that matters."

Togodumnus had been tempted to make some remark about what honour a gladiator could gain by killing a helpless victim, but he held his tongue because he had bumped into Serpicius earlier in the day and been cowed by the cold, heartless expression in the man's dark eyes. The Snake, he was convinced, would take pleasure in killing anyone, and would not concern himself with matters of honour.

The tenth day passed slowly. Several times, Togodumnus summoned the courage to venture outside, climbing up to the top of the earthen ramparts to gaze out to the north, expecting and dreading to see his father approach. Each time, the land remained empty.

It was growing late in the short afternoon when he heard a commotion outside, the sound of shouting accompanied by trumpet calls. Hurrying to the door of his self-imposed prison, he flung it open to see soldiers picking up their weapons and donning their helmets. The legionaries wore their articulated armour all day, even when building their barracks, so preparing for battle did not take long. Seeing them hurrying to their allotted stations around the perimeter, he went out to see what was happening.

Macrinus found him before he had gone more than half a dozen steps.

"Come with me!" the Tribune commanded, beckoning him.

"What's happening? Is it my father?"

"No. It's someone else."

"Who?"

"I don't know. That's why I want you with me. You can tell me who it is."

The two of them made for the north gate which led out to a wide, grassy plain that had once been dotted with trees but which now held only a few stumps because the Legion had cleared the land to provide timber for their fort.

Togodumnus shot an anxious glance up to the summit of a steep-sided hill that lay just to the north-east of the fort. The hilltop provided an eyrie for a watchtower with commanding views of the surrounding countryside. There was, though, no visible sign of alarm from the men on watch.

Puzzled, he asked Macrinus, "Why are the soldiers manning the walls?"

"Just a precaution," the Tribune replied unhelpfully.

The northern gates were open, but a crowd of armed soldiers was formed up in the entranceway. Macrinus marched past them, with Togodumnus struggling to match the Tribune's long strides. It was only when they passed outside the fort that Togodumnus saw a solitary figure standing beside a horse, around two hundred paces away. The man was waiting patiently, holding a pine branch in his hand as a signal that he came in peace.

"Do you recognise him?" Macrinus asked as they walked towards the lone figure.

Togodumnus stared, trying to make out the features of the face beneath the iron helmet the man wore.

"I'm not sure," he said, although he thought he recognised the figure's stance. His suspicion turned to certainty as they drew nearer.

"Adelligus!" he breathed.

"Who is he?" Macrinus demanded sharply.

"Commander of my father's bodyguard," Togodumnus explained, unwilling to provide the Roman with any more information than necessary.

Togodumnus' heart began to race. He and Adelligus had never been friends despite the close relationship between their fathers. His feet moved automatically, keeping pace with Macrinus, but he dreaded confronting his brother-in-law. He knew Adelligus was a fine warrior, an expert rider and a superb swordsman, but Togodumnus doubted whether he had the ability to keep Togodumnus' secret. One misplaced word or facial expression could alert Macrinus to where Togodumnus' true loyalties lay.

He need not have worried. As they came to within a few paces of man and horse, Adelligus tossed his peace branch aside and shot Togodumnus a withering look of disdain.

Adelligus was dressed for war, wearing a coat of chainmail and his iron helmet. A short, Roman *gladius* was at his hip, a long broadsword on his back, and an oval shield hung from the rear of his horse's saddle.

"Is this their gladiator?" he asked Togodumnus, jerking his chin to indicate Macrinus.

Before Togodumnus could respond, the Tribune answered in Brythonic, "No, I am not."

"Then go and send him out."

"Why?" Macrinus asked.

"Because I intend to kill him," Adelligus replied coldly.

"Does this mean that Calgacus is afraid to come?" Macrinus shot back.

"Calgacus does not need to come," Adelligus told him. "I will kill this gladiator of yours, and that will be an end to the matter."

"The challenge was issued to Calgacus," Macrinus pointed out.

"But your man was to fight someone else if Calgacus did not come," Adelligus retorted. "I am here. Let him fight me."

"If you are sure you want to die, I will fetch him," Macrinus said with a casual shrug.

"Then go and send him out. I will wait here."

"You're brave, lad," Macrinus told him. "Stupid, but brave."

Adelligus did not react to the jibe, simply cocking his head in expectation.

"All right," Macrinus nodded.

He turned away, signalling to Togodumnus to accompany him.

"Go on," Adelligus taunted. "Go with your Roman master."

Togodumnus stood his ground, hissing, "Why are you doing this? You have a daughter. And Fallar."

After his fears over whether Adelligus could keep his secret, Togodumnus felt foolish that it was he who was in danger of giving away too much, but he could not help himself. He knew his sister and the love she bore for the scar-faced young warrior, and his heart ached at the thought of the grief she would suffer if Adelligus were to die.

There was a glint of fierce pride in Adelligus' eye as he replied, "I am doing this for them. I have a better chance of winning than your father does."

Togodumnus could not argue. He held Adelligus' gaze, but the young swordsman's stare was implacable, forcing Togodumnus to turn away and meekly follow Macrinus.

"What was that about?" Macrinus asked when Togodumnus caught up with him.

"Nothing."

"Is he a friend of yours?"

"Hardly. He used to beat me up when we were younger. But he married a girl I liked, and they have a baby daughter."

Macrinus smiled, "You, my young friend, are too sensitive for this sort of life."

Togodumnus could not dispute that assessment. His heart was bleak as they passed back through the gates of the fort.

The Governor and his staff officers had gathered on the ramparts beside the gateway. Piso and Flaccus were also there, along with Serpicius who, apart from being bare-headed, was already attired in his gladiatorial costume, his bare torso gleaming with oil and marked by tiny goosebumps raised by the cold air.

Macrinus and Togodumnus climbed up to meet them.

"Well?" Flaccus demanded, the word mangled by his persistent cough.

Macrinus explained who the visitor was and what he wanted.

"Commander of Calgacus' bodyguard?" Flaccus demanded. "Does that mean he is a skilful warrior?"

All eyes turned to Togodumnus who shrugged, "I suppose so. He was always the best among the young men when we were growing up."

Macrinus put in, "Calgacus would not appoint a slouch to lead his personal guard. The lad may be young, but he has the look of a warrior about him."

"Excellent!" crowed Flaccus. "If he dies, Calgacus will be even more afraid to accept the challenge. His leadership will be completely undermined."

Togodumnus was appalled, but could think of nothing to say that could possibly prevent Adelligus' death.

"This might be an attempt to distract us," Piso warned. "There are reports of a large barbarian force coming this way."

Togodumnus looked up to the distant watchtower and, this time, could make out the large signal flags waving a message he could not decipher. His heart continued to pound and his breath became shorter as a sensation of utter helplessness coursed through his body.

Adelligus had come alone, but a large force was on its way? It made no sense.

He put a hand to his forehead, hoping nobody had noticed his confusion, but it was the Governor who held everyone's attention as he responded to Piso's warning.

"Then remind your Centurions to keep their men under arms and maintain a good watch," Agricola suggested. "And we should close all the gates."

"You think we are in danger?" Flaccus demanded anxiously.

"It might be an attempt to make us look the wrong way," Agricola nodded. "But we will be perfectly safe in here."

Flaccus dissolved into a fit of coughing which lasted a long time before he was able to gather his composure again. Eventually, he turned to Serpicius.

"Go and kill this barbarian. It seems Calgacus is not coming, but at least this saves us the trouble of seeking out a worthy opponent for you."

The gladiator stared back at him, his face impassive.

"You want me to go out there alone when there is a horde of barbarians on its way here?"

"Kill him quickly and you need not worry about them," Flaccus spluttered angrily.

Macrinus put in, "I will come with you. And I'll have a couple of hundred horsemen ready to ride out to protect us if need be."

Serpicius shot him a look of contempt before returning his icy stare to the Assistant Procurator.

"I want double the money," the gladiator stated flatly.

"What?" Flaccus barked, coughing loudly once again.

Serpicius ignored the nobleman's obvious physical discomfort as he said, "You heard. If I am about to risk my neck against a barbarian army in a fight which might end this war for you, I think ten thousand denarii is the least I can expect."

Everyone watched the confrontation in silence, the officers clearly enjoying Flaccus' discomfiture.

"Best decide quickly," Serpicius remarked, glancing up at the sky. "It will be dark in an hour or two."

Flaccus' mouth twisted in a grimace of distaste, but he knew he had no choice.

"Very well," he spat. "Ten thousand denarii."

Serpicius nodded once, then signalled to his slave to bring his helmet to him.

"Fetch your horsemen," he told Macrinus.

Togodumnus could not watch. As Macrinus hurried off to gather his cavalry, and Serpicius fastened his helmet with its iron face mask, he slipped away from the assembled officers, slowly making his way back to his room, his shoulders slumped under the weight of his despair.

Macrinus was too busy to notice Togodumnus' silent departure. He could have sent a junior officer to the Auxiliary Annexe but the current situation was fraught with potential danger and he wanted to be sure that his message would not be misinterpreted. Still, he knew better than to run, because the sight of a senior officer in a panic was not good for morale, so he forced himself to walk briskly without appearing to be in too much of a hurry.

Fortunately, he did not have too far to go because the western annexe was laid out not far from the north gate of the main fort. When he arrived, he found that his men were already mounted and waiting, having readied themselves as soon as they heard the Legion's calls to arms.

Around half of the Auxiliary cavalry were scattered across the newly-conquered territory of the northern province, but there were still over three hundred of them stationed here. They were arranged in a long column, four riders abreast, lances ready, while the horses stamped their feet and swished their tails in eagerness.

Macrinus sought out Sdapezi, the senior Centurion, who sat at the head of the column.

"Keep the northern exit open," Macrinus told him, "but don't come out unless you see me signal to you. With luck, this will all be over quickly."

"What if the barbarian army gets here?" Sdapezi asked.

"Then you might have to come out and rescue me. But don't get involved in a fight unless you have no choice. There could be thousands of them."

Sdapezi nodded his understanding.

"You could take a horse," he suggested.

"I could. But I don't want to let that barbarian think we are afraid of him."

Sdapezi shrugged.

Macrinus went on, "Have half the lads form up near the west gate. They can ride round to join you if you need to come outside. By using both gates, you'll be able to deploy twice as quickly."

"Already in hand," the Centurion informed him.

"Good. Well done. Now, I suppose I'd better go and escort our gladiator out to meet his opponent. Enjoy the show."

He returned to the main fortress where he found Serpicius waiting for him behind the now closed north gate.

"Ready?" Macrinus asked.

The helmeted head moved in a silent nod, so Macrinus signalled to the legionaries to open the gate to allow them to leave.

This time, as he walked through the high entrance beside the gladiator, he imagined this must be what it felt like to march into an arena. Except that, in an arena, the crowd was noisy and enthusiastic while, here, the audience comprised a few thousand soldiers who lined the ramparts in silent anticipation of a barbarian trick.

Macrinus looked up to the signal tower. The flags were not moving, no message being relayed. He guessed that meant the approaching barbarian army, if it existed, was still some way off. But how far was that?

"Best get it over with quickly," he suggested to Serpicius.

The gladiator walked on without giving so much as an acknowledgement that he had heard him speak.

Arrogant bastard," thought Macrinus as he realised that part of him hoped Serpicius would lose the fight. He disliked the man, and he detested Flaccus, yet he knew his thoughts were disloyal towards the Empire. If the war could be ended by a single death, it should be worth putting up with Flaccus' and Serpicius' superior smugness. Somehow, though, Macrinus felt cheapened by what they were doing. He doubted whether he would ever come to terms with it. Fighting and killing did not bother him at all, but using threats against civilians to lure out the enemy leader did not sit comfortably with his values.

At least the Briton Serpicius was going to meet was a warrior, he mused. That was some consolation.

Adelligus was ready for them. He had fetched his shield, a simple oval of iron-banded wicker, covered by a leather hide and with a central boss of iron. He had also drawn his longsword from his back, the blade held low across his body and legs, its rounded tip resting on the ground.

"I am Adelligus, son of Liscus," he announced formally as the two Romans approached him.

"What did he say?" The Snake demanded, his voice partly muted by the iron faceplate of his helmet.

"He is telling you his name," Macrinus explained.

"Tell him I am Death," Serpicius grunted as he drew his *gladius*.

Switching to the local language, Macrinus told Adelligus, "This is Serpicius. He is a killer, boy. You still have time to leave if you want. Know this, I have been a soldier most of my life, and I've seen a lot of men who are good with a sword. I've never seen one better than him."

Adelligus gave a soft smile as he replied, "You haven't seen me fight."

Macrinus shrugged. He had done his best. Now it was up to the Gods to decide the fate of the two men.

Both combatants adopted a fighting stance as Macrinus retreated a few paces to give them room. The grass was damp underfoot, treacherous with bumps and divots, and he wondered whether the combat might be decided by a slip or stumble at the wrong moment. Then he had no more time to wonder because Serpicius went on the attack.

Adelligus was good. He used his long, round-tipped blade expertly, attempting to keep The Snake at a distance and use the superior reach of his sword to cut past the gladiator's defence. Serpicius, though, moved and dodged so quickly that he was able to dart in as soon as the long weapon missed him, allowing him to deliver a short, vicious stab of his own. No matter how good Adelligus might be, the longer sword was heavy and took more time to reposition after each swing. Still, he was light on his feet and used his shield to block Serpicius' attacks.

The two men circled like dancers, watching for openings, occasionally feinting or lunging. Sword blades crashed onto shields, iron rang in the air as the weapons clashed, and the deadly dance continued.

Serpicius' body was largely unprotected. Apart from his large shield and iron helmet, only metal greaves, shoulder guard and girdle offered any ward against attack, but the lack of armour meant that he could move relatively quickly. In contrast, the chainmail tunic Adelligus wore was heavy, one of the reasons the Roman Legions had dispensed with it and used the segmented body armour that, while offering slightly less protection, was considerably lighter. Adelligus was young and fit, but fighting in chainmail was hard work and he soon began to tire as he wielded his heavy sword one-handed.

The young Briton must have realised his problem because he made an unexpected move. Sweeping his sword across his body towards his left shoulder, he backswung it in a ferocious arc but, instead of delivering a powerful blow, he released his hold on the leather-bound hilt and flung the sword at Serpicius' head.

The gladiator ducked, but was too slow. The great sword clattered onto his helmet, filling the air with a harsh, metallic clatter before it fell to the grass. The blow momentarily stunned Serpicius and forced him to take a step backwards.

In an instant, Adelligus had drawn his own *gladius* and stepped in, thrusting at the Roman as he attempted to make use of his temporary advantage.

The ploy almost worked. Serpicius had not expected Adelligus to throw his sword at him. The move had caught him off guard, but the gladiator's reflexes were inhumanly swift. He managed to block Adelligus' short sword with his shield, then retreated a few steps until he was able to regain his balance.

Adelligus closed in again, but The Snake was ready for him and the moment of opportunity passed.

Now the gladiator's experience and speed counted. No longer needing to watch for the greater reach of the longsword, he moved in close, stabbing with his sword and using his shield as a battering ram as he pummelled Adelligus' defence with a series of lightning blows. His *gladius* darted like a snake's tongue, left and right, high and low, flashing with incredible speed.

Adelligus was no longer attacking, merely defending in increasingly desperate attempts to prevent The Snake from striking a killing blow.

Serpicius was dancing round him, forcing him to twist and turn, never letting him rest, tiring him out with the constant movement.

It could only end one way.

Serpicius' sword dodged past Adelligus' guard and struck, needle point first, into the young man's side. The small iron rings of the chainmail coat popped and shattered, but did their work well enough to prevent the blade driving into Adelligus' flesh. Still, he staggered under the impact and winced at the pain, moving tentatively as he tried to counter the next attack.

This time, his unguarded right shoulder took the brunt, more chainmail rings shattering or coming loose as the *gladius* smashed down on the younger man's collarbone.

Adelligus could not summon the strength to drive his own sword into The Snake. It was all he could do to hold the weapon in his numbed, trembling fingers.

Another attack, another turn, another thrust which connected with Adelligus' left hip, forcing him to stumble. As he fell, Serpicius' shield crashed onto the top of his helmet, stunning him and driving him to the ground.

Somehow, incredibly, he recovered, sweeping his round shield up in a frantic block which prevented the killing stroke from being delivered. He surged upwards, stabbing his own sword, giving himself a short breathing space.

But his right arm was almost useless, numbed by the blow to his collar bone, and his breathing was ragged, his side throbbing with the pain of cracked ribs. No matter how he tried, he could not prevent Serpicius taking full advantage of his injuries. With two savage cuts, The Snake hammered his own blade into Adelligus' sword and sent it spinning high into the air, whirling end over end to land several paces away.

Adelligus now had only his shield to protect him. His chainmail had saved him from more fatal injuries, but Serpicius would soon beat him down sufficiently to deliver a deadly thrust to the Briton's face or throat.

Watching from only a few paces away, Macrinus knew the fight was as good as over.

Adelligus stood his ground, gripping his shield with both hands, crouching and twisting, blocking every attack, but Serpicius allowed him no respite. Barrelling in with his greater strength, the Roman knocked the Briton from his feet, thrusting his sword to catch Adelligus with a shallow cut to his unprotected leg as he fell backwards.

Adelligus sprawled on his back, his shield having fallen to the ground and rolled away. Frantically, he tried to rise, but Serpicius was coming for him, and his movements turned into a desperate, crab-like scuttle across the wet grass.

Macrinus chewed his lip, not sure why he felt so sorry for the boy who had only moments more to live. Adelligus had fought as well as anyone who had come up against The Snake, but he had been unable to do much more than delay the inevitable.

He must have realised it himself because he stopped trying to escape, knowing it was futile. Instead, he reached up with one hand and ripped off his helmet. Flinging it aside, he exposed his throat to his enemy as he stared at Serpicius from a distance of only three paces and called out, "Come on, then! Finish it! I am ready."

The gladiator could not understand the words, but he grasped their meaning. Slowly, he advanced.

And then the horns blared a warning.

The raucous sound was so unexpected and insistent that it froze Serpicius for a moment. Then he turned round and looked towards the fort.

"What is it?" he called to Macrinus.

The Tribune almost laughed aloud. He pointed beyond the gladiator and his fallen opponent, towards the distant line of low hills.

"Time to go!" he called. "Quickly, before they catch us."

Serpicius spun round again, staring into the distance. The crest of the hill, bathed in pale sunlight, was dark with a moving swarm of horsemen who were streaming down the nearer slope towards them.

Serpicius hesitated, took a faltering step towards the fallen Adelligus, but stopped uncertainly. Adelligus had heard the horns and guessed their meaning. Making use of Serpicius' momentary distraction, he had crawled a few paces towards the spot where his discarded longsword lay on the grass.

Deprived of the opportunity to make a quick kill, Serpicius seemed unable to resolve his dilemma.

"Leave him!" Macrinus shouted, running to catch the gladiator's shoulder. "We need to get back before they ride us down!"

The two men turned, breaking into a run as they headed for the safety of the fort, leaving an exhausted, battered Adelligus lying on the grass behind them.

Chapter XXXI

Sdapezi had seen them abandon the fight, so he had ordered the cavalry to deploy without waiting for Macrinus' signal. The horsemen streamed out of the camp, spreading into a long line of two ranks. They came at a fast gallop, but reined in as soon as Macrinus and Serpicius met them.

"I told you you should have brought a horse," Sdapezi remarked with a grim smile. "We need to get back inside quickly. There are thousands of the buggers."

Still trying to catch his breath, Macrinus turned to watch the approaching barbarians. It was impossible to estimate their true numbers, but they certainly outnumbered Sdapezi's force by a significant margin. Three thousand of them, at least, he guessed.

He nodded to Sdapezi.

"A dignified withdrawal if we can manage it," he ordered. "There's no point in committing suicide by trying to take on that many of them."

He was about to push between the horses and continue his walk back to the fort when Sdapezi muttered a surprised oath.

Spinning round, Macrinus saw that the vast throng of barbarians had come to a halt some four hundred paces away. They were unusually silent for savages, uttering no war cries and brandishing no weapons in threatening gestures. Instead, they sat on their horses in silent witness to the scene in front of them.

A scene into which two riders had come ahead, cantering towards the fallen figure of Adelligus. They reined in when they reached him, one of them leaping down to tend to the wounded young man, the other, much larger figure striding a few paces beyond him and then standing still with his arms folded across his massive chest while he stared at the line of Roman horsemen.

"What's going on?" Serpicius demanded, his voice metallic through the faceplate of his helmet.

"That," Macrinus informed him, "is Calgacus. I think he's just accepted your challenge."

Serpicius' face was invisible behind his iron mask, but his stance stiffened. His breathing was still coming hard after the exertion of their short run and his long fight with Adelligus.

"I can tell him you are too tired," Macrinus offered.

"I can beat him no matter how tired I am," Serpicius growled.

Unable to resist the temptation to undermine Flaccus' plan, Macrinus added softly, "You do know they say he cannot be killed?"

Serpicius snorted, "Every man can be killed. I just don't like the idea of fighting him while he's got an army at his back."

"You've got an army at your back, too," Macrinus pointed out.

Sdapezi put in, "We could try riding him down. We could probably reach him before his war host could stop us. They're a lot further away from him than we are."

"He's daring us to try something like that," Macrinus nodded. "Arrogant son of a bitch, isn't he?"

"It takes guts to stand there between two armies," Sdapezi agreed admiringly. "But I've seen him do something similar before."

Seeing Serpicius' interest, the Centurion went on, "He single-handedly charged at sixty of us when we thought we'd trapped him. He killed our Centurion, and all our so-called barbarian allies ran away from him."

The gladiator growled, "You all sound as if you are afraid of him."

"We are," Sdapezi admitted cheerfully.

"Well, I'm not!" Serpicius spat. "A taste of steel in the belly will kill anyone."

"Then we'd best go and meet him," said Macrinus. "Are you ready?"

The gladiator's head turned to face the distant barbarian horsemen.

"Are you sure they won't attack us?" he asked.

"They won't do anything unless we do," Macrinus assured him. "Calgacus obviously wants to talk."

"What makes you so sure we can trust him?" The Snake demanded, clearly unconvinced.

"A hunch," Macrinus shrugged.

"That's not much to place your faith in," the gladiator grunted.

"No, but I'm going to go and talk to him nonetheless. You don't need to come, but I suspect Popidius Flaccus might not be willing to pay you your ten thousand denarii if you stay here when Calgacus has come to accept your challenge."

He could see Serpicius' cold eyes regarding him through the holes in the iron mask, eyes that were as dark and unblinking as a viper's, and he wondered whether it had been wise to taunt a man who enjoyed killing.

Serpicius stood very still before giving a slow nod.

"All right. But make sure we are hauled out quickly if the rest of them decide to join in."

"We'll be ready," Sdapezi promised.

Serpicius took a deep breath, nodded once, then set off towards the waiting figure of Calgacus.

"Ten thousand denarii?" Sdapezi whispered incredulously. "I'd take on the whole bloody barbarian army for that amount."

"Don't tempt fate," Macrinus warned as he made to follow the gladiator. "You may have to fight them if anything goes wrong."

He soon caught up with Serpicius, falling into step beside him. Ahead of them, Calgacus had not moved. He simply stood with his arms folded across his broad chest while he waited for them to reach him.

"Be careful of him," Macrinus warned the gladiator. "He's not someone to underestimate. He's fast for a man of his size."

Serpicius merely grunted and kept walking.

As they drew near, Macrinus realised what it was that was different about Calgacus. Instead of a coat of chainmail, the Briton was wearing a massively bulky bearskin jerkin that covered his upper torso in a shaggy mass of fur. It made his shoulders look enormous and added considerable bulk to his already huge frame. Down its front, the jerkin was fastened by loops of cord wrapped over curved bear's teeth. His sword hung on his back, but he carried no shield and wore no helmet, his long, black hair tied back in a ponytail.

Macrinus silently acknowledged that Calgacus had not made the mistake of weighing himself down with armour, but whether that would be sufficient to give him enough speed and stamina to best The Snake was highly doubtful. Once Serpicius got past the reach of Calgacus' long blade, the Briton would be virtually defenceless.

His face bore no sign of any nervousness. He stood grimly, watching them with his sapphire eyes, his jaw set in a determined expression.

When they were within a few paces, the two Romans stopped.

"Good to see you again," Macrinus said in Brythonic.

Calgacus replied in his coarse, heavily accented Latin.

"You haven't brought any dogs this time?" he asked. "Just a snake?"

"This is Serpicius," Macrinus answered cautiously. "Our champion."

Calgacus turned a cold stare on the gladiator.

"I would normally give you a chance to reconsider whether you wish to fight me, but I think the only way to resolve this situation is for me to kill you."

"You can try," Serpicius rasped through his iron mask.

A smile touched Calgacus' lips as he said, "Has Macrinus not told you of my magic?"

"What magic?" Serpicius demanded uncertainly.

Calgacus gestured to his bearskin tunic.

"I wear the skin of a bear I killed with my bare hands. Its power is now mine. You must know how difficult it is to kill a bear. No matter how often you stab it, it takes a lot of punishment before it dies. That is why you cannot beat me."

Serpicius gave a snort of derision.

"Believe that superstitious nonsense if you will," he grunted. "You will soon learn that nothing can protect you from me. I will make you suffer a slow death to show you how wrong you are, and I will enjoy staring into your eyes and watching the life ebb from them when my sword is in your belly."

Calgacus returned an icy smile and his voice was as hard as iron as he told the gladiator, "I do not usually take the heads of my enemies, but in your case I will make an exception. Or, rather, I will have my shield-bearer remove your head once you are dead. That is his son you nearly killed. He deserves some recompense."

Serpicius spat, "If that boy is the best you've got, you won't last long at all."

Calgacus moved his gaze to Macrinus.

"None of my men will interfere," he said. "Do I have the same promise from you?"

"You do," the Tribune confirmed.

Calgacus nodded, "When your pet snake is dead, Liscus will take his head. You can do whatever you like with the rest of him."

"And if he wins?" Macrinus challenged.

Calgacus gave a shrug which was barely discernible beneath the bulk of his bearskin jacket.

"That's not going to happen. You know I can't be killed."

"You are full of talk," Serpicius rasped. "But words don't scare me."

"Then let us get on with it," said Calgacus. "I would like to return home before the midwinter solstice."

Macrinus stepped back, giving the two men room. Beyond them, he could see that Adelligus was now sitting on his horse, one hand clamped to his injured side. Beside him, the diminutive figure of Runt stood watching impassively.

For all Calgacus' apparent confidence, Macrinus recognised the sense of unease the two Britons were feeling about the outcome of the duel. In part, he shared their concern. If he had secretly wished for Adelligus to beat the gladiator, that desire was even greater now that The Snake was facing Calgacus. Macrinus liked and respected the British warrior. That did not mean he would not have killed him in battle, but this ritual combat was a different matter. In war, Calgacus was an opponent to be feared, but here he would be no match for a killer like Serpicius.

Unless, Macrinus reflected, he really was invulnerable. Macrinus had witnessed the scene when Calgacus had apparently been disembowelled, only to be brought back to life. It had made a powerful impression on the Romans who had seen it, and Macrinus was not immune to the feeling that he might have witnessed something supernatural, yet he had also been a soldier long enough to know that no man could live if a *gladius* bit him deeply. Besides, Calgacus did not have a sorceress with him this time. It had been her magic, not his, which had resurrected him. For all the legends surrounding him, Macrinus knew Calgacus could not survive this time.

Whatever the truth behind the stories, though, the fate of the campaign would be decided by the outcome of this duel.

The two combatants faced one another as if each of them was waiting for the other to make the first move. Then Serpicius reached across his body and drew his razor-sharp *gladius* before holding his large shield close to his body.

"I've got a bigger one than you," Calgacus declared, reaching back over his shoulder to draw his heavy longsword. The blade was polished, a central groove running down its length. Unlike the typical British swords, it broadened slightly towards the tip before tapering into a leaf-shaped point. It was an enormous weapon, capable of being wielded in one hand or two, its weight enough to smash through flesh and bone, its reach sufficient to keep a single opponent at a distance unless that opponent was very brave and very skilled. Against any normal adversary, the longsword gave its wielder a tremendous advantage.

But Serpicius had faced men armed with longswords twice now, and he had defeated both of them. Nevertheless, he moved cautiously at first, up on the balls of his feet but holding his shield high and his sword close to his side as he watched to see what Calgacus intended to do.

Calgacus attacked.

He leaped forwards, yelling ferociously in an attempt to intimidate the gladiator, swinging his huge sword back and bringing it crashing down on the Roman's shield, the edge ringing on the iron rim of the shield and knocking great splinters from the front of the painted wood.

The blow had been powerful enough to drive most men to the ground, but Serpicius had moved backwards, absorbing the worst of the impact. Yet, even as he moved, he was twisting his body and thrusting his own sword forwards in a vicious lunge aimed at Calgacus' belly.

Calgacus saw the blade coming for him and jumped backwards, sweeping his own weapon up as he tried to knock it aside. He missed because Serpicius drew his *gladius* back as quickly as he had made the lunge.

The two men stepped back, gathered themselves and moved forwards again, Serpicius crouching behind his shield, sword ready as ever.

This time, Calgacus used his greater height and the reach of his longsword to hold the gladiator at bay. Adopting a two-handed grip, he swept the great blade in rapid, weaving arcs, never allowing it to be still for a moment, flashing it in great circles, up and down, left and right, its tip grazing ever closer to the Roman.

Macrinus had seen such moves before, and again he marvelled at the skill and precision with which Calgacus wielded the sword, not to mention the sheer strength it required to keep such a heavy weapon constantly moving. It created a defence as much as an attack because there seemed no way for Serpicius to get past the deadly blade.

The gladiator, though, had trained for years, and had fought against all manner of opponents. He waited, poised like the snake that gave him his name, judging the moment to perfection. Calgacus' elegant sweeps were fast and deadly, but it would take only a slight deflection to his weaving patterns to leave him defenceless.

That deflection came when Serpicius launched himself forwards, crouching low to stay beneath the main sweep of Calgacus' great weapon, and thrusting out his shield, using the iron edge to knock Calgacus' sword high as it seared past him from his right to his left.

Driven by its own momentum, the longsword leaped like a salmon, silver against the dull sky, Calgacus barely able to retain his grip on the hilt. He almost lost his balance as the weight of the sword dragged his arms upwards. To compensate, he thrust his left leg back and planted his feet heavily on the damp grass.

The movement allowed him to retain his grip on the sword, but it also exposed his body to Serpicius' attack.

The gladiator did not waste the opportunity. His short sword jabbed forwards as fast as lightning, burying itself in Calgacus' belly, the sharpened point slicing through the bearskin as if it were simple linen.

Macrinus watched in fascination as the two men stood face to face, the tip of the gladiator's sword clearly stuck in Calgacus' stomach, its tip slicing up towards his heart as Serpicius delivered a fatal blow.

The gladiator kept pushing, thrusting his head close to Calgacus in order to keep his promise of looking him in the eye as he died.

Macrinus expected the Briton to stagger, to collapse at Serpicius' feet, and all he could feel was a sense of loss, as if witnessing the Briton's death was like watching the end of far more than a human life.

But Calgacus did not fall. Instead, his left arm dropped from its grip on his sword, and his hand clamped around The Snake's wrist. He yanked and twisted, pulling the *gladius* free and jerking Serpicius so fiercely that the Roman almost lost his footing. With a tremendous pull, Calgacus yanked Serpicius' arm across the front of his own body, forcing the gladiator to turn, rendering him incapable of slamming his shield into Calgacus because he was being dragged into an involuntary spin by the power of Calgacus' grip.

An instant later, before Serpicius could react, Calgacus' left leg lashed out, knocking the gladiator's feet from under him.

Serpicius crashed to the ground, landing heavily on top of his shield, but Calgacus still held his right wrist in a vice-like grip. He jerked it again, so fiercely that Serpicius' arm was almost yanked from its socket. The *gladius* fell from his hand, plunging into the grass, while Serpicius flailed on the ground at Calgacus' feet.

Calgacus released his hold, flinging the gladiator's arm free. At the same time, his own huge sword was moving, sweeping down to smash into the Roman's unprotected left shoulder, cleaving through flesh, muscle and bone, driving down into the gladiator's torso.

Serpicius screamed in agony, but Calgacus was not finished. He planted his right boot on the man's wriggling back and used both hands to wrench his sword free. As soon as it slid from the gore, he reversed his hold and plunged it back down again, skewering through the dying man's body with such power that the blade almost pinned Serpicius to the ground.

Calgacus stood very still for a moment, then heaved the sword free, needing several attempts to drag it out of the bloody corpse. Then, almost casually, he took a piece of cloth from under his belt and wiped the blade clean before unlooping his scabbard, carefully resheathing the sword and slinging it on his back.

Macrinus became aware that the watching tribesmen were cheering, the sound like a roaring wave rolling across the plain. Runt was already moving, drawing one of his own swords and kneeling to remove Serpicius' helmet so that he could hack off the man's head, just as Calgacus had promised.

Calgacus strolled towards Macrinus, his expression grim.

"Tell your man, Flaccus, that the next time he has any of my people murdered, I will come for him and remove his head, too."

Macrinus could not help smiling.

"I will take great pleasure in giving him that message," he said. "But how is it that you are still alive? I saw him stab you in the belly."

"Magic," Calgacus grinned. "You've seen me use it before."

Macrinus frowned. He could not help thinking Calgacus had played some trick or other, yet he could see that the bearskin tunic had a great rent in it, a flap which Calgacus held closed with his left hand as if it were nothing more than an inconvenient tear which could soon be stitched together.

"I don't know how you did it," Macrinus confessed, "but I think you cheated somehow."

"Call it what you like," Calgacus smiled. "Just tell your Governor what you saw, and tell him I said that your swords can't kill me."

Macrinus gave a helpless shake of his head.

"I will tell him," he sighed. "But I expect he will think I am an imbecile."

"Better a live imbecile than a dead gladiator," Calgacus told him.

"So, what happens now?"

"Now we both go back and tell our stories. We enjoy the winter feasts, and then we prepare for war again. Unless you can persuade your Governor to take your army back south. I offered him peace if he did that. The offer still stands."

"I doubt whether he will agree to that," Macrinus said.

Calgacus shrugged, "Then I expect I will need to kill you the next time we meet."

"I expect you will try."

"I'll cheat, you know."

"So will I."

Calgacus smiled. He held out his hand and Macrinus clasped forearms with him in the Roman fashion.

"Until next time, then," he said.

"Until next time," Calgacus echoed.

Then he turned away, joining Runt who now stood with Serpicius' severed head in his hands.

Macrinus watched the two of them walk over to Adelligus. They mounted their own horses, wheeled away and rode to join their war host.

Macrinus turned, walking back to the fort, unable to prevent himself grinning as he anticipated giving Calgacus' message to Popidius Flaccus.

Chapter XXXII

Flaccus was in a state of near shock. He demanded to know how Calgacus could have killed a trained gladiator with such apparent ease, shaking his head in disbelief when Macrinus reported how Serpicius' blade had failed to kill the Briton.

Macrinus could still not explain the mystery, but he took considerable pleasure from seeing the Assistant Procurator flounder in bewilderment. He took especial delight in relaying Calgacus' threat of what he would do if Flaccus tried to repeat his murderous ploy. When he heard this, the Assistant Procurator grew even more pale than he had been before.

"He cannot reach me!" he exclaimed in near panic, his breath coming in rasping wheezes.

Macrinus, enjoying himself immensely, and noticing that the Governor did not seem inclined to stop him tormenting Flaccus, responded, "I wouldn't be too sure about that. He stormed the Ninth Legion's camp a few months ago, and slaughtered hundreds of our soldiers. Who is to say what he can or cannot do?"

"This is intolerable!" Flaccus protested.

Turning to Agricola, he pleaded, "You must do something!"

Agricola nodded gravely.

"I shall order the cavalry to follow the barbarians to make sure they really are leaving. We'll also double the perimeter guards for the next few days."

Smiling, he added, "If it will reassure you, I will have guards allocated to protect you."

Flaccus frowned, but his imperious nod of assent was interrupted by another fit of coughing.

"Perhaps we should retire to my tent," Agricola suggested. "It will be dark shortly. We can discuss our next move over dinner."

Flaccus seemed keen to accept the offer, scurrying down from the top of the rampart and heading towards the Praetorium.

Once Flaccus was out of earshot, Agricola moved close to Macrinus, lowering his voice to enquire, "How did Calgacus really do it? I was sure The Snake had stabbed him."

Macrinus was compelled to admit that he did not know.

"He says he used magic," he informed the Governor.

"Keep that quiet," Agricola ordered with a scowl of disapproval. "I don't want any more rumours floating around. The fact that he killed a gladiator is bad enough for morale."

"The men saw what happened," Macrinus pointed out. "What do I say if anyone asks?"

"Tell them Calgacus was wounded, but that the sword missed anything vital."

Macrinus nodded, unhappy at the need to lie, but knowing that the alternative would be disastrous for the morale of the Legion.

"What about Serpicius' body?" he asked. "Do you want me to have it brought in?"

"I think not," Agricola said firmly. "Let the crows feast on him. Now, we should join the gallant Flaccus and have a meal of our own. Not that I expect it to be a festive occasion."

Agricola was correct in his assessment of the mood at dinner. Although the cooks prepared several savoury dishes, including some of the local grouse as well as more traditional larks and duck, the air in the large tent was sombre.

All the Tribunes were there, along with the senior Centurions, yet few of the men felt inclined to say very much. There were no fine couches to recline on, so they sat around a large table that was spread with many dishes and with ample wine available, although the Governor had the potent drink well watered to reduce the risk of anyone becoming too intoxicated.

He need not have worried, for nobody was in the mood to get drunk. Few of the officers had approved of Serpicius, yet his death at Calgacus' hands had shocked them, and they all realised that the campaign had reached a turning point. Calgacus, an enemy around whom legends and stories circulated like moths around a candle, had defeated a trained gladiator under the eyes of the entire army. More than that, men had seen Serpicius' sword plunge into the Briton's body with no apparent effect. No matter what orders the Governor might issue, the story would be repeated and would grow in the telling. What, they all wondered, would Flaccus do now that his plan had failed and his own life had been threatened by the enemy?

The Assistant Procurator seemed oblivious to the sidelong glances the officers were casting him. Silent and forlorn, he cut a sorry figure. He coughed and sneezed throughout the meal, picking at his food and contributing little to the conversation. Sitting opposite him, Togodumnus also appeared preoccupied, giving terse answers to any questions directed at him by the Governor.

Most of the talking was done by Agricola and Piso, but even that seemed forced, as if Serpicius' death had been more of a setback than they had anticipated. Their efforts to discuss mundane issues of duty rosters and building work could not distract men's thoughts from the real problem that faced them.

That problem was Calgacus. Every plan to capture or kill him was, it seemed, doomed to failure. The fact that the idea had been Flaccus' suggestion barely lessened the sense of frustration.

As the meal drew to a close and the slaves cleared away the dishes, the Governor's secretary, Donnatus, pushed aside the heavy flap of the door to the inner chamber and made his way to the Governor's side. In his hand, he held a leather scroll case.

"I apologise for the interruption," he said softly as he handed the container to Agricola. "This has just arrived on a galley. The messenger who brought it insists that the accompanying instructions are that it be given to you immediately."

An expectant hush fell over the table as Agricola opened the top of the cylindrical case and tipped out a parchment scroll.

"The Imperial seal," he observed as he broke the scroll open.

Everyone watched him intently as his eyes scanned the writing on the scroll. The message was not a long one, but its contents brought a slight tic to Agricola's neck as his pulse quickened and his features hardened.

When he had finished reading, he rolled the parchment up and handed it back to Donnatus.

"Draft a response for me," he said, his voice battling to conceal his disappointment. "Inform his Imperial Majesty that his orders will be obeyed immediately."

Donnatus inclined his head and left the chamber, scroll in hand.

Agricola sighed, placed his elbows on the table and steepled his hands in front of him. Looking around at the others, he informed them, "The Emperor has decided to recall me to Rome. I will depart in the morning."

He held up a hand, stifling the offers of sympathy that were forming on the lips of his officers.

He continued, "There is more. The Emperor has decided that he cannot spare reinforcements for us at the moment due to problems elsewhere in the Empire. He has decided that there is little point in continuing to fight barbarians who have no wealth worth exploiting. The army is therefore ordered to return south, back to that part of the province that was pacified two years ago."

Piso shook his head and Macrinus felt a hollow sensation in his stomach. All of the territory conquered in the past two years was simply to be abandoned.

Agricola went on, "There is no word on who my successor will be, gentlemen, but I am confident that you will give him the same loyal service you have given me over the past seven years. I wish to thank you for your efforts and your gallantry. I will remember my time here with pride and affection."

Some men murmured words of consolation, but Agricola stood up, raising his hands.

"I have a lot to do, gentlemen. I must board a ship in the morning so, if you will excuse me, I must leave you now."

He went to the doorway, his head held high, but Macrinus thought he looked somehow diminished as he left them. Julius Agricola had achieved so much in a few years, far more than any of his predecessors, but now most of his work had been rendered pointless by a single command from Rome.

Piso muttered, "Retreat? All the way back? That will take us to the territory of the Brigantes."

"It is the Emperor's will," Flaccus stated, his assertion issued through a dry, rasping throat. "But, since we are to depart, I, too, will take ship in the morning. I have duties to attend to within the province."

Once Flaccus had left, the officers voiced their disappointment more loudly. An imperial decree could not be ignored, but to retreat when their job was unfinished left a bitter taste in the mouth. They grumbled, complained and speculated on why the Emperor would issue such an order, but Piso, who was as disappointed as any of them, reminded them that it was their duty to obey, not to question orders.

"We will be busy tomorrow," he told them. "So, let us make some plans."

While the Legate and his officers discussed what needed to be done, Macrinus stood up and moved round the table to where Togodumnus was sitting with his eyes lowered, his face wearing a shocked expression as if he could not believe the Governor's news.

"What will you do now?" the tribune asked him.

Togodumnus shook his head and let out a resigned sigh.

"I must stay. My home is here. My wife is here. I cannot leave with you."

"What will your father do to you if you stay?" Macrinus asked.

Togodumnus' lips twisted in a wry smile.

"I doubt that he will do anything to me. He thinks I am beneath contempt. He will probably ignore me."

"But you are King of the Boresti," Macrinus reminded him.

"Not once you leave," Togodumnus replied with a hint of self-mockery. "But that does not matter. I never wanted to be a King in the first place. I only accepted the position because I wanted to help my people cope with Roman rule. There will be no need for that now."

Which was, Macrinus knew, all too true.

Togodumnus went on, "I think I will go to my room now. In the morning, I will take my horse and return home."

As he tried to rise, Macrinus laid a meaty hand on his shoulder, causing Togodumnus to flinch as if he had been caught stealing the silverware.

"Relax, lad," Macrinus told him. "I'd just like you to do something for me."

Togodumnus gave him a sheepish smile as he asked, "What is it?"

"When you see your father, give him a message from me, will you?"

"Of course."

"Tell him I am glad I won't need to kill him."

Togodumnus smiled at that. Standing, he clasped hands with the Tribune.

"I am sure he will be pleased to hear that," he said. "But what will you do?"

"I am a soldier," Macrinus shrugged. "I will do what I am ordered to do by whoever takes over."

"I wish my life were that simple," Togodumnus sighed.

At the far end of the table, Piso rose slowly to his feet, his expression stern.

"Gentlemen," he announced, "I suggest we should retire for the night. Tomorrow is going to be a busy day. You will need to be at your best because there will no doubt be unexpected problems to deal with. There always are when it comes to things like this."

He could not have known how accurate his prediction would prove to be. The fort lapsed into a watchful, restless slumber which was broken at dawn by the familiar blare of the horns and the unexpected news that Popidius Flaccus was dead.

Chapter XXXIII

"He simply passed away in his sleep," was the verdict of the Legion's senior medical orderly after he had examined Flaccus' body.

"It must have been that fever," Piso suggested.

The medical orderly did not contradict him, although they all knew that few people died from a bad cough.

"It was into his chest," Piso continued, as if feeling compelled to convince everyone.

The Assistant Procurator's freedman, Gracchus, was summoned. He looked terrified, shifting nervously from foot to foot and refusing to meet anyone's eye.

"The Master was very unwell," he confirmed, perhaps eager to ensure that no blame could accrue to him. "He went to bed early, almost as soon as he returned from dinner. All he did was dictate a couple of letters and take his usual warmed wine."

"Did anyone else come to see him?" Agricola asked.

"No, Sir. Only myself and the slaves who brought him his supper. He didn't even eat all of that, which was most unusual. I had to have one of the slaves remove it this morning."

Gracchus scowled as if the waste of food was a serious crime but, keen to reinforce his message, he repeated, "The Master really was not himself last night."

Piso told the Governor, "We had a guard posted at his door as you promised, Sir. He swears nobody else came in during the night."

"So, death was from natural causes, then?" Agricola asked.

His question was met by shrugs from everyone, including the medical orderly who was more used to treating wounds and infections than diagnosing sudden, unexplained deaths with no obvious symptoms.

"It must have been the fever," he eventually muttered.

"What do you want to do, Sir?" Piso asked the Governor. "Should we torture the slaves?"

"To what purpose?" Agricola asked, shaking his head. "Everyone could see he was not well. There is no need to create a problem where none exists."

He turned to Gracchus, saying, "I leave it to you to arrange a cremation. Take his ashes back to Rome."

Gracchus gave a nod, evidently relieved that he was not being blamed for Flaccus' death. The slaves would be even more relieved because any suspicion of foul play would have resulted in them being executed.

Piso asked, "What will the Emperor say about this?"

Agricola shrugged, "I will find out when I tell him. There is no point in writing a letter since I will be back in Rome in a few weeks."

Piso nodded gravely.

"I do not envy you that task," he said softly. "Flaccus was a close friend of the Emperor."

Agricola gave the Legate a wry smile.

"Emperors do not have friends," he declared. "They only have subjects. I doubt whether Popidius Flaccus will be missed overly much. Now, we had best get on. There is a great deal to be done."

They left the freedman to arrange Flaccus' cremation, warning him that he must hurry because the building, like all the others, would be burned to the ground before the Legion departed. Some of the destruction work had already begun, the wooden palisade around the fort being hauled down and cast into the deep ditches. Pits were being dug where materials such as nails and other equipment that would not burn could be buried. The tents of the Praetorium were already being dismantled, and the Governor's baggage was being loaded onto one of the galleys at the riverside.

"Macrinus has begun his work," Piso remarked, waving a hand to the distant hills where plumes of dark smoke showed that the outer forts and watchtowers were being set alight. Nothing would be left for the barbarians to use. If it could not be carried away, it would be burned, broken or buried deep in the earth where nobody would ever find it.

The Legion's advance guard had already left, heading out to identify a suitable site for a marching camp where the Legion would spend the first night of its long trek south. Wagons were lumbering out of the fort, the ramshackle village beyond the south gate was almost deserted, and messengers had gone out in every direction to summon in the outposts, giving orders for the withdrawal.

Agricola waited for Macrinus to return from his tour of the nearest auxiliary units, then said his farewells to his officers. That duty complete, he made his way out of the fort for the last time. With an honour guard from the Legion's First Century lining his route, he and his household boarded the galley and set off for Rome.

It was a sombre moment, every man present knowing that Julius Agricola, who had spent so many years of his life in Britannia, would probably never return to the island.

"He is a great man," Macrinus remarked to Piso.

The Legate nodded, his face grim.

"Too great, I think. Emperors dislike great men, especially when those men command large armies."

Macrinus watched the galley depart, the banks of oars slowly dipping into the water as they took Agricola on the first leg of his journey to the imperial city.

"May Mithras watch over you, Julius Agricola," he whispered, feeling a shiver of foreboding run down his spine at Piso's gloomy words.

The Legate blew out a long breath as the ship turned the bend in the river and disappeared from sight.

"Time for us to move out as well," he declared.

Within a few hours, the last of the soldiers had left, marching out of a ruined fort where nothing but blazing buildings remained. It had been the largest fortress ever constructed in Britannia, and now it was being abandoned after only a few months.

The last man to leave was Julius Macrinus, riding a horse and wearing his crested helmet and red cloak. As he passed through the ruined gateway, he turned in the saddle, looked beyond the pillars of writhing smoke to the distant hills, and smiled to himself.

"Farewell, Calgacus," he said to the empty air. "It seems you have won after all."

Epilogue

The following day, four men stood in the centre of the fort, the acrid smell of burning still hanging in the damp air, the ruined buildings now nothing more than piles of ash and charred, smouldering timbers.

"They've really gone," Runt said as if he could not believe it.

"All the way back to Brigantia," Togodumnus confirmed.

Bridei growled, "We should follow them and make sure they go."

"We will," Calgacus nodded. "The Venicones will want to return to their own lands anyway."

He sighed as he added wistfully, "It's a shame Gabrain is not here to see this."

"I can't believe we are here to see it," murmured Runt. "Thirty years we've been fighting the bastards, and I must admit I never thought I'd see the day they'd really go."

"They still rule all the south of the island," Calgacus reminded him.

Bridei chuckled, "That's a good thing. It means we can carry on raiding their lands and helping ourselves to their gold and silver."

Calgacus shook his head, smiling at Bridei's perpetual belligerence.

Togodumnus said, "I wonder what will happen to Agricola when he reaches Rome."

"I don't care," Calgacus snorted. "He's gone, and that's the main thing. Whoever comes in his place isn't likely to be as much of a problem for us, especially if the Emperor wants them to stick to protecting their southern province."

He paused, thinking to himself, then grinned, "It's Macrinus I feel sorry for. He'll never know how I tricked that gladiator."

"How did you do that?" Togodumnus asked. "I couldn't believe it when they told me you'd won."

"Thank you for your confidence in me," Calgacus chuckled.

"So how did you do it?" Togodumnus persisted. "I don't believe that nonsense about a magical bearskin."

"Oh, the bearskin wasn't magic in itself," Calgacus admitted. "The trick was in persuading The Snake to stab me there. If he'd gone for my legs or arms, he'd have won easily enough."

"But a bearskin can't stop a sword," Togodumnus insisted, frowning at the broad smiles on the faces of the others.

Calgacus laughed, "No, but it was bulky enough that I could wear my old breastplate underneath it."

"Your breastplate?"

"The one my brother, Caratacus, gave me years ago. It's an ancient thing now, but it's still good enough to ward off a blade, especially when the thick bearskin has absorbed some of the impact. Mind you, it's got another nasty dent in it now."

Togodumnus could not help joining in the laughter.

"You cheated!"

"Of course I did."

Calgacus clapped his son on the back.

"We have won. Maybe not in a great battle, but it doesn't matter why they've left. What matters is that we can live the rest of our lives in peace."

"Not if I can help it," grunted Bridei.

They laughed again, but Togodumnus quickly adopted a more serious expression.

"I'm sick of all the killing," he said. "I am glad it is over."

"The killing won't ever end," Bridei assured him. "As long as some men covet what others have, there will be fighting."

"Then I'll leave it to you to do the fighting," Togodumnus sighed. "I never killed a man before, and I'm not proud of what I did."

"One less Roman is nothing to be concerned about," Calgacus told him. "Especially a vicious weasel like Flaccus."

Runt asked, "How did you do it anyway? You promised to tell us."

Togodumnus chewed his lip before shrugging, "It was ridiculously easy. I slipped away from the wall before you began your fight with Serpicius. Everyone was watching you or manning the walls in case of an attack, so the camp was virtually deserted. The buildings hid me from most people's view. All I did was go into Flaccus' slaves' room. There was only one man there, the Nubian lad named Felix. I told him to make himself scarce for a while. As soon as he left, I simply tipped the rest of Emmelia's powder into Flaccus' wine jug. I knew nobody else was allowed to drink from it."

"Didn't the slave suspect you when Flaccus was found dead?" Calgacus asked.

"Probably. But I think he kept his mouth shut because I did him a favour earlier. Still, I didn't hang around to find out. I left the fort at first light and came to find you."

He frowned as he went on, "The thing is, if I'd known the Emperor was going to recall their entire Army, I wouldn't have needed to do anything at all, but by the time Agricola received the order, I'd already poisoned Flaccus' wine and it was too late to do anything about it."

"None of us can see into the future," Calgacus said. "You did what you thought was best at the time, which is all that any of us can ever do."

"So, what happens now?" Runt asked. "I know Bridei is desperate to chase the Romans all the way beyond the Bodotria, but the rest of us have families who are waiting for us at home."

"There's something I need to do first," Calgacus replied. "Let's go down to the river."

They walked out through the gap where the gates had once stood, then passed through the eerily deserted remains of the tiny village that had sprung up outside the fort.

When they reached the river, Calgacus stepped close to the bank, peering out at the dark, fast-flowing water.

"This will do," he said to nobody in particular.

He tugged at the thick leather belt that held his sword and pulled it off over his head.

He paused, holding the great longsword in both hands, looking down at the metal scabbard of bronze and tin which so many people believed was made of gold with a silver central spine.

"This has been in my family for generations," he told his companions.

Glancing at his son, he asked, "I don't suppose you would thank me for passing it on to you?"

"No," Togodumnus confirmed. "I have no need of a sword."

Calgacus nodded, "Then it is only fitting that it be offered to the Gods in thanks for their aid. They have kept me alive these past thirty years while a great many other men have not survived."

Each of the other three nodded their approval. Offerings of weapons were often given to the Gods by casting them into deep water. It was a tradition as old as time, and one that everyone understood.

Reverently, Calgacus drew the sword from its ornate sheath. He tested it in his hand, feeling the weight, lost in silent contemplation of how many times it had served him. Then he raised both hands, the sword held high in his right, the gleaming scabbard in his left.

"Camulos!" he shouted, invoking the War God of his people, the sound of his call echoing across the river.

He lowered his arms, hesitated for a moment, then hurled the scabbard out into the river. It spun in the air, the dull sunlight reflecting from its golden surface, then splashed into the centre of the deep water. For a moment, it floated on the surface, swirling downriver, but then the water flowed into the open sheath and it sank from sight.

"Camulos!" he called again, this time flinging the great sword high into the air. It tumbled end over end, arcing up before falling with a splash and vanishing beneath the water.

Slowly, he turned to his friends, placed his hands on his hips and, with a huge smile on his face, said, "Now we can go home."

Author's Note and Acknowledgements

The Battle of Mons Graupius, as outlined at the beginning of this book, is one of the most famous and controversial events in the early history of Scotland. Anyone familiar with that history will have realised from the beginning of the Calgacus series that this battle would feature in the story at some point, because the Roman writer, Tacitus, names the leader of the British forces as Calgacus the Swordsman.

There are, however, several problems with this battle, the most awkward of which is that there is some doubt as to whether it actually took place at all. Tacitus is the only source that mentions it and, as he was writing to promote and celebrate the career of his father-in-law, Julius Agricola, some people have claimed that he could have invented the entire battle. It is a story told to impress people, recounted by someone who was not even there. Another Roman writer, Tertullian, accused Tacitus of being, "loquacious in falsehood", although this could have been due as much to professional jealousy as a genuine criticism. That has not prevented some people claiming that taking Tacitus' word for the battle having occurred is like believing a story told in the pub by a man whose best mate swears it is true.

It is certainly true that Tacitus' description of the battle, while very detailed in some aspects, is frustratingly vague in others, and he gives no clue at all as to where the battle was actually fought, except that it must have been somewhere north of the Forth – Clyde isthmus. The problem, of course, is that Scotland has so many hills that Mons Graupius could be virtually anywhere.

This has not prevented people nominating prospective sites, and the search continues, with advocates of various locations often becoming quite heated in their arguments.

There are, however, some very fine researchers and anyone wishing a detailed analysis of the search for the site could do worse than review the information compiled on the website of RomanScotland.org.uk. Their research has produced a very strong candidate in a hill near the village of Dunning in Perthshire, which they claim is the only site that meets all the criteria necessary, including having a local name, "Dun Crubh", which could easily be Latinised into Mons Graupius".

While Dunning appears to meet all the criteria, I have some small reservations about it, not least of which is that the criteria were defined by RomanScotland.org.uk and, despite their meticulous research, other experts do not necessarily agree with their conclusions. For my own part, I think the nearby Roman fort is too close to the hill for there to have been any battle on the plain between them and, in addition, the hill itself is too steep and high for there to have been any effective pursuit by the Romans of the fleeing Britons.

However, it must be admitted that, of all the prospective sites, this one matches best. From a fictional narrative perspective, my main problem was that the Dunning site is, unfortunately, too far south for my own stories. Part of this is due to interpretation of where the various tribes of northern Britain were located. When I began writing the Calgacus series, I followed a theory which placed the Boresti on the northern bank of the River Tay. RomanScotland.org.uk, however, claim they were based on the northern bank of the Forth. This is important for locating Mons Graupius as, according to Tacitus, Agricola "withdrew to the lands of the Boresti" after the battle. If the battle was fought in Perthshire, he would have needed to advance, not withdraw, to the northern bank of the Tay, which presented me with some problems.

Since I began these stories, though, I have unearthed other, competing theories. The interpretation of the location of various tribes, including the Boresti, has tended to drift northwards in recent years, with some people now claiming they were based around Forres, near the Moray Firth, the town of Forres taking its name from the Boresti, a.k.a. the "Voresti".

For my part, the story required a northerly location for the battle, and there are several viable contenders. However, the problems do not stop there. One of the main arguments in favour of a southerly location is that the reputed size of Agricola's army would require a large fort, in excess of 100 acres, and there are no Agricolan forts of the right size north of Perthshire. This presented me with a real difficulty because, although my stories are fictional, I do like to try to base them on genuine facts. Fortunately, Professor David Mattingly of Leicester University came to my rescue with his opinion that the Agricolan army could have been accommodated within a fort of around 65 acres. So, although I still tend to believe Dunning remains the strongest contender from the long list of potential sites, I felt justified in using a more northerly location.

Which left me wondering which site to use. In 2013, Damien Bullen suggested that the Cluny Hills, in Forres, matched the description. I exchanged several emails with him about this and he made a strong case, although I was not entirely convinced. While the Cluny Hills met most of the criteria, there were two big problems with them from my perspective.

First, the hills are not large. Tacitus claims that Agricola was afraid of being outflanked and so extended his line of battle. In normal circumstances, his front line would have extended to around one kilometre, and lengthening this would obviously give a considerably longer frontage for his advance. The problem with Cluny Hills is that a Roman battle line in excess of one kilometre would extend beyond the sides of the hills. Far from being outflanked, Agricola could almost have surrounded the hills.

The other flaw with Cluny is the presence of a small stream running through the town of Forres itself, and thus lying between the hills and the known Roman marching camp. While this waterway may have been too insignificant to record, Tacitus does not mention any river or stream needing to be crossed.

I was still tempted to base my account of the battle on Cluny Hills when my mother and brother, who always become involved in my researches, suggested that Califer Hill, a little way beyond the Cluny Hills, is large enough and also further away so that the stream could have been crossed long before the battle began. We subjected this theory to some fairly rigorous scrutiny and the only flaw we could come up with was the lack of a local name that could have been rendered into Latin as "Graupius". As the same objection applies to every other prospective site other than Dunning, I felt there was no need to be too concerned over this. It also allowed me to incorporate the Cluny Hills, where there are possible ruins of an ancient hill fort, as the place where, according to Tacitus, the Legions were "Drawn up before the walls", so it fitted nicely.

I should state that we are not claiming to have identified the site of Mons Graupius, as we are not historians or archaeologists, but, with most of the credit going to Moira and Stuart Anthony, I think we did identify a plausible northern location that fits well enough to be used in my fictional account.

Wherever the battle was fought (if it ever happened at all), the most puzzling thing about it for me is that, although Agricola claimed a complete and overwhelming victory, he felt compelled to withdraw to friendly territory afterwards. There may have been strategic reasons for this, of course, but one possible theory is, as I have fictionalised, that the casualty figures claimed by Tacitus were adjusted for propaganda purposes. There is an account by Scottish "historian" Hector Boece that the Romans suffered around 12,000 casualties and were driven back as a result. Unfortunately, Boece has been rather discredited as a reliable source, but his claim did help me move my own story in that direction.

As for the reasons for the ultimate withdrawal of Roman forces from northern Scotland, there is certainly some justification for believing that Domitian was jealous of Agricola. The famous general had certainly enjoyed a longer than usual stint as Governor of Britannia, but he did not live long after his recall. There are some veiled suggestions that his death was not from natural causes, and it is not beyond the realms of possibility that Domitian had him executed either out of jealousy or from fear that he might pose a threat as a rival for the imperial throne.

The rest of the story, including the involvement of Caratacus and Cartimandua, is entirely fictional. However, I have always enjoyed writing about these two characters, along with Anderius Facilis, so it was nice to give them an important role as well as bringing some sort of closure to their fictional lives.

In terms of actual history, I must admit to shortening the period of time in which Agricola's fortress at Inchtuthil on the banks of the River Tay was occupied. This fort, together with the Gask Ridge series of watchtowers and the "Glen Blocking Forts" were probably in use for a period of several years rather than the condensed timeframe I have used. There is, though, considerable debate over who actually constructed these defences and when, so I used some artistic licence in shortening the occupation period in order to give Calgacus his ultimate victory.

What is true is that, after the Roman withdrawal, the Caledonian tribes continued to harass Roman troops and refused to submit to imperial rule. Later Emperors, Antoninus Pius and Septimius Severus, made attempts to conquer the northern tribes, with Severus conducting a particularly brutal and powerful invasion in the early years of the Third Century. However, none of these invasions were able to subdue the north. The Antonine Wall was abandoned after forty years, while Severus' campaign was cut short by his death in 211 A.D.. There were no more serious attempts to extend the borders of the Empire beyond Hadrian's Wall.

In fact, the reverse was true, with the province of Britannia coming under regular attack from the north. These incursions were so ferocious and wide-ranging that, after the Legions had finally been withdrawn in 409 A.D., the rulers of southern Britain invited mercenaries from Germany and the Low Countries to cross the sea and provide fighting men to hold off the depredations of the Picts. Those Anglo-Saxon mercenaries soon decided that they would stay permanently, with considerable impact on the future of what was soon to become England.

This, then, is the end of the Calgacus series. I started out wanting to tell the story of British resistance to Rome in a way that would entertain. I hope I have gone some way to achieving that. When I began, I thought I could create five separate stories. As things developed, I extended that to six, then seven, and finally eight. There will, however, be no more. I have decided to allow Calgacus a long and peaceful retirement.

As always, I must thank several people for their help and encouragement with this story, and indeed with the entire series. Moira and Stuart Anthony for reading the drafts and providing feedback, as well as helping with research. In addition, Ian Dron, Stewart Fenton and Liz Wright provided invaluable comments on the drafts of several stories. Professor David Mattingly, Damien Bullen, Ron Greer and the Antonine Guard, as well as Quintus, Rufus and Alexandra from Real Roman Tours, provided much valuable background and many useful insights. My thanks to them all.

RomanScotland.org.uk published a great deal of highly detailed information on their website, which I frequently referred to.

These books have become something of a family enterprise, with everyone in my immediate family contributing in no small way. From designing book covers, to driving me to various locations to give talks to all sorts of social groups, I could not have done this without them. So, enormous thanks are due to Alaine, Kevin, Philip and Sarah.

Many other people have assisted me with generous support. In particular, I would like to thank Susan Barrett, Moira Gee, Doreen Halley, Dianne Phinn, Gavin and Aileen Stewart, Alistair Stables, Ian Garden, Alan MacMillan and David Kennedy for their sterling efforts in helping to promote my books to a wider audience. To everyone else who has supported me in this long-running project, I would like to say a heartfelt thank you. There are too many of you to give a full roll call, but you know who you are.

I also owe thanks to other writers, most of whom had a much more difficult task than I did because they write genuine history books which I plundered for interpretations of the known facts, as well as for authentic names to use for the multitude of characters in my stories. The various writings of Mary Beard, Alastair Moffat, Stuart McHardy, Terry Jones, and Tim Clarkson were extremely valuable sources of background information.

As for the classical sources, English translations of most ancient writers are available. My main sources were Tacitus, Dio Cassius, and Suetonius, but I also gained background material from the writings of Plutarch, Livy, Polybius, Juvenal, Herodian, Apicius, and, of course, Julius Caesar himself. I would urge anyone who is interested in classical history to read as many of these works as they can although I should warn you that some of them can be pretty heavy going at times.

I would also like to thank everyone who has taken the time to get in touch with me over the past few years. It is always good to hear from readers, especially as, so far, most of the feedback has been very complimentary. It is not possible to please everyone, but if my stories have given some enjoyment to even a few readers, then this has been worthwhile. I hope some people will have learned a few things they did not know, but the main reason for writing these stories is to entertain. They are not history, but perhaps they will have inspired a few people to find out more about the known facts the stories are based on. Then again, with the passage of two thousand years and with few sources to go on, can we be certain what is fact and what is fiction?

    GA
    October, 2017

Other Books by Gordon Anthony

All titles are available in e-book format. Titles marked with an asterisk are also available in paperback.

In the Shadow of the Wall*
An Eye For An Eye

Hunting Icarus*
Home Fires*

A Walk in the Dark (Charity booklet)

The Calgacus Series:
World's End*
The Centurions*
Queen of Victory*
Druids' Gold*
Blood Ties*
The High King*
The Ghost War*
Last Of The Free*

The Constantine Investigates Series:
The Man in the Ironic Mask
The Lady of Shall Not
Gawain and the Green Nightshirt
A Tale of One City

ABOUT THE AUTHOR

Born in Watford, Hertfordshire, in 1957, Gordon's family moved to Broughty Ferry in the early 1960s. Gordon attended Grove Academy, leaving in 1974 to work for Bank of Scotland. After a long but undistinguished career, he retired on medical grounds in 2008 without having received any huge bankers' bonuses.

Registered blind, Gordon had more time on his hands after retiring so, with the aid of special computer software, he returned to his hobby of writing and had his debut novel, "In the Shadow of the Wall" published in 2010. Gordon's books are now being read by a world-wide audience. As well as his historical adventure stories, he has ventured into crime fiction with some spoof murder mysteries in the "Constantine Investigates" series. He is also kept busy with speaking engagements, visiting libraries, schools and community groups to talk about his books.

In addition to his novels, Gordon devotes some of his time to raising funds for the RNIB. As well as visiting schools and social clubs to talk about his sight loss, he has self-published a charity booklet titled, "A Walk in the Dark", a humorous account of his experiences since losing his eyesight. The booklet is available free from Gordon's website www.gordonanthony.net All Gordon asks is that readers make a donation to RNIB. This booklet can also be purchased from the Amazon Kindle Store. Gordon will donate all author royalties to RNIB.

Now completely blind, Gordon continues to write stories and, in his spare time, attempts to play the guitar and keyboard with varying degrees of success.

Gordon is married to Alaine. They have three children and one grandchild. The family lives in Livingston, West Lothian.

You can contact Gordon via his website or by sending an email to ga.author@sky.com

Printed in Great Britain
by Amazon